THE SNARES

RANDOM HOUSE   NEW YORK

THE SNARES

A NOVEL

RAV GREWAL-KÖK

Published in the United States by Random House, an imprint and
division of Penguin Random House LLC, New York.

RANDOM HOUSE and the HOUSE colophon are registered trademarks of
Penguin Random House LLC.

The FBI analyst's summary of Ibn Muhammed's case
(in chapters 30 and 46) originally appeared, in different form,
as a short story in *The White Review.*

Library of Congress Cataloging-in-Publication Data
Names: Grewal-Kök, Rav, author.
Title: The snares: a novel / Rav Grewal-Kök.
Description: First edition. | New York, NY: Random House, 2025. |
Includes bibliographical references.
Identifiers: LCCN 2024012628 (print) | LCCN 2024012629 (ebook) |
ISBN 9780593446034 (hardcover; acid-free paper) |
ISBN 9780593446041 (ebook)
Subjects: LCGFT: Action and adventure fiction. |
Thrillers (Fiction) | Novels.
Classification: LCC PS3607.R49877 S63 2025 (print) |
LCC PS3607.R49877 (ebook) |
DDC 813/.6—dc23/eng/20240419
LC record available at lccn.loc.gov/2024012628
LC ebook record available at lccn.loc.gov/2024012629

Printed in the United States of America on acid-free paper

randomhousebooks.com

1st Printing

First Edition

Book design by Fritz Metsch

For Yasmin

All my life
I have worshipped the wrong gods.

LOUISE GLÜCK

We tortured some folks.

BARACK OBAMA

THE SNARES

Jones angled the rearview mirror to cover the driveway, back door, deck, and most of the garden. The side mirrors showed the walkway and the street. His Nissan was eight years old, clean, unmemorable. Its license plates lay on the floor; he had the screws and a penknife in his breast pocket. He'd lowered his window a few inches but no breeze stirred the summer air. He heard distant traffic and the shouts of children at play. With a handkerchief, he wiped the sweat from his face. Even on a block with swept pavement and neat row houses, the air smelled of garbage.

He waited for his man. He had reviewed Chima's personnel file from the Justice Department, his naval service record, and his college and law school transcripts. He knew how much money Chima had in his bank account and retirement fund and how much his father-in-law had contributed toward the purchase of his house. He knew where Chima's two young daughters went to school. He'd skimmed the articles Chima's wife, a Georgetown Law professor, had published in scholarly journals. With the private assistance of one of the agency's technical analysts, he'd reviewed logs of Chima's internet search history and cellphone geolocation data. He'd peered into the recesses of Chima's past to find secrets and omissions that even his wife couldn't know.

All that wasn't enough. Jones had learned his art decades ago, in Greece and Lebanon. Now a veteran of the CIA's Senior Intelligence Service, he had access to more sophisticated tools and designed more elaborate operations than he had as a young officer, but he still trusted his intuition. Before he committed himself to this new project, he needed to see his subject (or partner, or agent, or volunteer; none of the old words quite fit) in the flesh. He needed to see how Chima carried himself when he came home: whether he ran up the steps, whether he smiled or scowled, whether he called to his children from the door or walked into the house in silence. It was the first rule. You didn't want someone who was satisfied with his life.

Afterward, Jones would drive home to spend the evening with his wife. He'd rest and reflect in the quiet of the country. And if all had gone well, he'd return to Langley the next day, mark an index card with a single check, and send it upstairs to his one trusted colleague by the agency's interoffice mail. Then the real work could begin.

ONE

NEEL WAS SITTING at his desk in the early afternoon when the telephone rang. He'd been working on a sentencing recommendation since nine A.M. Two Chinese-born Americans were pleading guilty to charges that they'd attempted to sell missile guidance software to a Turkish buyer unapproved by the State Department. Neel wanted twelve years, but his division chief thought Neel would be lucky to get the eight he'd offered as the lower bound of the plea deal. The chief, who'd stopped by on his way to lunch, counted off his reasons: first, the defendants were young and naive; second, the FBI had foiled the scheme at an early stage; third, the technology didn't work. What we had here was run-of-the-mill fraud, said the chief, not a breach of national security. Now Neel was struggling to convince himself that the judge would see things his way.

He was distracted, and a little irritated, when he spoke into the receiver. "Chima, Justice."

"I'd like us to talk," a man replied, in a grave voice.

"And you are?"

When he said his name, in that same implacable tone, Neel shiv-

ered. The caller worked at the highest levels of the CIA. He was re-
nowned, in government circles, for his celibacy, devotion, and fearsome
power. He was one of those men who, in consecrating their lives to the
agency, had entered a shadow priesthood. Though they'd never met, the
caller—this priest—said he'd been keeping an eye on Neel for years.

"Are you happy where you are?" the priest asked. "Toiling in the
trenches of the Justice Department?"

Neel had been a deputy assistant attorney general for most of
George W. Bush's second term. Though he occupied only a small room
in a massive building, he hardly considered himself a trench worker.

Before Neel could protest, the priest said he had an offer to make.
The Freedom Center, the newest federal intelligence agency, needed a
deputy director. The priest said that he *and many others* thought Neel
was an up-and-comer. Neel had an exemplary record, both as a naval
officer and as a federal prosecutor. The priest was fascinated by Neel's
Punjabi bloodlines. Neel could be a pioneer, he said, and a man of great
value to his government. He wanted Neel to visit him at Langley. If
Neel was interested, that is, in a change.

TWO

HE DROVE ACROSS the river the following afternoon. He had to show his identification at two separate checkpoints on the private road that opened off the parkway. A guard at the second checkpoint, a big man with a blond mustache and swollen face, ordered Neel to switch off the ignition and get out of the car. They would have to call to confirm Neel's appointment, he said. The guard looked Neel up and down while he rested one hand on his hip, above his holster. His partner was on the phone in the guard booth.

"I'm DOJ," Neel said.

"You just hold on, sir. We'll tell you when we're ready." The guard's drawl marked a childhood spent somewhere deeper in Virginia, or south of it.

Neel crossed his arms. The road had curved steeply away from the first checkpoint. Now the trees were dense on either side. He couldn't see the parking lot or the buildings he knew lay ahead. He was alone in the woods with these two men.

"We're clear," shouted the second guard, as he hung up the phone. "Visitors' Lot One."

The first guard smirked as he returned Neel's government ID. "Leave your phone in the glove box. Be safe now."

A man in a gray suit waited at the curb while Neel parked. He greeted Neel by his name and title but didn't introduce himself. Neel followed him across an empty lawn and up a set of granite steps into the building. They walked through metal detectors into a vast but nearly deserted foyer, then descended into a tunnel. An elevator lay a hundred yards ahead. Inside it, Neel's escort pressed the button for the third floor.

The doors opened onto a dimly lit hall. They walked past a woman, who stared resolutely at the carpet as she strode in the opposite direction. At the hall's far end, they turned into a secondary passage. Here the ceiling was so low Neel felt as if he'd entered a mining tunnel. They went left, left again, then right. All the while they passed unmarked doors. The escort walked faster. Neel broke into a trot to keep up. The building was immense. His companion seemed to be taking him to its very center.

They finally stopped at a door marked only with the number 020 on its nameplate. It opened before anyone knocked. A small man with white hair and blue eyes stood inside. He introduced himself to Neel, whispered a few additional words of welcome, and then, after shaking Neel's hand, reached up to squeeze his shoulder. Neel thanked him for the invitation, unconsciously dropping his own voice into a whisper as well. His escort had vanished.

Neel followed the priest into his office and sat in the lone visitor's chair. The room, though small and windowless, was brilliantly lit. Cold air blew through the vents. A whiteboard hung on one wall; the others were bare. Someone had drawn a triangle on the board in red marker, with the corners labeled VISION, VERIFY, and YEMEN. A desk, in black-grained wood, took up much of the space. On it sat a computer, a writing pad, an empty accordion file, and a silver pen. Neel saw his own name written in small, neat script on the pad's otherwise blank top page.

The priest smiled. He wore a slim-cut suit in royal blue—a youthful style Neel would have associated with an investment banker on the make rather than a government official.

"I ran the gauntlet outside," said Neel. "Security is fierce at Langley."

The priest laughed. "That's just for show. The real security is inside, within these walls, but you don't see it."

Neel resolved from then on not to say idiotic things.

The priest nodded toward the desk, where Neel was resting the fingers of one hand. "How does that feel to you?"

"I'm sorry," said Neel, as he snatched back his arm.

"Don't worry, everyone's drawn to it. Go on, touch it again." He explained that the wood had been milled from a species of Sumatran oak, extinct in the wild, that had been famed for its ability to resist both fire and flood. The local foresters called it the tiger tree. The desk was a gift to the agency from some of its closest friends in Indonesia, friends who'd shed blood in the struggle against global communism.

"It's lovely," said Neel.

"Scotch?" asked the priest.

Neel shook his head. He was unable to hide his surprise. Not only were they in the middle of a workday but he also couldn't see a place in that small, bare office where the priest might have kept a bottle and glasses.

The priest rubbed his face. "You're right, of course." Still, he said, he wanted to have Neel over soon to his D.C. apartment, which was not far from Neel's own house.

Neel shifted in his seat.

"I've reviewed your personnel file. Of course I know where you live."

"Of course," said Neel.

The priest said he hosted an occasional salon for men and women in the intelligence world—people who shared a certain cast of mind. If Neel came, the two of them could have a drink and talk in confidence. They would smoke a cigar on the terrace. "You do smoke, don't you? It's not proscribed by the Sikh gurus?"

"Tobacco is proscribed, but I'm not religious."

"I don't suppose you are," said the priest. He winked. Neel found it difficult to meet his gaze.

Suddenly he noticed a strange smell in the air, at once pungent and sweet. As it grew stronger he identified it as talc, or talc scent with potpourri, a dry, flowery smell that couldn't entirely mask an underlying odor of shit. In short, the office smelled like a nursery. Neel looked up at the vent. He tried not to let his unease show.

The priest held up both his palms, as if asking for silence, though Neel wasn't speaking. "Let's go on. Tell me, how's your faith?"

"I'm an atheist."

"I'm speaking of faith in our joint project." He offered Neel a bleached smile. "You'll understand soon enough. I'm going to tell you a story."

He cleared his throat, glanced once at the ceiling vent, and began.

"Like you, I've been in government service my whole working life. In 1970 I was commissioned as a first lieutenant into the Marine Corps. Everyone knew by then that the war in Vietnam could not be won, everyone, that is, except a handful of sociopaths and true believers. I commanded a platoon on a fire support base north of Hue. You've read the books and seen the movies. The reality was worse. We held a plateau. The Air Force had napalmed the hillside but it couldn't defoliate all that terrain. A few trees two hundred yards down the slope, with elephant grass in the hollows, became more trees and thicker grass, until soon you were back in blanketing, primeval jungle. We heard gongs in the night. I was green, you understand, I knew nothing. It was as if they'd dropped me into another century. The month before I arrived, a Marine out on patrol, a kid from Pittsburgh, fell into a pit and got himself impaled on a bamboo stake."

He shook his head. He had glowing, unlined skin, though he must have been at least sixty.

"Hue, a few miles back, was a den of nightmares. The civilians who'd stayed were starving. The surrounding fields burned or trampled. Biblical rain. We had a week on the firebase, then rotated back to Hue for a week in the ruins. Firebase, ruins, firebase, ruins. Two gates of hell." The priest rapped his knuckles on the desk. "We should have poured that drink."

"Awful," said Neel. He'd arranged his face into a patient, attentive expression—lips pressed together, eyebrows slightly raised. It was the expression he always assumed when an older man in a position of power wanted to tell him things.

The priest continued in the same soft voice. On the firebase, he said, the Marines lived knee-deep in slime. Leeches swam in their boots. They couldn't eat the food. Most of the men were on drugs. At the start, the platoon had thirty white soldiers, eight blacks, and two Mexicans. In Hue there was plenty of hate to go around but on the firebase they all suffered together. The priest didn't speak unless he had an order to give, in which case he yelled. Although the firebase was on the coast, near enough to the water that he could have pissed from the hilltop into the South China Sea, he never smelled the ocean, only mud and rot. He sent the men out on patrol, as he was ordered to, but they didn't go far. At the tree line they took a knee and smoked cigarettes until it was time to return. The radio operator transmitted fake coordinates back to the firebase and to Hue. If the priest had forced them to press on, one of the sergeants would have put a bullet into his back. And who could have blamed the shooter? It was a pointless war.

One night, the Vietcong or NVA scouts launched an attack against the firebase. Mortars thumped in the darkness, shells exploded, the Marines scrambled through mud—to the priest it all looked like chaos. But the sergeants shouted orders and the men slowly organized themselves. They shot flares, got down behind the sandbags, and opened up with the machine guns, though they had no targets. Then a shell hit one of the tents. The Marines ran to drag a screaming soldier from the flames. His skin was charred but he was still breathing.

Here the priest closed his eyes and whispered a name. It was a Greek name: *Condos* or *Christos*.

The priest followed his Marines to the casualty tent. He watched the medic work on the wounded man, or rather the wounded boy, for the soldier was only a teenager. He had been lying sick on his cot when the enemy attacked. Now the medic cut off what clothing wasn't already shredded or burned. His face was unmarked, but bomb fragments had torn his body open. The priest stood at the medic's shoulder. He put his hand on the boy's head. The skin had furled from his chest to his thighs. The priest could see everything within. He looked down past the shell fragments and burnt blood and organs and into the welling darkness of the boy whose life he'd been responsible for. Then the boy died. Soon the enemy mortars went silent. The American machine-gunners stopped firing. The patrol the priest sent to the tree line encountered no one. The flares dimmed, night returned, and the platoon was again alone on the plateau.

The priest stood up. Neel did too.

"What are you doing?" said the priest.

Neel sat. His ears were burning.

"That was my only firefight. Ten weeks in, I had infected feet and malarial seizures. They shipped me out. I never returned. But Vietnam changed me, as it changed everyone who fought. Sixty thousand dead Americans. Three million Vietnamese. The war was a disease."

"Yes, sir," said Neel. "It was a terrible mistake."

"What I've come to realize, Neel, is that every war is a mistake or an aberration. Even the ones we must fight. In war, men cease to exist as men. Two thousand years ago, the Romans barred their legions from the city. They understood that a soldier in uniform is an obscenity. In France today, citizens lower their eyes when recruits to the Foreign Legion come marching down a country road. I'm speaking of revulsion. Tell me, how do you feel when the Blue Angels streak over a stadium, or when the Defense Department sends a one-legged corporal to home plate for a standing ovation?"

"I'm not watching a lot of sports these days, with two little girls at home. But I find those displays embarrassing."

"Exactly. The sham patriotism, the spectacle. You understand because you're a veteran." The priest sat down. "And yet we remain under the thumbs of the generals. In Somalia, Afghanistan, Iraq. Eventually the Vietnamese moved on. The Muslims will not forgive or forget or move on."

"Sir, if I may. There are a billion and a half Muslims in the world. They don't all think and act as one."

The priest laughed. "I speak Arabic. I served in Cairo and Beirut. I've written manuals—books, really—for CIA officers on how to recruit agents in the Middle East. I'm not a racist, though you'll find many in this building. I think Arabs and Persians and North Africans in general are beautiful people. But Islam goes deeper than language or nationhood. You come from a family of Punjabi Sikhs. Don't tell me your father or grandfather never talked to you about the Muslims."

Somehow the room had become smaller. Neel forced himself to look the priest in the face.

"I've tried to overcome whatever prejudices my parents brought with them from India. I don't want to sound ridiculous, but I believe all men are created equal."

"Absolutely," said the priest, looking delighted. "Shouldn't we talk about the job?"

Immediately he started on a series of questions. He spoke rapidly, as if he were reading them from a list. He asked whether Neel valued loyalty, whether he was grateful to his mentors, whether he could keep a secret from his wife, and whether he feared death. Neel said yes each time. The priest hardly seemed to take note of his answers.

"Why did you join the Navy? That must have been an unusual choice for a Columbia University English major in 1990. What were you looking for? A good, clean war? Did you like the uniform, did you want to see the world, did you need to get away from your family? What was it?"

Neel gathered himself before he answered. He said there was the way he felt at the time, on the one hand, and the stories he told himself about his service now, on the other. "I was tired of being a student. I didn't want a graduate degree, didn't want to study law, which was what my father wanted me to do. At least, I didn't want to study law right away. Medicine—dealing with suffering and disease—wasn't for me."

"Yes," said the priest, interrupting Neel. "The practice of medicine is disgusting, for the practitioner."

Neel went on. "Finance was boring. I was interested in publishing, but that world didn't seem open to people who looked like me. In any case, I couldn't have told my parents I'd graduated from the Ivy League to work for eighteen thousand a year as an editorial assistant. But everyone admires a young officer. Plus, the Cold War was over. Saddam didn't invade Kuwait until I was already at Officer Candidate School. I didn't think I'd go into battle. And I'd seen *Top Gun*. I could envision myself as a naval airman—in a flying suit, standing on a carrier deck beside a Tomcat. Though I didn't end up in a fighter plane."

"Do you look back fondly on that period of your life?"

"I miss being young, feeling invincible, being able to go without sleep."

"I need to confirm that you didn't become a pacifist as a result of your service."

"I didn't."

"In hindsight, was signing up a mistake?"

"No," said Neel. "Why would you ask that?"

"You were older than most of your peers by the time you got to law school. And now you're older than most of the lawyers at your level in the Justice Department."

"I don't think of that as a sacrifice," said Neel.

The priest gave an almost imperceptible nod. "Do you still read novels?"

"When I'm on vacation."

"Are you close to your children?"

"I hope so."

"Did you support the president's decision to invade Iraq?"

Neel hesitated. "No," he said. "I didn't want Americans to die in an unnecessary war."

"Do you believe a public servant should vote?"

"Yes."

The priest crossed his arms. "And what are your politics, Neel?"

"I don't think you're allowed to ask."

The priest smiled. "Maybe not. But please answer."

Neel tried to suppress his irritation. The priest's questions seemed at once intrusive and pointless. Still, he decided to respond as honestly as he could. If he failed whatever test the priest was conducting, at least he wouldn't have to see this strange little man again.

"I vote for the most progressive Democrat in the primary, not that there's usually much choice. Democrat in the general."

"And how's that working out for you?" The priest laughed once more. "Don't worry. You don't have to answer that one. I'm curious, in fact I want to know everything about you, but you're not here for your politics."

Neel cleared his throat. "Why am I here, if you don't mind?"

"I meant it when I said I'd been keeping an eye on you. We want to refresh the intelligence world with new perspectives. We want outsiders. We like lawyers. The attention to detail, the ability to set aside personal qualms to serve your clients' interests. I'd have my pick of federal prosecutors, but there aren't many with combat experience, there aren't many naval airmen, and certainly none who are also Punjabis. So you flew in a radar jammer, not a fighter—that's all to the good. We don't want cowboys. You can work in a team, you understand signals intelligence, you know what it means to make decisions from imperfect evidence. The nature of our wars is going to change, no matter who wins this election. Fewer troops, more drones, more reliance on intelligence. You were a decent student at Harvard Law and you're a good lawyer but—you'll forgive me for saying this—you're never going to be a great one."

"I've gotten commendations," said Neel.

"Everyone gets commendations. This is the federal government. But you're not making it to the top at Main Justice. My sources say, 'Neel Chima, smart guy, good writer, but he doesn't have a flair for the courtroom.' You're not a trial lawyer."

"There are people who disagree with you."

"Fine. It's more than that. I like the pattern you're building—the pattern of your life."

Neel couldn't hide his confusion.

"You haven't told me the whole truth about why you became an airman. Perhaps you don't know the whole truth. And why did you marry a woman whose family can trace its ancestry back through centuries in this country? A woman who, despite her liberal credentials, happens to be the daughter of a wealthy Republican lawyer? Why was it so important to you, a brown-skinned son of immigrant parents, to join the Justice Department after the September 11th attacks?"

Neel tried to answer but the priest talked over him.

"You joined because you want to be inside. You've spent your entire adult life cladding yourself in layers of American armor. You want, on an almost primal level, to belong. I'm attracted to your hunger."

Neel shook his head.

The priest smiled. "Don't be offended. I'm offering you something better than anonymous toil. A way to vault past all the timekeepers at Main Justice. I'm offering a position that suits your abilities and temperament. You'll have the chance to work on a greater scale. I won't lie. There will be drudgery. It won't always be exciting to read and analyze intelligence reports, or to organize databases of suspected terrorists. But you'll have the opportunity to exercise judgment and discretion over the actions of agencies with billions of dollars at their disposal. You'll put drone attacks into motion. That's real power, Neel, killing power. You didn't have that even in the Navy."

"I never thought of my service that way."

"You'll only be one step away from me. You're aware of my influence in this community. It's a transformative moment. We're replacing the clumsiness of on-the-ground soldiering with an intelligence project that's clean, effective, and just. Maybe we'll even get bin Laden. I want you to lead external operations at the Freedom Center. How does that sound?" The priest's whole face was shining.

"Exciting."

"Good," said the priest. "You'll soon turn forty. You've done plenty of living but you're still fresh, still strong. It's the right time to make a change. Don't take on new work at Main Justice. Pay attention to the everyday things, the little things, look after your daughters, talk to Rebecca—that's your wife's name, right?—and then get ready to bear down for the country."

He stood to shake Neel's hand. He must also have pressed a hidden button because at that moment there was a knock at the door. The same man who'd escorted Neel into the building opened it, nodded once in Neel's direction, and turned to walk away.

"We'll talk soon," the priest said. "Hurry now to catch up to our friend. You don't want to get lost in this building."

Neel followed his escort to the elevators. They didn't speak during the descent or, after the doors opened, in the lower tunnel, the foyer, or the footpath to the visitors' lot. At the car, Neel's escort pointed in the direction of the exit road, nodded again, and turned back to the headquarters building. Neel looked up into the still-bright sky. He told himself he had no reason to be uneasy. The priest was asking him to trade an ordinary career, with its ordinary frustrations, for something great. Would a white man who stood in Neel's place question the favor a patron had shown? Or would that man look back on his years of service and think, yes, of course, these were the spoils, and this was his due?

THREE

FOR DAYS, THEN weeks, he heard nothing. Was that all, he wondered? It felt crueler to have a prize snatched away than never to have been offered the prize at all.

One night, as they were finishing dinner, Rebecca suggested that Neel was better off without the priest and the job he'd promised. She confessed that when Neel had gone to Langley for the interview, a shadow passed over her heart. Did Neel really want to work in intelligence at this point in history? After the lies that had led to the Iraq War, and the disgraces of Abu Ghraib, renditions, torture, and the rest? Wasn't intelligence work dirty work, in the end? Could the Freedom Center—whatever its professed function—really be the place for a principled lawyer like Neel? If he was burned out, if he found himself mired in the bureaucracy of the Justice Department, he could try the academy. Rebecca, newly tenured at Georgetown Law, had a warm relationship with her dean. She could secure Neel an appointment as a clinical instructor. He'd have more time for the girls and for himself. Wasn't he always talking about how he'd like to become a better cook and read more novels?

"I'm not ready to give up on a real career," Neel said.

"That's uncalled for," said Rebecca. "I was trying to help." She stood and began to clear the plates.

Neel apologized. "That was my disappointment talking. It's not that I liked the man, but after the interview my own job, my own life, seemed so drab. It wasn't only the novelty or the power he promised. His argument made sense. Don't we all want this country to turn away from war? Surely it's better to kill a few bad guys using targeted intelligence than to level entire cities. This is something good, something humanitarian."

"Right," said Rebecca. "The Freedom Center might as well be UNICEF."

"The point is, if we're ever going to get out of these wars, we'll need a more effective intelligence service."

"But that doesn't mean that you, Neel Chima, have to participate."

"You know how these jobs are. You put a few years in, everyone gets to know you. Later, after you leave the government, the living's good. Board seats, consulting gigs. It wouldn't be the worst thing to make some money of our own."

"We don't need more money."

"*You* don't need more money."

Rebecca sighed. "He'll call. He's just biding his time."

"I think the moment has passed," said Neel. "Go on. I'll do the dishes."

He tried to return to his life. He ate breakfast with his daughters, went to the office and the courthouse, watched television at night. That September the economy plunged into crisis. With tumult came change. The presidential polls turned. Neel discovered that he shared in the optimism of the moment, that unlikely optimism that surfaces in the wake of calamity. He wondered if his failure at Langley was a blessing. The priest was a man of the old order. He might find himself on the outside in the world that was to come. At dinner Neel talked with Rebecca of brighter days ahead.

———

On election night they watched the returns while the girls slept up-stairs. When it became clear that Obama—a man of dignity, an orator, a bodysurfer!—would win, and win in a landslide, they uncorked the Prosecco and drank a toast. Rebecca finished her glass quickly. Neel drank three. On the screen men and women danced in ballrooms and the streets. Rebecca and Neel made love on the couch for the first time in years.

FOUR

THE PRIEST CALLED Neel at Main Justice the morning after the election.

"Are you ready, son?" he said. "You start Monday at the Freedom Center. My advance scout. Survey the terrain, lay the groundwork."

"What groundwork?" asked Neel. "I didn't hear from you. I haven't met anyone at the agency." He needed, at the very least, to talk to his wife. He'd have to give proper notice at Main Justice. Two business days was an insult to his division chief. Neel was a key player, after all. He supervised investigations.

"Don't be silly," said the priest, and that was that.

He went in for the first time on Monday, November 10, 2008, six days after the election. It happened to be his fortieth birthday. Rebecca and the girls were at the table when he came downstairs. Maya, their older daughter, gave Neel a card she'd made herself. She'd written "I luv U" on the front and "I luv Hallawen" inside. Serena, the younger one, asked when they would eat the cake. Rebecca gave him a narrow, almost weightless box with a bow on it.

"New tie?" he asked, as he pulled apart the wrapping.

She laughed and covered her face.

The tie was dark green, skinny, and squared-off at the bottom. A skinny tie belonged on a skinny man, thought Neel, not someone as thick-chested as he was.

"It's a beauty," he said. He kissed Rebecca on the cheek.

"You'll look ten years younger when you wear it."

"I'll put it on tomorrow."

He poured coffee into a thermos, gave everyone another kiss, and went to the door.

"Walk in like you own the place," said Rebecca.

"I'm not nervous at all," he said, through a tight smile.

Traffic clogged the bridge. Going forward, he'd leave at dawn or even in darkness to shorten the commute. The traffic didn't move much faster on the Virginia side, on the parkway, but it was a pretty drive beneath autumn trees and a clear sky, with sunlight flashing on the river. He switched off the radio.

The new agency occupied fifteen acres of a northern Virginia office park. No one used its formal name ("Office for Counterterrorism Intelligence"). It was always the "Freedom Center," after the building that housed it, a five-story glass cube surrounded by paved lots, blast walls, and a security fence. The government had folded the Freedom Center's construction costs into the black budget for classified programs, so the numbers weren't public. Still, the final figure was rumored to have been spectacular. Neel had looked online for an aerial image of the Center but his search returned only a pixelated blur.

A guard met Neel at his designated parking spot, which was close to the building's entrance. He directed Neel to a lockbox where he could deposit his phone. Then they walked together into the atrium. High windows let in the light, but their thick glass left the outside world distant and dim. Neel felt as if he'd entered an aquarium or a space station. A pulse, originating somewhere deep underground, rose through the soles of his shoes. At the back of the atrium the guard swiped his key card and put his eye to a retina scanner. A door slid open.

"Pretty cool, right?" he said.

"Sure is," said Neel, though no intruder would have been able to get past the fence, walls, and guards he'd already passed that morning.

They walked together into a cavernous room.

"Operations," said the guard, waving his arm.

Dozens of analysts—most of them young white men—sat at work-stations arranged according to an intricate design. Each analyst had three or four monitors on his desk. Everything looked new: paint, furniture, computers, carpets. Massive screens covered the walls at the front and sides of the room.

"You'll meet the director now," said the guard.

Some of the analysts turned to look at Neel as he followed his escort to a short set of stairs. One of them saluted with two fingers to his forehead. Others smiled and nodded. Neel nodded back in their general direction. It wasn't a bad start.

The stairs rose to a hall with two glass-fronted offices. The door to one of the offices was open. The guard knocked on the glass, saluted the man inside, and left.

The director looked ten or fifteen years older than Neel. He had stringy red hair and a colorless face. When he stood, he revealed a surprising potbelly.

"Welcome, Mr. Principal Deputy," said the director. "What can I tell you?"

"Anything at all," said Neel, who already knew this was a man he would neither like nor fear. "Excited for day one. I'm at your service."

The director waved Neel over to the couch, which smelled of new plastic. He lowered himself into his own chair with a sigh.

"I'm a short-timer, as you know, given the scale of Senator McCain's defeat. I've had a great four-year run at the Center. But out with the old. My current deputy will be leaving too. And then a band of clean-cut Yankees will run the show." He smirked.

"Am I a Yankee? I was born in New Jersey."

"Good one," said the director, still smirking. "Now, do you know what we do?"

"I think so," said Neel.

The director continued as if Neel hadn't spoken. The government had built the Freedom Center, he said, in the wake of Al Qaeda's attacks on the World Trade Center and Pentagon. The new agency stood apart from the others (the NSA, CIA, Defense Intelligence Agency, and so on) in the vast national security apparatus. It gathered no intelligence of its own. Instead, it organized and evaluated the work of its sister agencies. In other words, said the director, the Freedom Center's analysts stood on a peak that overlooked many valleys. Their mission was to search for patterns and connections, however faint, that those closer to the front lines might have missed.

"We have the finest analysts down on that floor," he said. "Patriots. They hold your fate in their hands. They'll read a thousand field reports a day from the FBI and local police departments to find the ten that matter. They'll send those ten up to you. And if you can recognize which of those ten contains a real nugget, you'll have the keys to the White House. Though you'll hand the nugget over to me, of course, while I'm still here."

"Sir, of course," said Neel.

"Call me Smith."

Neel nodded.

"If a new name makes it up from the floor, if there's any chance whatsoever that the individual poses a threat, we put his name on a list. Domestic watch list, blacklist for government contractors, no-fly list, the works. No matter how tenuous the connection to terrorism. No matter how shaky the evidence. This is intelligence work, not criminal investigations, not prosecution. It's a low bar. Anything at all, a rumor, a footfall, we enter the name into the record. We don't want the bad guys to surprise us ever again."

"Understood."

"The Talibs are rearing their filthy heads in Afghanistan. It's boom times for opium." Smith rubbed a thumb and index finger together. "They have money for arms. They can safely rest and regroup across the border in tribal Pakistan. We need to nip this in the bud. You'll direct external operations. Take the fight to them so we don't have to fight here. We don't want any spillover into the homeland. No incidents. Okay?"

"Okay," said Neel.

"You've been anointed. You have your clearances. Now get your bio-metrics done, sign the forms, and go home. Come in early tomorrow and you'll have the run of the place."

They stood to shake hands. Then Smith raised one of his warm, thick palms to Neel's face. He gave Neel's cheek a little pinch. His hand smelled of lavender.

"So this is our young Turk," Smith said.

Though Neel was shocked by Smith's gesture, he thanked the director and turned away. But as he descended the stairs with the guard who had by now reappeared, he also recognized another feeling within: a new kind of self-regard, a new pride. Even this weak and vulgar man had been forced to acknowledge that Neel wasn't just a subordinate.

But the smell of Smith's hand, or Neel's memory of that smell, lingered. He spent the rest of the morning completing his paperwork, having his fingers and retina scanned, and testing his electronic swipe card. He began to feel unwell. Soon he developed a headache, which grew into a migraine. He finished his tasks before lunch, retrieved his phone, walked to his Honda sedan, and drove out to the other side of the blast walls. There he pulled over, though he was still on a restricted road. He opened the door, leaned out, and threw up onto the new blacktop. He wiped his lips with the back of his hand before he closed the door, swallowed a mouthful of tepid coffee from his thermos, and began the long drive home.

FIVE

HE CHECKED THE clock at midnight, an hour after he'd gone to bed. Then at 12:25, 12:40, 12:52. He tried not to disturb Rebecca when he turned to the nightstand. Sometimes fifteen minutes had passed, sometimes five. At two A.M. he wondered if he'd slept at all. Finally, after an interval that seemed as brief as any other, the digits moved from 2:16 to 3:28, so he knew that yes, he'd slept a little. At four he switched off the alarm. He reached under the covers for Rebecca, touching his fingertips to her thigh. He kissed her bare shoulder. She moaned in her sleep.

It was the darkest hour of the night. He crossed from the wool rug to the hardwood floor and then the bathroom tile. He closed the door as gently as he could, switched on the heat lamp, and opened the tap. He was dry-eyed and thirsty. As a young officer out on the USS *Nimitz* for combat exercises, he'd lived in such a state for days on end. He worked twenty hours, slept three, showered, dressed, and reported again for duty. Afterward, in port, he forgot about the suffering. What remained was a confidence that he could survive any trial. But he was older now. How long could he run on coffee and nerves? By nightfall, when he came home, he'd have nothing left for his family. He'd want music and a hot bath, with a tumbler of whiskey.

It was his third day on the job.

He was at his desk by 5:30 A.M. On the Operations floor, the analysts on night duty approached the end of their twelve-hour shifts. One of the large wall screens showed the number and path of every overseas flight that would reach the Eastern Seaboard that morning. A Freedom Center analyst had already cross-checked each passenger manifest against the national no-fly list. Another screen listed every passenger whom a border patrol or FBI agent would detain on arrival in the United States for a national security interrogation. The Freedom Center's analysts were transmitting, in real time, relevant queries from interested agencies to frontline officers at the airports. There were separate protocols for land crossings from Canada and Mexico and for land, sea, and air freight. Other analysts at the Center summarized overnight developments in surveillance, threat assessments, and critical investigations from anywhere in the federal government or local law enforcement.

Neel began by reading the daily intelligence briefs from the other agencies. The NSA warned that Hasni Sayyed, a citizen of both the United States and Yemen, continued to preach in a mosque in Aden of the duty of young Yemeni men to attack the infidels wherever they could be found. Sayyed placed weekly calls to two cellphone numbers associated with regional Al Qaeda commanders. The NSA nominated Sayyed for a targeted strike at the earliest opportunity. The FBI had infiltrated additional cells of angry young Somali Americans in Minneapolis. The Bureau's Intelligence Branch had "a high degree of confidence" that its penetration of those networks was comprehensive enough to forestall a domestic terrorist attack. Treasury had flagged a Lebanese-born currency trader in Houston who'd been transmitting deposits to formerly white-listed charities in Syria that may have been Hezbollah fronts. And so on.

Already, in his first week, Neel found reading the briefs to be a chore, from the abbreviations at the headers of the documents ("TS/SI/NF"—top secret, containing communications intelligence, and not for distribution to foreigners), to the opaque language within ("NSA noms OBJECTIVE CYPRESS to NATSEC PRINCIPALS COMTE for CAPTURE/KILL TGT AUTH; requests EXPEDITED ACTION WINDOW"), to the sheer volume of the material. He was impatient. But to generate targets and operations of his own he first had to learn the terrain. After reading the morning reports, he went on to edit the Freedom Center's brief, which ranked the threats the other agencies had identified in order of seriousness. He sent this brief to Smith for his approval. The priest, whom the president-elect had just named his special advisor on national security and a leader on his transition team, called at eight. Neel read him selections from the same document he'd sent Smith. The priest listened in silence, thanked Neel at the end, and told him to keep up the good work. "Remember," he said at the close, "nothing impresses like coming in early."

At ten minutes after eight, Neel dropped to the floor for the first of his three daily workouts. He did forty push-ups, rested a minute, and did forty more. In the late morning, he'd perform two hundred crunches; in the afternoon, a hundred squats. He couldn't run a mile without fighting for breath, he suffered backaches and heartburn and could no longer touch his toes, but he consoled himself with the knowledge that he still had a soldier's raw strength.

At eight thirty Neel met with Smith in a conference room. Neel's fellow deputy director, Jon Vanderhoof, a blond man with a long face, joined the meeting as well. Vanderhoof was technically Neel's subordinate—Neel had been hired as the Freedom Center's *principal* deputy director, a position that hadn't existed before his arrival—but the government had assigned the two men to the same pay grade. With Neel taking responsibility for the Freedom Center's external operations and liaisons with other agencies, Vanderhoof managed the Center's internal functions. He oversaw the floor analysts, organized them into working groups, and reviewed the summary reports they drafted. In their morning meeting, Neel, Vanderhoof, and Smith discussed the daily intelligence briefs, though Smith, in his blank passivity, seemed entirely unaware of their contents. Next Vanderhoof reported on the overnight additions to the threat matrix—the master list of suspected terrorists that it was the Freedom Center's duty to maintain. The matrix contained two categories, Violent Extremist U.S. Nationals ("VER-MIN") and Violent Extremist Foreign Nationals ("VERM-F"). The first list now held more than twenty thousand names; the second, close to a quarter million. Neel observed the other two men. He took notes but said little. At meeting's end, Smith said once again that the Freedom Center should always err on the side of inclusion. Its analysts must add every potential suspect to the threat matrix, with every name implicating more names as the algorithms that organized and cross-indexed the federal databases did their work. Always the lists grew longer, and the matrix deepened. "Never stop short," said Smith, through his stained teeth, "and never get soft." He stood, slapped Vanderhoof and Neel on their backs, and strode out of the room.

After the meeting, Neel went down to the Operations floor, though Vanderhoof told him there was no need. ("Downstairs you have the bookkeepers; up here we're the corporate titans," he'd said, on Neel's first full day. "They check the wiring. We have our fingers on the nuclear button. They fill the tank, we fly the jet." "I get it," said Neel, "thank you.") By now the night shift workers had logged out and left, and forty fresh analysts arrived for the day shift. Though the overhead lights were dim, Neel could see their faces by the glow of their screens. He knew they sensed his presence too, even when they didn't look at him. When he descended to the floor a secret tremor seemed to cross the room. The analysts sat up straighter in their chairs. They frowned more intently at their computers. Of course Neel liked the effect he had on them.

Now the large screens at the front and sides of the hall showed muted cable news programs and live aerial surveillance of Kabul, Baghdad, and D.C. Neel paused his walk across the floor to look over an analyst's shoulder. It must have been hard, dull work, this endless assembling of details. The various intelligence agencies captured a flood of electronic information every day—emails, text messages, chat logs, search histories, bank transactions, GPS coordinates, telephone metadata, and so on, from entire populations—and sent the cache to installations in Utah and New Mexico. There, in the western deserts, on machines that filled vast, air-conditioned halls, the government would store the data for decades to come. Most of the Freedom Center's analysts were recent college graduates who'd been hired for their technical or foreign-language skills. They were assigned to regional teams (Saudi Arabia, other Gulf states, Iraq, Afghanistan, Pakistan, the Horn of Africa, et cetera), and further divided by subject matter. One analyst in the Saudi group might be assigned to cover religious leaders, for example, while another would be responsible for reviewing suspicious financial transactions emanating from the Kingdom. Each analyst would receive a notification when another federal agency submitted an intelligence report that fell within his or her purview. The analyst would then cross-check that report against the national databases for possible connections and convergences. If, for example, the NSA was newly surveilling a cleric in Qatar—one who had both taken a radical turn and found an online following—a Freedom Center analyst would determine whether the cleric had any connection to people or entities of interest in the United States. Perhaps the cleric had a nephew in Michigan who'd attended a mosque under FBI surveillance. The analyst would immediately recommend that his supervisor nominate the nephew for the no-fly list and threat matrix. He'd request that the NSA surveil the nephew's international communications. He'd notify the FBI that a young American in a targeted mosque had a suspicious foreign connection. The FBI might investigate the nephew. Eventually, if the nephew was found not to be a terrorist sympathizer, the Bureau would seek to turn him into an informant, perhaps dangling as a reward the opportunity to one day exit the no-fly list and again enjoy the prospect of foreign travel.

"We want everything," said the analyst at whose desk Neel stood. "Where he goes, what he says, what he buys. We'll see what he's planning in the data before he acts."

If the Freedom Center failed, if some conspiracist or madman managed to kill Americans in another terrorist attack, the electronic record would remain. Eventually, an intelligence review board or congressional committee would convene. Someone in a position of authority at the Freedom Center—someone like Neel—would have to explain what had gone wrong. Why didn't the Freedom Center flag the pivotal phone call, internet search, knife purchase, or hotel stay? Why didn't the Center transmit an alert? Why had the Center let Americans die, when the other agencies had already collected the information it needed?

Vanderhoof told Neel that when he spoke to the analysts, which wasn't often, he uttered a single directive: "Don't fuck this up." Most of them would put in a year, said Vanderhoof, maybe eighteen months, before they'd burn out and quit. Some asked for a transfer to another agency. Others signed on with a private firm to do the same work at three times the pay. The Freedom Center couldn't retain enough analysts on a government salary, so it contracted with Lockheed and General Dynamics for additional talent at half a million a year per head. There were young men on the floor who made far more money than the brain trust, Vanderhoof said. "But we're still the bosses." He patted Neel on the back.

Upstairs, at his desk, Neel often saw Smith, whose glass-walled office faced his own, staring into space with a baffled expression. No terrorist had carried out a major attack on American soil on his watch. He'd already advised Neel to trust in the power of prayer. Smith took long lunch breaks every day. Vanderhoof warned Neel not to interrupt the director from two to three in the afternoon, when he napped on his couch. After Obama began his term, Smith would doubtless sign on with a defense contractor of his choosing. The government was spending billions every year on software and equipment. The technology evolved and enemies changed, but the playbook for contractors didn't: they hired insiders, asked them to call up their old friends in the agencies, and watched the money flow.

"They might as well pack that dude in ice," whispered Vanderhoof, in the break room late in the morning. He and Neel were standing in line for coffee.

"I thought Smith was your mentor," said Neel.

Vanderhoof smiled. "It's the government. Every man for himself."

Vanderhoof was next up at the machine. He poured all that was left in the pot into his oversized mug.

"Your turn to brew, Chima," he said. "Learn the ropes."

He winked at Neel on the way out.

SIX

VANDERHOOF CALLED ON a Friday afternoon. It was the end of Neel's first week at the Freedom Center. He was reading a stack of classified reports with a pen in his hand.

"My dude, my dog," Vanderhoof said.

"Jon."

"I have a cold one up here with your name on it."

"I don't know, Jon. I have work."

"It's Friday, my man. I have to go home to a fish dinner. At least give me a happy hour."

Neel sighed. "In twenty," he said.

Forty-five minutes later he walked to the elevator, got in, and pressed the button for the fifth floor, which was the top floor. He wondered if he was making a mistake. He was the higher-ranking official, after all. He could have told Vanderhoof to bring his beers down to the second floor, where they would still be within shouting distance of Operations. Or perhaps he should have reminded Vanderhoof that they were forbidden to drink on the job. They may have worked in a glass-fronted office complex in northern Virginia, under blanket surveillance and armed guard, surrounded by towns and suburbs unmarred by the looming recession, but they were still on duty. The nation was at war. American lives were always at stake.

Even as those words ran through his head, Neel laughed at himself. He was a lawyer and a bureaucrat. So far his new job had consisted of organizing databases and reading and drafting reports. No one would die that afternoon if he and Vanderhoof took their hands off their keyboards to open a beer.

Vanderhoof had a corner office, on a hall otherwise occupied by the Center's software engineers. Neel knocked on the door. Vanderhoof took a minute to open it.

"I was on the phone with the wife," he said, forming air quotes around the phrase "the wife." He rubbed his big face. "She's six months pregnant. Or like, five."

"Congratulations."

"He'll be our first. I was firing blanks for a few years. Phutt, putt," he said, making a gun with his fingers. "Then we went to the fertility clinic and shit got real expensive, even with federal benefits."

His shirt was rumpled, one of his eyes bloodshot, and his left cheek imprinted with the carpet's crosshatch.

Neel noticed that Vanderhoof's office, unlike his own, had a window to the outside. "Natural light," he said. "How did you swing that?"

"Seniority. Also, Smith wanted me up here to keep an eye on the nerds. He doesn't understand why a place that indexes and mines huge troves of electronic data might need some coders on staff. He thinks these guys are playing video games on the government's dime."

Vanderhoof blinked rapidly as he spoke. With his wide, pale irises, transparent eyebrows, and steep forehead, he looked like a fox: a handsome Arctic fox.

Neel sat down. "Maybe I should put in a request for this office. Get a little distance from the Operations floor and the new director, whoever he is. I could use some space to think."

"I'm sure you could, Neel. But you'll have to wait on that one because I'm staying right here." Vanderhoof grinned like a lottery winner. "I got the call two hours ago."

"You're not leaving?" asked Neel. He was unable to hide his surprise. Then, with Vanderhoof still smiling, he said, more gently now, "Smith said you'd be out the door with him. But this is great news."

"Yeah, you're stoked. The big dogs decided they want continuity into the new administration. They don't need Smith because he's an idiot. But you and me, that's a powerful combination. Look happier, man!"

He spun in his chair, opened the door to the mini fridge behind his desk, and took out two cans of beer. He pushed one across the desk.

"Please enjoy a fine domestic microbrew."

"How did you get your beer past the entrance scanners?"

"I'm an old pro, I know all the tricks. Though I'm younger than you in man years." He raised his can to Neel. "Government pay sucks, but with the kid coming it's not the right time to start a new gig."

Neel opened his beer and took a sip, trying not to let his irritation show.

Vanderhoof turned in his chair to look out the window. When he swiveled back to Neel, moments later, his eyelids were lower. "I'm so fucking tired," he said. "The wife has sciatica. I'm up at two in the morning to give her a back rub. She can't even take a crap. I hear her crying in the bathroom. What am I supposed to do? Go in there and say, 'Baby, if you could just unclench?'"

"I'm sorry. I've been there," said Neel, though in truth Rebecca's pregnancies had been uneventful.

"Sorry for the intimate details, but if we're going to be partnered up I want you to understand where I'm coming from."

"Everyone's a mystery, Jon. Please go on."

"I might be a goofball but I know what's what. I grew up in northern Michigan—woods and water, killer insects eight months a year, a deep freeze in winter. Every December I get an email from my mom telling me another truckful of teenagers skidded off black ice into the bay. They're hard people up there. Beards, flannel, firewood, hunting rifles. You get to thirteen, fourteen years old, you start drinking like a Soviet dockworker."

Neel looked at the beer in his own hand. He took a sip.

"There was this one skinny kid in my class. He had a lisp, floppy white hair, liked to sing and dance. Even the decent people called him Princess. And the jocks were like, 'Fag, fag, fag, you fucking fag.' He hung himself with an extension cord sophomore year of high school. His mom cut him down in the closet. She saved his life, but when he came out of the coma he had brain damage. I ran into him a few times afterward. He was in a wheelchair, had diapers on, smelled of shit—it was that kind of situation."

"This country really sucked in the eighties," said Neel.

"What I'm saying is you come out of a place like Sault Sainte Marie and if you're like me, someone who's not prejudiced, or at least someone who has tried to grow out of prejudice, you still might not want a gay son. Life's too hard. It's one thing to be gay in D.C. or San Francisco or Palm Springs, but what if your gay son wants to travel? What if he goes to Colombia or Uganda or some other place where they lynch people for being gay? What if my gay son gets offered a job in Dallas? You understand what I'm saying? People are full of hate."

"There are other ways to look at the issue, Jon."

"That's why I'm telling you this. I'm being vulnerable here. I'm fully aware that this whole line is a dullard's argument. Not only because gay men have a secret world straight men know nothing about, so that they live two lives while we live just one, or that they get to fuck like mice for as many years as they want to fuck like mice, but also because when you emerge from a crucible, when you survive that level of adversity, you come out stronger. I mean, look at you. Nails."

"Jon, I'm not gay."

"My point is, Neel, that it's the same thing with racism. You came here from the Navy and the Justice Department, places that are in a time capsule. Hillbillies, Scots-Irish, old line WASPs on top. Okay, there are some Jews in the Justice Department and blacks in the Navy but it's still America as she was. And then there's you. You got to Main Justice right after 9/11, correct? While Sikhs were getting shot up at gas stations because the yokels thought they were Taliban? Your father probably wears a turban. What did he do, drive a taxi?"

"He's an accountant."

"So I know you are fucking steel. I want to be on your team." Vanderhoof put his head back for a violent gulp of beer. "I've been in intelligence since '96. First at the Department of Energy, then the last four years in this shop. I know a lot of pros. Truth is, some were surprised you got this gig. You weren't the most obvious candidate. But word is you have a friend in a very high place. You're going somewhere. So bounce your ideas off me anytime you want. I'm going to ride your coattails."

Neel fought the urge to smile. "I'm feeling quite anonymous, to tell the truth."

"Together we can own this place, dude. Give it two years and then set your sights on the directorship. And when you get it, don't forget about your wingman."

"Let's not get ahead of ourselves, Jon. I'm still learning the job."

Vanderhoof waved his hand dismissively. They drank what remained of their beers. From outside, beyond the blast-proof windows, a jackhammer struck the pavement in regular bursts.

"You made the right choice in coming to the Freedom Center," said Vanderhoof, when Neel stood up to leave. "Hear that? Congress always has money for us. We'll build more and more. Intelligence is a growth industry."

Neel's first thought, on getting back to his office, was to tell Rebecca that he worked with the strangest men. But when he called, she didn't answer.

He looked at the papers on his desk. He had to read them before the weekend. He couldn't take classified documents home. That meant he would be working into the night. He'd long kept an irregular schedule. At the Justice Department he'd stayed late when preparing for a trial or sentencing hearing. Then, when the court proceedings ended, he'd go home in midafternoon for a week or two. It would be the same story now, he thought, only without any lulls. Rebecca picked up the girls at five from their after-school program. She was used to spending the evenings alone with them.

Downstairs, analysts were sparse on the Operations floor. It was four in the afternoon. He sipped lukewarm coffee to clear his head. The printouts on his desk held summaries of new FBI counterterrorism stings. Most of the subjects had attracted the Bureau's attention because they'd brushed up against other men or women in the national threat matrix. Neel had selected a few examples for Smith's inbox, more or less at random. A black Muslim convert in Long Beach had forwarded an email complaining about the secret cabal of Jews and Freemasons that controlled global banking to all two hundred and thirty contacts in his address book. Three Malians in Queens had been reading news articles from a West African website that featured contributors sympathetic to violent Islamic fundamentalism. An American-born Jordanian told a fellow worshipper at his mosque, who happened to be an NYPD informant, that he longed for the day when the Arab armies would push the Israelis into the sea. None of these men seemed likely to plan or execute an attack. But as Vanderhoof said, you had to show Smith you cared. Better to forward the director reports from unpromising investigations than no reports at all. Even if Smith didn't read the documents, he liked to see them on his desk.

The foreign threats were more significant, in Neel's eyes, not least because most arose in actual theaters of war. At the Justice Department, Neel had investigated attempts by Americans, or foreigners at American universities, to send restricted technology overseas. Many of his cases involved the transfer of software or industrial secrets to Chinese interests. The work was important to national security, but he wasn't hunting terrorists. Now he would be trying to identify and eliminate militants before they could harm Americans in conflict zones. That month, the Freedom Center had identified three actionable targets each in Somalia and Yemen, and nine in the tribal borderlands of Pakistan. It was this last set of targets, said the priest in his call with Neel that morning, the Pakistani targets, that had gripped the imagination of key players in the incoming administration. In Pakistan, the Taliban commanders had found a sanctuary where they could plan attacks, rest, and regroup. If there was a way out of the deepening mire in Afghanistan, it lay across the border, said the priest. And don't get me started on bin Laden and Al Qaeda, he added. Because we were not officially at war in Pakistan, American covert operatives and intelligence professionals had the field. The generals, with all their ponderousness and planning, could only interfere so much. In the new administration, a small group of White House decision-makers would approve the targets the Freedom Center chose. The United States was carrying out a drone strike every week; soon it would be a strike a day. Pakistan, said the priest, was where Neel would make his mark.

Neel clicked through intelligence reports relating to foreign targets, highlighting those he wished to print out and review more carefully. By seven thirty he had another stack of a hundred pages. He walked to the break room for a bag of popcorn and brought it back to his office to eat at the glass. Under the Government Accountability Office's guidelines, even the Freedom Center, awash in funding as it was, had to turn up its thermostats at five. Neel's skin felt greasy in the warmer air.

Below, twenty-five analysts had started on the late shift: nighthawks, loners. The largest wall screen showed a video feed from the surveillance blimp that hovered over the Virginia shore of the Potomac. Washington glowed on the opposite bank. Neel wanted to call Rebecca again, but it wasn't the right time. She would be giving the girls a bath or reading them bedtime stories. He wiped his hands on a paper towel and returned to his desk.

At nine Neel switched off his desk lamp. He'd read every report in his stack that pertained to Pakistani targets at least twice. An idea was forming. He walked downstairs and out of the building without speaking to anyone on the floor.

The Friday traffic moved slowly on the parkway, despite the late hour. Neel turned on the stereo. He'd left a Cannonball Adderley CD in the player. At home Neel would listen to whatever Rebecca wanted—classical, rock, pop hits on the radio—but when he was alone he chose jazz. His freshman roommate at Columbia kept his radio tuned to WBGO, the Newark jazz station, at all hours. It hadn't taken Neel long to fall in. He loved the intricacy of the music—an intricacy that didn't close off the musicians from their audience, and that always allowed for freedom. There were nights Neel lay in bed with the lights off, after his roommate had fallen asleep, when he listened to Monk or Coltrane through his headphones and told himself that he was at last discovering the real beauty of American life.

Now he listened to "Autumn Leaves," the first track of *Somethin' Else*. It was a melancholy song, a song for rain and darkness, with a melody so spare and lovely it made Neel's everyday concerns seem paltry. Why work so hard, why strive, when such grace existed for anyone who cared to listen? But now, at the song's five-minute mark, just as Miles Davis, who was in on Adderley's session, climbed to the high notes of his trumpet solo, Neel switched off the CD player. As always, he recognized the beauty of Davis's riff, but this time he didn't feel the ache. His own thoughts intruded. To listen to the album as background or mood was to dishonor it. He'd rather drive in silence.

He pressed and released the brake. The line rolled on. Red taillights glimmered on the water and through the trees. His mind wandered. He thought about the warehouses the government was building in the desert, to fill with servers and store all the data in the world. He thought about his daughters, by now asleep—he hoped—in their room. He thought about the boulders down in the river, which were ancient, and fixed, and would outlast them all.

He reached the bridge at a quarter to ten. Here the traffic moved more steadily. He coasted down the exit ramp and into the city.

On 18th Street, driving with his window down, he smelled cigarette smoke and heard dance music and laughter. At a red light, he watched a group of young women talking outside a bar. They wore tight sweaters and wool hats or scarves. One of them, her eyes brimming with the cold, stared back at him. And what if he pulled over, thought Neel, and parked, and asked that young woman if he could buy her a drink? Would she laugh at him? Would she look at his wedding ring and tell him to go home to his wife? The woman turned away just as the signal changed to green. Neel shook his head. You're a fool, he thought, you're washed up.

The house smelled of ashes. Neel found a note from Rebecca on the kitchen counter, telling him she'd run the self-clean cycle on the oven. She asked him to wipe the inside down with a wet rag before he came upstairs. "Kisses," she wrote.

Neel did as she asked. Afterward the burnt smell lingered on his hands. He decided to pour himself a glass of bourbon from an expensive bottle Rebecca's parents had given him at Christmas the year before.

The first sip brought warmth to his head. He could forget about drinking for a week or a month, but with one taste it always came back—the sense of well-being and wholeness, and of distance from all that troubled him. Each sip, each glass, posed a new question. Stop here, or go on? One small glass was always best. But some weekend nights he needed more from whiskey than a little heat. Then he'd drink four or five or six glasses, each bigger than the last, until he'd emptied half a bottle and raised a roar in his ears to drown out the world.

He looked around the kitchen and through to the living room: thick rugs, a green couch, heavy ceiling beams. It was all his wife's doing. She'd chosen the house, her parents had given them money for a down payment, she'd decorated it.

Her footsteps sounded on the floor above. He heard her open the bedroom door and walk to the head of the stairs. After working all week he'd come home to clean the grime from the oven. Now he wanted to enjoy his drink. It wasn't the time to talk. He sipped whiskey at the counter until he heard her return to their room. The darkness outside the kitchen window suddenly darkened. Rebecca had switched off the light and gone to bed.

One of the intelligence summaries he'd reviewed that evening pinpointed a group of men in Waziristan, in the Pakistani tribal regions. The men were anonymous but a Freedom Center analyst, cross-checking a CIA report against NSA intercepts, believed they represented a threat to the United States. One of the men regularly called red-listed numbers—numbers associated with known Taliban commanders—from his mobile phone. The caller, who was perhaps the group's leader, wore a tactical vest over his salwar kameez. His underlings had been carefully unloading boxes from the beds of two well-maintained pickup trucks they parked in the courtyard of the compound. Did the boxes contain weapons? Explosives? Occasionally, a luxury sedan sat in the compound too. Out in the open, the men scurried, rather than walked, between buildings. No women or children appeared in a surveillance drone's lengthy video feed. The CIA had no human intelligence on the group, no agents, no sources, but the signature seemed clear. These men formed a militant cell. Our soldiers across the border in Afghanistan were in danger. Neel had examined a series of still photos captured by the drone. From that great height the men looked like ants: their bodies were shadows, their faces could not be seen. Waziristan, the land itself, was as dry and stark as the moon.

This group or cell occupied too low a position on the threat matrix to qualify, at present, for a drone strike. The government had more important targets to hit. But Neel noted that in this instance the Freedom Center could issue a targeting recommendation based on the purely objective criteria of images, signals, and patterns. The fact that the CIA had no informants wasn't an obstacle. No local source had corrupted the targeting process by pursuing his own interests. No one was carrying out a vendetta. Neel decided to keep an eye on the group, and on any new intelligence that arose in its file, going forward. Perhaps his interest was arbitrary, a matter of chance, but wasn't so much of life, and even death itself, a matter of chance? The priest wanted him to do something bold in Pakistan. This remote borderland offered him a stage.

Neel's father was a quiet man, but occasionally he'd told Neel stories about his own childhood on the north Indian plains. He'd grown up in Punjab, three hundred miles from the mountains of Waziristan. He was nine years old in August 1947, a little Sikh boy with his hair in a topknot, when India won its independence. That whole summer was a bloodbath. Sikhs and Hindus slaughtered Muslims in east Punjab, on the Indian side of the new border; Muslims slaughtered Sikhs and Hindus in west Punjab, on the Pakistani side. There were no Muslims in Neel's father's village, in east Punjab, and his father witnessed no killings. But young men left the village on Sundays to join the pogroms in Ludhiana, the closest city. Neel's father watched the fires of the burning Muslim quarter at night, on the horizon, from the roof of his family home.

His father lived in Punjab until he finished college. Later he moved to Delhi to work as the bookkeeper of a manufacturing firm. The bosses let him know from the outset that a young Sikh—a Jat, a peasant by birth—could only hope to advance so far. In India, you needed the right name and caste, or the right connections with politicians and gangsters. In 1969, after Congress repealed the racially exclusionary provisions of the Immigration Act, he moved to the United States. He found economic freedom in New Jersey despite the bigotry he encountered. It was enough for him, he told Neel, to be out from under the thumbs of the Brahmins. His college friends who'd stayed in north India, Punjabi boys who once dreamed of glittering careers, ended up drowning themselves in the bottle, he said.

Neel considered his father to be a tolerant man. He'd never disparaged their black or Puerto Rican neighbors in Paramus. He voted Democrat, sent Neel to the local public schools, and donated to the food bank. Still, he was convinced that Islam was irredeemable, a religion of fanatics. The violence of his childhood had marked him forever. He warned Neel never to marry a Muslim woman. Neel thought this an old prejudice, a holdover from another country, and shrugged it off. But he wondered now whether it had left a trace. If he was being honest with himself, didn't he also resent that handful of Muslim terrorists who'd made life forever uncomfortable for other brown-skinned men in the United States? He'd never felt as self-conscious as he had in the first months after the September 11 attacks—at least not since his own childhood. Was it easier for him to work at the Freedom Center, knowing that most of its targets were Muslims? The question wasn't something he could discuss with Rebecca.

When he was sure she was asleep, he got off the counter stool and went to the refrigerator. He took out jars of pickles and olives, a wedge of Gouda, and a package of salami. Maya, their older daughter, had left a vanilla cupcake on a plate with the note "Lucky Dada."

He ate at the counter. Afterward he added water to his glass and a little more whiskey. He sipped and sipped again. Warmth spread through his body. He discovered certain insights. Though the life he and Rebecca shared was ordinary on the surface, with any couple's ordinary compromises and distance, a hidden grandeur lay beneath. For a moment he wanted to go upstairs to wake her, and tell her he was grateful. He thought of his aging parents, who still lived in his childhood home. He realized, with a shiver, that he wouldn't feel his father's absence when he died. Thoughts of home turned to thoughts of food. How he'd love a plate, right then, of his aunt's goat-and-spinach curry. He'd have dropped to his knees.

He finished his drink, poured himself a nightcap, and took the glass and his laptop to the couch. He'd just sat down when the stairs creaked. Moments later, Maya came into the living room on her tiptoes. She was six and in the first grade. Neel waved her over, pulled her onto the couch, and kissed her head. She had the softest hair.

"I like the way your breath smells, Dada. Did you find your cupcake?"

Neel said it was the most delicious thing he'd ever eaten.

"I know it was," said Maya, as she slipped back to the floor. "I heard you, and I wanted to make sure you got it. Don't be sad, Dada, but I'm going to bed now."

She climbed lightly up the stairs.

As a baby, she hadn't slept well. Neel used to carry her around their apartment after dinner so Rebecca could rest. He wouldn't forget the way Maya's tiny fist closed around his little finger, or how warm she was in his arms, or the strange, sweet smell that lingered on his shirt after he laid her in the bassinet.

And how much did he know of her life now?

The curtains were open to the night, which was cold and lovely as always. He swirled whiskey in his mouth.

He typed his password into the laptop. The security experts at the Freedom Center had installed software that masked what he did online. They assured Neel that no one—not the internet companies, not the Russians or Chinese, not even the NSA—could trace his activity. He wasn't sure how far he could trust them but for now the drink had pushed his qualms aside.

It was after eleven. Neel looked at a sports website, though he no longer followed sports. He watched a few highlights from that night's basketball games. Players he didn't recognize performed spectacular feats. He glanced at the *Post*'s home page, where the headlines focused on Obama's cabinet picks and the scale of the financial crisis. He read the entry for "Waziristan" on Wikipedia.

Then he opened a private window. He typed in the address for a website he hadn't visited in at least a year. On the website's home page, he entered the search terms for the clip he wanted. He found it easily. The clip had achieved a canonical position, being among the twenty most viewed scenes of all time in its category, with more than seven million views. Neel clicked through to the video. He silenced the audio.

The scene opened with a shot of a dim passage or tunnel taken from a low angle. Water trickled down mossy walls to a dirt floor. Lights sagged from an overhead electrical cord. The passage might have been the entrance to an abandoned subway station. Neel turned up the volume slightly. Machinery rumbled in the background. A voluptuous blonde in a short, tight dress entered the passage. She walked quickly in her platform shoes. Two shirtless black men followed. Both were tall and slender, though one of them, who was very dark, had a vanishing, African slenderness, perhaps a South Sudanese slenderness, while the other, who was lighter-skinned and freckled, had small, hard muscles across his chest and back. The three of them walked down the passage to a larger though still dim and filthy room. Here the noise of machinery grew louder. The three actors looked at one another. The woman and the darker man undressed while the light-skinned man watched. After the briefest preliminaries, the darker man pushed the woman against a pillar. He began to sodomize her. Presumably the second man would soon undress as well: the convention in these movies was that all three actors participated in the encounter. But Neel never watched the video long enough to find out. What compelled him wasn't only the woman's lively, wholesome face or her powerful thighs. Nor was it the ridged scar that curved from the darker man's neck to his lower back, a mark of suffering that imbued his presence with a survivor's mystery and grace. Nor that the acts performed onscreen, though portrayed as consensual, were vigorous to the point of roughness, or that the woman and the light-skinned man, who for these opening minutes remained a voyeur, shouted outrageous slurs at each other. What compelled Neel wasn't even the aesthetic appeal—the powerful contrast—of the silent, willowy man against the fleshy, pale-skinned blonde. No, he was waiting for a singular moment just past the six-minute mark of the clip. It occurred during a pause in the obscene exchange between the woman and the second man. The woman still had her hands on the pillar when she glanced over her shoulder at her partner, who continued to thrust away with a resigned expression. Then her own face changed. For a few seconds the action stopped. The woman and the darker man gazed at each other not in some imitation of lust, not in blank fury, but with understanding. Sadness met sadness. When Neel saw their twinned expressions, when he witnessed this evidence of human connection in the most sordid and extreme circumstances—then, as always, he could hold out no longer.

He cleaned himself off with a tissue from a box on the side table, closed the laptop, stood, and adjusted his pants. "So that's that," he said, out loud. Everyone had different selves, everyone contained multitudes, but now he was alone with his real self—alone and diminished. He couldn't help but feel ashamed. You drank down the bottle and saw what truths you saw. Was it really the sadness that had drawn him to the video, and not the power? Was it the empathy he'd discerned, in those few seconds of footage, or the fact that the entire scene was one of domination, and even of revenge? In adolescence, the years when cruelty took hold, and the terrible secrets of sex loomed closer, the other boys had taunted him for his race. Neel wondered sometimes whether he could trace every important decision he'd made since, and every desire, to the fact that when he was a New Jersey middle-schooler all the white girls looked past him.

At the window, he took a final, emptying gulp from his glass. His legs buckled but he did not fall. He remembered that he was exhausted. His mouth was burning as he leaned on the sill. He thought about Sudan, vastness, and exile. He thought about American drones over Pakistan. He thought about the stubbled wheat fields of his father's Punjab in winter. He considered the whiskey he'd drunk and why it was never enough. At that late, terrible hour, he would have liked to lie on the floor, as immobile as the root of a great tree, and fall into the stupor that awaited him. But what, then, could he have said to Maya and Serena when they found him in the morning?

He took a deep breath, walked to the hallway, and climbed the stairs. He moved with slow, careful steps to the bathroom and to bed.

SEVEN

SOMEHOW HE WAS standing on the tiles beside the YMCA's pool at five minutes to ten the next morning. Children splashed in the water while a coach shouted instructions. Parents sat in plastic chairs by the locker rooms, chatting and sipping coffee. For Neel, the sounds were muted. He felt as if his own head was submerged.

Serena knelt in the Astroturfed play area beside the pool deck. She held a picture book open to the dolls she'd arranged in a semicircle before her. She was four years old, with brown curls still tinged at the tips with her infant blond. In the car she'd told Neel she loved three people: her mother, her sister, and her preschool teacher. "And me?" asked Neel. His tongue stuck to his teeth. "And you, Dada," she said, "but not as much."

Another little girl, with brown hair in a lighter shade than Serena's, watched from behind. Then she stepped forward, picked up one of the dolls Serena had been playing with, and hugged it. Serena sprang to her feet. She grabbed the doll out of the little girl's hands. The girl's mouth trembled but she said nothing.

Neel was considering whether to intervene when the deck supervisor, clipboard in hand, called for the children in the Water Pixies class. Serena dropped the doll she'd seized and ran to Neel over the tiles. She performed a pirouette on the deck when she reached him. She slipped but caught herself.

"Careful!" said Neel, as he took her hand. "And let's remember to be friendly."

They walked to the low plastic gate that separated the deck from the lip of the pool. Neel gave Serena's name to the supervisor, who marked her list. They joined a line of six other children with their parents, all of whom happened to be men. Serena hopped on her toes. The little brown-haired girl, in line ahead of them, pulled on her own father's arm. She whispered something to him. The father glanced over his shoulder. He had the same brown hair as his daughter, a narrow face, and a thin upper lip. He was a familiar, sinister-looking D.C. type: a federal agent or an asset manager. He flicked his eyes over Neel. Neel maintained a blank expression as he considered the other man. He was lean but formless. Neel must have outweighed him by forty pounds. Even hungover, Neel would easily prevail in a fistfight. The other man grimaced. He bent down to his daughter.

After the last child from the nine thirty class climbed out, the supervisor opened the gate. The Water Pixies walked in. Most of them followed their fathers to the wall, which had hooks for T-shirts and towels. Serena, though, kicked off her flip-flops and jumped into the pool. The little brown-haired girl, who stood with her father while he undressed, looked on in anguish. Neel raised his palm to Serena, in a gesture he hoped she'd interpret as cautionary, and carried their towels to the wall hooks. Serena was doggy-paddling beside the ledge when Neel lowered himself in. The air was pungent with chlorine but the water soothing and cool. Neel gave Serena a squeeze. This was the only time they had alone together each week. He wondered if the other fathers were a more steadfast presence in the lives of their children, or if these Saturday-morning classes were also for them rituals of apology and penance.

The coach was a young woman in a purple one-piece. She descended into the pool after everyone else, clapping her hands for the children's attention. Then she led them, all three- and four-year-olds, through their exercises. The fathers were supposed to cheer and make sure the children didn't drown. The boys and girls kicked their legs while holding onto the side, blew bubbles underwater, attempted the breaststroke, floated on their backs, dove for plastic rings, and jumped into the pool from the ledge. Neel's rival, the cop or money man, behaved himself, but one of the other fathers, who had gelled hair and a lewd smile, quickly became an embarrassment. He cackled whenever the coach said anything. He complimented her on her athleticism. At one moment, he said he'd like her to critique his own stroke. Meanwhile his son, a tiny boy, sank whenever he pushed out from the side. Again and again, the coach lifted the boy to safety, though she stayed out of his father's reach.

Serena, already a better swimmer than the rest, didn't need Neel. He watched with his back to the wall. He liked to see her happy.

To close out the class, the coach led the group in a song. They performed a version of "The Wheels on the Bus" in which the children alternately churned their arms, spun in circles, and ducked their heads beneath the surface. At the end, each father had to throw his child into the air. Serena squealed when Neel tossed her. The coach led them through three rounds of the chorus. Each time, Neel threw Serena higher. His arms ached. He was ready for the showers and a cup of coffee.

The little brown-haired girl's father didn't stop, however, with everyone else.

"Here we go," Neel whispered to himself, as the man kept at it. He was throwing his daughter higher than Neel had thrown Serena. He smiled through his thin, sinister mouth while his daughter laughed.

Serena, seeing them, demanded that Neel throw her into the air too.

At first he refused, but when she made no movement toward the stairs, he took a deep breath and threw her higher than he had during the song. He made sure, in fact, to throw her higher than his rival was throwing his daughter.

"Again!" said Serena. She clapped her hands.

Neel threw her and caught her. She was tall at four years old and getting heavier. His arms were numb.

Now the man with gelled hair, who'd also remained in the pool, suddenly hurled his son skyward. He caught the tiny boy, who looked astonished, well above the waterline. The man flashed his lewd smile around.

"Again, Dada!" shouted Serena.

Neel said they had to get out.

"One last time!"

Neel decided to perform a toss that would settle any outstanding questions. He propelled Serena toward the ceiling with a mighty heave. She screamed before he caught her. He held her tightly when she came down.

"Again. Last one!"

By now the other two men, having accepted defeat, were towing their children to the steps. The deck supervisor called the next class to the entrance gate. Neel began to wade out as well.

"Please, Dada! One last, last time. But you have to throw me higher!"

Neel had never been able to say no to her. He glanced at the wall, where the other two men were reaching for their towels. They looked subdued. Well, he thought, let's put a cherry on it.

"This has to be it, darling. People are waiting."

He tossed her up high into the lights. As soon as she left his hands, he knew he'd misjudged the throw. For one dreadful moment he was sure Serena would fall on the tiles. He lurched backward. In desperation, he raised his arms. Then Serena's feet landed on his chest. He held on, gathering her body into his own, but her chin crashed into his forehead. The world dimmed. It was a few seconds before he noticed the pain. He held Serena with one arm while he felt for the wall with the other. When he had it, he looked at his daughter's face. She was pale, but he saw no blood.

"Baby, I'm so sorry," he said.

She just looked at him.

"Are you okay?"

She nodded. Her eyes were full of tears.

The pain spread from his temples to his neck. Someone put a hand on his shoulder. He forced himself to look up. He realized that Serena's coach, who was kneeling on the deck, had been talking to him.

"We're okay, thank you," said Neel.

He lifted Serena out. The coach spoke gently to her while he waded to the steps. The brown-haired girl's father came over from the wall. He offered Neel his arm but Neel shook his head. He climbed carefully out of the pool, walked to Serena, and took her hand. The men and women in the plastic chairs were watching. He saw their white faces turn to him even as he fixed his gaze on the locker-room doors. His ears burned all the way to the showers.

They used one of the large stalls in the family changing room. Neel's headache worsened by the minute. He felt ashamed, defeated; for a moment, as he raised his face to the warm water, he thought he would cry. What could he have told Rebecca if Serena had been hurt?

After they dressed, he bought Serena a chocolate milk in the cafeteria. She was smiling by the time they reached the parking lot. Neel found a bottle of children's Tylenol in the glove compartment of Rebecca's station wagon, which he'd borrowed that morning. He emptied the eight remaining pills into his mouth. They tasted of grape soda and chalk.

Neel wore Rebecca's sunglasses to drive. It was a sharp, cloudless day. Young people were lining up for brunch at the cafés. Even with Rebecca's glasses, and the lowered sun visor, he had to shade his eyes with one hand.

Serena asked if her mama and Maya were at home.

Neel said they were.

"Goody," said Serena. "Maybe Mama will take us to the park." She sang the rest of the way.

EIGHT

ONCE HE'D ASKED Rebecca whether she thought the girls were having a happy childhood. Of course, she said, just look at them, they're full of joy. If the girls were ever sad, they didn't stay sad.

It was still a miracle to him, and perhaps to Rebecca as well. When he was very young, his own mother had spoken gently as she fed him the staples of the north Indian plains: dudh, kheer, makkhani, dahi, dal. "So jana, beta, rana," she would say when she put him to bed. Sleep, little boy, little prince. After his first year at school he stopped answering her in Punjabi. English outside, English inside, his father said, it's the right approach. His mother understood the language but the words were heavy on her tongue.

What Neel remembered now was silence and the cold. It was always raining in New Jersey. He went to school in pants that were too short and too tight. His parents turned down the thermostats to save money. They wore sweaters and wool hats inside in winter. Neel didn't invite anyone to the house. His parents asked him if he had enough food on his plate and if he'd done his homework. Then they switched on the television. His father had a few friends, Punjabi immigrants like him, who'd come over to drink Scotch. But the friends visited less often as the years passed, and his father, who lost his taste for liquor, went on alone.

Much later, after Neel became a father himself, his mother apologized to him or at least tried to explain. Think what it was like, she said, to grow up in a Punjabi village in the forties and fifties. You spoke to other girls and women, but when the men came home you kept quiet. After sunset the plains went dark—dark villages, dark fields—for a thousand miles. There was no law in the countryside. You were always afraid. At least, said Neel's mother, your upbringing was better than that. Your father stopped drinking. He didn't shout at you or beat you.

She worked in her husband's accounting office. She organized his files, copied documents, and mailed tax returns for the two hundred families and small businesses he had as clients. She returned to him whatever salary he paid her. She didn't like to leave the house without him or, later, without Neel. She never learned to drive. You see, she told Neel, I didn't know enough. I didn't understand America. I didn't have the words, I didn't know what to say to you.

This was in Paramus, a working-class town turning middle-class in Neel's childhood. He went to school with the sons and daughters of plumbers, office managers, and policemen. When Neel was thirteen, with Reagan in his first term, his classmates' fathers were beating their chests. North Jersey was Republican; the men of Paramus looked across the Hudson to New York, the great, failed city, and congratulated themselves on having made the right choices in life. One of his classmates told Neel that his own father had stood outside Paramus High School at the morning bell to count the number of black teenagers who walked in, before he committed to buying a house in town. The boys told Neel he was a dothead, a raghead, and a sand n——r. Or that he was a curry boy, monkey boy, thumbtack Indian, Paki, Mowgli, shitskin, snake charmer, camel jockey, pump jockey, motel man, taxi driver, Mr. 7-11, and a hundred other names. But always they returned to their favorite refrain. Dothead, dothead, dothead, you fucking dothead. For years afterward the slur would run through his mind while he lay in bed. It was no use pleading that a Sikh boy wouldn't mark his forehead with the third eye any more than a rabbi would choose to wear a cross: "Shut up, dothead, go back to India Neel She-ma, no one cares." Neel couldn't tell his parents. For what humiliations had they suffered without complaint?

As Neel grew older, he watched his father, a big man at six-two, a strong man, become year by year more weightless. A war was on in north India. The Sikhs were fighting for a nation of their own in Punjab. In the summer of 1984, the Indian Armed Forces carried out Operation Blue Star in Amritsar, the second-largest city in Punjab, a few miles from the Pakistan border. The army attacked the Golden Temple, Sikhism's holiest shrine. They slaughtered the separatists who'd barricaded themselves in the temple grounds, as well as thousands of Sikh pilgrims. Afterward the Indian prime minister, Indira Gandhi, ignored intelligence warnings that she could no longer allow Sikh officers to serve in her personal security detail. On an October morning in 1984, two of those Sikh bodyguards shot her while she walked in her garden. When a great tree falls, said Gandhi's son Rajiv, the new prime minister, the ground must shake. Hindu mobs murdered Sikhs across north India in a weeks-long pogrom. They burned the Sikh neighborhoods of Delhi to the ground while the police watched. Khoon ka badla khoon, blood for blood, and on it went. Indian soldiers conducted night raids on Punjabi villages. Sikh separatists attacked police and military convoys and murdered Hindu civilians. For a decade Neel's uncle, his father's older brother, slept with a shotgun under his charpoy in his farmhouse in Ballowal village.

Gandhi's assassination led the news in America for a night or two before it was forgotten. For Neel's father, though, the killing marked the end of India. I'm finished with those people, he said, all of them. He used to fly back every three years to visit Ballowal, leaving his wife and son in Paramus, but no longer. Never a devout man, he stopped going to the temple altogether. He was sick of it, he said, both sides, Brahmins and Sikhs, hypocrites on the one side, drunkards on the other. He was sick of everything.

One night, he roused himself from his usual irritation, or immense silence, to make a speech. "In India, the Sikhs aren't free," he told Neel.

"The whole bastard Indian nation is a mistake. And in America, people hear my accent and think I'm a bumpkin. I studied Shakespeare in college while these bloody idiots were reading Superman comics, but to them I'm the clown. Son, I have no home. You must make one for yourself. I can't guide you here. I can only tell you what I learned in India. The poor have nothing, so they steal. The laws don't apply to the rich, so they steal. Therefore everyone steals. Whatever you do, remember that your friends are not your friends." Neel let his father talk but he didn't believe him. He read the novels his teachers assigned: Steinbeck, Hemingway, Stephen Crane. He was learning the language of intimacy and courage. He promised himself he'd make a different life in America.

They were lost years, iron years, years he wanted to leave behind even as he lived them. Grace came in the body. Neel grew four inches in the tenth grade and, with endless sets of push-ups and squats in his bedroom, put on twenty pounds of muscle. He'd always been quick but now he could outsprint everyone, white boys and black, across the state. He loved going to practice, loved lifting weights in the gym and running intervals on the track—he loved the rigor and the suffering. Now it begins, he thought, now I'm showing them who I am. He made the varsity baseball team his junior year. He had a hitch in his swing and batted ninth but in centerfield he ran down fly balls all game long. After he went under forty-nine seconds in the 400-meter dash his junior year, the recruiting letters from college track coaches started to arrive. His father didn't encourage him, but he sat in the stands for important meets, counting off Neel's time by the second hand on his watch. Pride surged in Neel when he shook out his legs and lowered himself into the starting blocks. As a senior, Neel won every 400-meter race he entered, and most 100- and 200-meter races too, until the state championship in South Plainfield. There he chose to compete in only the 400, his best event. In the final he led the field down the homestretch until a sophomore from Camden ran him down in the last twenty. His father said he wasn't surprised that Neel finished second. You've never been strong mentally, he said. By then Neel was a good student but not a great one. The head track coach at Columbia promised to put in a word with the admissions office. The college offered him a place.

He was still a dothead in Paramus, but he no longer heard the slur every hour or every day. He was different from the other Indians. Sports had become both shield and sword. On the track, girls watched him: strong, athletic girls who looked at his tall, strong body and smiled. He smiled too, but he was shy.

To celebrate his high school graduation, his father took Neel and his mother to Edison for dinner in Little India. Afterward they walked past the storefronts, looking at the displays of saris and jewelry in the windows. This was on a Sunday evening in June. The street was full. Neel listened to the crowds as they passed. He heard Punjabi, a language he still half knew, and others—Hindi, Gujarati, Bengali—he didn't understand but whose rhythms pleased him. The smell from the restaurants lingered for blocks: cardamom, cloves, onions frying in ghee. Neel saw the long black hair on the young women he passed, and their dark eyes and silver earrings, and he wondered why he'd never longed for them.

Perhaps two paths had always been open. Perhaps he could have held on to his parents' homeland even as he grew into adulthood. But what was Paramus to him, what was the silent house his parents kept, what was Punjab itself, when measured against the promise of a great, cleansing American freedom? Perhaps he would always carry a kernel of resentment against white men. Perhaps the tension that had marked his childhood would never entirely abate, and he would always listen for the whispers that he didn't belong. He could live with all of it, he decided. He would be a brown-skinned American but not a hyphenated one.

Neel lasted six weeks as a college sprinter before he tore his Achilles coming out of the blocks at fall practice. His athletic career had ended. He didn't mourn it. Another life beckoned.

NINE

. . .

DEEP, LOW-RISE BROOKLYN. Ibn Muhammed walked for three hours through Grand Army Plaza and Prospect Park to the cemetery, then back again into the heart of the borough. Relentless traffic, on streets without trees, gave way in the park to birdsong and a great beauty. Resting at the cemetery's verge he'd thought about death and the promise death held of peace. Now, on Coney Island Avenue, he walked through another kind of beauty. Immigrant shops sold paint, tires, sandwiches, jewelry. On the sidewalks, he heard Spanish, Bengali, Arabic, his own Punjabi. His thoughts floated above the fumes and noise.

He had been born in Massachusetts but his body was wrong for the country. At home, when he took off his shoes and socks, the skin between his toes itched and bled. The creams he applied did nothing or made his condition worse. You're a son of the Prophet, his mother once told him, you were made for the desert. She used to simmer mustard seeds in ghee for an ointment she applied to his feet with cotton swabs. Then she'd rest his feet on her lap, spacing his toes with her fingertips, until the inner skin dried. That was on her good days, the days she was herself, when the house smelled of onion pakoras and mutton stew, and when she sang ghazals while she cooked. Not on her dark days, which came more often as she grew older, the long, dark days when her chest and head hurt and she could not leave her room. Alone in his apartment, he still cried for her some nights, but only a little. Then, drying his tears, he reminded himself that the angel of death never sleeps. The angel will visit every house, again and again, until none are left.

No one in this city, he thought, looked at the sky. No one looked at the light that passed through the clouds. No one saw the light fall on the trickle of filth in the gutter—the light that transformed the filth. With his one eye he saw more than those who had two. He took care not to trip when he stepped off the curb. He waited to be sure of the traffic before he crossed. Although his blindness—his half-blindness—had opened other realms for him, he still forgot, from time to time, to turn his head. He didn't want to die crossing the street in West Midwood. But if he died in the street, then to die in the street was his fate, and it was written, alhamdulillah.

On the other side of the crossing, three young women, Latinas, maybe Puerto Ricans, walked out of the mini market. It was the corner of Coney Island and Ditmas. He heard car horns, jackhammers, rap music. Catching a whiff of marijuana, he remembered the calm sweet feeling that used to descend on him when he smoked. The girls stood on the corner in fake nails, tight jeans, and hoop earrings. They laughed and spoke loudly, as if the street belonged to them. And why not? thought Ibn Muhammed. Wasn't it fitting for them to revel in their own youth? He looked at them but in their world he didn't exist. Or did one of the young women tilt her head after all, and did she notice him when she glanced across the sidewalk? And in that moment, in the noticing, did she see a monster? Even now pride rose in him. It wasn't so long ago that girls fell for his dark curls and full lips. He was still a young man. The body remembered.

All this was vanity. He commanded himself to look at the sky as he left the women behind. The clouds remained. He wouldn't be this way forever. He'd chosen his present ugliness. He'd chosen not to groom his beard, chosen not to hide the scars on his forehead and cheek, chosen the unhemmed white pants he wore high over his ankles. He had chosen to wait for a wife. He was training himself to love as the Prophet did. When he was ready, he would honor women as the Prophet honored his concubines and wives.

Down the block, two police officers, patrolmen, leaned against the iron gate of an apartment building, staring at Ibn Muhammed as he passed. One shook his head. The other spat over his own shoulder, through the bars, into the bushes behind. Ibn Muhammed smiled at the patrolmen, for weren't they also his brothers, and didn't they also have immortal souls? He smiled though he knew they would never smile back. His beard, soft as the wool of a favored lamb, with a red tinge to the black, was in their eyes a provocation and a threat. He might as well have marched down the avenue brandishing an ax. So he humbled and diminished himself. He had chosen this most dangerous American life. It was right, he reminded himself, it was holy to be despised.

Eventually he reached the study center he was building. He paused a moment outside the storefront. Sailcloth hung over the windows but through the glass door Ibn Muhammed saw that the Ecuadorean had completed his tasks. The drop cloths, cans, and brushes, and the Ecuadorean himself, were gone. Inside, at the entry, he took off his shoes. He washed his hands and face under the tap. The room smelled of new paint. The walls glowed light blue. Ibn Muhammed trembled in anticipation of the work to come.

For he remained a novice. He had no religious learning. Prayer bored him. If the Quran was perfect, it was also inscrutable. Ibn Muhammed had to treat the sorrows of his life as stepping-stones. He had to follow the Prophet's example. He would trust in providence or fate. He would not fear the kings of this world. He would act as if the throne of every king was turned backward.

To live as a hermit in a great city. To be without fear because the book of his life was already written. To allow time to work on him as it worked on the rocks and trees. To wear the marks of solitude. To prefer tea without honey. To drink water instead of milk. To eat bread with no ghee. To walk all day in the rain. To dine on almonds and dates. To witness, in fasting, the disappearance of his own flesh. To live as a Sufi but dress like a fundamentalist. To stand out even in these neighborhoods. To be persecuted. To be humiliated. To perfume himself, nonetheless. To set aside the Quran and the prayer mat. To watch the sky. To long for the sky. To live as if there were no darkness below the air or water. To live without fear of the flagrant darkness at the bottom of the world. To refuse to fall in love with his own life. To write verses and to hope he had not written them but received them. To read Hafiz and Rumi. To read Khusrau. To read Bulleh Shah, who taught that the true holiness was to recognize that there were no unbelievers in creation. To be moved by lyrics he did not understand. To find, in a cold winter, the spring of love. To be a Muslim.

• • •

TEN

IN THEIR PHONE call on the morning of Monday, November 17, the priest spoke to Neel with greater urgency. The president-elect was alarmed by the escalating violence in Afghanistan. Coalition airstrikes in response to Taliban attacks had killed too many civilians. "The natives—Karzai, the provincial governors—are getting restless. We'll need to change the situation on the ground. I'm not as concerned with individual casualties as I am with making the war as a whole less dangerous. Find me some clean targets, write good memos, and we'll get those targets to the top of the list when we take charge. Let's hit the ground running after the inauguration."

Neel told the priest he had his first target in mind. He needed more signals intelligence but already the package looked promising.

"Good," said the priest. "The more data you put in the file, the better. Give the decision-makers confidence that you've built your recommendation on a solid foundation. All the same, don't let the fear of making mistakes stop you from taking action. Remember, every terrorist we take out from the air is one fewer terrorist who can harm Americans on the ground. That's what this is all about."

Neel promised he would be bold.

"Let's save some lives," said the priest.

"Have you heard?" Smith said, pointing his finger at Neel from across the table.

"Sir?"

"Your new director. They"—and here Smith waved vaguely at the world outside the conference room—"have made the call. Eliot Cone. Official announcement on Wednesday. You know him?"

Neel shook his head.

"You'll be peas in a pod." Smith patted himself on the belly. He walked out.

Vanderhoof stood up to follow.

"What did he mean by that?" asked Neel.

Vanderhoof looked back at Neel from the door. "Cone's a veteran, a lawyer, has a nice résumé. Guys like that make Smith insecure. Forget about it." He planted his middle finger between his eyebrows. "What happened to your face?"

A dark, soft lump had risen on Neel's forehead by the time he returned home from the pool on Saturday. It had grown darker and softer since.

"You should see the other guy," said Neel.

"You're a bad dude, Neel," said Vanderhoof, flashing a smile. But for the first time he looked unsure of himself. He lingered a moment before he left.

Neel spent the rest of the day alone in his office, reading and editing reports. Twice, the phone rang, with the caller's identity blocked, but Neel heard only static when he lifted the receiver.

"Who's this?" he asked, the second time. "You're dialing into a secure line." The caller didn't answer but laughed or coughed as Neel hung up.

Neel stared at the phone for a few moments before he went back to his work.

Late in the afternoon, Neel ran a set of searches for Eliot Cone in open-source and government records. He discovered that Cone was forty-six.

Unlike Neel, he'd attended a service academy, graduating from West Point in 1985. He'd served the minimum five years of active duty as a tank commander, mainly on a training ground outside Stuttgart, before enrolling at Harvard Law School, as Neel had also done following his stint in the Navy. After graduating, Cone clerked for a blind judge on the D.C. Circuit, a liberal lion famed for his intellect and generosity who nonetheless depended on his male law clerks to guide him into and out of his health club's swimming pool at five thirty each morning. Then Cone worked in the counsel's office of two different federal intelligence agencies. In his second position, at the NSA, he was detailed to the 9/11 Commission. Rumor held that Cone had been the lead author of those unsigned and incendiary sections of the commission's report that documented the CIA's institutional paranoia and general incompetence in the months prior to Al Qaeda's attacks. This, according to one anonymous but well-sourced blogger, proved to be a popular position with high-ranking members of the other intelligence agencies, as well as with certain elements within the CIA itself. Cone's career blossomed after the report's publication. In 2005, he moved from the NSA to the Office of the Director of National Intelligence, an agency established to advise the president on all intelligence matters, whether related to terrorism or not. Cone became that agency's principal deputy. Now, at the Freedom Center, he would coordinate the nation's counterterrorism response.

Neel looked at the picture of Cone on the ODNI's website. He had hollow cheeks, a high forehead, an ex-soldier's cropped gray hair, and a face creased by wind and sun. All this gave him a weary, even mournful expression. He had all the experience you could hope for in a director. Neel had no doubt that Cone would push the staff hard at the Freedom Center. He told himself that this was what he wanted, and that he was ready.

Neel rubbed his face with both hands. He looked at the framed picture on his desk, which he'd taken a year and a half earlier. Rebecca, Maya, and Serena sat with their toes in the water, on the Delaware shore. He thought, fleetingly, of leaving work early to see them. He stood to shake off his weakness. He walked through the Freedom Center's bright, quiet halls to the break room for more coffee.

ELEVEN

NEEL HAD FORGOTTEN about Thanksgiving. Now, in his third week at the Freedom Center, the holiday was upon him. They were going to visit Rebecca's parents in Chevy Chase. For the first time, Neel's own parents had decided to stay in New Jersey. The train fares had tripled by the time his father looked them up, the flights were full, and he'd grown afraid, in recent years, of driving on the freeway.

Rebecca dressed the girls in matching blouses and tights. It was too much, she said, but her mother would love it.

Neel loaded them into the station wagon at noon. His breath froze in the wind—the bleak days had begun.

"Try to enjoy yourself," said Rebecca, as Neel started up the car. "My parents are proud of you."

"Hopefully George won't be a dick."

"Neel, the girls!" said Rebecca. She'd spent years recovering from a moneyed but unhappy childhood. George Wallader, a litigation partner at Haines Strawbridge, was an office-and-country-club man. He'd made his name representing Republican officials in the banking scandals of the late eighties. Rebecca said her mother, Kay, had been bored for the entire span of her marriage, a span that covered most of her adult life. Kay wasn't interested in books or art or music and had never held a paying job. When Rebecca was a girl, Kay swam laps in the morning, took tennis lessons, and volunteered at Rebecca's school. George hired her a golf coach but she never became good enough for him to want to leave work early for nine holes with her. She helped her daughter with her homework until Rebecca outgrew her help. Later Kay would ask Rebecca to play cards or watch television at night. In the mornings, the family ate together at the breakfast table. They didn't argue, they dressed well, and they went to Nantucket for the summer. But every weekend the house reeked of gin.

It was a half-hour trip from the city in light traffic. The Walladers came out to the granite steps of their mansion while Neel steered to the top of the long, gravel-covered driveway. Kay was waving to the girls as Neel set the parking brake and switched off the engine. Through the glass, Neel noticed that George's nose was already glowing.

Outside, in the cold, they went through the hugs and handshakes. George smacked Neel between the shoulders. He wagged a finger in Neel's face.

"You're a dark horse, Neel, and not just in the literal sense."

"Oh, George," said Kay, slipping past her husband. "How long were you holding on to that line?" She kissed Neel with her small, hard mouth. "Don't mind him, you sweet boy. We were excited to hear your news. Are you happy?"

"Just trying to do my best with the opportunities I have," said Neel. "Onward and upward." He shrugged at Rebecca's amused expression. He never sounded like himself in her parents' company.

"Upward to a bigger house, one hopes," said George. "Take advantage of the downturn. Get your family away from that terrible city. I'm always happy to help. I don't see why my granddaughters should live with the smell of sidewalk piss."

"George!" said Kay.

"We feel lucky to live in Adams Morgan, actually," said Neel.

"Yes, well, let's go inside, shall we?" Rebecca said.

In the kitchen, the exhaust fans roared. The smell of roasting turkey and sweet potatoes filled the air. A chopped salad, bowls of cranberry sauce, and two uncooked pies sat on the kitchen table. The counters and sink were clean.

"We're on track," said Kay. "I'm timing all the dishes in the oven. Soledad, my angel, came in this morning to help me prepare."

Serena, noticing the pies, went over to have a sniff.

"Don't touch those, sweetie," said Neel.

The bird, said Kay, had an hour to go. Her voice was clear but her eyes distant.

"Apéritif, anyone?" she said. "I'm going to top up my Lillet. George has a pitcher of martinis going and there are glasses in the freezer."

Neel put an arm around Rebecca's shoulder. "Maybe later," he said.

"I'll just have a glass of water," said Rebecca. "Water for the girls too."

"I kept your games, you know," said Kay. "Snakes and Ladders, Ludo. I put them out in the family room. I thought the girls might be old enough by now."

"Snakes and Ladders!" said Serena.

"But I like Ludo," said Maya.

"We have time for both," said Rebecca, tapping Maya lightly on the arm. She and the girls followed Kay out. Neel took a few steps as well but George called him back.

"Now that my daughter has gone, what's your real answer? Martini? A Manhattan? I have beer in the icebox."

"No thank you," said Neel, though in truth he would have loved a drink.

"Odd choice," said George, scratching his head. He carried his glass and the pitcher of martinis to the door. "I hear there's a football game on. Let's try to hold on to some of the traditions, yes?"

The living room was enormous. A flat-screen television hung in the center of an otherwise bare wall.

"A friendly wager, Neel? A hundred dollars a quarter? You should be able to afford that. Mano a mano, no spread, no funny business. Tennessee or Detroit? Visitor's choice."

"Tennessee," said Neel, choosing at random. He'd stopped following football sometime in college, long before he'd given up on baseball and basketball, after he saw a player break his neck in a nationally televised game.

"The conventional wisdom. No surprise there. I'll cheer for the great American city of Detroit." He took a swallow from his glass and, after he put it down, thumped Neel on the thigh. "Let's go, Lions!"

Detroit had the ball first but a Lions running back fumbled on the second play from scrimmage.

"Overpaid bum," said George.

"Why, how much does he make?" said Neel.

George ignored him.

Tennessee scored almost immediately after the turnover and then kept on scoring. George quieted down but he still drank with purpose. "This isn't a fair fight," he said, with the Titans up 21–3 at the end of the first quarter.

"We can forget about the money," said Neel. "I had no idea Detroit was this bad."

"Nonsense!" shouted George. "You're not getting off so easy. The Titans will coast now. Overconfidence. Check your wallet, Mister Man." He stood up. "I'm refilling the pitcher. Keep my seat warm for me."

"Okay, Dad," said Neel.

"Ach," said George. He walked out.

Tennessee scored another touchdown less than a minute into the second quarter. George was muttering from deep in the sofa cushions, but soon he grew quiet. Neel watched the game without interest. George closed his eyes. He was breathing heavily. Before the quarter ended, he began to snore.

At halftime, Neel turned off the television. He stood and stretched his arms. The room, despite its immaculate furniture, smelled musty. George, still snoring, had turned his face up to the ceiling. His mouth was open, his lips wet.

Neel heard the clink of dishes and silverware from the kitchen. Kay called out instructions to Rebecca. Maya and Serena were strangely quiet.

Neel returned to the sofa.

"Come on, George," said Neel. He patted his father-in-law on the shoulder.

The old man rubbed his gin-reddened face. He wiped his eyes with his sleeve.

"What's the score?"

"35–10. Tennessee has the first two quarters."

"Hell," said George. "Next time we'll bet on golf."

"You know I don't play," said Neel.

"I used to drink all afternoon in the clubhouse, then all night at home. Can't now. Give me a hand."

Neel lifted George to his feet. He held him upright for a moment, until the older man found his balance. "Wait," said Neel, as George moved to the door. "You can keep your martini glass, but in the kitchen I'm going to fill it with ice water. Do you understand? My wife and daughters are here."

George looked at him with disgust but didn't argue.

At dinner, with the kitchen fans switched off, the silence thickened. Rebecca helped Maya with her slice of turkey breast. Neel helped Serena, or helped her as much as he could, since she refused most of what he cut. She whispered to him that she only wanted the cranberry sauce. Neel, who didn't like turkey himself, pushed his food around the plate. He wondered who had carved the bird.

George, at the head of the table, leaned forward in his chair. He ate with surprising vigor. He didn't touch his drink. Kay cradled her glass against her blouse. She gazed out with a pleasant, distracted expression. Neel allowed himself a few sips of wine. He shook his head when Kay tried to pass him the bottle.

"Eat, eat, everyone," said Kay, after a few minutes of quiet. "I'm glad to see you hungry, George. You've been so . . . depleted."

"De pee pee?" said Serena. She seemed surprised when no one scolded her.

The light had begun to wane. George's face took on a yellow tinge in the dimness. Neel, from across the table, blew Rebecca a silent kiss. That gesture, slight as it was, seemed to return her to herself. She took a deep breath, looked at Kay, and asked about one of their old neighbors. Kay said she didn't have any news. But she smiled at Rebecca and reached for her arm. Rebecca asked about the renovations to the gym and pool at the country club, and about Kay's health. Kay answered. She asked a few questions of her own. The conversation between mother and daughter trickled on. Neel relaxed into his chair. He ran his fork through his whipped potatoes and picked at his turkey drumstick. The house creaked. George murmured something about putting on an Aaron Copland record but didn't get up from his chair. In the gray light, beneath the soft, almost indiscernible voices of his wife and mother-in-law, and with his daughters strangely solemn and slow, it seemed to Neel that the room itself was fading. He was no longer at a holiday dinner but had become a character in someone else's dream of a dinner, in a dream of a holiday. He smiled as he watched his wife eat.

After the meal, with the overhead lights on, after the pies and ice cream and a brandy for Kay, Neel and Rebecca cleaned up together. They carried the dishes from the dining room to the kitchen, emptied the platters, and stacked the washer. George had recovered enough by now to perform a few magic tricks for his granddaughters with a handkerchief and the coins in his pocket. Maya and Serena laughed in a subdued way.

With the dishes done, Neel collected the girls and led them to the front hall. He helped them into their coats. Rebecca went to look for her mother.

"I wish your parents had come," said George to Neel, as the girls waited by the door. "They have beautiful accents."

"Okay, George." Neel patted his father-in-law on the shoulder. "Thank Kay for me."

"She's passed out somewhere. I'll tell her tomorrow." His lips trembled.

Neel reminded the girls to say good night to their grandfather. Rebecca came into the hall, put on her coat and gloves, and gave her father a hug. George held on. Rebecca kissed his swollen face before gently pulling away.

The wind swirled the leaves in the driveway. The mansion went dark as they walked to the car. Neel checked the football score on his phone while Rebecca helped the girls with their seat belts. The Titans had shut out the Lions in the second half, while kicking field goals in each of the third and fourth quarters.

"Your dad owes me four hundred dollars," said Neel, from the driver's seat, as Rebecca got in.

The girls fell asleep on the drive home, though it wasn't close to bedtime. The streets were empty.

"People don't change," said Rebecca, a few minutes into the drive. She spoke softly, more to herself than to Neel. After a pause, she said, "I should be in therapy."

"I've always thought you recovered so beautifully from your childhood," said Neel.

"Don't ever be like George."

"I think the casual racism puts him in a different category."

"I'm talking about everything else," said Rebecca. "Work. Drink. All that money. He spent too much time around the wrong men. I know you're just starting out at the Freedom Center, but you're there all the time. What I'm saying is, I don't want you to destroy yourself."

Neel drove through the gloom. In the rearview mirror, he looked at his sleeping daughters.

"I needed this job, Rebecca," he said. "I'm not young. I have to start achieving whatever it is I'm going to achieve in life. I'm forty years old and have never really pushed myself. Or I've only pushed myself physically and not at work. This is my chance to make a name. I'm tired of men like George condescending to me. I hate that he got us our house. I want to know things he doesn't know. I want to condescend to George for a change."

Rebecca reached over the gearshift. She squeezed his leg. When he glanced at her she smiled.

"And the human part of you, the part I love, is going to come through this quest for power or male fulfillment or whatever it is untouched?"

"Rebecca, this work is important. There are people who believe in me. Who knows where it will lead?"

"I'm not saying you can't have ambition. I'm ambitious. I want to be recognized as a scholar. But my work won't harm me as a person or as a mother. Your job is different. You need to be conscious of how you might change."

Neel dropped his right hand down to her hand, where it still rested on his thigh. He drove like that for a while.

TWELVE

AN ICE STORM howled over the weekend, laying waste to the capital's trees. There was early snow in New England and on the Great Plains. Neel heard whispers and giggles on the stairs. The girls exchanged meaningful looks at the kitchen table. Christmas approached; the mysteries deepened.

On Sunday morning, they went out to the yard, in their gloves and galoshes, to play bocce in the slush.

"Neel," said Rebecca, in a guarded tone. Her cheeks were bright. "What do you think about the holidays?" Serena hopped on her toes between them.

One of George's law partners had offered up his vacation house on St. Vincent for ten days, Rebecca said. George was on a case and couldn't leave, but Kay still wanted to go. It would be her pleasure, she'd said, to fly Rebecca, Neel, and the girls down with her. On business class, if that mattered.

"I wish I could," he said. But the priest had told him not to let down his guard. The nation was a soft target over the holidays. He could hardly take a sizable vacation after only working a month. "I don't want to hold you back."

Rebecca said she understood.

The girls were arguing over which ball was closest to the jack. Their loose curls, their little noses and tawny skin—Neel was always falling in love.

"They'll miss you in St. Vincent," said Rebecca. "You're fun on the beach. Sandcastles, flying a kite, digging for treasure. It's up your alley."

"I'm sorry."

She wasn't angry, she said, but he could see the disappointment in her face—or was it even disappointment, when she must have known how he'd respond?

By now the bocce game had run its course. Neel offered to make the girls hot chocolate.

In the kitchen, he thought about how, in a few words, and without any argument from Rebecca, he'd confirmed what once would've been unthinkable—that he'd choose to spend Christmas apart from his wife and daughters. But he would survive their absence just as they would survive his. It was a little frightening, he thought, that they could all accustom themselves so quickly to the new state of things.

He poured milk into a pan and set it on the gas. The girls were playing in the living room. Rebecca had gone upstairs for a dry pair of socks. They were all in the house together, a long afternoon lay open, and the winter holidays were many days ahead, but he felt, in those moments, as if he'd already said goodbye.

THIRTEEN

THE PHONE RANG in Neel's office early on Monday afternoon. The caller display was blank. Neel let it ring until it went silent. Ordinarily, this was the quietest time of day. He'd reviewed the new threat assessments that came in over the weekend, edited the Freedom Center's daily brief, had his regular call with the priest, met with Vanderhoof and Smith, checked in with the operations manager, and eaten lunch. Now he was working to update his Waziristan file. The Defense Department had supplied a trove of incident reports on roadside bombings in Nangarhar Province, Afghanistan, directly across the border from Waziristan. If the militants Neel was tracking were involved, their cell would immediately rate as a prime candidate for a drone strike.

The phone rang again. The caller display remained blank. Neel wondered whether it was the priest, on a masked line. But when he answered, no one responded to his greeting. He was going to hang up when he heard a sharp intake of breath and a long, weary sigh.

"It's time we talked, Neel."

"Who is this? Have you called before?"

"Sam Jones, CIA."

Neel recognized the pseudonym. "Sam Jones" was the author of occasional reports on the links between violent extremists in the Levant and imams in Europe and the United States—reports that, when they reached his desk, Neel had found to be uniformly conspiratorial and obscure.

"The two of us have a friend in common," said Jones, breathing heavily over the line.

Neel wondered if Jones were suffering from lung disease. "Are you sure? What is this?"

"I'm not talking about your everyday Washington or Langley friend who smiles and shakes your hand while he's secretly plotting your demise. I mean a friend who has both your and my interests at heart. I've always counted on his help to run special projects at CIA. His circumstances have recently changed—or improved, as it were."

Neel asked if Jones was referring to the priest.

Jones barked out a laugh, which gave way to a coughing fit.

"I'm busy," said Neel. "If you have something for us at the Center, there are official channels."

"You'll soon learn, Neel, that the agencies give certain professionals the space to experiment. There are official channels and unofficial ones, standard practices and special ones. The point is to find an approach that works."

"I don't know what you mean."

"The Executive Branch enjoys discretion when it comes to the conduct of war. Many past administrations have assembled small teams to carry out sensitive operations on foreign or domestic soil without the usual oversight. There have always been men of action willing to work directly for those at the highest levels of government. Men who'll do what it takes to eliminate threats to our national security. Now do you follow?"

"Not really," said Neel. He checked his watch. "Some presidents, in the past, made terrible mistakes. Then Congress instituted reforms." In his office, the track lights burned. He tapped his pen on the desk.

"Our idea, taking a page from history, is to see what happens when we vanish a given target. We can start with targets that don't even rise to the level of your Violent Extremist U.S. Nationals. Sub-vermin, if you will. I'm talking about undesirables rather than serious terrorists—your everyday hajjis, your everyday ragheads." Jones uttered these slurs dispassionately. "You target some Muhammed who has been making a lot of noise in San Diego or wherever—a preacher, a grandstander, but nonetheless someone who, if left unchecked, could punch a hole in the fabric of a free society. He's living his un-American life, thinking his un-American thoughts, while taking advantage of American liberties, until one day, poof, he's gone. What does that do to those radicals who remain? Maybe you've frightened them. Maybe they turn meek as mice."

"Maybe not," said Neel. "It doesn't matter. This is too ludicrous to discuss."

Jones continued as if Neel hadn't spoken. He wasn't asking Neel to be a gunslinger, he said. He already had volunteers—federal agents, police, ex-military—for the difficult work. But he needed help on the bureaucratic side. He would soon decide on an initial target. Next, over a period of weeks, Neel would push the selected name steadily down all the targeting lists until it was so low that nobody would notice if it disappeared from the threat matrix entirely.

"That isn't how we do things at the Center."

"It's not how some people do things. I won't be getting in touch with your new director. Eliot Cone, or Cohen, whatever his name is. I know the type. Too finicky."

"Are you making some kind of anti-Semitic insinuation?"

Jones had another coughing fit. "Do you like sitting in meetings?" he said, after he had recovered. "Do you always want to be the token minority, the window dressing, the note-taker? Do you want to be a yes-man? You meet people in this city who think it would be wonderful, just wonderful, to be the vice president."

"Thanks for calling," said Neel.

"I'll be in touch with the target's name," said Jones. "And Neel . . . I've been around this game a lot longer than you have. You'd do well to take me seriously."

Neel hung up. He sprang away from the desk. He had not agreed to anything. The caller might well have been unhinged. The CIA was a massive institution. Everyone knew there were old men who moldered in forgotten offices in Langley, holding on to their jobs as a kind of sinecure. Some officers became so paranoid after decades in their secret world, and so embittered, that they could no longer plan operations or produce reasoned analysis. Perhaps Jones was one of those ragged fantasists. If his plan had been serious, he'd never have discussed it on the phone. There was no reason for Neel to be afraid. He needn't call the priest for reassurance. That would seem weak. It would be best, he decided, to ignore the matter.

He sat down at his desk and returned to the Waziristan file.

FOURTEEN

THE FBI CAME in the next day. Two agents—muscular, heavyset white men—wanted to see him in his office. A routine update of his security clearance, they said. They didn't seem pleased.

"You know the drill," said one agent, the taller of the pair. "Infidelity, drug use, foreign entanglements."

The second agent, who had a military-style mustache, stared at Neel without blinking.

"None, none, and none," said Neel. He'd worked with FBI agents at Main Justice and didn't like them. They were reactionaries—prurient, fraternity types. Many were quite stupid.

"How much are you drinking?" said the taller agent.

"A modest amount." Neel kept his voice level.

The agents looked at each other. The one with the mustache wrote a few words on the notebook he held in his lap.

"What's modest? One drink a night? Three? Are you getting drunk?"

"No," said Neel. "I have a glass of wine at dinner." Never give an inch, went the mantra, never pull back the curtain on your private life.

You didn't take the FBI home with you. They couldn't see what you did at night.

"Do you ever wake up with a hangover? Ever need a pick-me-up in the mornings?"

Neel shook his head.

"We'd like a verbal response," said the taller agent.

"No, I don't drink in the morning."

"Have you ever consumed alcohol at work?"

Neel hesitated for a moment before he said he had not.

"Please describe your religious beliefs."

"I have none."

At this, the short man, the one with the mustache, snorted.

"What?" said Neel. He didn't try to hide his irritation.

"Have you ever considered converting to Islam?" said the taller agent.

"Of course not."

"Let's talk about your time in the Navy," said the taller agent. "Did you have a foreign girlfriend when you were an officer?"

Neel had answered questions about his service many times over the years.

"No," he said. "I was mostly in the middle of the ocean."

"And on shore leave?"

The *Nimitz* had sailed around the world. Neel had stepped off the ship in Colombia, Spain, the Philippines, Thailand.

"Come on," he said.

"Come on what? I will remind you, sir, that you are answering our questions under penalty of perjury. Did you make friends with or have sexual relations with foreign men or women in any of those places?"

"No," said Neel.

"Really?" said the man with the mustache, speaking for the first time. "Were you an asexual back then?"

"No."

"So when your carrier task force drops anchor in Manila Bay, and your brother officers are in the brothel getting their asses licked, you stay in your cabin to read paperbacks?"

"Yes," said Neel. "I was passionate about literature in those days." His mouth was dry but he was resolute. Any admission would remain in a government file for life.

"Are you currently faithful to your wife?"

"Yes."

"Do you wish to amend any of your responses today or any of your previous disclosures to the Bureau, reminding you again that you are speaking to us under penalty of perjury?"

"I do not."

"Okay. As you know, you will not be hearing from us."

The taller agent stood up. The other man scribbled a note before he stood too. Neither offered to shake Neel's hand.

Neel called Rebecca, wanting to express his distaste for the FBI, but she didn't answer. He was leaving her a voicemail when Vanderhoof walked in. He tried to wave Vanderhoof away.

"You can't come in here when I'm on the phone," said Neel, after he hung up. "This is an intelligence agency. I'll start locking my door."

"Heard the G-men were on the prowl."

"What is this, 1955? No one calls them G-men, Jon."

"Have you been putting that powder up your nose, Neel? Embezzling? Gambling? Whoremongering? They'll find you out."

"I'm always delighted to talk to federal policemen."

"I bet they have a lot of juicy material on you, my friend. They'll hold it close but if you ever make a mistake, watch out!" Vanderhoof pulled imaginary six-shooters from his belt, fired at Neel's chest ("Pow! Pow!"), spun the pistols on his index fingers, and holstered them.

"The nation is going to be a lot safer with you on paternity leave," Neel said.

That night, home after everyone had gone to bed, he played Charles Mingus's *The Black Saint and the Sinner Lady* on the living room turntable. He switched off the lights and kept the volume low while he stretched out on the rug. He hadn't listened to the album in years, but in the dark it all came back: the relentless bass line, the chaos of horns (a chaos that wasn't in fact chaos, but instead signified a deep, immeasurably complex order), a flamenco guitar breakdown so lovely and desolate that he had to close his eyes to listen. The FBI's visit had been nothing more than an unpleasant coincidence. He told himself to let go, to stop thinking, to fall into the well of music. Soon, he was dreaming.

He slept on the rug all night. In the morning, he woke to Serena sitting on his legs. Maya tickled him under his chin. They were both giggling. In the background, the needle clicked on the turntable.

"Silly Dada!" the girls said. "Silly, silly Dada!"

FIFTEEN

WHEN NEEL WOKE up on the morning of December 20, a Saturday, Rebecca and the girls were gone. They'd all signed the Christmas card Rebecca had left on the coffee table. There were two boxes wrapped in shiny blue paper in the living room and, as he discovered when he opened the front door to check the weather, red and green lights strung around the porch railing. In the kitchen, he tuned the radio to the weekend jazz program. He fried two eggs to Ellington on the piano, buttered a slice of toast, and—because he could—mixed water into a glass of cold red wine from the bottle Rebecca hadn't finished the night before. After he ate he stood awhile at the kitchen window. Ice glinted on the branches of bare trees. From the shelves in the living room he chose a detective novel, one of James M. Cain's that he'd read years earlier. He returned to bed. He read and slept, read and slept, until it was time to come down for dinner.

There was Kung Pao chicken, broccoli, and rice in takeout boxes in the refrigerator. He warmed up the food, opened a bottle of beer, and sat at the counter to eat and drink. He tried Rebecca's phone after he cleaned up but the call went straight to her voicemail. Neel left a message asking about her flight, the girls, and the weather. He said he was a little lonely at home and that, strangely enough, he was looking forward to work on Monday. He went on too long, felt suddenly embarrassed, and ended in a mumble. He was going to sleep now but maybe they could talk on Sunday, he said.

He called his parents the next morning. They invited him again to Paramus, so he wouldn't have to spend Christmas alone. He reminded them that he'd stayed in D.C. to work. His mother asked him what the point was of moving up in the world if he couldn't even go on holiday with his family. It was complicated, replied Neel. He had to sacrifice now to secure a greater reward in the future. When does the future begin? she asked. He let the question lie.

Afterward he walked the neighborhood streets. It was sharp outside but clear, with the wind having driven off the early scud. Neel gave way to couples who strolled hand-in-hand. At the bakery he bought a fruit tart and a baguette, which, with the butter and olives in the refrigerator, would be enough for the day.

He passed the afternoon on the couch with the Cain novel and the Sunday papers, making sure to keep his phone at hand. He got up only to flip the record in the player or change it out, or to use the bathroom. He was still listening to jazz but chose singers now, Ella Fitzgerald, Nina Simone, Crosby and Armstrong in *Bing & Satchmo*. He wanted voices in the room.

At four, the light was spent. He remembered that it was the winter solstice. Rebecca hadn't called back. Despite his wounded pride, he tried her again. More than anything, he wanted to speak to his daughters. The call went straight to voicemail for a second time. He hung up without leaving a message then, seconds later, threw his phone against the sofa cushions. The big clock ticked over the fireplace. Outside, the wind had started up. Gusts whistled under the front door. His thoughts began to turn. He knew the girls would sleep easily after full days on the beach. His mother-in-law would be happy with her magazines and a bottle. Rebecca had told him that the vacation house stood on a hill at one end of a small, picturesque town, a short walk from the central square. He wondered if she would go out that evening, perhaps to a hotel bar, and drink a rum punch while she listened to the distant surf. He imagined an elegant little place with ceiling fans and island music. Along with the tourists, there would be handsome local men. What would stop her from having a night or a few nights for herself? She would be discreet. He hadn't been a perfect husband. No one could blame her.

The loneliness was driving him mad. He stood, turned on the lights, and went to the kitchen. He ate quickly, returned to the living room, browsed the shelves for a book to follow Cain's, but nothing appealed to him. It was too early to go upstairs; the morning was impossibly distant. He went to the foyer, put on his jacket and scarf, and laced up his ankle boots. He was going for a walk.

He went east, past the park, into the heart of Adams Morgan. There was little traffic now, and the sidewalks were empty. The wind cut through his clothes. A bar on the corner of Kalorama and 18th looked warm and welcoming in the dark. All right, he told himself, just a round or two. He pushed open the door.

It was a small, pleasant space. Five stools at a zinc-topped counter, a gas fireplace, three booths and a couple of tables at the back. The bartender had set up a checkerboard on the counter. There were three other customers. A young man and woman huddled together in a booth, while a woman about Neel's age, wearing a leather skirt and white sweater, sat on one of the stools. Neel took another stool at the counter. A new man entered a few minutes after Neel arrived. He stamped his boots at the entrance, though the sidewalks were clear of snow. His eyes flitted around the room. He was in his thirties, with a taut face, wearing jeans and a neon-orange parka. He was obviously an outsider in that neighborhood, but didn't seem self-conscious. If anything, he looked at the others with disdain. He sauntered up to the bar, stopping at Neel's side. He ordered Irish whiskey, picked up his change without leaving a tip, and took his glass to drink alone in the back corner.

Neel and the bartender exchanged a shrug. They had started a game of checkers. The bartender was winning out. When the game ended, they began another one. The bartender won that game too, as well as the next. They didn't rush. The woman at the counter, who wasn't playing, joined in their loose conversation. She had a low, friendly voice. She'd been watching movies all day in her apartment, she said, until she'd gone stir-crazy. The three of them covered the weather, the quietness of the city in December, and the general optimism about the president-elect.

When Neel finally forced a stalemate, the bartender poured him a pint on the house. By then his two allotted rounds had become four. The woman, drinking lime soda and gin, was matching Neel's pace. Twice, Neel looked into the mirror behind the bar and saw the man with the taut face staring at him. When he caught the man staring a third time, Neel winked. The man didn't look away. Though his glass was empty he didn't return to the counter.

At eight, Neel turned down a sixth beer. He paid his tab, congratulated the barman on his skill at checkers, and shook hands. The woman at the counter said she had to leave too. She was an economist at the Federal Reserve. She liked to arrive at the office early, she said. She did her hard thinking in the hour before the phone started to ring.

Neel stood with her at the curb while she waited for a cab. When one arrived he offered her his hand, but she stepped close to hug him instead. She held him tightly for a few seconds. He turned his face to her. The night had put color in her cheeks. He smelled the gin on her breath and her sweet, unfamiliar perfume as she kissed him on the cheek.

"We'll keep it at that," she said, as the taxi driver tapped his horn. "I wouldn't want to upset your wife."

Neel hadn't mentioned Rebecca but he wore his wedding band. "She's far, far away," he said.

He held the door for her as she got into the cab. He wasn't sure what he would have done if she'd invited him to join her. She blew him another kiss through the window as the cab pulled away.

He walked home with quick strides in the cold. It was a friendly, harmless episode. Anyone could receive a holiday kiss with a clear conscience. Twice while he walked he heard a rustling or crunching in the darkness, but each time, when he looked over his shoulder, the sidewalk was empty. The wind had risen in the night. There were squirrels in the trees, rats in the gutters. The noise could have been anything.

SIXTEEN

ON CHRISTMAS EVE, Neel found the connection he'd been looking for. A Freedom Center analyst had mapped telephone metadata captured by the NSA against an expanded set of the military's incident reports from Paktika, Khost, and Nangarhar Provinces in Afghanistan. The analyst discovered that the putative leader of the Waziristani cell—"Captain Z"—had, on three occasions, called telephone numbers associated with Taliban commanders in the hours leading up to an IED attack against coalition forces. On each occasion, the Taliban commander who received the call had been within a mile of the corresponding bomb blast.

"This is the smoking gun," said the priest, when Neel called to deliver the news. "Captain Z is directing the show. He may well be making the bombs himself. We already have video evidence that his men are up to no good."

"I love it," said Neel. "But a cautionary note: we don't have drone footage of the cell members delivering or planting a roadside bomb."

"You'll never assemble a perfect intelligence report, Neel. You decide based on the data you have. Don't hold back just because you didn't get everything on your wish list. Move Captain Z to the highest tier of the threat matrix. Let's get his name out there to the agencies. We'll gather more intel—more drone surveillance, more call data—before launching a strike. You'll have everything you need to make your case. I know you'll write a great brief."

Neel logged into the threat matrix after the call ended. He moved Captain Z up the targeting list, as the priest had requested. Other bureaucrats, at other agencies, would immediately take note. He took a moment to marvel at his success. A few weeks ago, a single intelligence report had caught his eye. Since then, he'd initiated a process that now promised one result: the elimination of a high-level target in central Asia. It was possible he'd misinterpreted the evidence, that the call pattern Neel's analyst had identified had some different, more benign significance, and that Captain Z was not directing cross-border attacks, but Neel couldn't afford to linger on his doubts. As the priest had said, there were no certainties in intelligence work. He would push on.

That night he left work earlier than usual. The Operations floor was quiet, with the Center running skeleton shifts for the holiday. When he retrieved his cellphone from the lockbox outside, he saw he had a voicemail. He'd finally spoken to Rebecca the evening before. He thought she must have called again. He waited to play the message until he got into his car. But it wasn't his wife. Instead, he recognized Jones's voice, with its lewd drawl.

> With the cat away the mouse is playing, am I right? Ha, ha, ha . . . [coughing]. . . . Good for you, Neel, nothing wrong with blowing off a little steam. You've got red blood in your veins. Only I thought you'd have chosen a younger . . . companion. Anyway, things are falling into place on our end. We're almost ready for you to jump in. Until then, keep on enjoying the holidays, ha, ha! Delete this message after you've listened. I'll call soon.

Three weeks had passed since they'd spoken. The long silence had confirmed for Neel that Jones was a crank, who would—if ignored—

leave him alone. Now Neel knew he'd been fooling himself. There were eyes on him in his own city. He remembered the taut-faced man at the bar on Sunday night and his sense that someone had been following him on the sidewalk. And what now? Was this blackmail? Coercion? His hands shook as he started the car. He turned up the heater but did not begin to drive. Instead, he looked through the windshield at the near-empty lot. He felt very far from home.

SEVENTEEN

REBECCA AND THE girls flew back to Washington on New Year's Eve. Neel was waiting on the stoop when their taxi arrived. They were tanned and tired. It had been a wonderful holiday, Rebecca said, but she was happy to return. She'd brought him a bottle of island rum and a beach shirt printed with a tropical pattern. The girls hugged him at the door and again when he put them to bed. Serena made him promise he'd never miss a family trip again. He woke early on New Year's Day, while they slept, and went to work.

As the days passed, his shock at Jones's message receded. He looked up and down the block when he got into his car in the morning and around the parking lot at the Freedom Center at night, but no one was watching. Although he still took Serena to the pool on Saturdays, he otherwise avoided public places. It was as if he was suffering from a persistent but low-grade illness. He lived in a kind of middle state, without the confidence with which he had begun work at the Freedom Center, but still with the hope that he could forestall the worst. It was a vaguely familiar feeling. Over the years, he'd often felt a sense of estrangement from those around him—whether as a high school sprinter, lowering himself into the blocks for a final for which he'd been the fastest qualifier, or as a Navy flier, or as a Harvard student in some distinguished professor's seminar. Despite his dominance on the track, he feared defeat. In the Navy and at law school, he was never free from self-doubt. There was always the chance he would say or do the wrong thing, fail some inscrutable test, and show everyone that he was a pretender.

But doubts lessen, feelings shift, and even a middling man can redeem himself. Neel's glass-walled office was a sanctuary. He went in early, stayed late, pushed his boulder up the slope. He wanted a great success in Waziristan. Then, perhaps, he could trust in a bright future. Every morning, the priest told him he was doing great work.

EIGHTEEN

CONE VISITED THE Freedom Center in January, a week before the inauguration. He was a man of average size, who spoke at modest volume, but anyone could see he was ready to command. There was something unconditional about him. He introduced his incoming chief of staff, Monica Gallant, to Vanderhoof and Neel. Monica had earned his absolute trust, said Cone, in the three years she'd assisted him at the Office of the Director of National Intelligence. She had shoulder-length brown hair and a small gap between her front teeth. When they shook hands, Neel thought he detected a catch or pause. It was a tiny gesture of recognition, even interest, not that it mattered.

Obama was sworn in on the twentieth. His young family stood proudly at his side. Cone testified before the Senate Intelligence Committee six days after the inauguration. Neel went to the Capitol for the hearing. He saw the priest outside the chamber. "Pay close attention," said the priest. "You might find yourself in that seat one day." But he said this with an ironic smile, and Neel wasn't sure if the priest was jesting about his ambitions or encouraging them.

Neel sat in the second row of the gallery, behind Cone's wife and two sons. The chairman thanked Cone for his years of service to the nation, in the military and intelligence. Then Cone read his opening statement in a firm tone. He emphasized the need to balance kinetic action with soft power. He promised to deliver accurate, impartial intelligence assessments to the other spy agencies, the White House, and Congress. He spoke about the lethality and reach of American drones. He said, in response to the chairman's questions, that the United States should never torture enemy combatants. He agreed with the president's pledge to close the prison camp at Guantánamo Bay, but also testified that the nation had to move on from the mistakes of the past. He did not believe the attorney general should prosecute any CIA officers or contractors who had—out of a sense of duty—abused prisoners in this long and difficult war.

"We can never forget the nature of the enemy we face," said Cone.

"Wise words," said the chairman, looking left and right at his fellow senators.

In the gallery, Neel nodded too, though he didn't think that Cone's pronouncements were entirely sincere. The committee hearing itself was a performance. Cone was the president's man and would follow the president's lead. The senators were complicit in the Bush administration's failures. The responsibility for Iraq and Guantánamo lay equally on their shoulders. It was best to close the book. Neel wasn't going to protest. More and more he felt himself divorced from policy, ideology, even history. Iraq was a disaster, and torture a stain, but what had all that to do with him? He was girding himself for new battles. He had the priest in his ear and Jones watching from the shadows. He had to find his way in a world of bureaucrats and operators he only dimly understood. Most of all, he had a career to make.

The Intelligence Committee reported Cone's nomination to the Senate with a unanimous recommendation in his favor. Two days later ninety-seven senators voted to confirm his appointment as director of the Freedom Center, with three absent and none opposed.

Neel called Cone to congratulate him.

"You dream, you prepare, and then it's nothing," said Cone, in a strangely wistful voice. "See you at work."

NINETEEN

ON SATURDAY, JANUARY 31, Neel walked from his house to Georgetown to attend the priest's monthly salon. Cone would begin his tenure at the Freedom Center after the weekend. Neel was only going to the party because he wanted to ask the priest about Jones. He couldn't talk about blackmail and a murder plot on the phone; they had to speak face-to-face.

He'd wrapped himself against the cold in a wool coat and hat. Snow began to fall soon after he set out. It took him half an hour to cross Kalorama and Rock Creek and skirt Dumbarton Oaks. As he drew closer to the priest's apartment, his pace slowed.

He paused at the corner of Dent Place. Down the block, lights glimmered behind a row house's third-story windows. Even from a distance, Neel could sense that a party was in progress. A black sedan with tinted windows sat double-parked before the entrance. As Neel started up again, he heard laughter drift down from a balcony or roof deck. He smelled woodsmoke and pipe tobacco. It was a pretty scene for a winter's night. But as he walked closer, the air filled with diesel exhaust from the idling black sedan. Neel was peering at the car's windows, trying to make out the driver, when a man in a trench coat surprised him by stepping out from the façade of a neighboring brownstone.

The man said nothing as he looked Neel up and down. His barrel chest, gray skin, crew cut, and wired earpiece marked him as a government agent or private bodyguard. After a few seconds, Neel shrugged. He walked the few remaining yards to what he assumed was the priest's building. When he looked back, the bodyguard had disappeared. The black car didn't move.

He was checking the building's address when the lobby door swung open. Out came a man wearing a ski jacket and tan work boots. He was black, and about Neel's height, but older and bulkier. He held the door for Neel.

"You here for the salon?"

"Arriving midstream." Neel took the door as the other man released it.

"You haven't missed anything. Make an appearance, have a drink, shake a hand or two. But it's not a place to get loose-lipped in. I'm off to drink a couple more cocktails someplace I don't have to worry about the career consequences."

Neel smiled. "You're really getting me excited to go upstairs."

"You'll be all right. Louie Horn, by the way. Call me Horn."

"Neel Chima. Office for Counterterrorism Intelligence."

Neel propped open the door with his foot while they shook hands. He'd decided he liked Horn.

"I heard about you," said Horn. "Outsider, special hire. It surprised some people when they brought you in. You don't have the typical background for the intelligence side of things. If you don't mind me saying."

"You're fine. They brought me in *because* I'm an outsider. For the fresh perspective and so on."

"No doubt." Horn glanced down the block. "Listen, be smart in there."

"What's your connection to all this?"

"I was NSA. Now I'm a contractor. Same job, better pay. Software, systems architecture, the technical stuff on the front and back end."

Horn stepped farther out on the sidewalk. The wind had picked up. Gusts turned the branches of the curbside trees. "It got cold," he said.

"Maybe I'll catch you at the next one of these," said Neel.

"I've said my goodbyes, amigo. Monday I head west on a contract. Massive data storage at the Utah site. You know the project."

Neel wished Horn good luck.

"We'll ride another place, another time." Horn offered Neel his fist and Neel bumped it with his own.

A taxi pulled softly up to the curb, behind the black car.

"Safe travels," said Neel, as Horn climbed into the back seat.

The building was a triplex, with each apartment occupying an entire floor. Neel took the stairs to the top. Voices carried to the landing. Neel stamped his feet on the mat. The door was ajar. Though his face was still cold, he was wet under the arms. He noticed, to his annoyance, that his heart was racing. Here he was, a forty-year-old man who'd been invited to a cocktail party, and he felt like a college freshman calling on a girl for a first date.

It seemed, when he entered, that everyone turned their heads, and that all their voices dipped. In the quiet, Neel heard a familiar snippet of Beethoven on the stereo. Two blond women, both in gray pantsuits, stared at him from the love seat. For a few awful moments he saw unspoken questions on the faces of white people he didn't know. Then Vanderhoof raised his glass in greeting from the far corner of the room. A moment later the priest appeared. He took Neel by the biceps to draw him aside.

"You're still a specimen, aren't you? I'm amazed you have time for the gym."

The guests turned away. Their voices rose and again drowned out the music.

"You have a lovely apartment," said Neel. "It's good to see you. I was hoping we could talk."

"Later." The priest smiled. "You'll have a wonderful time. I'm always joyous at these gatherings. I find the free exchange of ideas exhilarating." He released Neel's arm.

"I've been looking forward to the salon," said Neel, hoping he sounded sincere.

He took off his hat and held it in both hands while he looked around the room. There were fifteen or twenty people talking in small groups. Vanderhoof had returned to his conversation with Monica Gallant and an older woman Neel didn't know. Smith, the Freedom Center's former director, sat alone in a corner armchair. He was smiling into space while he sipped from a can of diet cola.

"Put your coat in the back bedroom, get a drink, and then we can have some fun. I'll introduce you to the important players. Or, if you prefer, the ideas men." The priest licked his brilliantly red lips. His face was so unlined and youthful that Neel wondered if he'd applied makeup before the party.

"And we can have that private chat too," Neel said.

"Off you go," said the priest, tapping his watch. "Double time, sailor."

Neel crossed the living room to the apartment's central hallway. Vanderhoof blew him a kiss as he went by. Neel frowned back. Monica, looking with quick eyes over her shoulder, smiled at him. There was boldness in her gaze. Neel shivered a little before admonishing himself.

The hall was as crowded as the living room. Neel felt impatient and vaguely unwell as he slipped past the other guests. Two men in sports coats and khakis stood at the door to the back bedroom. They were whispering to each other. They fell silent when Neel approached, but only moved to let him into the room when he asked if they'd step aside.

He didn't close the door behind him. He took off his coat, put his hat in one of the pockets, and added it to the pile on the bed. Then he adjusted his shirt while he looked around. There was a curtained window, striped wallpaper, a nightstand, a wooden stool in the corner, and a bookcase whose shelves, when he stepped closer to look, seemed only to hold histories of the Second World War. A Christ figure on a large silver cross hung over the bed. There were two framed photographs on the wall. The rest was bare.

One photograph, in black and white, showed a young couple dressed in the styles of the immediate postwar years: a boxy, patterned sports coat and narrow tie for the man; a darker sweater over a cream or white calf-length skirt for the woman. They might have been newlyweds, in their best clothes, but they looked weary and dour. If these were the priest's parents, thought Neel, his childhood must have been as grim as Neel's own.

The second, color photograph showed the priest himself in early middle age. He stood on a sand dune, wearing a straw fedora over an untucked white shirt. In the background, on a lower plane, a camel stood tethered to a palm tree. The priest had one hand on his waist and the other around the grip of the pistol holstered on his belt. He was flashing a smile Neel recognized. But his mirrored sunglasses also froze his expression into something icy or blank. He looked every inch the clandestine officer out, on foreign soil, for secrets and blood.

Neel walked back through the hall. He didn't look anyone in the eyes as he slipped into the kitchen.

A younger man was examining the bottles on the bar cart. Neel was relieved to find beer in the refrigerator. He'd promised himself, coming in, that he'd stay away from liquor. He uncapped his bottle with an opener that lay on the counter.

The young man asked Neel if he wanted a pint glass. The glasses were in the cabinet beside the sink, he said. He seemed proud to know the priest's apartment so well.

"I'm good," said Neel, raising his bottle.

The priest waited in the living room. He wanted to introduce Neel to "a pair of fascinating men"—one a journalist, the other a thinker. The two guests stood at his side with anticipatory smiles.

"Peter Moore," said the taller man, who looked a few years older than Neel. He wore a pink shirt unbuttoned to halfway down his chest. He might have been handsome in his youth but now he'd come apart.

"I write for the magazines, so I qualify as the journalist, but I hope I do a bit of thinking as well. I'm very interested in you, Neel Chima." He had an English accent—an upper-class accent, to Neel's ear.

"I'm not that interesting," said Neel, as they shook hands. "I think I've seen you on the cable news."

"The producers do love to book themselves a posh Englishman," said Moore, dipping his jowls.

"Transatlantic affirmative action," said the second man, with a peeved expression. "We should all be so lucky." He was younger than his companion, fat, and entirely bald, with oily skin and large, black-rimmed glasses.

"Don't hate the player," replied Moore. He seemed to enjoy how ridiculous the phrase sounded on his tongue. "I use my opportunities, deserved or not, to urge America to fight her good fight."

"Thanks for doing your part," said Neel. He said this without a smirk, in a warm tone, and Moore didn't flinch. "I'll watch what I say. I don't want to read my cocktail party chatter in the *Times Magazine*."

"You won't find me in there. All the New York editors have switched sides. I'm having a better run with *The Atlantic* and the English press. Stiffer backs, you know. Regardless, it's all off the record at our friend's gatherings." Moore bowed in the priest's direction.

"Peter's a good contact," said the priest. He again took Neel by the arm. "You'll want to make a friend or two in the fourth estate."

"Of course," said Neel, as he pulled free of the priest's grip. "My pleasure."

Moore seized a handful of peanuts from a bowl on the nearby side table. He shook the nuts up in his palm before flicking one into his mouth with his thumb. In his other hand he swirled a martini glass. There was only a little of the drink left.

"My turn," said the second man. He rocked childishly on his heels. He put down the slice of cake he'd been holding to shake Neel's hand. "Tim Osborne, American Institute for Global Democracy."

The priest excused himself to throw another log on the fire. Moore stepped forward to close the gap that had appeared in their little circle. With the side table blocking him on his left, and Moore and Osborne standing close, Neel had no way out. He leaned against the wall.

Osborne looked at the bottle in Neel's hand. "I'd leave the Mexican beer for your backyard barbecues. I know Peter will be exploring the brown liquors after he finishes his second martini."

Despite the frank repulsiveness of his physical appearance, Osborne exuded a strange charisma. Neel, whose childhood had conditioned him to be self-conscious, was always amazed to meet men as baselessly confident as this.

"Third," said Moore, after a pause. "Third martini."

"I'm all right with beer," said Neel.

"We indulge," said Moore. "The Islamofascists do not. We drink liquor, we even flirt with Dionysian madness, but we don't succumb. It's one definition of civilization." He closed his fist around the stem of his glass and raised it before him like a shield.

"At this point in history, drinking is a patriotic act," Osborne said.

"To wine in an age of struggle."

Moore and Osborne clinked their glasses.

Neel shifted across the wall. Osborne noticed his movement at once.

"Let's talk a little shop before we lose you. I'm interested in what the Obama people are doing in Afghanistan."

"The key issue being the Durand Line," said Moore, turning to Neel. "It's something you, I'm sure, have considered at length."

Neel looked blankly at Moore.

"The Durand Line. The border between Afghanistan and Pakistan. A notional barrier for the Taliban, but a very real constraint for the American military."

"Right," said Neel. He felt slightly embarrassed by his own ignorance. But he also knew that Osborne and Moore, recognizing his power, had to attend to him regardless. He could affect the outcome of the war in a way they could not. "Before I tip my hand—or the government's hand—why don't you tell me what you're thinking?"

"Me first," said Osborne. His eyes were wet behind his glasses. Neel, smelling his breath, realized he was very drunk. "There are two problems with the Afghan War."

"I'm sure this will be fascinating," said Moore. "But since you're speaking, and not Neel, I'll go for refills. Tim, another Scotch?"

Osborne nodded, though he had an ample measure in his glass.

"And don't you go anywhere, Neel Chima."

"Problem number one," said Osborne, "is the terrain." He'd taken advantage of Moore's absence to move a half step closer. "Afghanistan is a country of little grass. You have rock and rubble, gray rivers, endless

mountains. Out on patrol, you look up a ridge and see the enemy sil-
houetted against the dawn. Men with guns watch your every move. You
experience the elemental fear of being a stranger in a strange land."

"You've been there," said Neel. "I didn't know. Setting aside the danger, you make it sound beautiful."

Osborne looked delighted. "I had to do an embed if I wanted to keep
calling myself an area expert. Afghanistan *is* beautiful, at least in the
Hindu Kush—beautiful and austere. Conventional military action is
impossible. By the time you climb far enough up the ridge to get him in
your sights, the enemy has disappeared. You look through your binocu-
lars and see ridge after ridge, peak after peak of empty land. It's just
wind, snow, and ghosts."

A gap appeared in the crowd behind Osborne. On the other side of
the room, a sickly-looking man, his face mottled with liver spots, sat
alone on a dining chair. His gaze met Neel's. Moments later, other
guests entered the living room, the gap in the crowd closed, and the
man disappeared from view.

Moore returned with two large whiskies. "I prefer the British countryside myself," he said. He passed one of the glasses to Osborne, who
gulped the remnants of the drink he'd been holding.

"Or give me your Maryland shore or your Virginia hills. Afghanistan
doesn't appeal to me, in the physical sense, for the same reason I've
never been inclined to visit Alaska. Nature should be restful, not overwhelming."

"What's the second problem with the war?" Neel asked.

Osborne put down his empty glass. He held his new drink in the
palm of his hand. He brought the whiskey up to his nose to sniff at it
before he answered.

"Like all guerrillas, the Taliban turn darkness to their advantage.
They move at will in country they know while our men hunker on their
bases. The border that so concerns our friend Peter here is another veil,
another night. For American soldiers, who cannot cross the Durand
Line, Pakistan is in permanent shadow."

"Brilliant," said Moore. He'd collected another palmful of peanuts,
and shot a few into his mouth.

"But we won't despair," said Osborne, pushing his glasses up his oily nose.

"Surely not," said Moore.

"We've put the time in. We've been up close to the people. We know the enemy. You've seen the green-eyed girl in the famous photograph. Afghans have the most beautiful children. You can't tell as much with the adults because, outside of Kabul, you don't see the women, and the men disappear beneath their beards. But once in a while, you'll meet an ANA soldier with a face out of Greek myth."

"Hiding women is an offense against creation," Moore said.

"Then you get up close to an Afghan. The two of you cannot imagine the stench," said Osborne.

"I wish you hadn't said that," said Neel.

"Don't take umbrage," said Moore. "Tim's only telling you what he witnessed. We all know that with the women secluded, the men bugger the boys, and the boys bugger the sheep. You'll find more deviant sexuality in a pastoral Islamic society than in the novels of the Marquis de Sade."

"It's a moral question," said Osborne. "We must win because our way of life is better."

"We're not trying to change anyone's way of life," said Neel. "We're seeking peace and security."

Osborne looked momentarily startled. He bowed his head in an exaggerated apology. "In any case, we have a solution to the conflict. Just as the atomic bomb overcame Japanese terrain and imperial fanaticism in World War Two, the drone, if used correctly, can negate the Afghan mountains and the Afghan night. It can fly anywhere, at any time, and of course it can kill anything on the ground. We have secret agencies— the CIA, your Freedom Center—that can plan missions over a border the military is not permitted to cross. What do you say, Neel?"

"That's the hope. I'm not disclosing any government secrets when I tell you we have high expectations of the drone program."

For a moment, as the crowd shifted again behind Osborne, Neel glanced across the room to the sickly-looking man on his dining chair. He was still staring impassively at Neel. But the opening closed so quickly that Neel wondered, even as he recoiled, if he'd only imagined what he'd seen.

Osborne was still talking. "We cannot accept random, ideological violence in perpetuity. From September 11, to Madrid on March 11, 2004, to the 7/7 bombings in London, to a hundred different suicide attacks in Iraq. We must change the calculus. Of course the drone can be a precision weapon, a widow-maker. Fine, carry out your strike on the terrorist driving alone on a dirt road. But that's not enough. The terrorists may accept, even embrace, the martyrdom of an individual commander. So learn from our Israeli friends. Our enemies live in family compounds. When you kill a militant at home you pull him out at the root. Hurt the tribe—hurt the fanatics in generational terms—and you inflict a lasting wound."

Moore giggled. "Tim, you really are a bloodthirsty bastard."

"I'm saying we must speak the Taliban's own language. There is no alternative, unless we plan to colonize the natives with a million American soldiers. But I think the Tenth Mountain Division has sustained enough casualties for this war."

"Thanks for the insights," said Neel. "We're not planning to slaughter innocents."

Osborne rocked on his heels. "No one is calling for the elimination of the Pashtun people. But a little clumsiness in targeting the Talibs wouldn't be the worst thing."

"Naughty," said Moore. "I have a slightly different view, though we may end up in the same place. It makes perfect sense for a Pashtun goatherd to take up arms against the invader. It also makes perfect sense for Neel Chima to call in a drone strike against that goatherd when he shoots at Marines on patrol. In the end we're all agents of history. The beauty of war by data is that it takes the moral question out of the discourse. If you want to get on television, Tim, I suggest you not talk about the necessity for the collective punishment of savage tribes. This is about risk management in the age of Barack Hussein Obama."

"I couldn't have put it better myself," said the priest, who'd rejoined their group. "I heard just enough of that little speech, Peter, to understand that the two of us are in alignment."

"We need to be as ruthless as our enemies if we want to prevail," said Osborne. He looked hurt.

"The dream is to end all wars," said the priest. "But you dream of the future. In the short-term, at present, I agree that a measure of ruthlessness might help. Of course, we needn't linger on that aspect."

"Only the short-term—only this moment—exists." Osborne raised his voice. "Remember the Greeks. The people fear the gods *because* the gods are fickle. We should worry less about justice. Trust in power!" Osborne raised his glass high.

The priest gave him a reassuring smile. At that moment, Monica— drawn, perhaps, by Osborne's excitement—appeared at the priest's side. She twirled an empty wineglass in one hand.

"The muse of the foreign policy establishment," said Moore. "I would offer you a kiss, but I'm afraid I have peanut oil on my mouth." He smiled wolfishly while he rattled the nuts in his palm.

"Thank you, Peter," said Monica. She wore slim-fitting pants and a short-sleeved blouse. She must have been in her mid-thirties, or about Rebecca's age, but she looked younger and more delicate. "This is your first visit to the salon, isn't that right, Neel? Is Peter talking your ear off?"

"Not at all," said Neel. "It's been . . . interesting . . . to hear where we are in the anti-terrorism discourse."

"What you're hearing is the avant-garde, Neel," said Moore. "We're at least two weeks ahead of the public conversation."

Osborne was staring at his feet. His eyelids drooped. He mumbled something about another drink, turned abruptly, and walked away. Moore used the opportunity to sidle closer to Monica until the priest stepped forward to block him.

"A bit of a schoolboy, that one," said Moore, who seemed unabashed. "Monica scared him off."

"A brutally violent schoolboy," said Neel.

The priest clucked his tongue. "His heart is in the right place. We disagree on certain tactical points, but we all share the same values."

"Hear, hear." Moore swirled the whiskey in his glass.

Neel had finished his beer by now. He told the others that he was going to get another from the kitchen. He'd had enough of Moore.

"I'll come with you," said Monica. "I need more wine." Neel noticed that she and the priest shared a smile. He would ask her how well she knew him, when he got the chance.

Moore drew himself up. "It was a pleasure, Neel Chima. It's good to have someone like you on board. You make this whole enterprise look better."

"And better in substance," said the priest, with a proprietary smile.

"That goes without saying," said Moore.

"Run along, you two," said the priest. He touched Monica on her lower back. "You and Neel might as well get acquainted."

Neel followed Monica to the kitchen. As he crossed the room he looked for the liver-spotted man who'd been staring at him, but the dining chair by the wall was empty, and the man himself had vanished.

Monica poured herself more wine. She and Neel were alone. He put his empty bottle on the counter but didn't go to the refrigerator for another.

"That wasn't a subtle exit," Monica said.

"I needed space. There's at least one psychopath back there."

"Don't take Tim Osborne too seriously. The American Institute for Global Democracy runs on Gulf money. The sheikhs like the talk of fire and brimstone. Threats of mass violence make them feel more secure in their palaces. Tim's harmless, deep down."

"Strange way to make a living."

Vanderhoof walked into the kitchen, rubbing his palms. "I thought I'd nip whatever plan the two of you are hatching right in the bud." He smelled of cigars.

"I just spent fifteen minutes with Smith, who remains a halfwit but now has a board seat on a cyberwar contractor. He's also making fifty thousand a month in consulting fees."

"That explains the grin on his face," said Neel. "He didn't seem to recognize me."

"Oh, he recognized you. But he's not wasting his time on small fry."

"That kind of insolence would have gotten you a court-martial in the Navy, Jon."

Vanderhoof shrugged. "I wish the music was a little more lively."

"I don't think Aerosmith is right for this crowd," said Neel.

"I want something with a beat. I may look like an albino lumberjack but baby, these hips don't lie." Vanderhoof gyrated in place while he shook his fists in the air.

"Don't ever do that again," said Neel, as Monica covered her mouth with her hand.

Vanderhoof took a beer from the refrigerator. "Jealousy is a very ugly emotion, Neel. Enough chitchat. I've got networking to do." He offered a final gyration before he walked out.

"And you?" said Monica to Neel. "Don't you have networking to do?"

"I'm not the social type. I came to speak to our host."

"About what?" Her face betrayed nothing.

"Advice on a work matter."

"Why don't you try me? We're in the same shop now. We have the same clearance. I can keep your secrets."

Neel shook his head.

"Suit yourself," Monica said. She didn't seem offended. "I'll find him for you."

The priest came into the kitchen a minute later. Neel apologized for taking him away from his guests. But he needed help, he said.

"That's why I'm here."

"A man from CIA is calling. The pseudonym is Sam Jones. He mentioned you on the phone."

The priest's nostrils flared but when he responded, his voice was gentle. "I can only advise you on matters that concern the two of us, together—namely, your official duties at the Freedom Center. Your private affairs must remain private. You'll excuse me." He patted Neel on the arm, turned, and walked out.

Neel stared after him. Of course the priest knew Jones. They'd been colleagues at CIA for a quarter century. His curtness had been deliberate.

Monica returned to the kitchen. "You're upset," she said. "You didn't get what you wanted."

"No."

"You're a big boy. You know it's good to have important friends. Just understand that friendships like these come with conditions."

"This goddamn city," said Neel.

"My offer to talk always stands. No conditions."

There was an openness in her expression, but Neel wanted to leave. He offered his hand. Instead of taking it, she leaned forward to give him a hug.

"See you Monday," she said.

The black car had left the curb. Snow covered the sidewalks. Neel walked a few blocks to find a taxi. His mind churned during the ride home. Monica, the priest, Jones—he couldn't fix on anything. But as the minutes passed, and the short drive came to its end, he found himself thinking more about Monica. She was attractive, yes, but it was her generosity he found most appealing. She'd offered friendship and understanding. They would be working long hours together at the Freedom Center. Perhaps they could rely on each other. It would be a relief finally to have someone to trust.

Everyone was asleep when he walked into the house, though it wasn't late. He emptied his pockets at the kitchen island. It was then that he noticed he had a voicemail on his cellphone. The caller had dialed from a private number. When Neel played the message, he immediately recognized Jones, despite the static on the line, and the liquor in his voice.

. . . wanted to lay eyes on you again . . . due diligence, as it were. . . . You're a big guy, you could do the deed yourself, take care of the vermin, ha ha, just kidding. The program is up and running. We'll need you soon. . . . Make yourself look good, make everyone happy [cough]. . . . Oh, I saw you and that little minx having a tête-à-tête in the kitchen. You just can't help yourself, ha, ha! Wonderful stuff, Neel, no problem at all. We'll talk soon.

Neel put down the phone. Nothing, he felt, could surprise him now. Jones had emerged from the shadows. The two of them had attended the same party, shared the same room. He thought about the people he'd spoken to and the faces he'd seen. He remembered, with a flash of certainty, the sickly, liver-spotted man who'd stared at him from across the crowd. Neel put his hands on the kitchen counter. Though he couldn't know what lay ahead, he was no longer walking in blindness.

TWENTY

ON MONDAY, NEEL forwent his usual call with the priest. Instead he spent the early morning combing the weekend reports for data with which to buttress his targeting brief on the Waziristan cell. After he updated it, he sent the brief to Cone, with a recommendation that the Freedom Center nominate the cell for an immediate strike. For now, Neel's part was complete. He took a moment to consider his own state of mind. Beyond all else, he felt satisfaction at having completed a difficult and tedious task. The new administration wanted to replace dangerous ground operations against Taliban irregulars with unmanned attacks from the air. Not only the priest but—as Neel had witnessed at the salon—an entire class of officials and hangers-on expected the Freedom Center to lead that effort. In this case, Neel was calling for the assassination of a militant leader whose identity he did not know. If the government carried out the strike, unknown others would die too. But he'd learned years earlier, as a young naval officer, to divide himself— to sever emotion from duty. His role was to implement the government's tactics, not to question them. In this work, skill counted more than conscience. You did what you could for the mission.

Seven years in the Navy had changed him forever. His father hadn't argued when Neel told him, his senior year in college, that he was applying to the Aviation Officer Candidate School, but he asked why Neel hadn't chosen his path earlier. "Hell's bells, you could have gone to bloody Columbia for free. At least you're not wasting your life."

Now he remembered dry weeks on the carrier, endless briefings, the roar of the nuclear reactors that made ordinary conversation an ordeal, the smell on the upper decks of aviation fuel and engine exhaust. He kept his books in a milk crate under his bunk, with his package of rubber earplugs. He had Kabir, a verse translation of *The Odyssey*, Raymond Chandler, Shakespeare's tragedies, and three or four depraved French novels he could masturbate to. They were always tired at sea, and there were never enough hours for sleep, but he read every night.

"Man's life is a dancing shadow, amounting to nothing," wrote Kabir, and Neel wanted to believe. How else could he withstand the fear? In February 1993, on Operation Southern Watch, the *Nimitz* sailed to the Persian Gulf. It joined the mission to secure American aerial dominance over Iraq. Neel sat in the rear seats of a Prowler, a soft, slow beast of a plane. His task was to jam Iraqi radar so that the Hornets, in formation ahead of and behind the Prowler, could fly unhindered to Saddam's missile sites. He didn't dwell on whether the operation was necessary or just. He wanted to do his duty and to live.

He could hardly breathe as he dressed for the mission briefing. Above his head, Hornets slammed onto the carrier deck at three-minute intervals. In the squadron room he looked across a row of blank white faces. Some of the officers were his friends but in those moments every man sat alone.

They cruised into enemy airspace at 420 knots, the sky at 35,000 feet a deeper, more luminous shade of black. Through his night-vision goggles he watched green stars stream overhead and green satellites flash in their orbits. The Prowler flew over the desert. When it reached the villages and cities of the Euphrates Valley, Neel began to work his switches and dials. One by one, the Iraqi radar installations fell silent. The jet faced no antiaircraft fire. Neel imagined technicians on the ground, with clipped mustaches, shaking their fists at their snow-filled screens. All told, it was two hours in and back. Neel said nothing—he was not permitted to say anything—as they dropped down to the *Nimitz* in the Gulf. The pilot, Lewis Maycock, call sign Yoda, who must have stood on his toes to clear the minimum height for naval aviation, caught the Prowler's tail hook on the second trap wire on the deck. It was a perfect landing. Neel's eyes welled behind his goggles.

He flew his missions, earned his badges. He'd never felt more American, never as secure, as when he stood in his flight suit on the carrier deck. The black and brown and Asian sailors smiled when they saluted him. He knew they were proud to see one of their own with an officer's stripes on his sleeve. He listened to the men chatter while they worked on the Prowler in the hangars—a Filipino seaman from Long Beach, say, or a black petty officer from Mobile. You learned the patois, the American tongues, and you knew the country.

Dawn on a calm sea. Steel under his feet, the radar antennas turning on the towers. On his first tour, he never thought of the future. He was twenty-four. The days stretched without end.

On his third tour, the carrier group sailed the North Atlantic for winter exercises. Past Scotland, the ocean turned the color of iron. Its swells deepened. The airmen watched the sky during short, dark days. Neel landed with bile in his throat. The taste of rubber and sweat lingered after he removed his oxygen mask. One morning, a mechanic fell off the deck into sixty-foot seas. At night, in Neel's berth, the walls were like ice. He heard strange cries from the stairwell. According to rumor, the enlisted sailors ran a prostitution ring on the lower decks. If you dared descend you could buy methamphetamines or prison wine. Men reeled into the infirmary with broken jaws and teeth. Don't ever go down there, warned Yoda. Stay on the upper decks where you belong.

They tallied the dead. A Prowler overshot the trap wires on another carrier and plunged into the Red Sea. Two countermeasures officers drowned, though the pilot and a third officer ejected safely. The same week another Prowler collided with a Seahawk helicopter on a cloudless morning off Oahu. Pilots died in their Hornets at the rate of matadors. No one could shoot them down but the machines failed, and even the best pilot could miss his landing with the ship rolling on the waves.

Everyone waited for Asia. In summer you could smell flowers from ten miles out at sea. Once, off an anonymous Philippine island, with an afternoon's dispensation to go to the beach, Neel swam through a cloud of tiny jellyfish. They crackled against his skin like sheaves of wheat in the wind. On another day, in Flores, Indonesia, an orange-and-black snake wound itself around Neel's calf in shallow water, then slowly uncoiled and swam away. He mentioned the incident to a medical officer on the carrier the next day. Neel was lucky, said the doctor, both to have seen the snake, which was a rare specimen, and to have lived. The animals were territorial. If Neel had stepped on it or tried to pull it off his calf, the bite would have turned his whole leg blue. An antidote existed but they didn't stock it in the *Nimitz's* infirmary. He would have suffered, the doctor said, while they flew him to an onshore hospital. He should never forget that there were still wild places in the world.

He'd just turned twenty-five when the *Nimitz* reached Thailand. Neel and Yoda motored into Phuket City harbor on the carrier's launch. The ship loomed in the deep channel behind them, on a different scale than every other vessel in sight. The Malay Peninsula stretched to the south, and beyond it the Strait of Malacca, through which the carrier group would sail in three days. For now they rested at the rim of the Islamic world. Their orders were to dress in civilian clothes on shore.

Neel followed Yoda into the back seat of a taxi. They lowered the windows to let the warm air course over their faces. Cologne rose from their skin with the heat. In ten minutes all traces of the port disappeared. They stepped out from the car at a night market. Cicadas screamed in the trees. Middle-aged women as slender as girls worked in the stalls. Men sat on crates or plastic stools to slurp noodles, leaving the tables for families. People spoke to one another in their impossible language. *Ka, ka,* the women called. Neel smiled and looked at his shoes. Yoda pointed out the ribbons hanging from the branches of the banyan trees, and the tiny altars on windowsills and street corners. It was a land of ghosts, he said, ghosts that came out after dark. Once, years earlier, he'd been drinking through the afternoon at an outdoor bar in a tourist district of Bangkok. Before night fell, in the fleeting tropical dusk, he'd watched a Thai youth pour out the last drops of his beer at one of the street-corner shrines and bow his head in prayer. A minute later, the same youth smashed the empty bottle on the head of an Englishman who'd chosen to relieve himself farther down the alley. The Englishman dropped to his knees, piss staining his shorts, while blood trickled from the gash on his bald pink head. No one on the street paid the least attention.

"We can't know this place," said Yoda. He wasn't yet thirty, but the few years of experience he had over Neel made him a patriarch. "The Thais love us and hate us. We have to walk gently here."

"I'm following your lead," said Neel. Before joining the Navy, he'd only left the United States once, to drive to Montreal on a weekend road trip with a friend from Columbia. Now he wanted the whole world. With three hundred dollars in his breast pocket, he was untouchable. He walked with his chest forward, his shoulders back. You take off the uniform but the rest remains.

Yoda led him through the lanes to a floodlit building. The guards waved them through the front gate. The place was called Nightflower. Americans, officers, had ruined themselves for the women who worked there. If you fall in love, said Yoda, you can redeem the woman for a hundred thousand baht, rent a cabin on the beach, and forget, for however long it takes the shore police to catch up to you, that there ever was a U.S. Navy.

The hostess pointed them upstairs to the VIP floor. German and Russian men crowded the lower level. They drank and laughed, pointing at the women who danced in bikinis on stage. On the higher tier, where Yoda and Neel were the only customers, women in evening dresses lounged behind a glass wall.

"Watch how I do it," Yoda said.

"Are we sure?" said Neel, but Yoda was already at the glass.

He held his face right up to the pane, looking dispassionately at the dozen or so women on display. Some of them smiled at him but most continued to file their nails or rub lotion on their arms. Moments later Yoda whispered a few words to an attendant who spoke, in turn, through an intercom. A woman in a yellow dress stood, walked to the door at one end of the glass wall, and stepped out. She took Yoda's arm. She was taller than him in her heels.

Yoda winked at Neel over his shoulder. He paid at the cashier's desk before he disappeared with his companion into the elevator.

Neel glanced over the remaining women. They were all black-haired and slender. He couldn't choose. He could hardly look at them.

The attendant materialized at his side.

"Orange dress," said Neel, picking the woman closest to the door.

Upstairs, in the room, she turned on the water and told him to undress. She massaged his shoulders while he soaked himself in the tub.

"Dark man," she said. "I like dark man."

Neel asked her what else she liked and she said, "Hello Kitty."

Unclothed, on the bed, her skin smelled of mangoes. She whispered in his ear. The words sounded sweet though he could not understand.

"Shh," he said, and went on in the silence that fell.

Afterward she let him sleep until his two hours were up. A ceiling fan stirred the air. The room had no windows. It could have been midnight or midday. He'd have lain there forever.

He dressed unhurriedly. This was a new kind of power. To be like Yoda and the others. To take what he wanted, to feel no shame.

She asked if she'd see him again. He said he hoped so. Then he asked if this was her home, if she was from Phuket.

She said no, she'd come from far away, from the hill country in the north. They all had. The land up there was poor. Families lived on small farms and had many children.

"I'm sorry," said Neel.

She smiled at him as she shook her head.

"Please tip," she said.

Yoda was drinking in the VIP lounge. The women were gone from behind the glass and the main floor emptied of tourists and dancers.

"You don't live just one life," said Yoda, smiling wistfully. "You're an officer, you fly, you command. Then on shore leave in a country like this, in secret, behind a closed door, you become someone else. We'll remember these nights when we're old."

"When I was a boy I wanted to escape New Jersey," said Neel. "I dreamed of marrying a nice-looking girl and moving to California. I didn't envision this."

Yoda stood to put his hand on Neel's shoulder. He had to reach up to the taller man. "No one is who they thought they were," he said. "There's freedom out here."

"I think the girl I was with really liked me," said Neel.

Yoda laughed. "Of course she did."

He led Neel into the street.

At a restaurant he knew, which never closed, and where the cook slept on the kitchen floor, Yoda told the waiter to bring all the dishes on the menu and a bottle of rum. Neel and Yoda didn't stop eating. They must have looked strange, the two of them, one short and pale, the other tall and dark, in the otherwise empty room. The cook, who was an old woman, came out to watch the Americans gorge themselves.

Yoda talked through the meal, even while his mouth was filled with rice and curried beef, or while he dabbed the sweat off his forehead with a napkin. He stopped talking only to drink shots of rum. He told Neel that government pay was the best kind of pay because it came in the right amount. There was always enough in your account for you to have a good time on shore leave, but if you went too far and spent it all you wouldn't hate yourself. He said that looking back he'd learned three important things in his twenties: first, always be direct with women about what you want; second, don't be afraid of death, because the ones who are afraid are the ones who make the mistakes that get them dead; and third, if you want a career in the Navy, loyalty and having the right friends are more important than ability.

Neel knew Yoda enjoyed having him as a disciple. He could listen. He didn't argue. He was learning Yoda's lessons and another of his own. You let an older man savor the wisdom he's earned. Watch him fall more deeply in love with himself, and he'll love you as well.

Neel and Yoda left the restaurant at sunrise and slept through the day at their hotel. The next night, they did it all again.

TWENTY-ONE

A WHITE HOUSE staffer led Cone and Neel down to the West Wing's basement. They took their seats in the Situation Room, joining a dozen other military and intelligence types. It was eleven in the morning.

"Terror Tuesday," Cone whispered. "Freedom Center in the house. Ready to get after it?"

"I'm ready to read from the brief," Neel said.

"You're ready to *sell* that brief. Whatever intelligence gaps we've talked about don't matter now." Cone punched Neel lightly on the arm. "The Center needs this target."

The president walked in behind the vice president and the priest a minute after the hour. The three of them sat at the head of the table.

A National Security Council staffer, an austere woman who looked to be in her late forties, opened with an overview of the most pressing threats faced by the United States. Then officers from the CIA and Defense Intelligence appeared on a video screen at the foot of the table. They listed the high-level terrorist suspects they wished the Air Force to target. They showed satellite images of buildings and vehicles in Pakistan, Yemen, and Somalia. Neel had already seen the pictures. His attention drifted. The vice president, three chairs away from Neel, seemed to be falling asleep.

A special operations officer made his own presentation from the video screen, focusing on the areas of greatest unrest in Iraq, followed by the NSA director. Finally it was the Freedom Center's turn. The meeting had already run long. Cone nodded at Neel. Around the room, bodies shifted in their chairs.

Neel turned to the first page of his brief. As a lawyer, he always began an oral argument by reading from the page. That way he'd speak clearly, without faltering, until the inevitable interruption. "Our first actionable target is in Waziristan," said Neel, "on the Pakistani side of the Af-Pak border. We've identified a bomb maker or supplier of bomb-making materials, and his militant cell, in a village a stone's throw from the Durand Line, and sixty miles south of the primary road link between the two countries, through the Khyber Pass. Despite its remote location, the cell appears to be a wellspring of anti-Coalition violence. The bomb maker, codenamed Captain Z, is perhaps the single greatest threat to the security of American soldiers in the Afghan theater."

The man facing Neel, a small, lean general with little hands and a smooth head, snorted.

Neel looked up to meet the general's gaze before he went on. "Through forensic analysis we can trace a notable percentage of the explosives that are killing and maiming our soldiers in the border provinces of Nangarhar, Paktika, and Khost to the work of a single skilled technician. The bombs he makes are among the deadliest we've encountered."

"It's speculation," said the bald general.

The president, at the head of the table, kept a neutral expression.

Cone spoke for the first time. "With respect, sir. It's not speculation that American soldiers in Afghanistan are taking casualties from a cowardly campaign of terror."

"CIA confirms that the operation falls under the blanket clearance the Pakistanis have given for strikes in the tribal borderlands," Neel said.

"You don't even know the target's name," said the general. "All you have is pattern-of-life surveillance. No human intelligence, no reports from the field. The target could be a local gangster for all you know."

He reminded Neel of a creature from a nature documentary he'd watched with Maya. There were worms in the deep ocean that waited for the bones of dead fish to drift down to the floor. They were ugly, translucent things that could live years between meals.

"We can't afford to take our eyes off the largest Taliban training camps," said the general. "Kill the fighters. Destroy their trucks and matériel. Grind the enemy down."

Cone spoke after a moment's silence. "If you read my deputy's brief you'll find that the intelligence is solid. Phone intercepts confirm the visual evidence that members of the cell are transporting scrap metal and nails to the compound. That's the same deadly shrapnel these animals pack into their pipe bombs. The phone chatter we've been able to translate reveals that they hold virulently anti-American views. CIA identifies a movement signature associated with terrorist groups, of late-night travel and all-male gatherings in the courtyard. There isn't an economic base in the region to support the purchase of the high-grade rifles and trucks and the Mercedes we've seen in the pictures. There's no civilian presence. The cell leader, our Captain Z, has repeatedly called known Talibs from across the border shortly before a bomb goes off. All this adds up to extreme derogatory evidence. We have more than we need."

"The NatSec Principals Committee has approved the action for a reason," said Neel. "This meets every definition of an imminent threat."

"It's Swiss cheese. Full of holes," said the general. "And I'll remind you that the Committee's list of approved targets far exceeds our capacity to carry out operations. This room is where the final decisions get made. It's too risky to waste a strike on the basis of a threadbare intelligence package."

The priest, who had been looking at Neel with an indulgent expression, now turned to the president.

"We should accept the Freedom Center's recommendation," he said. "My Pakistani contacts think we're on to something. In a dangerous environment, with little opportunity to source human intelligence, this is the type of data-driven proposal we should embrace." He pressed a handkerchief to his lips.

"I agree," said the vice president, who suddenly sat upright. He smiled at Neel as if at his own good fortune. "Great work, team."

"My lawyers will look at the file," said the president. "Thanks, every-one."

He stood up and they all did.

Neel followed Cone out. He felt an overwhelming sense of relief.

"Nailed that," Cone said, as they climbed the stairs.

The White House issued an approval that afternoon. The operation was scheduled for nine P.M. on the East Coast of the United States, which was seven A.M. in Pakistan. Satellite imagery showed a beautiful morn-ing in the Hindu Kush.

Cone knocked on Neel's door at five minutes to nine. Neel was just finishing an extra set of thirty push-ups. Monica stood at Cone's shoul-der. Vanderhoof waited at the top of the stairs. They all went down.

The floor manager had put the drone pilot's video feed up on the main screen. The images were blurred, and sometimes pixelated, but Neel could make out the buildings. The drone circled high above a large compound set off from the other houses in the village. The silver Mercedes he'd seen in surveillance photographs sat in the rear court-yard. Dirt footpaths snaked through the boulders, with larger outcrop-pings in the near distance. It was a hard, dry country, of stunted trees and wind-stripped soil. On one side of the screen a cloaked figure walked with a dozen smaller, darker forms. Neel realized, after watch-ing for a few seconds, that it was a shepherd leading his goats out to graze.

"He has no idea," said Vanderhoof, at Neel's shoulder. "Good morn-ing, motherfucker."

Most of the daytime analysts had stayed on to watch. They gathered in the aisles while the arrivals for the overnight shift took the desks. Neel could see the anticipation—an almost erotic charge—in the ana-lysts' faces. He followed Cone to the back of the room. The floor man-ager dimmed the lights. Onscreen, the day brightened. Cone asked the manager to pipe in the drone operators' audio feed. Everyone on the floor fell silent.

A voice crackled in the static. "Place the target. Place the target, S.O." It was the pilot speaking. He was an Air Force officer, flying the drone from a trailer on a base in Nevada. This was nothing like naval aviation. The drone pilot faced no danger. On the other hand, Neel had never had to fire a missile.

The video field narrowed to show only the compound where Captain Z lived. A two-story house faced a smaller building, perhaps an animal pen, across an empty courtyard. White crosshairs appeared over the house.

"Eyes on," said a second voice, which presumably belonged to the sensor operator.

"Hold," said the pilot, who was communicating with the CIA officers who had operational control of all strikes outside official combat zones. Under the classification rules, their voices could not be piped into the Freedom Center. "Mission intel clears us," the pilot said, seconds later. "On my signal."

Neel held his breath.

"Fire now!" shouted the pilot. "Fire!"

"Splash," said the sensor operator.

Neel counted silently. One one thousand, two one thousand. . . . At seven seconds a column of white smoke erupted, blotting out the other images on the screen.

"Contact," said the pilot.

When the smoke cleared, Neel saw that both the house and the animal pen had collapsed into rubble. A sheep or goat lay with its legs splayed beside what remained of the courtyard wall.

"Jesus," said Monica, who'd slipped in between Neel and Cone.

On the floor, the analysts clapped solemnly. A few of them shook hands, even hugged. Neel stood still. It was a moment of triumph for him, yet he felt a strange ambivalence within. It was one thing to plan a killing, another to witness it.

"This shit is nuts," said Vanderhoof, elbowing Neel in his side. "It's not over."

Four men or boys had run into the courtyard from offscreen. A fifth figure arrived, then a sixth.

The pilot's voice crackled. The static, and the noise from the Operations floor, made it difficult to make out the words. Neel heard him say "Rifle," and then, "S.O., can you confirm weapons?"

Neel saw nothing incriminating. The images were blurry. On the other hand, he didn't have the training.

"Two rifles," said the sensor operator. "Unless those are crowbars or staffs."

"Positive ID," said the pilot. "I see rifles. Request permission to strike."

Static filled the air. The figures, whose faces were indistinct, moved over the rubble. The crosshairs hovered in the center of the group.

"Repeat, do we have permission?" said the pilot. "Targets are moving to the edge of the frame. Two squirters. The window is closing." Moments later he said, "Yes, affirmative," in response to questions he was hearing from the CIA officers through his headset. Finally, he had the order he wanted. "We're clear. S.O., fire when you can."

"Now!" said the sensor operator. "Splash."

Again Neel counted in his head. At seven, the missile hit. This time, when the smoke cleared, he saw three bodies on the ground. Another figure dragged itself from a crater in the center of the courtyard, leaving a dark trail on the dirt. The other two figures seemed to have evaporated.

"Lotta bugsplat," said the sensor operator.

There was more applause from the crowd at the Freedom Center. Neel grimaced. He'd never liked the mission patois, the brave talk, when he was a Navy flier.

The pilot, sounding relaxed now, said he'd continue to circle and observe the compound.

At the Freedom Center, the floor manager switched off the feed. Light returned to the room. The analysts looked around. Vanderhoof was grinning in a dead-eyed way. Monica wiped her face.

"Thank you, everyone," said Cone, without raising his voice. "That was teamwork. For those going home, sleep well tonight knowing you saved American lives. We'll do more great work tomorrow."

There was applause, backslapping, hugs. Slowly, the analysts returned to their desks or headed for the door.

Cone walked up to Vanderhoof. "You're good, Jon. We'll need you fresh and rested tomorrow. I'm going to debrief here with the targeting crew but you're free to go."

Vanderhoof looked surprised, but he said good night to them.

Cone watched him walk to the exit. Then he tapped Neel on the arm. "Come upstairs. Say hi to someone."

The priest stood outside Cone's office. "I watched the show from up here," he said, with his schoolboy's smile.

He shook hands with Cone and Monica before he turned to Neel. They hadn't spoken since their brief exchange about Jones at the salon, three nights earlier.

"And you, the architect of all that carnage. *Gratias tibi ago.*"

"Thank you," said Neel, though he didn't understand the Latin phrase.

"The director and I are going to have a little chat now. Good night to the two of you. You should feel very proud." He patted Neel on the shoulder, smiled at Monica, and turned away.

Cone unlocked his office. He followed the priest in, closing the door behind him.

"Enjoying your triumph?" asked Monica, alone now with Neel in the hall.

Neel exhaled. "It's strange to see the enemy die in real time."

"If that was the enemy."

Neel frowned. "I think we were all in agreement on that. Everyone signed off on the targeting brief."

"Of course we're in agreement. And if you—or we—made a mistake, it's not as if we'd ever know. A Waziristani tribesman has no one to complain to."

"No," said Neel.

"Rest easy. The work isn't subject to review."

"Let's just keep on getting it right."

She held his gaze. "Word is, the green light stays on for new targets."

The phone began to ring in Neel's office.

"Are you going to get that?" Monica asked.

"I've done enough for one day. I'm going home to see my wife."

Outside, the wind bit into his face. He was so tired of winter. Traffic was light on the parkway and, later, on the city streets. He saw, when he pulled into the driveway, that the light was on in their bedroom. He went upstairs to say good night to Rebecca. When she asked him how his day had been, he kissed her and didn't answer.

Downstairs, he took the stopper out from a bottle of wine Rebecca must have opened at dinner. He'd done his duty, followed the data where it led him. And if he felt uneasy at what he'd witnessed that night, if the fact that he didn't know who'd died in the drone attack weighed on his conscience—well, he wouldn't be a human being otherwise. Ambition had its cost. He could bear the consequences.

His laptop waited in the living room. It wasn't a night for music. He'd wait half an hour until he was sure Rebecca was asleep. Then he'd find the right website and watch a forbidden video or two. What he wanted now was to forget.

TWENTY-TWO

. . .

AN OLD MAN came to the masjid. Sometimes he brought his grandson. The old man taught the boy, who was very young, how to prostrate himself before Allah and how to be still. Ibn Muhammed watched them from the mihrab. After prayers, he offered the old man tea.

Eventually, Ibn Muhammed confessed. He was not a hafiz. He had no claim on the jamm'ah, his tongue was heavy, he had nothing to teach.

"I'm eighty, my son," replied the old man, in a Punjabi thickened with the Saraiki dialect of southern Pakistan.

Ibn Muhammed was always asking him to speak slowly. Even then he strained to understand.

"What can the mullahs teach me?" asked the old man. "Does any mullah in New York have a prayer mark like mine?" He touched the callus that darkened his forehead. "What more do I need to know? 'Wherever you turn, there is the face of Allah.'" He circled his arm in the air. "If Allah called you to this work, then, little brother, you have nothing to be ashamed of."

The old man's smile revealed a paan-chewer's crimson tongue and ruined teeth. On the other side of the room, the little boy spun a plastic top on Ibn Muhammed's desk.

"Come closer, brother," said the old man.

Ibn Muhammed leaned across the table.

"Beware the stranger." The old man beckoned Ibn Muhammed still closer.

He tilted his ear to the old man's lips.

The old man pointed a finger to the world outside the storefront masjid. He whispered what must have been one of the handful of English words he knew: "Gov'ment."

It was a neighborhood of spies, of tipsters and brutes, in a city run by the police. One night someone broke into the masjid, stole the eighty or one hundred dollars Ibn Muhammed kept in a desk drawer, pissed on the cushions. He knew there were eyes and ears everywhere—cameras, wiretaps, patrol cars. But he had nothing to hide. This country—his only country, his native land—had damaged him enough. He would fear no devil or beast.

Frozen mornings opened to dark, rain-filled days. His thighs chafed, the skin bled between his toes, and his unseeing eye burned in its socket. Every morning he walked the dirty sidewalks to the masjid, removed his shoes, performed his ablutions, and prayed or—more often—read. When he looked at the light-blue walls, when he leaned back against the softness of the cushions, peace descended. He felt as he'd once felt when he listened to his mother sing from an upstairs room, or when she pressed his legs on the sofa. But hymns and idylls must end. Soon he would leave his cave for the untamed country. He wondered, some nights, whether all this was a Christian affectation—a kind of monkishness—this self-denial and penance.

The old man told Ibn Muhammed not to waste his youth. Allah had imbued him with vigor for a reason. "Ramadan will not come for months. Don't eat dry chapatis. Spread butter, eat pickles and curds. Eat pakoras, eat samosas. Eat kheer with raisins. Sweeten your tea. Don't turn your back on the blessings."

The old man paid five dollars a week in zakat.

The loneliness weighed on him. Was it the wettest month on record? He looked out the window, to the black streets with their clogged gutters. He looked to the computer on his desk. He didn't want to read about the wars. The screen tempted him with another promise. Down the avenue, the curtained windows and neon signs of the massage parlors tempted him. At any moment he could clip his beard, trade his robes for jeans and a baseball cap, and walk through the foul weather to a bar to drink beer, and later tequila, and talk to women as he once did.

The old man didn't trust the Syrian. Ibn Muhammed didn't trust him either. He had pale skin, sleepy eyes, and a wallet that bulged in his breast pocket—he looked like a villain. But a week earlier, the Syrian had put three hundred dollars into the box, and going forward he promised to pay three hundred every week. When Ibn Muhammed asked why, the Syrian said three hundred was nothing to him, it wasn't even loose change in his pockets. Allah had blessed him in his business dealings.

The Syrian lived, he said, in three places at once. His hands were in New York. His mind dwelled on his own suffering country. And his heart rested in Hejaz and Najd, in the country of the two holy mosques. "And why are you so angry, Ibn Muhammed al-Punjabi? I sense your confusion and hurt. Who took your eye? In the masjid, we must be holy, but on Saturday night let me take you to a certain club in Queens. You're a young man. Don't resist your passions. Everything in nature comes from Allah. Everything in nature is holy."

Ibn Muhammed shook his head. He said the streets the Syrian talked about, the "certain club" in Queens, and the back rooms the Syrian would undoubtedly explore, held nothing for him. He didn't tell the Syrian his real fear—that at night, in some forbidden place, his animal spirits would emerge, never to submit to piety again. He thanked the Syrian for the donation.

"You read the news," said the Syrian. "You watch the video clips, you hear our brothers' cries. Help me help them."

Ibn Muhammed al-Punjabi replied that he was nothing but a half-blind Sufi. He had no vengeance in his heart. He loved the saints, not the martyrs. He told the Syrian what he told the old man: he had no learning. His mother used to say that Allah had imbued every human life, believer or not, with infinite value. Because every life was infinite, the taking of a single life destroyed the universe. Ibn Muhammed was not a man of action. He deplored violence of any kind. But to appease the Syrian, he agreed to call from the mihrab for the safety of the Afghan children.

When the Pakistani arrived, it was as if Ibn Muhammed's own brother, Faisal the apostate, had returned in a gentler guise. The Pakistani told Ibn Muhammed that he washed dishes in two restaurants. He slept on a cot in a Flatbush basement. He had no papers. He feared the government. He lived, he said, on chapatis and tea. Still, he had perfect teeth.

No one who grew up in a Lahore jhuggi could have a mouth like that, said Ibn Muhammed. "Did you have your teeth bleached? Did you straighten them? I see the face of God in your face."

The Pakistani replied that he had never set foot in a dentist's office. "When I was a boy," he said, "the mullahs taught us that Allah desires to be known. Allah is nearer to us than our own pulse. Why shouldn't he bless me with the mouth of a king? Why shouldn't I be the most fortunate dishwasher in America? I'll save the money I make in the country of the kafirs and one day go home to marry a girl with black eyes and a red dress, alhamdulillah."

At home, Ibn Muhammed lay naked on the sheets. He looked down at his own body without touching himself. But if he were to stray, if he left the path of righteousness and found himself not only fatherless and motherless but with no protection at all, wouldn't that also be Allah's doing? Weren't all lives, for all time, already written? And if the shard of doubt he had never been able to expel, that remained lodged in his chest, near his heart, if that shard turned, if it opened or deepened a wound, and the wound festered and swelled and overcame him, what then? What if Allah didn't exist?

Or was that question itself meaningless, if the divine was everywhere in creation? When a Sufi loves a woman, he loves God. When a Sufi admires a flower or a mountain, he admires God. Because a Sufi never turns from creation, he never turns from God. The nature of his belief couldn't matter less.

The dishwasher promised Ibn Muhammed that one day they would fly together to Lahore for the dishwasher's wedding. They'd spend a week in his village, in the countryside. "We'll drink warm buffalo milk from the pail, bhai-sahib, and eat my mama's mutton saag."

The old man never raised his eyes to the Syrian, but neither would he acknowledge the dishwasher, who was, after all, his countryman. The dishwasher took no offense. He shrugged and then touched Ibn Muhammed's arm. He asked Ibn Muhammed al-Punjabi for his real name, the name his father chose. Ibn Muhammed told him.

The dishwasher promised to help Ibn Muhammed translate his verses into a Punjabi that would drip with honey.

The Syrian kept his promise to give three hundred a week. After making his donations he lowered himself to the cushions, beneath the light-blue walls. He smiled without moving his sleepy eyes.

The old man and his grandson no longer came.

ONE DAY, BELOVED

—Ibn Muhammed al-Punjabi—

One day, beloved, I'll lead you to the mountain,
to watch the sun rise over all Kashmir
in air purer than air.

Or you will watch the horizon
while I watch you
in a dawn that catches the silver on your ears.

No cold wind, beloved, can touch us,
when love drums in my heart
and all creation is aflame.

TWENTY-THREE

IT WAS THE middle of February. Neel had been the principal deputy at the Freedom Center for three months. In the days since the Waziristan operation, he had prepared three additional briefs on militant commanders in the Pakistani tribal areas. He'd asked the Center's analysts to collate data on at least five other potential targets in the region. But although the NatSec Principals Committee had approved Neel's targets, the White House didn't schedule them for drone strikes. Nor were the targets likely to appear on the schedule in the near future, said Cone. Apparently, the Pakistani generals had decided that the presence of high-level Al Qaeda figures in the tribal regions posed a threat to Pakistan's own stability. The generals were passing information on regional targets to their contacts in the CIA. Thus the CIA could produce targeting briefs that cited human intelligence. Neel's briefs, built entirely on surveillance data, looked thin by comparison. The priest encouraged Neel to keep going. But for now the CIA was directing the drone war. Like his predecessors, Obama had turned his eyes to Langley. Meanwhile, Neel worried that the data underlying his own recommendations would go stale, and his targets disappear. He was losing ground even before the priest added him on short notice to a delegation the government was sending to Thailand. Overseas, he'd have no access to the targeting data. He didn't want to go, but Cone told him he had no choice.

Now he sat in a conference room in Bangkok, listening to an Australian software engineer talk about massive data harvesting. The air smelled of bodies. Neel's hands left an imprint on everything he touched: table, paper, shirtfront. Vanderhoof, in the chair across from him, kept falling asleep. They'd arrived at noon, which was midnight in D.C., after twenty-one hours of travel. Cone had flown in with them but was elsewhere now. Officially, they'd come to renew the agreement granting the NSA a tap on the fiber-optic cable running beneath the Gulf of Thailand. The tap gave the American government unfettered access to the electronic communications of 140 million Southeast Asians. In exchange for the renewal, American operatives, along with a handful of British and Australian spies, were to provide software and training to Thai intelligence. Neither Neel nor Vanderhoof had been assigned a speaking role at the conference. Monica hadn't made the trip at all. The Thais preferred to deal with men, the priest said, and it was best to avoid awkwardness with foreign allies.

They took a break in the afternoon, following a lecture on encryption standards by an NSA mathematician who stared at the ceiling the entire time he spoke. Women in white blazers, white skirts with black piping, low-heeled black shoes, and squared blue hats brought sliced mangoes, cookies, and mugs filled with orange-colored tea.

"Hot tea?" said Vanderhoof. "Even the walls are sweating. I have high blood pressure, sleep apnea, pre-diabetes. I'm at risk for gout. Do you know CPR?"

"You'll die before I touch my lips to yours," said Neel.

"If I have a stroke, promise you'll take care of my unborn son."

They adjourned at seven. Outside, vans idled in the tropical night. The heavy air, the damp smell in the sudden darkness, the trees noisy with insects—for Neel, the memories stirred.

They had half an hour at the hotel to shower and change. Then the vans took them, under an escort of Army jeeps, to an ornate building that might once have been the palace of some lesser royal but had now been requisitioned by Thai intelligence. Two long tables draped in red cloth stood in the center of the grass courtyard. String lights hung from above. There was already a crowd.

Waiters in pressed khakis carried trays of cold Champagne.

"Sweetness," said Vanderhoof, taking two glasses.

Over Vanderhoof's shoulder, Neel saw Cone talking with a Thai officer. Cone beckoned to Neel.

"The boss is calling."

"You screwed something up," said Vanderhoof. "Don't try to blame me."

Neel crossed the grass.

Cone patted Neel woodenly on the shoulder. "I've had two cocktails with Colonel Watakeekul already. You've got to catch up."

"Call me Sunny," said the colonel, with a bow. He gestured to the nearer of the two banquet tables. "Will you join Director Cone and me for dinner? We were just talking about you. I'm very interested to find a fellow Asian in the U.S. intelligence services."

A waiter pulled out three chairs for them. Sunny took the one in the middle. Cone and Neel sat on either side.

The waiter returned with a bottle of gold-colored liquid. He filled their glasses.

"To friendship," said Sunny. He drained his glass in one gulp. Cone, with a quick shake of his head, did the same.

"Packs a punch," Cone said.

Neel needed two attempts to empty his own glass. The liquor was oily and sweet and burned all the way down.

"Mekhong rum," said Sunny. "The Thai soldier will drink this into the next life."

Three full glasses appeared before them. Sunny raised his arms. He turned his hands in a signal, apparently, that the others were to take their seats.

Vanderhoof sat with the remaining Americans and the British and Australian guests at the second table. He scowled when Neel saluted him. Thai officers took the open seats at Sunny's table. They did not speak to the two Americans but talked among themselves in their own language. Waiters brought out the courses in quick order: papaya salad, fried chicken, coconut soup, beef and peppers, platters of rice topped with river shrimp the size of a man's fist. All the dishes were fiery. From time to time Sunny proposed a toast and everyone drank. Neel stopped counting after the fifth round. The chatter grew louder and less distinct. Cone and Sunny talked intently, their heads close. The liquor had reddened their eyes. Occasionally, Sunny looked over at Neel, but didn't address him. Still, Neel felt as if he were the hidden object of his host's attention. Everywhere, the shadows deepened. Animals scurried through the branches of mysterious trees. The rum carried him like a tide.

At one point, Neel looked over at Vanderhoof, who smiled back before he raised his middle finger. At Vanderhoof's side, a big, crop-headed Australian was weeping. The Australian stuck his tongue out and plunged it repeatedly into the pitcher of water he held in front of his face. The others at the table laughed. The waiters came around with platters of sweet rice and sliced mangoes. Liquor flowed.

Neel checked his watch when the waiters cleared the dishes. He read the dial and then forgot the time at once. The voices of the Thai officers had softened now. They smoked with their legs crossed and their seats pushed back from the table. At the second table, the white men, swollen with food and drink, and away from the company of women, continued to roar under the string lights. Soldiers stood guard at the walls.

Cone excused himself to go to the bathroom. He stumbled when he stood.

"Mekhong rum is unforgiving for foreigners," said Sunny.

"I won't even try to get up," said Neel.

"I drank what you drank and I weigh much less than Americans, but I'm fine. You just have to believe in yourself. Watch." Sunny stood up. He raised one leg in the air. After a few seconds, he put that leg down and raised the other. He closed his eyes, touching his nose with each index finger in succession.

"You're cleared to drive," said Neel.

"Thai officers have chauffeurs," said Sunny, as he sat down. "We can talk privately now. You have other things to learn from me. Thais are survivors. Why did we escape colonization when the bigger nations— China, your India—did not?"

"That's a difficult question, sir, at this time of night." Neel drew a deep breath. "I suppose it was some combination of political leadership, national unity, and geography."

"Nonsense. You've heard of the Thai smile? We are hospitable, we know how to treat our guests, but on the inside we are hard. Foreigners underestimate us. In old Thailand, when a new prince took the throne, his retainers tied the prince's male relatives into sacks, beat them with sandalwood paddles, and threw them into the river. This way they killed the prince's rivals without spilling royal blood."

"In that case, I don't think I'd have wanted to be a minor prince."

"Of course you cannot be a prince." Sunny laughed. "The point of my story is that you must be ruthless if you wish to safeguard your position. Consider your situation."

"Me?" said Neel.

"You are younger than your director, so it's right that he is first and you are second. And yet . . . you are not *so* much younger than him. Are you thinking ahead? How will you take command?"

Neel couldn't conceal his shock. "You have it wrong," he managed to say, after a moment's pause. "I'm not looking to usurp anyone. It's out of my hands. The president nominates the director."

"Don't be silly, Neel." Sunny's eyes darted around. "I have contacts in U.S. intelligence. I understand the arrangement. The president relies on his advisors. Everything depends on which advisor has the president's trust and who that advisor favors. You must be ready to sacrifice. You must do what's required of you. This is a very complicated game."

"What are you saying?" asked Neel. "Did someone ask you to speak to me?"

Sunny erupted in more laughter. "Eliot!" he shouted.

Cone was walking back to the table. His step was firmer now. Before he sat down, he lifted his glass. "To Thailand! To his majesty and our gracious hosts!"

The Thais stood at the mention of their king. Neel, after a few seconds in which he was the only one still sitting, rose too.

When they were all in their chairs again, Sunny put his hand over Cone's on the table. "And what do you know of Thailand, Eliot?" he said. A strange smile crossed his lips.

At the other table, a man fell out of his chair with a crash. His companions laughed. Neel looked over but Cone and Sunny didn't turn their heads.

"Because I know America," said Sunny. "I went twice for training. First Maryland, then Fort Benning. Georgia was as hot as Thailand. They taught me counterinsurgency and interrogation techniques. I was just mentioning to your deputy that I made friendships in America I will keep my whole life."

A bull-necked waiter approached with a tray of cigars. Cone and Sunny each took one. Neel declined.

"And Neel, of course, has spent time in Thailand," said Sunny.

"I came onshore once or twice when I was in the Navy, yes. How did you know?"

"I'm an intelligence officer, my friend!" Sunny laughed again. He cut and lit his cigar with practiced gestures before he passed the implements to Cone.

"Eliot, we face a common enemy in the Muslims. It's important for us to understand each other."

Cone said the country was at war with terrorists, not the Muslim people.

Sunny winked at Neel. "Your director is a funny man. As I said to you just now, we can speak politely but inside we must be—is this the right word?—*pitiless.*"

He drew on his cigar. Cone, his face dimming, smoked as well.

A truck entered the courtyard through a side gate. Neel heard shouted commands and the clink of chains. One of the Thai officers at the table looked over at the truck and said something. The other officers laughed.

Sunny went on. "I will give an example from my own life. Now I am happily married, like you both. I have two sons. But things were different before."

"Everyone has a past," said Cone.

"I made a terrible mistake. When I was a young man I knew nothing." Sunny drew again on his cigar.

Neel's mouth was dry. He put his empty glass between his legs so the waiter wouldn't refill it.

Sunny told them about his life as a young officer. Military intelligence sent him away for his first posting, he said, as far away as it was possible to go, to Chiang Saen, in the distant north. It was gangster country. Sunny dealt with unlicensed casinos, money laundering, the poppy trade, poaching, illegal logging. He was twenty-two and lonely. Everyone he'd ever known was hundreds of miles away in Bangkok. Within a month he'd fallen in love with a waitress. She was a tribeswoman—a Red Karen and an animist.

"Neel, she had darker skin than you."

"Fascinating," said Neel.

Until Sunny arrived, the girl had lived in terrible poverty. She was grateful to him. Actually, she was more than grateful. At times she seemed to worship him, as if he were one of her Karen gods. She knew how to please him. He couldn't leave her behind.

"So I married her. What do you men think of that?"

"You're a romantic," Cone said.

"I was stupid."

At the far wall, by the truck, the chains were clinking again. A man shouted something unintelligible. Neel heard a series of sharp cracks. It was as if a cane were striking tile or bone. Were Thai soldiers abusing a prisoner in the midst of a banquet? Absurd as it seemed, Neel could think of no other explanation. He looked at Cone but the director had fixed his gaze on the tablecloth.

Meanwhile, Sunny continued with his story. After a year, he said, the army returned him to the main branch of military intelligence in Bangkok. Now his family met his new wife. They weren't pleased. Sunny didn't dwell on their unhappiness at the beginning. He thought they'd accept the situation in time. But as the months passed, their disapproval began to grate. He preferred not to bring his wife to family events, for when she did come the other women commented on her dark skin and country manners. His cousins called her Cocoa Bean. His mother said his wife was going to give her little monkeys for grand-children, little black monkeys. One of Sunny's uncles openly proposi-tioned her. The other men laughed. Everyone knew a Red Karen would sell anything for a few banknotes. Sunny was ashamed. He began to realize the enormity of what he'd done.

"I'd behaved like a greedy little boy," he said.

For his second wedding anniversary, he took his wife south to Phuket. Those were the happiest four days of their marriage.

"You've been to Phuket, isn't that right, Neel? That's where your ship stopped. You know it's a beautiful place, full of delights." His voice seemed to be arriving from a great distance.

Neel didn't respond. Eliot tilted his head back to look up into the night sky. He turned the cigar in his mouth.

On their holiday, said Sunny, he and his wife swam every day. They ate at a restaurant in the harbor, smiled at English tourists, walked on the sand. On the fifth day, the day before they were to leave, Sunny rented a small yacht. He was a skilled sailor, having learned at the mili-tary prep school. He steered the boat into the Andaman Sea, not so far from shore, but far enough that the land disappeared on the eastern horizon. He furled the sails but didn't drop anchor. The boat bobbed on the swell. It was a warm afternoon. Sunny told his wife she could jump in. She wore the white bikini she'd bought in Phuket Town on the first day of the trip. The bikini contrasted beautifully with her brown skin. Sunny said he'd jump in as well, once he changed into his own bathing suit. All of a sudden, the breeze dropped. The sea itself flattened. Now it looked like green glass. There were no other boats. Sunny's wife didn't question him. She jumped feet first into the green water. He watched her swim a few strokes. She smiled at him and waved. Sunny waved back. Then he went to the wheel, started the engine and, without look-ing over his shoulder, motored off to the south.

Eliot cleared his throat.

Sunny steered the boat with a smile on his face. After thirty minutes he turned around and motored back to the spot he'd left his wife, or where he thought he'd left her, to the best of his reckoning. The sea was empty though the surface rippled again with the afternoon breeze. Sunny waited a few minutes before he unfurled the sails and set a course for Phuket. He didn't need the engine. There was an astonishing silence in the cabin. Outside, the rigging creaked and the water slapped softly at the hull. Back at the marina, he reported that his wife had disappeared while he was in the bathroom. He'd searched the sea for hours to no avail. He hadn't known there was an emergency radio on board. That evening, he visited the harbor police chief, thanked him for his efforts, and slipped him an envelope with a week of his own salary inside. Then he took the express bus home to Bangkok.

Sunny extinguished his cigar on his plate.

"The Army gave me a month's leave. I went to the monastery, shaved my head, put on robes. My parents gave a donation. I did penance and made merit. Then I went back to work. A year later I married a proper Thai girl from an old Bangkok family. The generals came to the wedding. Everyone forgot about the past."

The vans that had brought the guests to the banquet were idling now at the courtyard entrance. The men at the other table stood, stretched, made signs they were ready to leave.

"My wife and I have two sons. The older boy is studying business. The younger one has been accepted into the military prep school. I have all this because I took my last chance to save my own life. I was pitiless."

Vanderhoof was walking gingerly toward them.

"One last thought," said Sunny. He raised his palm to Vanderhoof, who stopped at once, spun on his heel, and retreated to the gate.

"When the Red Karen girl watched me motor away from her, as she paddled alone in the sea, as the minutes passed and the strength left her arms and legs, I'm sure—I've always been sure—that she thought it was all a game. She believed I would come back. I know she was loyal to me until the end."

"My God," said Neel.

Eliot grunted as he rose to his feet. He thanked the colonel for his hospitality. There was a catch in his voice.

Neel stood too. He said nothing to Sunny before he followed Cone out.

Vanderhoof sat alone on the rear bench seat of one of the vans. Cone and Neel slid in beside him.

"Neel, this is for the country," said Cone. "You have to hold your nose."

"What happened?" said Vanderhoof.

"We're in bed with some very bad people," Neel said.

"Just remember that we're different," said Cone. "We don't kill innocents. We don't kill for selfish reasons."

Neel felt sick with exhaustion and disgust. But even in that state, even drunk, he'd recognized another quality in their host. The colonel, in his confidence and clarity, reminded Neel of the priest. Were those two men friends, wondered Neel, and had the priest whispered in the colonel's ear? He wondered whether he was succumbing to paranoia. There was no way to know the truth.

He rested his head on the window for the drive back to the hotel. The others slept.

TWENTY-FOUR

A HAMMERING REACHED him in the depths. Can't be, thought Neel. He rolled his head across the pillow.

"Sir! Wake up, sir!"

Neel opened his eyes. The lights were on. He wore his shirt, tie, pants, and shoes. The hammering continued.

"No," whispered Neel.

"Sir! Sir!"

He checked his watch. It was five A.M.

"We need to move now!"

He put his feet on the floor, raised himself, and walked to the bathroom. He dropped to his knees in front of the toilet to throw up.

The man at the door was shouting about a transport.

"Food poisoning," said Neel, as loudly as he could manage. "I need ten minutes."

"Negative," came the reply. "I have to come in now."

Neel wiped his lips with a handful of toilet paper. He flushed, stood, and left the bathroom. He unlocked the door to his room, walked eight steps, and dropped back onto the bed.

His visitor, an American security contractor, strode across the carpet. "Sir, you have ninety seconds."

"I can't move," said Neel.

"I see your briefcase. I will pack your bag. Go to the bathroom and brush your teeth. Keep those pants on. Take off the tie. We'll change your shirt. Sir, now!"

"Fuck this," said Neel. He let the contractor pull him to his feet.

In the bathroom he put his head under the tap, brushed his teeth, and tried to piss but couldn't. He threw his shirt and tie into the bathtub. He walked out with water streaming from his hair.

His bag stood by the door. The contractor held out one of his shirts with an impassive look on his face.

"It's go time, sir."

Neel buttoned the shirt, took a few steps down the hall, then stopped. The contractor, who was carrying Neel's bag, stopped too.

"We're late," said the contractor.

"My briefcase," said Neel. "Under the coffee table."

"Wait here, sir."

A minute passed, then another. Neel roused himself to knock on the door.

"Is there a problem?" he said. "Hello?"

The contractor shouted back something unintelligible. Moments later he emerged with Neel's briefcase. He handed it to Neel.

"Why so long?" asked Neel. "Wasn't the briefcase where I said it would be?"

The contractor picked up Neel's bag. "Hustle," he said.

Vanderhoof was sprawled across the van's rear bench seat. "Cone left," he said. "If we miss the flight you are going to call my wife."

Neel took the front passenger seat, giving himself the greatest possible distance from Vanderhoof. He nodded to the driver, a Thai man in a blue cotton suit, reclined the seat as far as it would go, and passed out.

Vanderhoof shook him awake at the airport. They walked morosely into the terminal. Another security contractor materialized at Vanderhoof's side to lead them around the line at the X-ray machines and straight to the departure gate. Cone stood at the windows overlooking the runway. He was talking on his phone. Neel went to the bathroom, found a clean stall, and vomited again. His throat burned with Mekhong and chili peppers. By the time he came out, the others had boarded.

He'd been assigned a window seat. Vanderhoof, still in his sunglasses, had the aisle. The middle seat was vacant.

"This is a blessing," said Vanderhoof, pointing to the space between them.

"Can't talk," said Neel. He locked his seatbelt.

"Dude," said Vanderhoof. He was rubbing his head.

They both slept for the seven-hour flight to the Emirates.

The security people gave them lanyards to wear in the Dubai airport. Neel and Vanderhoof followed their compatriots through a glassed-in vastness. There were throngs everywhere, moving with purpose, yet somehow the terminal didn't feel crowded. No one gave the Americans a second look.

"This place is so . . . capacious," said Vanderhoof, who'd pushed his sunglasses to the top of his head.

Neel was walking with his head lowered. He said nothing.

"Do we even matter?" Vanderhoof asked. "Americans, I mean? Look at all these people. I feel like a Sioux tribesman watching the wagons roll by."

"I don't know what you're talking about, Jon."

"I'm talking about Arabs, Asians. There are so goddamn many of you."

"First, you're a very stupid man. Second, I'm trying not to shit my pants before we get on the plane. Please don't say anything else."

"We're gonna be overrun."

On the plane, while Vanderhoof considered the menu card, Neel turned his face to the window. He slept over Europe and most of the Atlantic, waking only to drink water and use the bathroom.

They landed at Dulles at four in the afternoon. Vanderhoof jabbed Neel in the arm as the plane rolled to its gate.

"It's on." His face had color in it. "Afghanistan, baby, it's happening."

"You need to stop calling me 'baby,'" said Neel.

"The White House leaked the plans. Troop surge. Seventeen thousand soldiers. Obama wants to take the fight to the Talibs, man. We're in business."

"Seventeen thousand is nothing. You've seen the same intelligence I have. We'd need a hundred thousand troops just to secure the southern provinces. Drone operations against high-value targets are one thing, but how is this troop increase going to change the security situation?"

"Traitor."

"Maybe with more Americans in theater we'll collect more data for targeting. Otherwise, this doesn't move the needle."

"It's time to grind. Let's go straight to the Center. Show the boss he can count on us even after the longest flight in history."

"I'm going home to see my daughters."

"The vaunted Neel Chima doesn't have the stomach for the job?" Vanderhoof flexed his long, lean arms. "You need to be a Marine, bro."

"You're not a Marine, Jon."

Cone, who'd been sitting a few rows ahead, already stood with his bag in the aisle. He was on his phone. The passengers filed off the plane. Neel slipped past Cone in the terminal with a wave.

Rebecca had a string quartet playing through the kitchen speakers. She sat on a barstool at the counter, in a sleeveless blouse that revealed her muscular shoulders. The girls were eating omelets at the table. They ran to him. He gathered them into his arms. Then he hugged Rebecca.

"I've missed you," she said. Her face was dark with wine. "Take your time upstairs. I'll make dinner."

He showered, wrapped his towel around his hips, lay down for a moment on the bed, and fell asleep. When he opened his eyes the girls, dressed now in their pajamas, were whispering at the door. Neel asked them to come in. He sat up. His body seemed to belong to someone else.

Then Rebecca appeared. She switched on the lights. "Should I let you sleep?" she asked.

Neel kissed his daughters. Maya complained about his breath. They ran from the room.

"Day is night, night is day," Neel said, in a thick voice, as he dropped back onto the covers. "I want to have dinner with you."

He went to the bathroom, brushed his teeth, and put on an old sweatshirt and corduroys. He tiptoed out of the room and along the darkened hall.

Downstairs, in the kitchen, Rebecca tasted the sauce with a long-handled spoon. Neel walked up behind to kiss her neck.

At the counter he poured himself the last glass from the open bottle, and sipped wine while he watched Rebecca work. She added salt and cream to the sauce, licked her index finger, and added more salt. She hadn't known how to cook when they married. Now she was better, or at least more adventurous, than he was.

"The sauce is close," she said. "I'm making lovers' pasta."

She'd already put the salad—shaved beets with chopped parsley—on the kitchen table.

Neel considered the wine rack. He asked Rebecca if she wanted something Italian to go with the food. She said he could pull whichever bottle he liked, since she'd already drunk too much while she cooked. She switched the music from classical to jazz for his sake, choosing the album by Getz and Gilberto.

"How was the conference?" she asked. "How was Bangkok?"

She opened a package of penne and dropped it into boiling water. She added two pinches of salt, stirred, stood back.

"All the policy stuff had been worked out ahead of time. I sat through a day of presentations I didn't understand. It was too technical."

"Did you have good Thai food?"

"I couldn't even taste it, it was so hot. My ass will burn for weeks."

She shook her head. "Thank you for that."

She was silent for a few seconds as she stirred the pasta. Then she told him she'd finished her new article while he was gone.

"Remind me about that one."

"Workplace arbitration agreements and the death of collective action."

"A page-turner."

"Don't be mean. I left a copy in the living room if you want to take a look. It's a first step. This is not just egghead law-professor stuff. Workplace arbitration agreements limit the basic freedoms of millions of Americans."

"Maybe you should write a treatise."

"I'd like to, if we can make time. With the girls, your work, my classes. We'd have to talk about it."

"Not tonight, though."

Rain tapped at the windows while they ate.

"We should have done this in the dining room, with candles," she said.

She was wearing the teardrop earrings he'd given her as an anniversary present. She rarely put them in. They were heavy and hurt her ears. Out on the avenue, a siren faded into the rain.

"I like it here," he said. "Let's keep it close." He squeezed her leg under the table. Through the speakers, Astrud Gilberto sung about quietness, beauty, the night.

"My God, her voice," said Neel. "I thought this record had lost its hold on me." He lifted Rebecca's hand to give it a kiss. He drank the wine.

She asked him more questions while they cleaned up in the kitchen. She said it was crazy to travel that distance and do nothing but sit in meetings. Had he really not seen more of Bangkok?

"Not more than the inside of a conference room."

"You did nothing at night? No drinking in karaoke bars?"

"Just dinner with some Thai officers. There was plenty of drinking there. What are you getting at?"

Suddenly, she seemed embarrassed. "Nothing," she said. "I'm glad you're home."

He ran his fingers down her back when she came to bed but she whispered that it was late. She fell asleep quickly. He listened to her breathe for what seemed like a long time until he slept too.

He woke to a different sound—a rustling or scratching in the dark. Now the rain had stopped. He was alone in bed. For a moment he was still in Bangkok. Then, turning his head, he saw Rebecca's silhouette at the far wall. She was on her knees, doing something with his travel bag. She stood to switch on the bathroom light, partly closing the door to keep the bed in shadow. Neel could see more clearly now. Rebecca lifted his clothes from the bag, piling them on the rug. She took out his deodorant, headphones, and charger. She unzipped the side pocket, where he'd stuffed his dirty laundry. She pulled out a few balled-up pieces of clothing. She discarded the undershirt and socks but smoothed a pair of his boxer briefs on her lap. She lifted them to the light, holding them carefully between her fingers. Then she brought them close to her face, as if she were a forensic scientist. She sniffed, turned the underwear inside out, and sniffed again.

His heart broke for her. He could hardly remember the night or two he'd been unfaithful, early on in their marriage. Rebecca had never found him out. Those were a younger man's mistakes, meaningless now. So why was she afraid? Was she looking for confirmation of the distance she herself felt from him?

Neel might have shifted his weight on the mattress, or moved the covers, or perhaps Rebecca sensed a change in his breathing—whatever the cause, she looked over. She saw that he was watching her. She put down his underwear, stood, switched off the light, and came back to bed. Neel lifted the covers for her. He wanted to make a joke but couldn't think of what to say. Instead, he put his arm around her waist. They went back to sleep without speaking, in the warmth between the sheets.

TWENTY-FIVE

THE SUN WAS bright at the curtains. He sensed that the house was empty. Rolling onto his side to look at the clock, he saw that it was after ten.

Rebecca had left a note on the nightstand: "You were sleeping like an angel. I'm sorry about last night, what was I thinking?—XOXOX."

He found his phone on the floor. He called Vanderhoof and Monica at work, leaving voicemails to apologize for missing the early meeting. If Cone asked, he'd be there in an hour, he said.

The kitchen smelled of strawberry tops and burnt toast. Rebecca had stacked the dishes in the sink, refolded the *Times,* and left a lidded coffee cup for him on the counter. Neel glanced at the newspaper without opening it. The headlines announced Obama's troop surge in Afghanistan and a request from the automakers for billions more in bailout money. There were crayons loose on the kitchen table, crumbs and a bread knife on the butcher block, and a Toni Morrison novel facedown on one of the stools.

Though he was hopelessly late for work, he lingered. The room held him. It was the weave and wash, the everyday order and disorder his wife and little daughters had left behind. He swept the crumbs, wiped off the knife. He lifted Rebecca's book to the counter, marking her page with an old business card he found in a drawer. He poured coffee into the tumbler. He put an apple in his pocket and walked to the living room.

He'd left his briefcase on the floor. Now he turned the combination to unlock it. He removed a file folder and leafed through the documents it contained. The papers were classified. Under the rules, he should have turned them over to the security contractors for transport back to the United States. But no one had asked him for the folder in the rush to leave. Neel paused, returned to the first document in the file, and reviewed the papers with greater care. Checking the index, he cursed aloud. Two items—spec sheets on the NSA's capacity to collect emails, chat messages, and phone conversations in Southeast Asia—were missing from the file. They were technical documents, barely comprehensible to him, but of value to foreign adversaries. What the NSA could do in Southeast Asia it could do anywhere it had a fiber-optic tap. A Russian or Chinese spy—or a militant Islamist—could learn things from those documents the NSA would not want revealed.

Neel closed his eyes as he tried to remember what had happened. He'd woken up in Bangkok with his passport in his pocket. He had not taken the passport to the palace banquet the night before. That meant he must have unlocked his briefcase when he returned to his hotel room, taken out the passport so he'd have it in the morning, and closed the briefcase again. He could easily have picked up the file folder and dropped the spec sheets during that process. It had been dark, after all, and he'd been drunk. The contractor who'd retrieved the briefcase in the predawn scramble might have overlooked two pages lying on the floor or under the couch. It was possible that the security team had performed a final sweep of the room after Neel left but there was no way to be sure. What he couldn't deny was that he'd mishandled secret documents. He might have committed a felony. The classification laws required him to report the breach immediately.

Neel sat on the armchair. He closed his eyes. He needed to analyze the situation objectively. He'd carried out the government's business in

Thailand under difficult conditions. He'd endured fatigue and tedium. He'd drunk a preposterous amount of liquor not of his own volition but to appease an important ally. Surely the responsibility for the breach lay with the contractors whose job it was to safeguard the members of the delegation, and their documents and effects. Whatever his own transgressions, it was those contractors—in the strictest, moral sense—who bore the blame.

Given those truths, he wondered if it wasn't safer for now to remain silent. He saw no reason to draw attention to himself. He could return the folder to the secured locker for classified documents at the Freedom Center, where it would slot in as one among thousands. He doubted anyone would check the folder's index or look inside its covers. If someone did open it days or weeks hence, and if that person consulted the index, discerned that two pages were missing, and, in reviewing the sign-in ledger, noted that Neel had been the folder's most recent custodian; if, at that stage, Neel were asked to explain himself, time and distance could only work in his favor. Perhaps he would have come to a different decision if he were still at Main Justice. But in his new life, compromise and risk were in the air he breathed.

On the parkway, he played his voicemail over the speaker. He had two identical messages in which a woman asked him to extend his car's warranty. A chill ran through him when he recognized Sam Jones's voice on the third message. Jones apologized for calling again on an insecure channel. Static crackled through the recording. Neel lost some of Jones's words while he fumbled with the volume control but heard, in quick succession, the phrases "innate violence," and "a real dirtbag." Then Jones's voice became clear. "I'm giving you the target now," he said. "Copy this down."

Neel stopped the playback. He did not want to hear a name. He deleted the message while he drove. Then he lowered the windows to let the cold air in. Below, the gray river rolled.

He and his fellow ensigns used to run every morning in Pensacola, four abreast on an asphalt path, during flight officer training. They wore crew cuts and nylon shorts. He was only months out from his Columbia graduation. He remembered the purple dawn, steam rising from the sawgrass, and the bottomless skies of the Gulf of Mexico. He was quiet around his fellow officers—the onetime quarterback from the Dallas suburbs, the hollow-cheeked engineering graduate, the Pac-10 cross-country champion, the youngest son of a state senator from Wisconsin. Though he liked these handsome, earnest young men, he was wary. They had come from another America. The wounds he'd suffered in New Jersey weren't so far in the past. He wanted the Navy—the uniform above all else—as a shield against his own foreignness.

While they ran the instructors shouted out cadences—snippets of pornography, boasts, childish or brutal jokes—and the men shouted back. His own body was supple and strong. He kept his shoulders loose, his stride easy. He could do anything they asked. The air carried the distant stink of the marshes.

We're the boys from the fleet that you heard so much about,
Mothers lock their daughters in when we come on out.
Your wives call us crazy 'cause the crazy things we do,
We're the boys from the fleet now who the fuck are you?

Neel whispered the cadence as he drove high over the Potomac. The lines had never been his own, but he repeated them nonetheless. Now, as he drove, he raised his voice to a chant. Soon he was shouting. He held the wheel steady while his eyes watered in the wind.

Vanderhoof and Monica looked startled when he appeared at the top of the stairs. He'd already signed his classified file into the secured locker on the ground floor.

He apologized for being late. He slipped past the others to unlock the door to his office.

Vanderhoof caught his arm. "Happy to see you alive, brother," he said.

"I'm glad you're back," said Monica. "Eliot left for the White House. He wanted to take you with him."

They followed Neel into his office.

Neel asked them what he'd missed.

Jon launched into a summary of that morning's threat assessment meeting. He spoke of suspects and targets and the progress of the war in Afghanistan. Deaths and data, timelines and goals. Neel fought the urge to close his eyes. He wished he'd seen his daughters that morning. Once Maya told him that she loved the lunches her mama packed her for school. She said she wanted to eat butter-and-honey sandwiches and seedless green grapes every day for the rest of her life.

Finally Vanderhoof stopped talking. He and Monica looked carefully at Neel.

"I think this dude is still drunk," Vanderhoof said. "Or he suffered permanent brain damage in Bangkok."

"I'm having a hard time with jet lag," Neel said.

"Eliot will be back soon," said Monica. "He wants to meet in the conference room in twenty." She gave Neel a sympathetic smile before she walked out.

"My man, what happens in Thailand stays in Thailand," said Vanderhoof. He followed Monica into the hall.

To Neel's surprise, the priest came back with Cone from the White House. He said he wanted to address the Center's leadership in person. He took reports from all seventeen intelligence agencies but the executive team at the Freedom Center was the one closest, he said, to his heart.

He spoke from the head of the conference table. They faced a difficult situation in eastern Afghanistan, he said. Roadside bombs continued to take their toll on American forces—forces that would soon swell by many thousands. Every soldier the president sent to Afghanistan represented another potential victim of a terrorist attack. It was the sacred duty of each analyst, programmer, manager, and leader at the Freedom Center to do everything in his or her power to save those young American lives.

Vanderhoof raised his hand.

"Wait," said the priest. The way forward, he said, lay with better management and deeper analysis of the data. The NSA was sweeping up the signals, surveillance drones were in the skies over Kandahar and Kabul, and there was a camera on every paved road into the cities and towns. "Trust the data," said the priest. "See what the others have missed. Tell us what's there. Find the targets. Send them up the chain." His eyes were like blue stones. "I want you to change the course of this war. I look at every American body bag as a personal failure. We have technology on our side. Science. Use it!"

"We will," said Cone. He was sitting up stiffly in his chair.

"Wonderful," said the priest. "And—this goes for all of you—don't believe any old rumor that reaches your ears. The White House remains satisfied with the outcome of the Waziristan operation. Eliot, let's keep a lid on things in this shop."

Neel had not heard any rumors. He looked across the table. Sweat marks showed on Cone's shirt collar.

Cone cleared his throat. "To your point, we are not going to stream targeting operations on the big screen downstairs in the future. We'll limit discretionary access to live video feeds to the people in this room. Analysts will be invited to watch on an as-needed basis."

"A wise move," said the priest.

"What happened?" asked Neel. He did not like the way Cone was staring at the table.

It was Monica who replied. "An independent journalist is asking questions about the Waziristan strike. Why were there so many bodies? Who were they? How did we make the decision to attack? Et cetera. This journalist has either seen video of the strike or has listened to an insider describe the images in detail. The journalist has apparently made contact with a village headman who claims the first missile strike killed an entire family, including at least one woman and three children, and the second killed four men and two boys who arrived to help. The tribals are also angry because we hit some livestock."

Neel glared across the table at Monica. "And where are my reports on this? You didn't think to mention anything to me twenty minutes ago in the hallway?" He turned to Vanderhoof, in the seat beside him. "Did you know?"

Vanderhoof nodded.

"I'm sorry," Monica said. "I didn't think we were going to discuss the leak today."

Cone broke in. "No one's keeping secrets from you, Neel. You would have known, if you'd made it in on time. Your hurt feelings aren't the issue."

"Please," said the priest. "The man we are talking about is a quote-unquote 'independent journalist.' He's a troublemaker, but he's not important. He hasn't verified anything. The story is a long way from publication. If and when the piece does appear, it'll be on a left-wing website with a tiny readership. There's no need to obsess over problems that have yet to materialize. At least we know the rumor is out there. All agencies, even small, top-secret intelligence outfits, have to deal with leaks. They come with the territory. You just tighten up and move on."

Neel struggled to control his voice. At first he'd been angry but now another, thicker feeling—not fear alone but fear mixed with shame—was rising in him. He resisted a sudden urge to bow his head. "What do you think? Sir?" He looked at the priest. "Did we hit the wrong people?"

The priest raised his eyebrows. "Without agents on the ground we're in the dark. The signals are always jumbled. You're in as good a position as anyone to assess the strike, Neel. You did your homework, you gave it your best shot. Now move on. The terrorists will always try to spin the narrative in their own favor." He checked his watch. "Jon, I want to commend you on your management of the Freedom Center's internal operations. The process of allocating incoming data to your analysts, distributing raw reports within the Center, and working with Neel to transmit a usable intelligence product to your clients, including me, has been superb. Keep it up."

Vanderhoof blushed like a schoolboy.

"I couldn't have hit the ground running without you," Cone said. He flashed Vanderhoof a thumbs-up.

The priest went on. "Chin up, Neel. The president may be hesitating right now but he won't be gun-shy forever. Keep the pipeline filled. Be more careful when it comes to pattern-of-life targeting, improve your documentation, but don't stop."

A brief silence fell. Until that morning, Neel hadn't brooded over the Waziristan strike. When he'd thought of it at all, which wasn't often, he felt only a vague unease. It was as if he'd woken up after an office party at which he offended a colleague with some unthinking comment, the phrasing of which he couldn't recall in the sober light of day. Now this seemed an absurdly flippant response. He considered a series of basic questions—questions he would have done well to ask in the immediate aftermath of the attack. How many people had died? Were they adults or children? Did the strike eliminate the anonymous man— the presumed militant commander—Neel had targeted? He couldn't answer. But even as he tried, even as his throat narrowed and his temples throbbed, he also knew that the urgency would fade. Everyone in the intelligence complex had to live with the unknown. Everyone had to accept the possibility of a mistake.

The others stood and moved to the door. Neel stood too.

"Before we close, I have something for you all," said the priest. He took a small purple bag from inside his suit jacket, loosened the cord, and overturned it on the conference table. Four coins fell out. "Take them."

They picked up the coins. Neel weighed his in his palm. It was the size of a silver dollar but had a plastic lightness. The image of a Predator drone, with lightning bolts over the nose and tail, appeared on one side. A snarling dragon held the earth in its talons on the other, above the inscription UBIQUE VIDEMUS.

"We see everywhere," said the priest, who was looking at Neel. "To mark this team's first strike under Eliot's leadership."

"It's an honor," said Cone.

Neel put his coin into his shirt pocket.

"A word, Neel?" said the priest. "We'll go to your office."

"How was Bangkok?" he asked, once Neel had closed the door.

"A little tiring."

"And demoralizing? It's okay to say that."

Neel shrugged before he sat down.

The priest was still standing. His eyes never left Neel's face. "Travel, pointless meetings, disgusting liquor. Dinner with a man you didn't like. Actually, I know Colonel Watakeekul quite well. He's an acquired taste."

Neel's heart thudded.

"I understand you had some trouble the next morning. Getting ready on time, gathering your things, all those details."

Neel's mouth twitched. It was as if the priest had uncovered a single card from a deck he was holding behind his back. He could easily have engineered a security lapse in Bangkok. He could have arranged for the contractors not to retrieve Neel's classified documents after the meetings, or asked the man who came to Neel's room in the early morning to tamper with the file. Neel resisted the urge to confess. He waved at the chairs on the other side of the desk.

The priest stayed on his feet. "I once asked myself the same questions you must be asking. When I first went overseas as a CIA officer I wondered why we had to deal with criminals. With experience you see those relationships in context. We made friends with the Northern Alliance before landing in Afghanistan. We knew the leadership had its share of pederasts and thieves. But sometimes you join hands with monsters to defeat a greater monster. We're allocating billions of dollars here. If you stare at your shoes, fretting over the mud, you'll step on a mine."

"One has to be a realist," said Neel.

"Exactly."

"So why is the president doubling down in Afghanistan?"

"When you find yourself in a fight, it's better to win than to lose. If you lose you embolden the enemy. Win with as little pain as possible, as leanly as possible—but win."

The priest rapped his knuckles on Neel's desk. "It's okay to make a mistake. It's okay to see a pattern that isn't there. Maybe after we carry out a strike there's no change in the volume of militant activity. Maybe the roadside bombings continue. Okay, so you got the wrong guy. Take it on the chin. Learn from failure. Get smarter, go back to work, deliver more targets."

"Who really died in Waziristan?"

The priest shrugged. "I don't know. I'm sure there was a bad actor or two in the building. The Pakistanis haven't complained. Neel, I'll speak bluntly. Be a slave, if you like, to guilt, fear, doubt. Exhaust yourself in the tumult of your conscience. But I decided long ago that my mind wasn't a battleground. I wasn't going to let emotion distract me from duty. With time you realize that so much of what other people consider the bedrock of their existence—money, prestige, sex, love, family—is mere decoration. It's not that you're immune to the comforts, but you understand that they are peripheral. People in this line obsess about *power*—its accumulation, its exercise—but even that word is only a metaphor. What I'm really talking about is *fate*. Who shapes the course of a man's life or a nation's life? Who decides when others should die? Who decides that a certain country should no longer exist? You, Neel, are on the cusp of entering a very small circle. You can become an agent of history. Don't throw away the opportunity."

Neel looked at the priest in wonder. Neel's own family could never be peripheral; Serena and Maya were not decorations to his life. Yet there the priest stood, in the center of the room, watching Neel with a grave expression. He had not made a joke. He was a man, Neel thought, who was incapable of joking. As they looked at each other, the priest smiled. It seemed to Neel a proprietary smile—the smile of a master who wished to recognize his apprentice. Even as Neel shuddered, he wondered whether a tiny part of him, the cruelest and most hidden part, was quickening to the priest's offer of freedom.

Finally, Neel broke the silence. "You're not talking about the drone campaign. You're not talking about targets in Pakistan."

"I'm talking about the targets and everything else. Every opportunity that has come your way. Do your duty and you'll be safe. Work without fear. Know that we take care of our own."

"And if I don't want to do what I've been asked to do?"

"Maybe your protection disappears. Maybe, if you transgress, you'll find yourself exposed."

"That sounds like a threat."

"I was merely answering a hypothetical. Why, have you transgressed?"

Neel shook his head.

"Then you have nothing to worry about." The priest extended his hand. "Don't get up. I'll see myself out."

TWENTY-SIX

HIS WINDOW WAS closing. The NatSec Principals Committee had declined to advance the Freedom Center's targets. Neel decided to give everything in one final drive for relevance.

He ordered a cot for his office. He slept on it four nights in a two-week span, brushing his teeth beside Cone in the mezzanine bathroom. He spoke to his daughters on the phone in the afternoons but didn't see them for days on end. His appetite for office catering—Caesar salads, BLT sandwiches, teriyaki chicken skewers—soon waned. He was too tired for real exercise. Though he'd still drop to the floor for a few reps during a mid-morning break, his old regime of eighty push-ups, two hundred crunches, and a hundred squats, a program that had ordered his days and kept up his strength through years of desk work, no longer seemed possible.

By the end of the first week of March, Neel had selected five new targets in the Pakistani tribal regions. He wrote three briefs himself and delegated the other two to senior analysts on the floor. Each brief contained fifty pages summarizing the human and signals intelligence gathered by the relevant agencies. Cone forwarded all five briefs to the

NatSec Principals Committee. He requested approval for capture-or-kill operations, arguing that the named targets posed an imminent threat to Coalition forces in Afghanistan. The Principals Committee approved Neel's three targets but returned the other two with a request for additional evidence and analysis.

Cone went alone to the White House on March 10, 2009. The priest had instituted a new policy limiting each agency to one representative at the weekly Terror Tuesday meeting.

Later that day, Cone returned with bad news. The president would continue to prioritize the targets nominated by the CIA. Though Neel's targets were sound, they would have to wait. He should refresh his current briefing with new intelligence as it came in and continue to scour the matrix for new leads, but the White House would not order any immediate strikes from the Freedom Center's recommendations. The priest, said Cone, nonetheless commended the Freedom Center for organizing the databases on which every agency relied.

"So all our hard work hasn't been wasted," Cone said. "If that's any consolation."

"I don't think it is," said Neel. He checked his watch. It was four in the afternoon. "Vanderhoof has been solid. You should buy him a beer."

"You've also done a good job on targeting. But redundancy is built into this business. You want to give the decision-makers multiple options. It's all for the greater good."

Neel felt like a man whose wallet was empty, whose cards had been declined. He told Cone he wasn't feeling well. He would work another hour and then go home.

TWENTY-SEVEN

A LONG WINTER was ending in Afghanistan. As the high passes of the Hindu Kush cleared of snow, violence grew. Roadside bombings mounted in Paktika Province. In the restive south, in Kandahar and Helmand, American soldiers came under attack as soon as they left the perimeter wire of their bases and outposts. The data soon confirmed the whispers Neel heard on the Operations floor: there had never been a more dangerous time to be a Coalition soldier, or an Afghan civilian, in this long war.

Cone surprised Neel one afternoon on the smokers' patio. Neel was sitting on the lone steel bench, reading area reports from the FBI's counterterrorism branch. The small patch of sky he could see from there had turned a late, pale blue.

"I've found your secret garden," said Cone, as he joined Neel on the bench. He had the eyes of a gambler who'd stayed too late at the tables. "Only the U.S. government would put a smokers' patio in a nonsmoking building." He asked what Neel was reading.

Neel showed him his stack of reports. "Domestic investigations."

"Can't forget about the homeland. But you know where my head's at."

"My head's in Afghanistan too. I'm reading everything they send up from the floor. Some of it looks juicy, but no one at the top agrees."

Cone sighed as he rubbed his head. His hairline had visibly receded in his three months at the Freedom Center. Now he was bald on top, with just a horseshoe of gray-and-white stubble that wrapped from his temples to the back of his skull. The two men shared a brief silence.

Neel spoke first. "I thought the agency that organized the surveillance data was supposed to have the inside track on picking targets. Wasn't that the promise?"

"Maybe we were all dreaming. CIA saw what we had cooking at the Freedom Center. With Iraq winding down, leadership at Langley understood that target selection in Afghanistan was something that could bring our shop closer to the president. But CIA always needs to be closest to the president. So they assign ten, twenty people to do what you're doing. Ten people to do what I'm doing. Three analysts for every analyst we have on the floor. And proprietary human intelligence from Af-Pak that they don't share with other agencies. They always add something to their target packages we can't match."

"Even if the HUMINT is worthless," said Neel.

"It probably is. Score-settling between Afghan warlords, tribal feuds, Pakistani officers marking names on a list. All dog shit."

"But it counts at the White House."

"Sure. If you're giving the order to blow up half a tribal village, wouldn't you want to cite a personal attestation from ISI Colonel Blah Blah Khan in Rawalpindi that the place is crawling with Taliban commanders?"

They lapsed into silence again.

"You're not in the worst situation," Cone said. "You're a smart guy. You can see where this war is headed. Best case for the middle-to-long term, we secure the cities while the Afghan countryside remains a free-fire zone."

"Wait, we can say that?" asked Neel.

"This is a private conversation between the two of us. At West Point I learned that the only way to achieve security in the face of a popular insurgency is domination and slaughter. White settlers versus the Plains

Indians, the U.S. Army against native guerrillas in the Philippine-American War, the Brits against the Chinese in Malaya and the Mau Maus in Kenya. Since we can't go to those extremes in the twenty-first century, it follows that we're not going to win total victory over the Taliban. So tell me, are you going to regret ten years from now that the president didn't act on more of your proposed targets? Are you going to be upset that you didn't kill more people to achieve what will end up being—again, in the best-case scenario—a stalemate?"

Neel laughed. When he replied he couldn't keep the bitterness out of his voice. "I haven't found a way out of that cognitive dissonance. So why am I staying up until three A.M. to cull raw intelligence for my next targeting brief?"

Cone turned his head to Neel. He'd missed a few silver flecks of stubble in his morning shave.

"Remember that I started out as a tank commander. You couldn't have found a young officer more eager to fight a decisive battle against the Soviets on the Central European plains. I spent four years on a base in Germany before the Evil Empire collapsed on its own. But I don't think I wasted my time. The billions we spent on bases and military equipment weren't a waste. The Russians had to build tanks and bases and draft soldiers and train officers to keep up with us. We bled them out."

"I don't think the Taliban are spending in the same way. Roadside bombs are cheaper than fighter jets."

"Granted. But the enemy is still bleeding. Every day we kill their commanders from the air. At some point, months or years from now, the pipeline will run dry. Maybe we'll see a drop in violence as soon as this summer, after the election. If we can't defeat the Taliban at least we have the resources to wait until they sue for peace. I'm playing a long game here."

"I was hoping for better."

"It would be nice to get bin Laden at some point, too." Cone stood up, cracked his knuckles, and released a strange giggle. "But I'm reminding you that the system has its own logic. More importantly, it will offer its own rewards. Lockheed Martin took forty billion in defense contracts last year. Boeing took twenty-two billion. Northrup Grumman, General Dynamics, Raytheon. Billions on billions. The two of us will be dealt into that game when we leave this place. I know I deserve it. For all the years I've sacrificed to work, for not seeing my wife, for never getting to coach Little League or any of that shit."

Neel looked up again at the patch of sky. "It always comes down to money." He felt vaguely ashamed. It was better, he thought, when your bosses held to the fiction that government service was its own reward.

"We just have to stay out of trouble. Be good soldiers, keep our heads down, maintain the important relationships we've made. Our time will come." Cone's shoes crunched on the white gravel. "Come on. Let's get back to our desks."

Neel followed him inside.

TWENTY-EIGHT

A SHIVER RAN through the grass. Neel sipped his Champagne. Then he passed the plastic flute to Rebecca and watched her drink. She wore a peach-colored sundress that was too brief, perhaps, for late spring. To the west, the hills glowed with orange light. This was central Virginia: horse country, wedding country. They'd seen Confederate flags on two front porches after they left the interstate at Fredericksburg.

Neel took the flute again. He moved his hand up Rebecca's back. A bass line came thumping across the meadow. "I wish I could be like them." He waved his hand in the direction of the music. "I wish I liked parties, dancing, all that stuff."

"Don't worry, I like sad people," said Rebecca. "Tortured souls, artists."

"Not that I'm an artist."

"I like sad lawyers too." She ran her fingers over his cheek.

They looked at the sunset.

"I'm sorry," said Neel. "I haven't been there for the girls."

Rebecca squeezed his hand.

"Now you look sad," he said.

"The girls love you, Neel, even if you're never home. You're the handsome stranger who plays with their alphabet blocks once a month."

"I need help. I'm beginning to wonder if this job is good for me."

"Leave," Rebecca said. "Be brave. You were a fighter pilot."

"The Prowler isn't a fighter. And I wasn't the pilot."

"I'm saying you'll find a way."

"If I leave after five months I won't get the next gig, the gig I'm due, whatever that is. But if I stick it out for two, three years, put in a solid effort, at least I'll get paid on the other end."

"It's not worth it."

"I'm worried that I'll make a terrible mistake."

"Quit before you make that mistake, Neel. One day George will die and we'll inherit his ill-gotten fortune. We'll be fine."

Neel shook his head.

Rebecca let go of his hand. She said, "I wish I'd told you, when we were young, that if you don't do the work you love, your job is just a dream. It never becomes real."

"We're dropping bombs on Afghanistan, Rebecca."

She sighed. "I suppose death is real."

"Let's join the celebrations," he said.

In the reception tent they steered through strangers. The music made it difficult to talk. It was the wedding of Neel's second or third cousin; Neel might have met the groom once in his life. He'd come as a favor to his father, who'd recently announced that he'd never again leave New Jersey. ("I'm sorry, Neel," his father had said, when they spoke on the phone. "You'll have a miserable time. It can't be helped. Go in, leave some money for the married couple, and get out.") The ceremony, which ended an hour earlier, had been brief. The guests sat in another tent, shoeless and cross-legged, with the men and women separated by the long carpet that formed an aisle. Dampness seeped up through the ground sheets. Those guests who'd come without a turban or scarf had been asked to cover their heads with the small white cloths the attendants handed out at the entrance. For a few minutes, a reader on a raised platform sang prayers out of the holy book. Neel felt as bored as he always felt during Sikh rites, but looking around he saw quietude, and even bliss, in the faces of some of the older guests. Then Neel's cousin and his bride stood up in front of the congregation, the cousin in a blue turban and cream-colored kurta, the bride in a red-and-gold sari. No one clapped or cheered. The guests rose to their feet, bowed in the direction of the newlyweds and the holy book, and filed out of the tent. At the flaps, the attendants dispensed unwrapped sweets from a steel bowl with their bare hands. Afterward, the guests ate a bland vegetarian lunch at communal tables in the main tent. Then, as soon as the reader and attendants left, taking the holy book with them, the caterers opened the bar.

Neel ordered whiskies, neat.

"When in Rome," he said, in Rebecca's ear.

A middle-aged woman stumbled into him as he lifted the drinks. Liquor splashed over his hands. The woman wore a sari in a lurid shade of green. Her blouse was cropped high over her naked belly.

A tall man—the woman's husband, presumably—pushed her aside. He gripped Neel by the wrist. "Sorry, very sorry," he said, with a Punjabi accent. He'd smeared kohl around his eyes. He had a mustache and a gangster's scowl.

"Don't worry about it, bhai-sahib. We're in a crowd."

The man clapped his hands. "Good boy," he said, though he couldn't have been more than a decade older than Neel. He nodded to Rebecca. "Hello missus."

"You'll have to excuse us," said Neel.

Rebecca took his hand. They weaved through the crowd. Neel realized, with some concern, that she was leading him to the dance floor. On the way, a man with wet lips and sparse white hair grabbed Neel's arm. He looked vaguely familiar.

"Hello soldier, sat sri akal," the man shouted. He kissed Neel on the cheek.

"Sat sri akal-ji," said Neel, repeating the traditional Punjabi greeting. He'd been saying it his entire childhood before he finally asked his father what it meant. "God is truth," said his father, "or truth is God. There are different interpretations."

The white-haired man smacked Neel on his buttocks as he passed. "We're in hell," said Neel.

"What did you say?" asked Rebecca.

Neel put his lips to her ear. "Welcome to Punjab."

They drank their whiskies near the DJ's table. The music was playing at a shocking volume. Young people covered the floor but the middle-aged were dancing too, at the sides and on the grass between the tables—men alone or with other men, women with women. Most of the men wore shirts and ties but the women, even the handful of young white women among the guests, had chosen saris and salwar kameezes in extravagant colors. Many of the women wore earrings that dangled to their shoulders, gold necklaces, and bracelets stacked to their forearms. Rebecca was the only one Neel saw in a dress. She was undaunted.

"Finish your drink," she said. "We're going in."

Neel shook his head, but he followed her onto the floor. Moments later he was holding his arms above his head and rapidly twisting his wrists in the only bhangra move he knew.

"You're full of surprises!" Rebecca shouted.

A group of children, jumping in pagan joy, came between them. Rebecca took a little girl by the hands. Together they did a version of the twist.

The DJ drawled into his microphone. "Bride and groom are accepting felicitations. While we wait for them, let's conga! Grab your mummy, grab your aunty, grab your dadiji. I want everybody now!"

Neel lost Rebecca as the crowd rushed onto the floor. Someone shoved him from behind. He fell against a young man.

"Shake it, bro!" shouted the young man, over his shoulder. "Don't be shy."

Neel grabbed the young man by his love handles. The line began to move. It must have been a hundred guests long. They made one lap around the inner ring of tables before the line fragmented. Men fell to their knees. Some lay laughing on their backs. The music had gotten even louder. Now a tabla beat played on a loop. The crowd cleared. In the center of the dance floor, a middle-aged man in a sweat-stained purple shirt and matching turban danced alone. He crouched, bobbed his head, and began to chop his arms with an expression of profound concentration. A circle of men, index fingers held high, formed around him.

"Do it, yaar!" one of them screamed.

"Yes, uncle!" said the DJ into his microphone. "The hosts provide the venue but you bring the party!"

The dancer repeated his chopping move a few more times before he sprinted past his admirers to launch a karate kick. He slipped on landing but didn't fall. Then he threw back his head and howled. His face was wet, his eyes open wide. His friends seized him. One poured a shot of liquor down his throat. They kissed his face while he wept.

"Give it up for uncle-ji!" shouted the DJ. "Who's next?"

The tabla loop gave way to a synthesizer. A woman with a girl's voice sang high above the music.

Rebecca was at Neel's side again. She asked what the lyrics meant.

"She's singing about love. Her mother, her husband's motorcycle, gold. 'Nashaa' means booze. Honestly I don't know what the song's about. The same as all the songs—money and marriage."

Rebecca's face and shoulders were flushed. "Why haven't you taken me to India? Indians are awesome."

"We're not Indian, my dear, we're Punjabi."

She put her arms around his waist. He smelled whiskey, cotton, sweat. Other guests stared. Punjabi husbands and wives did not touch in public.

"Let's get something to eat," he said.

The receiving line blocked the main entrance to the tent.

"I'll get this part over with," said Neel.

Rebecca needed air. She told him she'd wait outside.

It was some time before he reached the newlyweds. The groom clasped Neel's right hand between both of his own. He was young, perhaps in his mid-twenties, with a crazed expression. It was clear to Neel that the young man had no idea who he was.

"My father sends his regrets," said Neel. He slipped the envelope he'd been carrying in his jacket into the already stuffed breast pocket of the young man's kurta.

The groom nodded frantically.

"You'll be okay," said Neel, patting him on the arm.

The bride stood a step behind, with her scarf draped over her head. She looked terrified.

"Congratulations," Neel said. "It was a lovely wedding."

She pulled her scarf lower over her face.

"You two have fun!" said Neel, as he walked out.

He found Rebecca near the toilet trailers. One of the guests, a man in his thirties, sat on the grass nearby. He was vomiting into his own lap. An older woman stood over him. She wiped her tears with her scarf.

"He won't be the only casualty tonight," said Neel.

"I don't understand why that woman is crying," Rebecca said. "Shouldn't we try to help?"

Neel led her away. "It's the shame, the family honor—men are supposed to hold their liquor. They'll be fine. One of their relatives will get them home."

"It's getting cold." Rebecca crossed her arms in front of her chest.

They reached the smaller tent, where the priest had conducted the wedding ceremony that afternoon. Now caterers had rolled up the ground sheets and set out buffet stations, folding tables, and plastic chairs. Lamps buzzed in the corners. It was almost eight but the only people eating were a few white-bearded men hunched in their shawls. Neel led Rebecca to the food. The caterers stared with open hostility as he piled lamb curry on buttered rice. Rebecca took lentils and salad. They sat at an empty table. Rebecca said she felt tired all of a sudden. She wasn't used to being out at night. Neel asked her how she liked the food. After she said it wasn't as good as the takeout they ordered in D.C., they lapsed into silence.

They'd almost finished when someone thumped Neel between his shoulder blades.

"How are you, son? I've been looking for you. You remember your

Baljeet uncle?" It was the older, wet-lipped man who'd greeted Neel in the other tent.

He sat in the open chair beside Neel. He didn't acknowledge Rebecca or even look at her.

One of the caterers jogged over from his position at the buffet station. "Uncle-ji, can I get you a whiskey?" he asked.

"Does a poor man love God?"

The caterer shook his head.

"Yes, idiot." Baljeet snapped his fingers twice.

The caterer sprinted away.

"The only thing these donkeys understand is a slap. But it's best not to hit people in America."

Neel concentrated on the last forkfuls of lamb curry on his plate.

"There are nice girls here. Your papa should have come."

"I'm sure he would have liked to see his old friends," said Neel. With a glance at Rebecca, he pushed his chair back from the table.

Baljeet reached for Neel's arm. "Your papa never missed a wedding in the old days. When they saw us, everyone knew the drinking would begin."

Neel moved his arm but the old man only tightened his grip.

"He's not a drinker anymore," said Neel.

"It's been years, son. Seeing you now is like seeing your papa again. I knew all his secrets in the bachelor times."

"We have a long drive," said Rebecca.

Baljeet dropped his hand to Neel's thigh. "Back in Punjab, if you had a problem, you had to solve it yourself. Someone owes you money, you beat the scoundrel up. You don't involve the constables—they want bribes." Baljeet rubbed the thumb and forefinger of his free hand together. "The boys take lathis, you know, big sticks, and off we go for fisticuffs. Your papa Bhagwant Chima was a good boxer. He was even stronger than you. But you are solid."

The caterer returned with a plastic cup filled high with whiskey. Neel could smell the drink from his chair.

"Good," said Baljeet. He took a long sip. "When Bhagwant went off to Chandigarh for college I used to mark the holiday dates on my calendar. Before he came back to the village I did some looking around, you know, in harvest season. Different crews came every year from Bihar, different pickers. I will go to the fields at lunchtime, see the new girls, see which one likes her ghee. I smile at her, make sure she gets a little more ghee, extra roti, another spoonful of curds. When Bhagwant comes home for his holiday he asks me how is the wildlife this year. And I tell him, just wait and see. After dinner we go to the fields. We stand in the trees. When the Bihari girl comes to do her business we are there to say hello. We are very nice, we bring buffalo milk and sweets. The Biharis are kali kali, dark girls, you know? They want to make a bit of pocket money too. We had happy days as boys."

Rebecca pushed back her chair and stood up. "That's a terrible story. Are you talking about rape?"

Baljeet had a shocked expression. "Of course not, missus. The Bihari girls like to meet young sardars. You know what a sardar is, missus? A real Sikh."

"Excuse us," said Neel, as he stood too.

"You're not leaving? What would Papa say?"

"I don't want to hear any more," said Neel, in Punjabi.

"Don't be rude, yaar," said Baljeet, but Neel and Rebecca were already walking away.

They found their car in the dirt lot near the meadow.

"It's not always like this," said Neel. "Scotch makes these old guys crazy."

"What's sad is that I've always liked your father," said Rebecca. "Was that man telling the truth?"

They got in, fastened their seatbelts. Neel paused before he turned the ignition key.

"Maybe he was, in his own way. They lived in a different world. It's impossible to understand them now."

They had thirty miles on a country highway before they returned to the interstate. Neel drove carefully. The road twisted and dipped in his headlights.

"The Indians you've met in America don't come from the same place my family came from," said Neel, at one point. "High-caste Hindus from Mumbai or Hyderabad or Bangalore—your doctors and software engineers—they don't know the Punjabi villages any more than you do."

Rebecca said nothing.

Even today, said Neel, a young woman from Bihar might toil all day on a Punjabi farm for two dollars. When his father was young, it was worse. In the eyes of a harvest worker, the son of a small Punjabi land-owner would have seemed unimaginably wealthy.

"My parents didn't grow up with the idea of girlfriends and boy-friends," said Neel, as he glanced across at Rebecca. "A Punjabi girl could get killed for taking a lover. So young men like my father made other arrangements."

"That's one way to put it," Rebecca said.

"He's a different person now." A few minutes later Neel said he'd never liked weddings. He was glad they'd gotten married at the court-house.

Rebecca murmured that she didn't like weddings either. She'd closed her eyes.

"Sleep," said Neel.

They had an hour to go. He stayed in the passing lane, away from the semis and the slower traffic. The lamb curry was giving him heart-burn. On the other side of the windows, the landscape vanished into the night.

TWENTY-NINE

AGENT MILLER HAD come, she said, for a friendly chat. She was a small woman, in her thirties, with cropped red hair and a pinched face. In her limp blue pantsuit she looked to Neel like a border guard from some dismal Eastern European republic.

While she understood that conversations like these could be awkward, she said, her interviews of Cone and Vanderhoof earlier that morning had been perfectly collegial. But Neel had seen Vanderhoof walk out of the third-floor conference room with a haunted expression. "Be careful in there," he'd whispered in the hallway. "Don't let her pin anything on you."

Neel rested his palms on the table. He took slow, deep breaths through his nose. He held in his mind the defense lawyer's first commandment to a client: the best response to any question is, "I don't remember."

Agent Miller asked Neel whether a security contractor had approached him, at the close of the Bangkok meetings, to collect the classified documents he held.

"Not that I recall," said Neel.

"Did you realize at the time that you were in breach of security protocols?" Agent Miller looked down at her writing pad as she spoke. A digital recorder sat on the table.

"I don't remember what I was thinking at the time."

"Do you realize now, two months later, that you were in breach?"

"You defer to your handlers when you're on government business. They're the experts. You do what they say."

"There's no question we saw a breakdown on the part of the security team. But right now I'm asking about you. When you left your hotel room on your last morning in Bangkok, did you know whether classified documents were missing from the file that was still improperly in your possession?"

"No."

"Did you think to turn the file over to the officer who assisted you that morning?"

"No. I was trying to make a flight."

"Do you think it strange, in hindsight, that your two colleagues from the Freedom Center managed to return all classified materials to the security team, while you did not?"

"I trusted the handlers. I was following instructions."

"Excuse me," said Agent Miller. She wrote a few words on her notepad. Then she said, "What was your physical condition that morning?"

"I don't remember."

Agent Miller raised her eyebrows.

"I was tired," said Neel.

"Were you intoxicated? Were you vomiting?"

"The meal we ate the night before didn't agree with me." Impatience, even anger, had entered his voice. He drummed his fingers on the table, frowned, clenched his jaw. But all these signs were part of a performance—a performance he'd witnessed from the other side, as a prosecutor conducting interviews of his own. In truth, he was afraid.

Agent Miller cleared her throat. She pressed a button on the digital recorder. "I wish you would tell the truth. We're talking about the mishandling of classified documents in a foreign country. You, of all people, know how important this is. It wasn't so long ago that you were investigating government employees for breaches of secrecy."

"I'm not under investigation."

"Not yet," said Agent Miller. She picked up the digital recorder, pressed a button again, and set it back on the table. "On the record. We're trying to establish what happened on your trip. But I'll warn you that the reckless consumption of alcohol is an aggravating factor. Don't take my questions lightly. Thailand is a frontline state. The government is dealing with an Islamic insurgency in the south. Though it's an ally, it's also leaky and corrupt. Individual military or intelligence officers in the Thai security apparatus might be willing to sell secrets to our adversaries. China, Russia, and Iran all run covert operations in that country. So tell me what the Thais know about you. Do they have any leverage?"

"They don't have leverage because I haven't done anything."

"All right. We'll get back to that. Let's finish talking about the documents. Did anyone else have access to the folder before you returned it to the secured locker at the Freedom Center?"

"No. I discovered the file when I opened my briefcase at home. I took it straight to work that same morning."

"Did you first check whether documents were missing?"

Neel hesitated before he replied. If he told the truth he would be admitting to a more serious breach. But if he held the line here, he could at least claim that he'd remedied the security team's failures as best he could. He chose the latter course. "I had no reason to check. Are you suggesting the file wasn't complete? The point is, I used my best judgment to remedy someone else's mistake."

"Your best judgment?" Agent Miller laughed. She turned back the pages of her pad to read a note she'd written earlier. Then she resumed her questioning. "We at the FBI have conducted routine security interviews with you in the past."

"Yes," said Neel.

"Have you ever said anything to the Bureau that wasn't true? Have you told us everything about your previous trips to Thailand while you were in the Navy—who you met, what you did?"

"Of course I told the truth." Neel wanted nothing more than to get out of the room. In fact, he never wanted to see Agent Miller again. "If you don't mind, I have a meeting to get to."

"You're an important man." She smiled. "A final question. Would you volunteer to submit your government-issued laptop for a forensic examination?"

Anger curled his lips but he kept his voice steady. He said he wouldn't give up his laptop. He was too busy. He couldn't disrupt the Center's work.

"Thank you for your cooperation, Mr. Chima." Agent Miller stood to shake his hand. "You won't be notified of the status or result of this inquiry."

Neel walked to the door.

"Please be careful from now on," she said, before he left.

The interview had gone poorly but he wasn't going to panic. Agent Miller had confirmed that he wasn't under investigation. He didn't need to hire a lawyer. Any disinterested observer would understand that his own role in the breach was secondary. At worst, Cone would be directed to place an administrative note—a minor reprimand—in his personnel file. At best, Neel would never hear of the matter again.

He dropped to the floor of his office for a quick set of thirty push-ups. Be strong, he told himself. Admit to nothing. Don't show weakness.

He was raising himself from the carpet when he heard two knocks at the door. He opened it, slightly breathless now from the push-ups.

To his surprise, the priest walked in. He held a bottle of bourbon with a ribbon around its neck.

"I come bearing gifts," the priest said. "I met with Eliot down in Operations. I have a moment now before I head over to Langley. Then it's back to the White House. I'm running ragged these days." He handed Neel the bottle. "I noticed you didn't drink the Scotch or Japanese whisky at my salon, all those weeks ago. So I brought something American. For the sacrifices you're making." He wagged a finger in the air. "Just don't drink at work."

Neel thanked him. He asked the priest to sit.

"I can't stay. But please, make yourself comfortable."

Neel sat. The priest walked around Neel's desk to stand behind his chair. He put his hands on Neel's shoulders.

"My boy," said the priest. His breath, on Neel's neck, smelled of mints. "What have you gotten yourself into? What does the FBI want to know?"

Neel shook his head. "The security team failed in Bangkok. I carried a classified folder back to the States. I turned it in here."

"Documents are missing." The priest's voice had dropped almost to a whisper. "Documents that reveal NSA sources and methods, and that are broadly applicable. An adversary could look at those documents and draw conclusions about how we collect signals intelligence across the globe. And though this isn't something I personally believe, one could draw the inference that you tried to cover up the breach."

"No," said Neel. He knew these few moments in his office were crucial.

"Without question, you were in a difficult position in Bangkok. You were required, more or less, to drink heavily. But so was everyone else. Somehow you came out worse, didn't you?"

"It's a mistake," said Neel. He tugged at his collar.

"I've managed to silo the inquiry thus far. All Eliot knows is that there was a problem with the document collection. He's not angry with you. We do, however, have some zealous agents and prosecutors in the Eastern District of Virginia. One young man in the U.S. Attorney's Office thinks he's going to invoke the Espionage Act."

"The contractors were at fault. The prosecutors should look to them."

"There's always plenty of blame to go around in these situations. It will be apportioned in due course. You know the drill. Potential charges float around. Sometimes they disappear. Prosecutorial discretion is a wonderful tool. I think the question for you to consider is how you can continue to be of use. Which avenues are open? Isn't that always the question? How best to serve?"

He finally lifted his hands from Neel's shoulders. Neel watched him walk around the desk to the door.

"I've been sending a stream of targets up the chain," Neel said. "It's what you wanted."

The priest nodded. He had a resigned expression now. "I'm only one man, Neel. As the Afghan conflict has escalated, you must understand that the Freedom Center's role has changed. My dream of refashioning this place into a boutique operation, a targeting shop with a direct line to the White House, seems to have stalled. There are too many voices in the room. The generals, the seventh floor at Langley—everyone wants their say. But you've been given other opportunities to make an impact. Special projects, unique possibilities. You might act while there's still time."

Neel looked at him in amazement. "You're talking about Jones? You know I won't do it."

"Choose freely, my boy. Just think on what I said. Think about your family, at least."

He walked out, closing the door behind him.

Neel rested a few moments, with his eyes closed. Alone now, he felt calm. But this was a calmness without hope—the calmness of a survivor adrift at sea.

THIRTY

THE CALL CAME a week later. It was late in the morning.

"Time's up," said Jones, in his rusted voice. "What do you have for me?"

Neel felt a strange sense of relief. Waiting had become its own ordeal. The prisoner in the box, the revolutionary blindfolded at the wall—eventually he's ready for the gavel to strike, or the bullet to fire.

"I want to meet," said Neel.

"Sure," said Jones. He named a coffee shop on Chain Bridge Road. "Fifteen minutes."

Monica was standing at his office door when he hung up.

"I have to run," he said. He slipped past her into the hall.

"You're needed here. We had a scheduling change."

Vanderhoof's wife had given birth to a son at the beginning of the week. He'd gone out on a month's paternity leave. In his absence, Cone had asked Neel to manage the Center's internal operations.

"What should I tell Eliot?" Monica asked. "We're meeting at one today."

Neel was already at the stairs. "I'll be back soon!" he shouted.

———

Outside, the air had thickened. He turned up the air conditioner for the short drive.

He parked at the far end of the strip mall's lot. Sweat trickled down his back as he walked past brick-accented storefronts. No one was waiting for him in front of the coffee shop.

He didn't see Jones among the handful of customers inside. But moments after he joined the short line at the counter, he heard a voice he knew.

"Nice to see you again."

Neel spun around.

Jones was at Neel's shoulder. "We have the armchairs. Coffee's on the table."

Neel followed him to the far side of the room. Heat radiated through the glass.

"I came to tell you I want no part of this," said Neel, as soon as they reached their seats.

"Slow down, sailor." Jones grinned, showing yellow and brown teeth. He wore a faded blue suit with a beige shirt and no tie.

"I haven't spoken about your scheme to anyone."

"First things first. Milk and sugar?"

"Black is fine."

"I like sweetness, myself, at my age." Jones stirred two packets of sugar into his cup. "Usually I'm the one who's too direct. My superiors used to say I had poor tradecraft. One shouldn't rush these things."

"I have to get back to the Center. I'm meeting the director."

Jones made a dismissive gesture. "Neel, you're here for a reason. What do you think I learned in my years in the field? What do you think I learned from Iraq?"

"That's irrelevant."

"Irrelevant? This guy." When Jones laughed, his mouth was the only part of him that moved. "Five years ago I watched the Second Battle of Fallujah from Langley. Live, minute-by-minute, for days on end. I had all the video feeds going—from our choppers, from the helmet cams of the Marines—all the images, all the logs, everything. Our soldiers advanced in darkness, one house at a time. They took fire from the rooftops, they laid fire. It was fierce, methodical urban warfare. We had the manpower advantage, the guns, the air support, the night vision. The battle could only go one way. By the end, the insurgents were out of food and medicine. They were dying four or five to a room but they refused to surrender. Insurgent snipers were drinking their own piss to stay alive long enough to fire one last bullet at an American's head. I saw one hajji who was spitting blood—a man literally choking in his death rattle—try to bite a Marine as his final act on Earth. All for a pile of rubble. For shit and dust."

"I've heard this story. Vietnam was a slaughterhouse too. But Fallujah has nothing to do with my concerns, which are the watch lists and threat matrix we maintain at the Freedom Center and the ongoing search for actionable targets in the Hindu Kush. Haven't you heard? Even the president thinks Iraq was a dumb war."

"That dumb war revealed the nature of the enemy we face." When Jones frowned, his forehead crumpled like old newspaper.

"The young men we track in the U.S. are not in the same category as hardened warriors in Iraq. This whole conversation is pointless. By law, CIA can't involve itself in domestic operations. Enacting a program of disappearance and assassination on American soil would be profoundly immoral. I could go on."

Jones blinked twice, very slowly, without averting his gaze. He seemed to be waiting for Neel to flinch. Eventually, he allowed himself another little smile. "I'll be back," he said.

On the way to the counter Jones took out his phone, typed a brief message, and replaced it in his pocket. He put in an order at the register. He returned a minute later with a plate that held three cookies.

"Chocolate, chocolate chip, lemon-glazed."

He put the plate down on the little table between the armchairs. He sat, picked up the lemon cookie, and began to chew on it.

"Let's start over," he said. Crumbs fell from his mouth to his collar and shirtfront. "First, I apologize for the surveillance we put on you. But you understand the process. One has to review the signals, collect the facts, build a file. Our work—yours and mine—is in this sense the same."

"I'm not a suspect. You had no right."

Jones made the same dismissive gesture—a flick or wave—with his free hand. "That's done with. But the wheels are in motion. If I delay our first operation, our test case so to speak, your name will come up. My friends won't like that."

"I want your friends to forget about me."

Jones brushed a napkin across his lips. More crumbs fell to his shirt. "I came to you, Neel, with a proposal of dubious legality. The action I planned would interfere with your agency's work. By your own admission you said nothing. You didn't report me up the chain. You didn't tell Eliot Cone. You didn't contact the inspector general. What does that say about your judgment? You might find yourself having to answer some hard questions. And it's not as if this is the first such lapse on your part. What's your record when it comes to basic operational security? Taking care of classified documents and such?"

It was Neel's turn to laugh. "The FBI has interviewed me about the mistakes our security team made in Bangkok. Dozens of other people—Canadians, Australians, Thais—had copies of the same documents I had. They were hardly the NSA's crown jewels. I'm not the target of an investigation. As for the rest, you're bluffing. So I didn't report the heinous crimes you've dreamed up. Tell me what comes next. You'll call Main Justice to outline a criminal conspiracy that you personally directed, whose discovery would send you to prison for the rest of your life, all to implicate me in an alleged crime of omission? If anyone asks, I'll tell them the truth, which is that I saw no reason to encourage an old man in his delusions."

Jones picked up the chocolate cookie, snapped it in half, and returned both pieces to the plate. His face betrayed no emotion. "I know how to handle lawyers, careerists, bureaucrats—all you upper-floor, key-punching types. You like a soft touch. Gentle inducement. That's what I started with here. I prefer not to have to spell things out."

He lowered his voice. Neel leaned forward to listen.

"But if you want me to treat you like a little brown rabbit in the field, an animal to bully and trap, I can do that. Do you want me to be brutal?"

He withdrew an envelope from the inside pocket of his suit jacket and tossed it onto the table.

"We have pictures of you and that leather-clad hussy at a bar while your wife and daughters were away. As I said, you might have chosen a younger woman. But I'll be happy to drop the package off at Georgetown Law so your wife can weigh in."

"Nothing happened," Neel said.

Jones's voice hovered somewhere between a whisper and a snarl. "Sure. You were lonely, you needed a break, so you went out to flirt with a middle-aged barfly. It's understandable."

Neel shook his head.

"Take a look at the other pictures in that envelope. Stroll down memory lane. We had one of our men meet your old friend Lieutenant Maycock—Yoda, right?—down in Houston. Funny guy. Misses the Navy—the uniform, the perks. Has a short man's chip on his shoulder. Likes to talk about what a great high school wrestler he was. Apparently Yoda became a bit of a loudmouth after a few drinks. He bragged about the whorehouses you used to visit in Phuket, Olangapo City, all the red-light districts. So we had our local agents take pictures of those joints. We've got the topless bar girls with their neon skirts, the prostitutes behind glass, the drunken johns making obscene gestures from the floor. Are you so sure those girls were tested for HIV, hepatitis B, syphilis, what have you, back in the nineties? Those diseases can be latent for a long time. Rebecca might want to get some bloodwork done."

Neel thought about punching Jones in the jaw.

"What else can I offer? We'll have the FBI ramp up its inquiry into the documents you lost in Bangkok. Get you named as a primary target of the investigation. That would earn you a suspension from the Freedom Center. Who knows? Maybe you could use a break from work. Frankly, you look tired. But hiring a good defense lawyer is going to cost you everything you have. You'll probably have to beg or borrow from your father-in-law. And remind me, how did you end up with a top-level security clearance in the first place? Have you told the truth, and nothing but, in every background check over the years? Sailors go boozing and whoring all the time. You weren't the only one, but you have to disclose. Did you?"

Neel stared across the table.

"I'm just getting warmed up, Neel. Let's keep this going. If you're the target of an investigation, the Bureau will seize your laptop. Give the pope's laptop to digital forensics at the Bureau and they'll find something amiss—and you, Neel, are not the pope. How about your bank accounts, the financing for your house, the trusts your father-in-law has set up for his granddaughters? I'd hate to see anything get frozen while the government pokes around. They'll send agents in for a dawn raid while the girls are sleeping. Tear your house up to look for evidence. Wailing children, wife in her nightie on the sidewalk—that's never pleasant. The neighbors will talk about it for months. I'm sure you and Rebecca have always filled out your tax returns with perfect honesty and competence, so an audit wouldn't hurt you. And then we have the Chimas of New Jersey. Should the IRS audit them as well? That might upset their quiet, well-deserved retirement."

Jones spread his hands in a benevolent gesture. "Tell me what matters most to you, Neel. Money, family, name, career, freedom, health? I can take it away."

"You don't have the power."

"Don't gamble your own life." Jones picked up one of the chocolate cookie halves and sniffed at it. "Truth is, you're not so important. There's always a backup option. But we don't like it when a minor bureaucrat refuses to do his part. Even if you survive the hell that we'll unleash, your life will never be the same. You'll always hear whispers. Your wife won't stick around. Your pretty little girls—Maya, in first grade, am I right?, and Serena?—will grow up with a father who fell from grace."

"Never say my daughters' names again."

"Okay, tough guy," said Jones. He chewed his cookie, licked his lips. "Don't kid yourself. You were always going to do this job for us. Shall we get down to business?"

Neel said nothing.

"Good," said Jones. "This remains a country of patriots. The young men who signed up by the tens of thousands after 9/11 are coming home. But it's one thing to come home in victory. In 1945 you were a hero, a hometown legend. The country was shiny and new; all the jobs paid. You got your girl and tore off into life. It's a different thing to come home to a country that doesn't care, with the economy in shambles, after fighting a war you didn't win. Maybe you don't see it in D.C. Maybe they don't see it in Manhattan or San Francisco or the west side of Los Angeles. But drive through Appalachia or the Florida panhandle. Take a walk up the Grand Concourse in the Bronx. Get a beer at a VFW post, go to a gym or shooting range in any small town, hang out at the barbershop. You'll realize that we have a massive pool of angry young veterans to draw from. Men who didn't like the way the enemy fought in Iraq or the way they're fighting in Afghanistan now. They're angry at the cowards who laid IEDs for military convoys. They're angry at the mullahs who directed the suicide bombers. They hate radicals. They hate Arabs. They hate Muslims in general. They don't like the fact that their brother soldiers are missing legs or hands or penises or had their faces blown off. These veterans are trained and dangerous and ready to serve. They know we have unfinished business stateside. They'll do the work. We're starting small but we have the capacity to operate at scale."

It was almost noon. The tables were filling with customers eating sandwiches and salads. With the added bustle and noise, Neel had to lean ever closer to hear Jones's words. His breath was hot and sour at close range.

Jones was still whispering. "We have assembled teams—cells, in the correct parlance—of three men each. The men in any given cell only know the others in that cell. To each cell leader I'm a code name and a voice on the phone. Then we've enlisted a layer of auxiliaries, bureaucrats, to carry out certain functions. Men who can push buttons."

"Men like me."

"Correct. This is an opportunity. There's more to national security work than indexing Suspicious Activity Reports and updating databases."

"Enough with that. The Center assists in antiterrorist operations. We target foreign militants for drone strikes."

"That little experiment has run its course. The Freedom Center was never going to be a paramilitary outfit. You guys are back to building a search engine. You're a filing cabinet and a phone book. What I'm planning is something grand. Power without recourse. Hooded figures in the night. The tools of dictatorship in the hands of freedom-loving patriots."

"The CIA tried to liquidate Communist sympathizers in Vietnam. It didn't work then. It won't now with militant Islamists."

Jones grimaced. The liver spots at his eyes disappeared into yellow folds of skin. "People like you refer to the Phoenix Program as if it was something shameful. You think you've learned the lessons of history. You're so very informed, so civilized. But you don't know what you're talking about. That program was run by men of courage and imagination. If they'd had today's CIA toolkit—the population-level data, the surveillance capacity—they'd have succeeded. Today we know what we need to know. There's no need for interrogations, coercion, cross-checking, all that painful, grinding effort. Our project will be efficient. Take your first target. We already have the complete picture. He's a lonely young dreamer by the name of Ibn Muhammed al-Punjabi. A grotesque figure, as you'll discover."

Jones passed a slip of paper across the table.

"Al-Punjabi. You're serious."

"Elegant, isn't it? We use our Punjabi—you—to neutralize one from the other side. Briefly: Ibn Muhammed was born Manshoor Jalaluddin in Somerville, Massachusetts, in 1985. Today he's a twenty-four-year-old imam preaching in a storefront mosque in Brooklyn. He has internet contacts with overseas militants. His only family is an older brother in Chicago, not religious, busy making money. The brother thinks Ibn Muhammed is a fool. No one will miss him when he's gone."

"What's he done?"

"He's a bitter seed. He will continue to radicalize. Once they're on a trajectory, these men don't turn back. You slip his name down the watch lists, starting today. If anyone notices that you've been snooping around the file, you have a ready-made explanation. You took an interest in your

Punjabi brother, reviewed the investigation, and realized the suspect didn't merit a high level of federal scrutiny. You're Abel, he's Cain, except you realized he wasn't much of a Cain. After his name drops off the lists, we'll take care of the body. No one in the agencies will notice. Then we rinse, repeat, and scale."

"You have no evidence that your target is planning a terrorist act?"

"We can't go after a kingpin right off the top. But make no mistake, Ibn Muhammed is a dangerous man. They're all dangerous men. Remember the Quranic injunction: 'When the sacred months have passed, slay the idolators wherever you find them.'"

"You're talking about disappearing an American citizen off the streets of New York. We have laws. A constitution."

"Spare me. Five years ago we were shoving tubes up prisoners' asses with the full approval of the Justice Department. Does it matter now? How about the Predator strikes you planned in Pakistan? You don't even know the names of the people you killed. Someone calls a red-listed phone number, drives a truck, marches around in the company of other men. That's enough, in your eyes, to liquidate him and his family. Now, I have no problem with the drone attacks. In fact, I'm eagerly anticipating more. But don't kid yourself. Legality has nothing to do with whether what you're doing is just."

"I can live with myself," said Neel.

"You can't hide from your conscience forever. You can't cower behind legalisms. You have to make the choice. Either embrace the work we do with a clear heart—and I mean *embrace* it, in all its power and fury—or retreat from the intelligence community in disgrace."

Neel looked at the table.

"I know what path you'll take," Jones said. "You were an English major. Remember Macbeth. You've stepped so far in blood that you can't return."

"Macbeth dies at the end."

"We all die at the end, Neel."

"There'll be investigations. Local police, the Bureau."

Jones laughed. This time he looked around to the tables on either side, as if the other diners might join in his mirth. "Come on, Neel!

Crimes in America don't get solved. Not even ordinary crimes, crimes committed by morons who leave their blood and saliva and semen all over their victims and who carry cellphones that track their location and who brag about what they did on Facebook. No, the police and the Bureau are not going to look too closely at an elimination event carried out by anonymous professionals. They'll shrug their shoulders. In the end, they want the vermin to disappear."

"Someone will leak."

"Nonsense. This kind of project isn't new. We know how to run secret ops." Jones eyed his remaining cookie and a half. "You'll do the right thing. You want to get back on that yellow brick road."

Rain began to hit the glass. They both looked out.

"Spring storm," said Jones. "It was coming."

Neel stood up. Jones stood too. His pants hung loosely from his hips.

"So nice to speak in person, Neel. I'll stay to finish my snack."

Neel glanced back once from the door. Jones chewed methodically on his cookies.

Neel returned seven minutes late for the afternoon meeting. Cone frowned when Neel walked into the conference room but didn't admonish him. In his absence, Monica had been leading the discussion. Cone asked her to continue. Neel said nothing for the remainder. He was anxious to get back to his own office.

He was at his desk forty minutes later. He reached into his pocket for the slip of paper Jones had given him. It was damp from the rain, though the ink hadn't smudged. He typed Ibn Muhammed's name into the cross-agency search engine.

The results filled many rows. The NSA, FBI, and NYPD had each, at various times, taken an interest in the target. The FBI had assigned a junior analyst to prepare a summary report of the investigation. The analyst, according to her linked personnel file, was a recent NYU graduate with a degree in creative writing. She'd been hired under a Bureau initiative to recruit elite college students from diverse backgrounds, as part of its effort to bring fresh perspectives to domestic intelligence work. Neel printed the junior analyst's report. He knew his actions would leave a trail in the databases, but there was no other way.

He began to read.

. . .

Subject: Ibn Muhammed al-Punjabi (A.K.A. Ibn One-Eye),
    F.K.A. Manshoor Jalaluddin (F.A.K.A. El-Habibi;
    Manny; Manny Boy; Tiger)

DOB: 6.4.1985

Residence: Brooklyn, NY

I. Background

The NYPD's demographics unit opened an investigation
into Manshoor Jalaluddin in February 2008, when
Jalaluddin petitioned for a change of name in the
Brooklyn courts—an inherently suspicious act, for a
Muslim man of fighting age. The investigating officer
raised the standard questions: Was the subject's new
name a *nom de guerre*? Did he wish to distance himself from
crimes he had already committed? Did he intend to
apply for a passport? And so on. The investigator
found nothing of significance. The file remained open.

His petition approved, Jalaluddin began to post brief
devotional poems on the internet under his new name, Ibn
Muhammed al-Punjabi—"a Punjabi son of Muhammed." He
composed some of these in the native tongue of his
Pakistani immigrant parents, expressing—according to a
department translator—childish sentiments in error-strewn
syntax and crude vocabulary. Still, a few pundits posted
comments to the poems in online forums. Ibn Muhammed
responded to those comments with questions of his own.
Because some of the commentators lived overseas, these
communications brought Ibn Muhammed under the purview of
the foreign surveillance rules. The government now had
legal authority to monitor Ibn Muhammed without a
warrant. The NYPD forwarded its file to the FBI,
recommending a parallel federal investigation.

II. Early Life

Bureau analysts excavated Ibn Muhammed's past. His
father, Samir Jalaluddin, moved from Lahore to the
Boston suburbs in the 1970s, after completing his PhD
in organic chemistry at Punjab University. Dr.
Jalaluddin found work as a technical associate in the
MIT laboratories. The following year he sent for his
young wife, Nurmein Jalaluddin (née Khan). They bought
a row house on a quiet Somerville street. Eventually,
Nurmein gave birth to two American sons: Faisal in
1979 and, after many setbacks, Manshoor in 1985.

Dr. Jalaluddin's employee file at MIT contained two
reprimands for drinking at work, a mandatory counseling
order, and an advisory that the faculty excuse him from
working alone with female students. The union protected
his job but he never advanced from the staff position
that for most would have been a stepping stone. Nurmein,
for her part, suffered from obesity, hypertension,
diabetes, and bleeding ulcers. She was twice
institutionalized during bouts of depression, the first
time when Manshoor was still an infant.

Both Jalaluddin sons thrived, despite the conditions
at home. Faisal earned honors at Somerville High,
enrolled at Penn, and eventually joined an investment
bank in Chicago. Manshoor, though not the student his
brother had been, won a place on Somerville's varsity
soccer team. This was in September 2001, at the
beginning of his junior year. The team photograph shows
a slender young man with wavy black hair and striking,
gray-green eyes. The caption to the team photo gives his
nickname: "Tiger."

None of his former classmates remembered Manshoor
ever mentioning his religious beliefs. Few of them even
seemed aware, in the immediate aftermath of Al Qaeda's
attacks on the World Trade Center and Pentagon, that
Manshoor was a Muslim.

On a windy afternoon in November 2001, Manshoor spun
past a Boston Latin fullback in the waning moments of an

away game. Off-balance, and desperate to preserve a
scoreless tie against league-leading Somerville, the
fullback thrust out a leg. Cleats met shin; the Tiger
flew. He landed on a drought-hardened field with torn
cartilage and a fractured knee.

Manshoor never played again. He found other passions
during his long recovery: nu metal, alternative comics,
marijuana. He grew a beard, which came in with a copper
tint, and gained thirty pounds in a year. His grades
slid toward mediocrity. Still, a surprising performance
on the verbal portion of the SAT helped him win
admission to Syracuse off the waiting list.

III. Graduation

In June 2003 a neighbor called the Somerville police
to report a loud argument in the Jalaluddin household.
The neighbor heard shouting, a woman's screams, and
breaking glass.

When officers arrived sixteen minutes later, all was
quiet. Nurmein Jalaluddin answered the door but refused
to make a statement. She wore a headscarf and long
sleeves. Her face showed no visible injury. The police
report states that Dr. Jalaluddin lay unresponsive on
the living room couch, that the room smelled of liquor,
and that Manshoor came downstairs with bloodshot eyes
and dilated pupils. Slurring his words, Manshoor said
his mother didn't understand English and that, despite
the neighbor's emergency call, his parents hadn't
argued.

In late July 2003, her family doctor referred Nurmein
to both a nephrologist and a psychiatrist. The former
found advanced kidney disease; the latter diagnosed a
mood disorder. In response to the psychiatrist's
questions, with Manshoor translating, Nurmein admitted
that she had neither a job nor friends, and that she
rarely left the house. She said she spent her days
cooking, eating, and listening to recorded sermons.
Above all, she prayed.

She disappeared on a humid night in early August.
Neither Dr. Jalaluddin nor Manshoor realized she'd left
the house until the next morning. Two days later, a
police diver recovered Nurmein's body, clothed but
horribly bloated, from the Charles River. "So it was
written," said Dr. Jalaluddin to the reporting officer.
The coroner noted that Nurmein had sewn a mortar,
whetstone, and pestle into the pockets of her abaya.
Cause of death: suicide by drowning. Though Nurmein was
literate in Punjabi, she'd left no note.

Faisal returned from Chicago to deliver a brief and
impassive eulogy. Neither Dr. Jalaluddin nor Manshoor
spoke to the handful of mourners who'd gathered for the
funeral. Eight days later Manshoor left for welcome week
at Syracuse.

IV. College

At college, Manshoor, now Manny, remained an
indifferent student. He veered close to academic
probation in the fall semester of his freshman year.
Still, he rushed Sigma Chi, one of the lesser
fraternities, in the spring. With his new brothers he
drank, smoked, and went to all the games. He formed no
intimate friendships. One of the brothers remembered
Manny as "a layabout"; another said Manny was okay,
"but not really a Sigma guy in the end." He had no
recorded contacts with the Muslim student groups on
campus, which state and federal agencies kept under
surveillance.

As a sophomore, and declared business major, Manny
inherited Sigma Chi's marijuana connection from a
departing senior. His drug use increased from habitual
to heavy. Nevertheless, he made a personable enough
impression in on-campus interviews to secure
internships, over successive summers, with lower-tier
investment firms in New York.

Bureau analysts found two red flags, with the benefit

of hindsight. First, for an elective on mysticism in the
religious studies department, Manny turned in a paper on
Sufi Islam that was uncritical of the practice and even,
in its conclusion, admiring. Second, in his senior year,
Manny submitted a poem under the pseudonym "El-Habibi"
("The Beloved") to *Brick Bat,* the student literary annual.
Most of the contributors were disciples of Bukowski and
Plath. They described, in plain language, episodes of
erotic despair and extreme violence. Not El-Habibi. He
wrote, in an elevated style, of love and devotion (or
perhaps, on closer reading, of childhood trauma and the
first stirrings of fanaticism). Under the title "The Rose
in My Room," El-Habibi offered a dedication: "In
Memoriam: N.J." The poem opened with the lines "My
Lord's arrow pierces my heart / through smoke, my
sorrow, and my doubt." Twelve stanzas later, it ended
with the couplet: "My faith in thee glows bright. With
you / I'm blessed. Still weak but ever true." The
editors rejected the poem.

On a frigid Tuesday night in early December 2006,
Manny left the Sigma Chi house with one of his
fraternity brothers. They walked six blocks through
sleet to an empty bar. Manny and the brother stationed
themselves at the foosball table. They drank three
pitchers of beer in ninety minutes. It was shortly after
ten when the brother, swaying on his feet, went to the
bathroom. He emerged to see Manny arguing with a new
arrival, a small man in a black baseball cap. The
brother stood thirty feet away. He heard the small man
shout a series of slurs—"dirty Arab," "raghead
motherfucker," and the like—while Manny retreated. The
brother moved as quickly as he could on his "beer legs,"
as he stated to a Syracuse police officer later that
night, but in vain. The brother remembered how casually
the small man raised his beer bottle over Manny's head
("like he was swinging a bat in the on-deck circle") and
the silence that descended moments later, after the
small man had run out of the bar, and Manny lay on the

floor. The reporting officer noted the green glass scattered in a blast pattern on the tiles and the impressive quantity of blood.

Manny did not regain consciousness on the ambulance ride from bar to hospital. Later, he could offer no details of what had happened that night. During the weeks he lay in the recovery rooms of Upstate University Hospital, he posted two photographs to his lightly-used social media account. The first showed him as an infant in a diaper, balancing on his brother's knee. Manny, or Manshoor as he once again preferred, wrote a caption: "This world is the prison of the believers." The second photo showed Manshoor at age seven. He lay shirtless on a couch, his head in his mother's lap, while Nurmein, in a sweat-ringed salwar kameez, her scarf fallen to her shoulders, smiled and stroked his hair. For this picture, Manshoor wrote, "Allah will offer the traveler a path, even in the sea." By all accounts he was a model patient. A pair of operations failed to restore sight to his injured eye.

The dean of students offered every accommodation: an extended leave, tuition credit for his interrupted semester, trauma counseling, academic advising. But though Manshoor was only six classes short of a degree, he chose not to return to campus. The Syracuse police never arrested his assailant.

V. Brooklyn

In April 2007, upon his discharge from the hospital, Manshoor returned to his father's house. By then, Dr. Jalaluddin had accepted early retirement from MIT. Over the course of that spring and summer, Dr. Jalaluddin became at first sluggish, then inert. In late July, according to Manshoor's subsequent account, his father's skin took on a greenish tinge. Dr. Jalaluddin's limbs swelled one night in early August. Only then did he permit Manshoor to call an ambulance. Emergency room physicians at Massachusetts General diagnosed Dr. Jalaluddin with neurotoxicity and liver failure. He died within the week.

The Jalaluddin brothers sold their father's house at the height of the market. Each received a $300,000 windfall. Manshoor took his new fortune to Brooklyn, where he rented a small apartment on a shabby block of Crown Heights. He didn't contact his former classmates or fraternity brothers, though many of them had also moved to New York. The pictures he posted to social media, at long intervals, showed that he lived with bare walls and cheap furniture. He didn't seek work. Instead, he studied religious texts and registered for an online Punjabi-language course. When he left his apartment he wore a zealot's white robes, high trousers, and checkered kerchief. His neighbors noted the starburst scar on one side of his face and the arresting contrast between his clouded eye and his gray-green one. At night, Manshoor read dispatches from the wars in Iraq and Afghanistan. Occasionally, he reposted a story to his social media account. None of Manshoor's posts portrayed the U.S. military in a favorable light. An *Al Jazeera* article on an American airstrike in Helmand, for example, featured a photograph of a four-year-old Pashtun girl whose face had been so badly burned that she no longer had eyelids, lips, or a nose. Above the link, Manshoor typed, "Is this collateral damage?" No one in his limited circle of contacts wrote a response.

In the fall of 2008, Manshoor, now Ibn Muhammed al-Punjabi, toured small commercial properties in north and central Brooklyn. Vacancies abounded in the unfolding financial crisis. Entire business districts had devolved into regions of despair. Landlords offered four free months on a year's lease to tenants with ready money. In late November, Ibn Muhammed signed for a storefront on Avenue H in West Midwood.

Three weeks later, Ibn Muhammed pulled away the sailcloth he'd draped over the street-facing windows. He'd had the rooms painted light blue, laid carpets, piled mats and cushions along a wall, and adorned the

front door with the inscription Υ∧١, or 786, an esoteric
and disfavored reference to the Basmala.

From the lectern of the Masjid-e-Shuhuda, Ibn
Muhammed delivered his first sermon. It was two years to
the day since the attack that had partially blinded him.
In a near-empty room—a near-empty room that nonetheless
held an NYPD informant—Ibn Muhammed thanked Allah, the
most gracious, the most merciful. Allah, who had brought
a cooling wind into the desert of Ibn Muhammed's own
life. Allah, who had blessed the new mosque with a
snowfall as pure and sweet as mother's milk: "Bismillah
ir-rahmani ir-rahim. Bismillah Allahu Akbar."

VI. Investigation

The NYPD trained a high-resolution camera on the
mosque's entrance. The police informant, a Syrian-born
U.S. citizen who'd embezzled funds from an Islamic
charity in Queens, continued to attend Friday prayers.
Some days, he was the only worshipper present. He
reported that Ibn Muhammed mixed occasional homilies
on Islamic values with intense, if naïve, religious
hymns he may have composed himself.

The NYPD was on the verge of clearing the mosque from
manned surveillance when, in February 2009, the signals
changed. The informant reported that Ibn Muhammed had
paused his sermon, "with a veiled look in his eyes," to
make an unusual request. He asked the seven worshippers
present to pray for their Afghan brothers and sisters,
"who lived in fear of American bullets and bombs." On
receiving this report, the detective supervising the
investigation immediately asked for more resources from
the department and its federal partners. The FBI moved
Ibn Muhammed al-Punjabi to a more prominent position on
its national watch list. Because the list featured
three other men with substantially similar names, a
Bureau analyst added the designation "a/k/a Ibn One-
Eye," though the record doesn't indicate that any of
Ibn Muhammed's contacts actually referred to him by

such a nickname. The Bureau's Brooklyn field office
earmarked two and a half million dollars in federal
funds to the NYPD to support the investigation. It
detailed a federal informant—a young Pakistani
immigrant without papers, whose deportation the
government was holding in abeyance—to join the NYPD
informant on the case.

An agent in the Brooklyn field office planned the
operation. The two informants began separately to attend
Ibn Muhammed's prayer services. They made a show of
their newfound friendship before jointly seeking closer
relations with the imam. After Friday services they went
to Ibn Muhammed for advice on spiritual and domestic
matters. The supervising agent choreographed each
interaction in minute detail. For example, the young
Pakistani, who claimed to struggle to survive on a
dishwasher's earnings (though in truth he enjoyed a
generous federal stipend), asked Ibn Muhammed how much
of his income he should give to charity. Meanwhile, the
Syrian, a businessman locked in a struggle against his
own libertine nature, asked—"tremblingly, haltingly"—
whether the sex acts he wished to perform on his wife
were in fact forbidden to a believer. The Syrian brought
sweets on each visit. The informants always accepted a
second cup of tea.

Within weeks, after earning the imam's trust, the
informants began to talk of foreign wars. They railed
against the supreme cowardice of drone warfare. They
spoke of the dead women and children of the Muslim
nations. They asked the imam if believers were required
to make jihad when they lived in an infidel land. The
Pakistani sowed certain words into their conversations:
fertilizer, nails, subway, Nazarene, Jew. He described to Ibn
Muhammed the sense of futility and shame—the burning
horror, in other words—that rose in him when he walked
past the federal courthouse or the Prospect Heights
shul. To balance his co-informant's ardor, the Syrian
talked of offshore accounts, wire transfers, and Islamic
foundations. The two of them sought to enmesh Ibn

Muhammed in a violent conspiracy, on the one hand, or a
scheme to channel funds to foreign terrorists, on the
other. In either case, if he said the operative words
("Brother, I will"), if he rented a van or purchased a
bag of ball bearings for the Pakistani, or deposited a
check for the Syrian, Ibn Muhammed faced decades in
prison. And if not, if through luck or grace Ibn
Muhammed managed to slip the traps, the supervising
agent hoped surveillance would uncover other missteps—a
false statement on a tax return; a pornography habit;
visits to a massage parlor; pills; liquor; gambling
losses—that would give the government leverage to turn
the imam into an informant himself.

"I will get results," promised the Syrian, "La ilaha
illa Allah."

VII. Current Status

Two months into the operation, Ibn Muhammed has shown
himself to be an elusive target. In response to the
Pakistani informant's overtures, the target repeated
that "Allah gave [him] a voice, not a gun." Although
the Syrian made weekly donations to the Masjid-e-
Shuhuda and held open the possibility of greater
largesse, Ibn Muhammed refused to transmit any portion
of those funds to overseas accounts. He said he planned
to self-publish a collection of spiritual and ecstatic
verse, and that he needed to save for advertising and
associated costs. "Man can only meet God in work in
which he has lost himself," he said. Yet the poems
themselves contain images of, for example, a world in
flames, dagger-like eyes, and the infamous rivers of
honey invoked by Wahhabi suicide bombers. Ibn Muhammed
may remain vulnerable to the violent fantasies that
arise from an apocalyptic imagination.

In sum, while Ibn Muhammed holds anti-American views
and may yet reveal himself to be a material supporter of
terrorists, and while his private austerity may obscure
a deeper anti-capitalism or even nihilism, we can as yet

```
neither confirm nor discount his personal propensity for
violence.
     The operation continues, at a reduced priority.

[Updated April 30, 2009, 1:45 P.M. ET]
```

. . .

Neel put the report on his desk. He stood, walked to the wall, and rested his forehead on the glass. It was mid-afternoon, though of course neither daylight nor dark showed on the Operations floor. Analysts sat at their terminals, typed on their keyboards, and spoke quietly into their headsets.

There was nothing in the report. Reading it, Neel had felt empathy for Manshoor Jalaluddin, as the victim of a racist attack, and then distaste as he read of Jalaluddin's growing religiosity. But the young man who now called himself Ibn Muhammed had committed no crime. The government should never have surveilled him at all. He didn't belong on a watch list. Vanderhoof, as deputy director responsible for internal operations, would receive a notification if Neel removed Ibn Muhammed from the databases. But Vanderhoof wouldn't be back at the Center for weeks. And when he did, it was unlikely that he'd pass his time reviewing old logs and activity reports.

Neel's telephone rang. He walked back to his desk and picked up the receiver, knowing who it would be on the other end.

"You read the file?" said Jones.

"You've got the wrong guy. Ibn Muhammed is no one's idea of a real target."

"Precisely. Even the local field office has given up on him. But I won't. You have every warning sign: a devout mother; a history of loss; early drug use; social isolation; racial victimization; literary pretensions; an idiosyncratic theology that usurps secular education; a hunger for fame. He's the perfect age for a jihadi. And did you notice that he's a handsome kid but has no wife or girlfriend? As far as we can tell, he's never even visited a hooker. He's dealing with some kind of sexual confusion. Probably hates women."

"Even if you're right about all that, you could say the same for tens of thousands of men in this country who haven't done anything."

"Close your eyes," said Jones. "Do you see that small, ugly apartment, on an ugly block, in an ugly neighborhood? Do you see our target? Maybe he looks like you. But he's fifteen or twenty years younger. He grew up in a different America. He never had to prove himself like you did. Look at his ugly beard. Look at his disfigured face. Think of the thick robes he wears in the heat of a New York summer."

Neel shuddered, despite himself. He'd spent a lifetime making himself invisible, or at least putting himself beyond a certain kind of reproach. And here was a young brown man who, though given every opportunity to belong, had chosen to become a stranger.

Jones went on. "One day our young man reads the news on his favorite website. His heart races, his ears turn red. He grows angry. In fact, he's always angry. Let's say this is July. By now the Bureau has forgotten about him. Even the NYPD has pulled its informant. No one's watching. Outside, the pavement burns. Have you smelled a Brooklyn street in summer? In the neighborhoods, up in the tenements, the air reeks of shit. Our young man is suffocating in his little room. He's had enough. He calls the nearest rental agency to ask for a pickup truck. The clerk tells him there isn't one on the lot. Ibn Muhammed throws his phone on the counter. Then he sees the kitchen drawer. At once, he knows what to do. He takes the longest knife he owns. He walks out of his apartment without bothering to lock the door. He descends into the terrible heat. On the sidewalk, he plunges his right hand into his pocket, runs a finger on the blade. With every step he feels stronger."

"This is a fantasy."

"You know what these animals tell each other? 'A civilian corpse is worth twenty in uniform.' The French learned in Algeria that the enemy we face prefers to kill women and children. Innocents are more of a prize than armed men."

"If I remove the target from the national threat matrix it's because he shouldn't have been on any list in the first place."

"Is that a yes, Neel? Have you discovered a way out of your moral dilemma?"

"The Freedom Center has the authority to manage the nation's consolidated watch, threat, and targeting databases. As the principal deputy director of this agency, I can exercise my lawful discretion to protect the privacy of individual citizens who are mistakenly targeted. The government has no compelling interest in tracking Ibn Muhammed through the intelligence services. What happens next has nothing to do with me."

"I told you earlier, Neel. You can't hide behind legalities forever. Embrace this work. Be proud of what you do."

Neel hung up the phone. If he wiped Ibn Muhammed from the Freedom Center's databases, the NYPD and individual federal agencies could still investigate him but he wouldn't face automatic scrutiny whenever he encountered a government official. Now, if he heard footsteps, he could board an international flight or buy a bus ticket to Canada. He would have a chance to flee.

But even as Neel considered these possibilities, he knew he was deceiving himself. What he really wanted was for the clouds to pass. What he wanted was the return of the future he'd been promised. He was acting for his family and most of all for himself.

Neel logged into the threat matrix and removed Ibn Muhammed al-Punjabi, a.k.a. Ibn One-Eye, from every list.

THIRTY-ONE

ON NEEL'S FIRST day at Officer Candidate School, a drill sergeant told him there'd be no A-rabs in his Navy. Neel had just turned twenty-two.

"I'm not an Arab, Sergeant Instructor," said Neel.

"I don't give a cooked shit," said the sergeant. "You don't belong."

Right off the top, the instructors put them through boxing drills. After two weeks, satisfied that no one would die in the ring, they paired the officer candidates by weight and had them fight three rounds. Halfway through his first round, Neel's gloves weighed on his arms like fetters. He looked out over the ropes at the other candidates. Most cheered but some were rigid in their seats. Neel shuffled his feet across the canvas. He held his opponent when he could. The clock was too slow. "Fight!" screamed the referee, pulling Neel off his opponent, "Now, fight!" The other man held him too. Neel tried to speak but the mouth guard blocked his tongue. The only sound he could make was a grunt or cry. His opponent, with his lips on Neel's ear, answered with cries of his own. Neel hoped he was saying what Neel was saying. *I'm here. I see you. We are men, not beasts.* The referee thumped them on their backs and chests. "Fight! Fight! Fight!"

There was a moment in the second round when the referee separated them for the eighth or ninth time—with the clock running close to its limit and his opponent pulling on his arms—that Neel thought the other man understood. Neel tapped his opponent's ribs with a glove and looked him in the face. They both moaned. Neel wanted his opponent to know the truth. He whispered, *I won't hurt you, look at me!* But the headgear squeezed the other man's cheeks and brow. His eyes vanished under the leather and sweat. Neel didn't raise his hands as the instructors had taught. He shook his head, *no, no,* and tried to smile. The opponent moaned again. He leaned back, dropped his front shoulder, and hooked his right fist into Neel's chin.

Neel saw the flash you read about. Every sound stopped. Then darkness closed. He fell backward and did not land.

His concussion kept him out of drills for three days. His legs came back before his head did, but the lesson was clear to him even in the fog. Don't play the fool. You won't connect. No man is your brother. Next time, save yourself.

THIRTY-TWO

NEEL SIPPED HIS third bourbon on the rocks. He leaned away from the pool of light on the table. The liquor gave him a little distance from the world. Some people pedaled an exercise bike at six A.M. Others played chess online after dinner or pulled weeds in the vegetable patch on Sunday. Neel would sit on stolen time in the back corner of a bar, waiting for his blood and breath to slow. If only the lull could last. If only the clock didn't drive on, if only whiskey brought warmth without pain, if only real life wasn't waiting at the door.

He'd chosen a dive on the edge of Adams Morgan, a small, cash-only place with splintered booths, a dry-rotted sofa against the far wall, and a reeking passage that led to a single, broken toilet. He'd half-expected a tail, but no one followed him inside or looked his way after he claimed the sofa. A few men drank on the stools, ignoring the muted West Coast baseball on the television. The bartender filled his own plastic cup from the soda gun, stacked glasses, wiped the counters.

Rebecca had called Neel at work late that afternoon. Agent Miller had visited her unannounced at Georgetown to ask about Neel's behavior before and after his trip to Thailand. What, Rebecca asked Neel in a

clenched voice, had he done in Bangkok? Why hadn't he told her about
the documents he'd lost? Would he have to resign from the Freedom
Center? Did he fear prosecution? She'd spoken to her father. He'd offered to retain counsel for her separate defense. He wanted Rebecca to
bar Neel from the house and find a divorce lawyer. It was sensible advice even if she wasn't ready to act on it. "I hate that you're making me
talk this way," she said.

Neel asked her to calm down. He said the Bangkok incident had
little to do with him. Security contractors bore responsibility for the
breach. Rebecca should never even have heard about it.

"So why is the FBI interviewing me?"

"The bureaucracies are always clawing over turf, undercutting one
another's leadership, fighting for the president's attention. An overzeal-
ous special agent at the FBI decided this was his chance to get noticed.
So he took his dick out and gave it a shake, sent Agent Miller your way."

"Why did you say that?" asked Rebecca. "It's not the time to be vulgar."

"Agent Miller is an operative out on her boss's bidding. She isn't
someone you need to fear."

"Why are they picking on you?"

Neel sighed. He was just a fall guy, he said. It could have been anyone.

"It's not because you drink too much? It's not because you're reckless? You're a mark, Neel."

Neel said he'd been living with the inquiry for weeks. By now, it had
faded into background noise. "Believe me, I've taken the measures I
need to take. I have assurances from the top. This will go away."

She didn't believe him, she said. She wanted him to come home
early but he said that was impossible. He was behind, as always, at
work.

"Let's get through the week, okay?" It was a Wednesday. "We'll discuss everything on the weekend."

Rebecca hung up without saying goodbye.

An hour later he saw Monica in the break room. On an impulse, he
asked if her offer to talk in confidence still stood, all these months after

they'd spoken at the priest's salon. He could use a friend, he said. She showed no surprise at his question. She had work to finish, but said she could meet for a late drink.

She walked in at ten. By then he was on his fourth and—he promised himself—final glass. She stopped at the counter. The bartender flicked his eyes over her while he took her order. She walked to where Neel sat in the shadows.

"Charming place," she said. The sofa was narrow for the two of them.

"I didn't want to go somewhere we might be recognized."

"No one knows who we are. No one cares."

She had tired eyes. The hours were taking their toll.

"Your nose is glowing," she said. "What round are you on?"

"I'm too dark to have a red nose."

"Right away with the race card." She patted him on the leg. "I'm not against social drinking, for the record." She raised her glass.

Neel tilted his whiskey. "I'll schedule a dry month for myself at some point. Maybe in 2020."

Monica brushed her hair back from her face. "It's not that I don't enjoy this kind of repartee, Neel, but it's a school night. What do you want to talk about?"

He swallowed some whiskey. Now that the moment had arrived, his instinct for self-preservation stirred. Though they'd worked together for months he had no reason to confide in her. He felt like the sprinter he used to be, fighting his own nerves while he lowered himself into the blocks for an important final. There were always those few seconds—before it was too late, before the gun sounded and adrenaline and instinct took over—when he wanted to stand up and walk away.

"Neel?"

He drew a deep breath. "The FBI keeps snooping around. Agent Miller went to see my wife today at Georgetown." Though he was three and a half whiskies in, his voice trembled.

"This is the Bangkok investigation?"

"What serious prosecutor wants to waste time on a case like this?

Fire a couple of security contractors if you have to, but to me this is file-cabinet stuff."

"The missing material is top secret. NSA sources and methods."

"A hundred other people had copies of the documents. Those copies went out from Bangkok to Yorkshire, Ottawa, I don't know, fucking Perth. Do we track every piece of paper we hand over to our allies? Are we asking the Thais if their vaults are secure? Come on. The NSA doesn't share critical information at international conferences. The pages that went missing from my folder are top secret the same way a billion other government documents are top secret. No one at Fort Meade is losing sleep over this."

Monica tilted her head. "If the U.S. Attorney brings a charge it won't be a defense to say the top-secret documents you lost weren't all that important."

"A charge." Neel drained what was left of his whiskey. He put the empty glass down by his feet. "My wife's father is a defense lawyer at Haines Strawbridge. He thinks I'm the second coming of Benedict Arnold. He wants my wife to cut me loose."

"If she leaves you, Neel, it won't be because Agent Miller asked for a twenty-minute interview." She paused. "You don't seem to like your father-in-law very much."

"He bought us a house. I'm bound to resent him forever."

"What a terrible man." She shrugged. "Okay. So you committed a minor transgression."

"At worst."

"The problem is that this minor transgression leaves you open to criminal penalty. Someone's putting the heat on you, but why? You're probably right that no one cares about the documents. I'm guessing that what someone does care about is having leverage over you. Someone wants to make you do something."

"That's right," said Neel. Now he hesitated. He reached for his glass on the floor, forgetting for a moment that it was empty. When he sat up, he had a question of his own. How far back, he asked Monica, did she go with the priest?

"He recruited me to ODNI and then the Freedom Center. I've been to his salon four or five times. I know work is his whole life. He's not married, has no girlfriend or boyfriend, no children. On a personal level, he's a mystery."

"He said—or suggested—I had a way out. That way out required a sacrifice. I had to do something I did not want to do. Now I'm haunted by it." Neel ran both his hands through his hair. "I can't share the details. I'm confiding in you but I'm not insane."

Monica had finished her own drink. She sat back for a few seconds before she spoke. "I don't think that's it," she said. "You're not suffering because of what you did. It's a little late to get high-minded." Now she turned so she could look into his eyes. There was, he thought, a hint of contempt in her face. "I've seen you call for a drone strike in a Pakistani village against anonymous targets. You could live with the six or seven or dozen bodies we left in the rubble. You can live with whatever you've done now. No, you're worried for yourself. You're worried about your family. Don't lie to me, Neel. What do you want?"

He clasped his hands, looked at the table. Then he asked Monica if she thought the priest would keep his word. "I did what he wanted me to do. Now will he, or whatever cabal he belongs to, get the FBI off my back?"

"He has a long arm, Neel. But only the president or attorney general can stop the FBI on a dime. You'll need patience." She was still looking intently at him. "He'll help you if helping you serves his own interests. He's supremely ambitious and supremely confident. He believes that the more power he gathers, the safer this country is going to be. If you're useful to him, you can count on his support. That's what D.C. is: America in its purest form. No loyalty, no love, just favors. There's a reason why people like you and me ended up here."

She looked away and raised her index finger in the air. Apparently the bartender saw and understood her gesture. "Can you collect my vodka soda without ordering another whiskey for yourself? I don't want you to drive into a lamppost when you leave."

The bartender's scowl grew deeper when he saw that it was Neel, and not Monica, who'd come for the drink. He didn't acknowledge the two singles Neel left on the counter as a tip. Neel handed Monica the glass before he sat down again. He draped his arm across the top of the sofa. When she turned to him he let it fall to her shoulders.

"Family man," she said. "Let's wait on that one. You don't need to complicate your life right now." Her voice was gentle.

He took his hand away. Monica was looking at him without judgment. As for Rebecca, well, the gulf between them, when they last spoke, had seemed too vast for words.

"I think you should keep your interests aligned with those of our powerful friend." Monica was speaking as if Neel hadn't just touched her. "Keep doing what he wants. But don't forget that you have leverage too. You know what he's asked you to do. That gives *you* power. We're each, in our own way, a ticking bomb."

"Christ. Don't you wonder sometimes how you got into this work?"

"I wanted—I want—to rise. One day rooms will fall quiet when I walk in. I'll make decisions you read about in the *Times*. And later still I'll get paid." She tilted her head back and drained her full glass.

"Coming out of law school, I thought I was going to do something honorable."

"And when I was twelve I thought I was going to be on the cover of *Vogue*. We grow up, Neel." She leaned over to kiss him on the cheek. "Let's go our separate ways now. But don't be a stranger."

"Thank you."

"I like you, Neel. You've seen a lot. You can survive the pressure. But in talking to you, I almost feel like I'm the older and wiser one. You should be careful who you trust."

They'd both parked down the block. He walked Monica to her car. Before he started up his own Honda, he gave himself a hard slap on each cheek and checked his eyes in the drop-down mirror. He lowered the windows and kept both hands on the wheel as he drove. At home, Rebecca and the girls would be asleep. It wasn't far, but he went slowly. He had dark hair, dark enough skin. He didn't want to draw the attention of a bored D.C. cop.

THIRTY-THREE

ON SATURDAY, NEEL, Rebecca, and the girls walked the eight blocks from their house to the park. Away from the pavement, a new sweetness filled the air. Bees flew low over the meadow. Neel carried a tarp to lay beneath their picnic blanket. Rebecca had packed strawberries, hard cheese, olives, and the croissants she loved from the corner bakery. Maya and Serena wore their little straw hats. Rebecca said she'd play hide-and-seek with them after lunch. The girls didn't ask their father to join. They knew by now to excuse him from their games, just as they sought only Rebecca's hands when they crossed the street, or asked her and not him if they could buy popsicles from the ice-cream man. It had all happened so quickly. Neel had done his share, more or less, in Maya's first year. He hadn't tried as hard with Serena.

Rebecca told the girls they could run around for a few minutes before they ate. Neel lay on his back and closed his eyes while she arranged the plates and cups. She paused to run her fingers through his hair.

"Kay told me a secret once," she said. "This was years ago. I brought a boyfriend home from Amherst. She told me to watch him while he slept. Then I'd see him as he really was."

"I'm awake," said Neel, without opening his eyes. "So my inner self remains a mystery."

"I have a pretty good idea by now."

Neel cleared his throat. He propped himself up on his elbow, opened the olive jar, and sniffed at the contents. "Your mother wasn't too excited about me."

"She was born in 1948. She hadn't envisioned someone like you for her daughter. But she came around."

"She was afraid of me. Or afraid for you. She thought I would be domineering, violent. A hot-tempered savage." Neel rolled an olive against his teeth.

"That was never you." Rebecca shaded her eyes while she looked across the meadow for their daughters. "That's not the problem."

"But there is a problem." Neel dropped back to the picnic blanket. The day was bright. The high clouds didn't move.

"You shouldn't have kept me in the dark, Neel. You should have trusted me to help you."

From the far end of the park came the first soundings of the weekend drum circle. He closed his eyes. "It's hard when you reproach me," he said.

Rebecca was serving the food now, onto paper plates. "Can you bring the girls in?" she asked.

He stood and called for their daughters to return.

The girls ate their strawberries and croissants but struggled with the cheese. Neel, who wasn't hungry, pulled his croissant into two pieces for Maya and Serena. He lay down again. This time he fell asleep.

He woke to Serena poking at his face. She was trying to fit her index finger into one of his nostrils.

"You can't sleep in the park, Daddy. Maya says it's against the law."

He moved her hand away. He asked how long he'd been out.

Rebecca was rooting around in the hamper. "The girls want more strawberries," she said.

"Actually, I want honey," said Serena.

"You have a funny face, Dada," said Maya. "Your nose is too big."

Neel patted her on the arm. She ate her last strawberry, then stood and sprinted off across the meadow. Serena ran after her.

"We could have brought wine," said Neel, as he sat up.

"We could have," said Rebecca. Her face was flushed with the sun. She was thirty-five, healthy, excited for what lay ahead. Neel felt a sudden yearning for her.

He reached for her hand. "Do you worry about terrorism?" he asked.

"I didn't expect that question," she said. "I worry about climate change, clean air, clean water. I worry about the misogyny our daughters will face. I worry about racism, the Republican party, the Supreme Court, *Roe v. Wade,* sexual assault, cervical cancer, breast cancer. I worry that you'll develop heart disease. You're Indian, you drink too much, you've stopped exercising, you hate salad. You're overdue for a checkup."

"I do push-ups and crunches in my office."

"Well, it's your life," she said. She was silent for a few moments as she gazed across the meadow. Then she told him that Serena had been asking for a puppy.

He grunted. "Let's think on that for about five years."

His phone was buzzing. He reached into his pocket to silence it.

On the far side of the meadow, Maya and Serena were petting a big, long-haired dog. An older girl held the leash.

"I should check on them," Neel said.

"It's all right," said Rebecca. She stood and walked across the grass.

They went home late in the afternoon, after hide-and-seek, a Frisbee game in which even Neel joined, and a family nap on the blanket. Neel said he'd unpack while Rebecca ran a bath for Maya and Serena.

They came downstairs half an hour later, smelling of peppermint. Neel was slicing zucchini on a chopping board. He had a glass of beer on the counter. The kitchen smelled of roasting chicken. The girls wanted to go outside to look at the vegetables growing in the garden. Neel said he'd keep an eye on the oven.

He watched them through the window. Maya and Serena took turns with the copper watering can. Rebecca had transplanted kale, spinach, and pepper seedlings three weeks earlier. Now she was showing the girls how to pick caterpillars from the kale. They watched solemnly while Rebecca crushed the pests beneath her flip-flops. At one point she glanced back at the house and saw Neel watching them. She beckoned to him to come out. But he only shook his head and waved. She turned away. The girls, who were still kneeling in the vegetable bed, hadn't seen him. Rebecca picked Serena up to kiss her. Maya hugged her mother at the waist. The years were turning fast. Rebecca had told him that the wonderful thing about children was that they always let you begin again. Didn't Neel know that if he took one step forward, his daughters would take three or four? It was the easiest and most natural thing in the world, she said. Why didn't he do it? He replied that he would, when he had more time.

They ate together in the dining room: roast chicken and potatoes, sautéed zucchini with parsley and mint. Maya and Serena had their own sides of sliced bananas and yogurt. Neel carved the chicken at the table. He chopped one breast into pieces for the girls and put the other on Rebecca's plate. He took the wings himself—cook's privilege, he said. He'd opened a bottle of red wine but Rebecca only wanted cold water after a day in the sun. The girls had an appetite. Neel drank his wine and listened to their chatter.

When they were almost finished, Maya asked Rebecca why her daddy never talked at dinner.

"Because you and your sister do all the talking for him," Rebecca said. She turned her gaze on Neel.

Maya frowned to show she was unhappy with such a flippant response. "That doesn't make sense. You can say as many words as you want."

"You're right," said Rebecca.

"I'm sorry," said Neel. "I just love listening to all of you."

"You can talk sometimes and then listen too," Maya said.

Serena laid her head on the table. Rebecca asked Neel if he'd put the girls to bed.

"No!" cried Maya. "I want you!"

Serena said she wanted her mama too.

It was all right, Neel said. He'd clean up while Rebecca read them their stories.

When Rebecca returned to the kitchen, Neel was wiping down the stove.

"Dishwasher's stacked," he said. He had been steadily sipping wine. He had a last half-glass on the counter. The bottle was empty.

She asked if he was ready to talk.

"Almost there." He'd join her in the living room in a few minutes, he said.

He brought a glass of whiskey in with him. Before he sat, he put a record on. He wanted to soften the atmosphere.

"Thelonious Monk," he said. "'Easy Street.' It's the sweetest song. Just wait until the bass comes in."

She was on the couch. He sat in the armchair across from her, swirling the whiskey in his glass.

She looked at him with an unhappy expression. "Beer, wine, whiskey. It's the triple crown every weekend. I know this world, Neel. I grew up in it."

"I'm dealing with a lot at work. Guilt, pressure." He smiled. "But I love you."

"What guilt? You said you did nothing wrong in Thailand. Not that you've told me anything." She crossed her arms.

He took a long, slow sip of his whiskey, closing his eyes while he swallowed. It was a provocation.

"You brought your work home," she said. "That was never part of the deal. What's the fallout going to be, Neel? You're not acting like some-one who's in trouble with the FBI."

"How should someone in trouble with the FBI act?" He shook his head. "I was offered clemency, protection—call it what you like—if I did someone important a favor."

"What favor?"

"I can't talk about that part. But I did it to protect all of us. The FBI will go away."

"You're making this sound like the Mafia. Favors, protection, tit for tat. It's not how federal investigations work."

"You set the thermostat too high," he said. "It's almost summer, for Chrissakes. This room is a coffin."

"I'll turn it down. But I'm not finished. You need to tell me what actually happened in Thailand."

"Nothing," said Neel. "Nothing happened. We went to a banquet after a day of meetings. They made us drink. The hospitality culture of the East. It turns out Thai booze doesn't agree with me. Unrelatedly, a couple of pages disappeared from a file in my hotel room. I hadn't looked at them. I shouldn't even have had the file after the meetings ended. Security people were supposed to collect the documents." Suddenly, he'd had enough. "It's all so pointless. I want to listen to music now, Rebecca. The deep stuff. I want to get clean after a hard week. Fuck it, it's fine."

"'Fuck it'?" she said, in a voice that held no bitterness. "'Fuck it'? That's what you're saying to me now? Oh, Neel."

She left the room.

He followed a few minutes later. He waited while she brushed her teeth and washed her face. She wore a T-shirt to bed. He watched her rub lotion on her sun-reddened neck and legs. They had the bedside lamps on but no other light. There was darkness by the walls. He moved closer to her. His body and breath radiated heat. When he put his hand on her shoulder she shook him off. She put the lotion down on the nightstand, turned out her light, and slipped between the sheets.

"Drink a glass of water," she whispered. "Drink two glasses before you come to bed."

THIRTY-FOUR

"I HAVE TWO massive problems," said Cone. He stood on the carpet in the middle of Neel's office. Monica leaned against the doorframe with a bemused expression. They'd both ignored Neel's invitation to sit.

"Massive problem number one: I got an email yesterday from Adam Buford. Heard of him?"

"Yes," said Neel.

"He's the reporter who was sniffing around a couple of months back. Hates the 'military-industrial complex' and the intelligence agencies. Not someone we'd usually pay attention to. But he went deep into our Waziristan strike. He sent me a list of questions informed enough that I felt compelled to call him back. We spoke this morning for half an hour. He spent most of that time reading excerpts from his draft article to me. This thing is a goddamn dossier. Buford has an anonymous source in this building, a self-styled 'whistleblower' who didn't like what he saw when we carried out the operation. The whistleblower leaked your targeting memo, Neel. Last month Buford flew out to Kabul. He hired himself a fixer, donned a burka, and traveled all over eastern Afghanistan pretending to be the fixer's wife. At some point Buford and the fixer crossed over to Pakistan. He rode sidesaddle on the back of a Honda CD70 to the village we hit."

"And?" asked Neel, from behind his desk. At the door, Monica stared into space. For a few moments—moments that for Neel, when he returned his gaze to Cone, slowed to an icy stillness—no one spoke.

Cone puckered his cheeks while he looked down at the carpet. He seemed to be considering whether to spit. "And, Neel, it doesn't look great for us. Buford has counted sixteen dead and wounded. His fixer took photos of an orphaned eight-year-old boy who lost a foot. The boy has bandages on the stump and on his head. His uncle, who's taking care of him, isn't sure if his brain still works. He hasn't spoken since he regained consciousness. There are four other villagers with shrapnel wounds, including two women and another child. Those casualties are on top of eleven dead in the two strikes: five men, one woman, two teenage boys, and three young children. The victims are all related. The villagers admit they have guns but they say the weapons are for protection. There's no government in the mountains; it's not as if they can call the police when they're in danger. Everyone the fixer talked to swore no militants lived in the village but one of the survivors said he now prays for the Taliban to bring America to her knees. The story will be published online in the next couple of weeks."

"Where?" asked Neel.

"As a freelancer, Buford didn't want to tip his hand. But my name will be in the story, since I direct this agency. Your name will be in there as well."

Neel asked what Cone planned to do.

"Since we can't publicly acknowledge that we have civilian agencies leading drone strikes in Pakistan, a nation where we aren't at war, we also can't comment when one of those strikes goes wrong. The White House understands we're in an awkward position but they won't get us out of it. Let's hope no one pays attention when the story appears."

"Is the reporting accurate?"

"No question there was collateral damage. That in itself isn't a career killer for you or me. It's hard to get clean targets. Plenty of civilians have died in this war. But the fact that our names will be attached to this particular fiasco is not great."

"That doesn't seem so important right now," said Neel. He felt sick. Monica gave him a sympathetic smile.

"Big-boy pants, Neel. Okay, moving on. Massive problem number two: the Global War on Terror, or whatever we're calling it now, has gone to shit." Cone began to read from a briefing paper in his hand. The paper summarized a set of intelligence reports he'd already discussed with Monica and Neel in their meetings that week. Defense Intelligence attributed a high casualty count among Coalition forces to the early onset of spring in the Hindu Kush. Isolated skirmishes had swelled within days into the full onset of the Afghan fighting season. The Taliban struck before Coalition preparations were complete. The American response, well-intentioned as it was, suffered from intelligence failures. A B-1 leveled half a village in Farah Province on May 4. Signals indicated the place was a Taliban stronghold, but the signals were wrong. The bombing killed more than a hundred civilians, including forty or so children who'd been sleeping in the adjoining compounds of a large extended family. The provincial governor had demanded a personal apology from an American general. The Freedom Center's analysts weren't uniquely at fault, but neither had they warned the Pentagon of the risk of massive collateral damage. Meanwhile, twice as many American soldiers had died in the first four months of 2009 as in the same period of 2008. This year promised to be the bloodiest of the campaign. In Iraq, where the violence between locals and American troops had at last abated, a U.S. Army sergeant on his third tour in-country gunned down five of his fellow soldiers at a combat stress clinic in Baghdad. Cone tossed the briefing paper down on Neel's desk. "War is costing the United States at every level," he said. "I'm personally feeling the heat from above."

Neel cleared his throat, but Cone shook his head before he could speak.

"The Freedom Center is supposed to consolidate actionable intelligence from across the agencies," Cone said. "As you know, our community has incredible reach. Every cellphone and smartphone on the planet is a tracking device. The NSA can see what's on your computer, online or off; Treasury knows when money moves; the National Geospatial-Intelligence Agency scans the most remote regions on Earth down to the square foot. And yet we're being caught unawares by terrorists and militants. Why, with all this information, can't we deliver the intelligence product the White House needs? I'm not just talking about targets for capture or kill operations. You've been doing your best with that, Neel, even if to limited effect. I mean the basics. We don't know where the Taliban is going to strike next. We don't know when the next big attack is going to happen in Europe or the Middle East. We have Muslim neighborhoods in American cities under blanket surveillance, and we hope we've scared those communities into submission, but we can't offer the president any assurances. What's wrong with this picture?"

"Reality is always going to be more chaotic than the data," Neel said. "Though we try to get better, the future is by definition unknowable."

"Wrong answer," said Cone, "even if, technically speaking, you're correct. The White House claims that leadership at the Center has failed to develop high-level relationships with our sister agencies. We're sitting in our offices, tapping keyboards, looking at screens, holding our dicks—sorry, Monica—and no one even knows who we are. We comb the data, but we don't get the inside view from the other shops. Where are our tips, where's the hot stuff? To change the situation, the White House wants us to send emissaries out on the road. Okay?"

Neel didn't respond.

"I admit that right off the top this diagnosis sounded far-fetched to me. We're looking for patterns and convergences in the signals, not selling used cars. Why does one of our people need to swap stories with the chief scientist at the National Reconnaissance Office? I pushed back to the extent I could. I asked if we could at least hold off until Vanderhoof gets back from paternity leave next month."

"They want us to act now," said Monica, to Neel.

"The bosses say that since the wars aren't going to wait, neither can we. They're adamant that I need to designate someone at the deputy director level. Given that you, Neel, are the only deputy director on hand, I have to designate you our traveling salesman. Start out west. Swing through Utah, New Mexico, Arizona, Wyoming, the whole damn constellation of data centers, air bases, satellite launchpads, the works. Your first trip is in ten days. Salt Lake City. There will be many more. Vanderhoof might take some of the assignments when he gets back, but I need him to run our internal processes. Plan on living the rest of the year out of your suitcase."

Neel shook his head. "I don't see the value in this, Eliot. It'll be tough on my family."

"It won't be so bad. You'll come home most weekends. Let's face it, you weren't seeing your girls all that much as it is."

"What you're asking for is different."

"I was skeptical at first, but I've come around. The White House is tapping into a deep American wisdom. In the end, we're all family. You have to slap a guy on the back, ask about his son's Pop Warner team, know that his wife is sick, congratulate him on his daughter getting into her top choice for college. Go to Utah. See what's actually happening in the NSA's data centers. Build relationships with senior managers and engineers in the facility. Streamline the Freedom Center's access to the NSA's servers. Get our analysts the same level of permissions as the NSA's own analysts to the daily data collections. Don't frame it as competition but as collaboration. The NSA should want us to cross-check its reports. If we highlight suspicious activity the NSA's analysts have overlooked, we help that agency demonstrate the value of its signals intelligence. Let's set up a hotline for NSA managers to alert our shop to irregularities, unexpected data threads, clusters of suspicious activity, anything, even if their analysts have yet to file a formal submission. Our two agencies are natural allies. Data collection and interpretation are at the core of both our missions. If this end of the intelligence community coheres around those values, we can form a real counterweight to the CIA. Give the NSA men the personal touch, Neel. Make them like you. Then move on and do the same thing wherever we send you next."

"Relationships take time," said Neel. "You have to be realistic."

"We have White House support to seek more flexible arrangements with our sister agencies. This is another chance to create a legacy, Neel. We'll make the Freedom Center a top-tier intelligence agency yet. Whether or not we alter the course of the Afghan war, whether or not the White House acts on our targeting recommendations, I'm determined to make our product impeccable."

Monica, in the doorway, was tapping her heel.

"Oh, and you won't be alone, at least on the first trip. Monica will go with you. Our contact at the White House told me to give you reinforcements at the outset. Everyone wants you to succeed."

Monica smiled at Neel again.

Neel crossed his arms while he considered the matter. "Sure," he said at last. "It's not as if we have a choice."

THIRTY-FIVE

IT WAS THE end of May. The mosquitoes drove Maya and Serena inside. They took out their sketchbooks in the living room. Neel was in the kitchen, chopping vegetables for soup. Rebecca had a sourdough loaf in the oven. She was cracking eggs for a cake. A Brahms piano concerto played on the speakers. The weekend had arrived.

Neel had put off the conversation for a few days but couldn't any longer. He told Rebecca that Cone was sending him on the road. He would be traveling across the country for months, mostly in the far west. There was nothing he could do. The real order had come from on high.

Rebecca put down the mixing bowl she'd been holding.

There was more, Neel said. A news story naming him in connection with a botched drone strike in Pakistan would soon appear online. The story would cite a flawed targeting memo Neel had drafted. The reporter had visited the village where the missiles landed. He claimed that many civilians, including children, had died. The story would include images of some of the maimed survivors.

"I don't know what to say." Rebecca moved closer. "This is awful.

How can you sleep?" She wore an orange T-shirt. Her face was flushed in the warmth of the kitchen. When she touched his arm, he shivered.

Neel said he didn't think he was in trouble for the drone strike. It was an embarrassment but not a crime. Everyone had approved the operation, including the president. There would be no consequences. But he was reeling, he said. For two days he'd walked around like a zombie.

"You should never have taken this job," she said.

"I can't leave now. I'm too vulnerable. As far as we know, the FBI hasn't cleared me on the document inquiry." He looked up at the clock. It was 11:30. He had to get through five and a half hours before he could have a drink. "This is a dark time, but we'll make it."

He couldn't tell her about the other catastrophe, the one he had set in motion but could still, perhaps, avert. A young man was alive today in Brooklyn. Next week, or in two weeks, he wouldn't be.

She walked away. She opened the oven door to look at her bread, went to the counter, picked up the mixing bowl, and put it down. He felt her anger from across the kitchen. It had been gathering for months and even years. He had put her in an impossible place.

"I was going to ask you today if we could take a trip," she said. "It'll be our ten-year anniversary this summer. I thought your mother could come down to look after the girls. Did you even notice that I spent spring break alone with Maya and Serena?" She said all this in a tight voice.

Neel looked up at the ceiling. He was sweating under his shirt. "A trip is a good idea," he said, as her face opened in surprise. "I'll call Mom after lunch."

THIRTY-SIX

REBECCA CHOSE LOS Angeles. She thought of the city after reading a travel feature in the *Post*. She wanted to see the Pacific and the mountains in the western light. They could take day hikes, she told Neel, go to an art gallery and the beach, eat at one of the famed restaurants. Neither of them had visited California in years.

His mother took the train down on a Thursday. It was the day before Neel and Rebecca were to leave. That night, Neel parked in the driveway but didn't immediately get out of the car. Instead, he switched on the interior light, opened his briefcase, and took out two sheets of paper. The headers marked each sheet as top secret. The documents bore time stamps demonstrating that Neel had printed them within the span of a few minutes earlier that evening. One printout showed a log of Ibn Muhammed al-Punjabi's progression through the national threat matrix. The last row of the log noted that "FC-PDD"—Neel himself, the Freedom Center's principal deputy director—had removed Ibn Muhammed from the threat matrix three weeks earlier. The second sheet showed an index of files relating to Ibn Muhammed's case uploaded by the FBI to the cross-agency intelligence register. The most recent entry on that index was an analyst's update to her summary of the investigation, dated April 30, 2009. The index listed the case as open.

Neel took photographs of each page with his phone camera. Then he toggled the video function and trained the camera on himself. He stated his name and title. He said he had been coerced by two men—an officer in the CIA's Senior Intelligence Service, and a White House advisor—into removing a watch-listed subject from the national threat matrix. Those two men intended to send operatives to murder Ibn Muhammed in Brooklyn. The killing would be the test case of a program to assassinate suspected terrorists, terrorist sympathizers, and other undesirables within the American Muslim community. As of that night, said Neel, May 28, 2009, and as evidenced by the index of FBI files he had just photographed, an investigation of Ibn Muhammed remained open, and the subject was still alive.

Neel stopped the recording. He played the video once for himself. Then he took a zip drive out of his shirt pocket and attached it to his phone. He copied the two images and one video from phone to drive, deleted the three original files from his phone, returned the drive to his shirt pocket, and stepped out.

He walked to the compost bin behind his wife's vegetable garden. A full moon shone above the yellow street lamps. He lifted the cover from the bin. A rich, strangely sweet scent rose to his nostrils. Neel picked up the small shovel that lay beside the bin. He dug into the heap of decaying scraps, peels, newsprint, and coffee grounds. The worms he uncovered arced away from the blade, toward the safety of the dark. Neel put the shovel down, opened his briefcase, removed the two classified printouts he'd photographed, and tore them into pieces over the hole he'd made. Then he picked up the shovel and filled the hole. He covered the bin, took up his briefcase, and walked to the back door. The lights were on in the kitchen but not upstairs.

He checked his watch when he entered the house. It was a few minutes after ten. He put his briefcase down in the kitchen before he went to the living room. His mother was sitting on the couch with needles and yarn in her lap. He asked her not to get up. She'd almost finished knitting a blanket for Serena, she said, as he leaned down to give her a hug. The blanket would match the one she'd knitted for Maya the year before. A cup of masala chai and a plate of the fennel seeds she chewed at night, to help with digestion, sat on the side table. She was wearing pants and a sweater instead of one of the salwar kameezes she usually chose.

He loosened his tie, said he was happy to see her, and that he'd like to talk with her awhile. But first he went back to the kitchen to pour a glass of bourbon.

She peered at him over her reading glasses when he returned. "The best thing about Papaji is that he doesn't drink," she said. Her long black hair showed no gray. She had been dyeing it for years.

He said the whiskey helped him sleep.

"I've always thought you should have been a bit stupider in life," she said.

Neel laughed. "That's a random thing to say."

"You might have done accounting like Papaji instead of this late-night government business. Papaji made good money. You could have taken his clients when he retired. It's easy work, nine to four, ten to four, except one-two months at tax time. I would have helped in the office. Or you could have been a city engineer like Tejinder's son or a dentist or doctor. Those are good jobs. We would have introduced you to a Punjabi girl and you would have stayed in Paramus and been happy. Instead you live in a far-far place and we don't see our granddaughters." She put her knitting down, lifted a bowl from the side table, and spat out some seeds. "It's not good to be so ambitious."

"If I'd married someone else, I wouldn't have Maya and Serena now."

"There would be different children. You might have had a son. But I said to Papaji before I came down that it's time for you to grow up. You made your choices. All this moping and doping afterward is wrong."

Neel looked at her in astonishment. He'd always thought of his mother as a brittle, frightened woman, who'd been silenced by a village childhood and the hardships of immigration, but here she was speaking with the full weight of her sixty-two years. From what Neel could discern on the telephone, his father, at seventy-seven, was in frail health. Perhaps his mother was gaining in confidence as her husband faded.

She raised her palm before Neel could reply.

"Anha kuttha hirana magar," she said. She took off her reading glasses and put them on the side table. "Samajanha?" She was asking if he understood.

He shook his head. "Probably some village nonsense."

"No need to be rude. I said you're a blind dog chasing the deer. You'll never catch this thing you're after, whatever it is. You must learn to be happy, no matter the circumstances. Look at me, I'm happy. Papaji is old, but he's happy. In Paramus we have a car, washing machine, dishwasher. When I was a girl I couldn't imagine this life. I made buffalo patties for the oven with my bare hands."

"You packed shit. I know."

"There was no wood, no gas. The girls went to the field or the animal pens with baskets to pick up the waste. This was our main job. Make bricks out of dung, line the bricks against the walls to dry, burn them in the oven. The roti tasted of it. You never got the smell off your hands."

"To Punjab," said Neel. He raised his glass.

"Don't be funny," his mother said. She inserted another pinch of fennel seeds into her cheek. "And you, don't you have salt? Don't your daughters drink milk? Look at this house. Expensive cars up-down the street. You think I don't know what houses like this cost? Your father-in-law is a big man. Can't you look on the bright side?"

"Jesus, Mom. You've said more to me tonight than in the past five years combined. I'm happy you have a washing machine. It's good to hear that you and Dad are happy. But that's today. I haven't forgotten that Papaji was irritable all the time when I was a boy and that we were afraid of him and that the three of us never talked to one another about anything."

She spoke again in Punjabi. This boy is forty years old and still angry at his papa, she said. She spat her seeds into the bowl.

"Was he a good father, Mom? Is he a good man? I don't know." He swallowed whiskey.

"He would chew the pieces of mutton before he put them in your mouth. When his friends came over, those drinkers, he held you on his lap and gave you peanuts and the two of you sipped his one beer together. He went to all your running races. He didn't understand baseball, but he still left the office to watch you play. He was proud of you."

"He always thought I'd lose," said Neel. "He told me I'd squander my gifts. I was a tragic fellow, he said, like Hamlet."

"He paid for Columbia when all the other boys and girls were going to Rutgers or Trenton State. He went to the temple to tell everyone when you joined the Navy. He kept the picture of you in a white uniform in his office."

"You know what he asked me? 'Why do you sit behind the pilot, how come you're the bloody passenger after all that training?'"

"He was making a joke, son. That's how he shows his love."

"The last time I visited, I went for a walk with him in the neighborhood and it all came back—Paramus, school, home, all of it. I stopped right there on the street and looked him up and down. I said it was all so goddamn hard when I was a kid. Why did he have to be such a dick, on top of everything else?"

"You need to respect your Papaji, even if you think you've gone past him. Life was hard for everyone back then." There were tears in her eyes.

"So we're standing on the street. He smiles, puts his hand on my arm. 'I sleep well at night,' he says." Neel's voice cracked. He swallowed a mouthful of whiskey. "No one fucking sleeps well, Mom."

"Neel, your language." She wiped her sleeve across her eyes. "Why are you like this?"

Neel suddenly felt very tired. "I am who I am, Mom. New Jersey made me, you guys made me. And now I've put my own cherry on top."

"I don't know what that means."

"I've had a rough couple of months at work. Look, if I don't move now, I'm going to pass out on the couch."

"Leave your glass. I'll clean up."

He stood to give her a hug. "Sat sri akal-ji," he said. "Do you have everything you need?"

"Sat sri akal, son." She picked up her knitting. "The girls are very nice. Rebecca has done a good job. I'll teach them to sing a shahbad this weekend."

"Good night," he said.

THIRTY-SEVEN

. . .

IBN MUHAMMED'S MOTHER had lived in a world of omens. She brooded on the tremor in her left eyelid, a strange silence at dawn, the feral cat sitting on the porch with its back to the house. His father, the scientist, used to laugh. But now Ibn Muhammed's own mind was unquiet. His phantom eye burned in its socket. His feet bled in his socks. A foul smell lingered in his apartment. Trouble was coming. He searched the faces of men he passed on the street. He held his breath when he unlocked the door to the masjid. Daily he whispered the du'a his mother had favored. Allahummak finni'him bimaa shi'ta. O Allah, suffice me against them however you wish.

One afternoon he came home to find the light on in his bedroom, though he'd turned it off before he left. The same thing happened the next day and the day after that. Finally, on a Friday morning, he duct-taped the switch. When he returned that evening, the tape remained on the switch and the light was still off, but water was running from the bathroom taps. It wasn't djinns who were tormenting him.

———

He searched the online classifieds for a used car. A man in Midwood offered a nine-year-old Toyota for eleven thousand dollars. The car had new tires and a service record. But couldn't they watch him just as easily—or even more easily—if he tried to drive away? And where would he go? Chicago? Did Faisal want him there? Could he drive to Canada? Was Canada safe? Wouldn't the Canadians deport him when they wished? He didn't buy the car.

Brooklyn was expensive, even for a man who bought nothing. He wasn't at the end of his money, but he could see the end. He paid rent on his apartment and a monthly lease on the storefront mosque. He'd already repaid the four years of loans he took out to go to Syracuse. He ate, he gave alms. By late spring, the Syrian and his weekly donation had disappeared. The Pakistani dishwasher, who had pledged Ibn Muhammed his eternal brotherhood, disappeared too.

When Ibn Muhammed spoke on the phone to Faisal, his real brother, asking if he wished to donate to the Masjid-e-Shuhuda, Faisal shouted at him.

"I won't help you, Manny, until you stop wasting your life."

"My name is Ibn Muhammed al-Punjabi."

"You'll bring the FBI to my house."

"And you, you're not wasting your life?" asked Ibn Muhammed. "You have no trade. There's no honor in your wealth. You're a vulture, a usurer. Mamaji would have been ashamed of you."

Faisal hung up.

If no one came, if no one prayed, was the masjid still a masjid? In truth, he liked solitude. There were moments, when he leaned on the cushions between the pale-blue walls, while the ceiling fan moved warm air over his face, that love transported him. Then Allah was as close as his own breath. Ibn Muhammed had found what the great Sufis promised he would find. From Khusrau: *Come, beloved, that I may hold on to this life*. Ibn Muhammed inscribed the sentiments into his own poems, in English and an artless Punjabi. From Bulleh Shah: *I must run, for my beloved calls me*.

If he was half blind, weren't the others fully blind? If Allah wasn't in the mosque or the book, could Ibn Muhammed find him in the rhythms of his own life? In the quiet of the storefront masjid he had become a different man. When, in months or a year, he gave up the lease, when he exchanged his unhemmed white pants for jeans, when he cut his beard and turned his gray-green eye back to the world, he wanted the calmness to remain.

He would bear witness to beauty. He would help others. He'd return to his studies, but at Brooklyn College, not Syracuse. He would renounce business and instead train to be a teacher or a nurse. He had learned patience. If the watchers released him, he would tell a different tale to the world.

On the morning of Friday, May 29, on the Jummah, he saw a Ford sedan parked at the red-painted curb outside the masjid. A bearded, well-muscled man sat inside. The Ford was still at the curb when Ibn Muhammed left at noon to buy a sandwich. On his return, he walked around to the driver's side. He knocked twice on the glass. The man lowered the window. He wore aviator sunglasses and a golf shirt: his appearance was a parody. Ibn Muhammed smiled as he offered the man his testimony: "There is no God but God, and Muhammed is his messenger." "Fuck off," the man replied. Ibn Muhammed warned him that he couldn't park in a red zone. The man raised the window.

Ibn Muhammed went into the masjid. He tasted bitter almonds on his tongue. The watchers wanted him to be afraid. He whispered a prayer. Inna lillahi wa inna ilayhi raji'un. To Allah we belong and to him we shall return.

· · ·

THIRTY-EIGHT

THEIR FLIGHT LANDED on a Friday night. They picked up the rental car Rebecca had reserved, drove downtown, checked into their hotel. They ate a light dinner in the ground-floor restaurant. Back upstairs, they took quick turns in the shower. It was long past midnight in the East. They slept.

Rebecca raised the blackout blinds early the next morning. Light filled the room but, eighteen floors above the street, the windows blocked all sound. Neel gazed at his wife. He'd awakened to a new feeling. A continent separated him from Agent Miller, the priest, Jones, Ibn Muhammed—all those who haunted him. He had no weekend duties— he didn't have to make breakfast or take his daughters to the park or pool. For the next two days he would live with Rebecca in the sun.

He tugged on Rebecca's arm as she walked past the bed. It had been weeks since they'd made love.

"No way," she said. "Get dressed. We're going out."

They drove up Sunset to Silver Lake, stopped for coffee and pastries, walked around the reservoir, looked up at the mountains in the famous light. Later they returned to the hotel to shower and change. They ate street tacos, browsed the galleries of the Arts District, stayed on to eat at a restaurant where Rebecca had booked a table. All day they were gentle with each other. They moved among attractive people, in glorious weather. But although Neel never looked at his phone, though he smiled, held his wife's hand, spoke quietly to her—though any observer would have said he looked as tranquil and pleased as any other visitor with money to spend—he couldn't set aside the suspicion that he was an actor playing a role. What's more, he sensed that Rebecca was playing a role as well—playing beautifully, perhaps, but playing all the same. Even after they drank martinis and wine at the restaurant, ate risotto and lamb chops, shared a slice of chocolate cake over shots of Drambuie, and then returned, mellow now with liquor, to the hotel, he felt he was an imposter. There was always a sliver near his heart. For the hours turn, darkness falls, and warmth fades. Conscience and crime outlast a change in the weather.

He woke at one A.M. to a sour smell. The blinds were up, the curtains open. A yellow moon hung at the window. Rebecca sat in bed beside him, watching television.

He put his hand on her thigh. The sheets were cold.

She glanced across. "We drank too much," she said. "My head hurts. I'm waiting for the ibuprofen to kick in."

Neel raised himself to his elbows. He looked at the screen. Rebecca had landed on an interview program on BBC World. The host, a middle-aged white man Neel vaguely recognized, was speaking with a bearded guest in his early thirties. Neel watched in silence for a few minutes. The guest had an arresting presence. Neel thought of a marble Hercules he'd once seen at the Metropolitan Museum. It wasn't only the curls in the guest's hair and beard, his Greek nose, and broad chest. There was something vacant, even statuary, in his expression, though he spoke in gentle tones. He had a British accent but not, to Neel's ear, an upper-class one. He told the host that he went to Afghanistan to volunteer for an Islamic charity in the summer of 2002. The charity was delivering blankets and medicine to poor villagers, he said. Back home, in the Midlands, he'd been studying to become a nurse. He was in Afghanistan for two weeks before local militiamen kidnapped him and turned him over to American operatives.

"The Americans did this to me," the guest said, pointing to his left eye. A caption appeared at the bottom of the screen: "FAWAD BASRA RECOUNTS ABUSE IN AMERICAN CUSTODY."

Now Neel identified what was uncanny in his expression. One of the guest's eyelids was frozen in a half-lowered position. An entire region of his face seemed to be paralyzed.

"Does your eye always weep, Mr. Basra?" asked the host.

"I can't stop the water. I'm blind on this side." Basra waved his hand in the air. His nose was not quite in the center of his face. Faint pink scars crossed his forehead. He said the CIA and the U.S. military imprisoned him for three years, in Afghanistan and Guantánamo, before his release.

"Were you ever charged with a crime?"

Basra shook his head. "They did this to me," he repeated. He wiped his cheek with a handkerchief.

"What happened exactly?"

"A guard put his thumb into my eye. No reason. I wasn't under interrogation. He brought me my supper. Usually, they put the tray through a slot in the bars, but this time he unlocked the cell door and came in. I was hungry. They didn't feed us enough. I shuffled across the cell, in my shackles, for the food. Then, without warning, the guard grabbed the back of my head with one hand and pushed under my eyelid with the thumb of his other hand. I screamed but he wouldn't stop. The force was incredible. It felt like he was trying to fit his whole hand into my brain."

"Monstrous," said the interviewer. "What happened next?"

"Nothing. I collapsed on the ground. The guard left. No one came. When I got up, I couldn't see out of this eye."

"Did a doctor examine you?"

"Later. But not my eye. He wanted to make sure I was strong enough to withstand the torture."

"This was in Afghanistan? At what we now know was Bagram Air Base?"

"Yes. They punched me, choked me, broke my nose, dislocated my shoulder. They dragged me facedown across a concrete floor. They drowned me. They pulled off my wedding ring and threw it away like it was garbage. They put drugs in my food and then, when I was too drowsy to resist, they beat me. Months of this. Now I can't breathe properly. I smell nothing, taste nothing. Sleeping is difficult. I don't like to go outside. My children are afraid of me." He gestured at his face. "They did this to me."

"Americans," said the interviewer.

"The cell had a bucket for a toilet." Basra looked away from the camera. "They gave me a kind of liquid food that went right through. Sometimes they chained me to the wall and I couldn't reach the bucket. So they put me in diapers. Then they chained me up without diapers. I was trapped in my own filth. After a few days they'd use a hose to wash out the cell with freezing water." Basra's voice wavered. "We don't treat animals like this."

"Do you need a minute?"

Basra shook his head. "I was underground. I didn't have clothes. It was cold, dark, like living in a root cellar. They played loud music all the time. It hurt my ears and my head."

"What music?"

"Metal. Men were screaming. It wasn't music. They didn't want me to sleep."

Rebecca shifted so that Neel's hand fell away. She folded her arms over her stomach.

"The guards wore ski masks. They put on rubber gloves and put their fingers into me. My ears, nose, private places. They put tubes into me."

"They tried to take away your human dignity."

"Later, in Guantánamo, I saw them beat children and old men. You go crazy in these conditions. You forget who you are. When they give you a shirt or a blanket or the Quran or a few pieces of toilet paper or a bar of soap you thank them as if they are angels."

"You mention the infamous prison camp at Guantánamo Bay. Did your conditions improve after you were flown there from Afghanistan?"

"Of course not," said Basra.

"The British government has paid you compensation, is that correct? For its failure to get you home sooner? For its failure to ensure that its ally, the United States, safeguarded your basic human rights?"

"Yes. I need the money because I cannot study or work. My head isn't right."

"But the Americans haven't paid you."

"No."

"Has the American government apologized?"

"Never." Basra ran his hand down his long, mournful face. "They did this to me."

Neel reached for the remote, which lay on the bed between them. He switched off the television, turned on the bedside lamp, and rubbed his forehead. "It's the middle of the night," he said.

"Neel, that man is broken."

"Yes?"

"People you work with gave the orders."

Neel sat up. "Is this really the right time to talk about the treatment of detainees during the Bush administration?"

She lifted the glass of water from her nightstand and drank half of it. She offered the rest to Neel. He drank.

She waited until he put the empty glass down on the opposite nightstand. "We mutilated him."

"It was all before my time. Rebecca, we talked this through after I interviewed for the job. I joined the Freedom Center to push our antiterrorist policy in a different direction."

"Where's the justice for him? We haven't made amends, paid reparations, held anyone to account. You're in a position to do something, Neel. You talk about gathering power and influence. Why don't you speak to the director about Basra? Or bring his case to the White House?"

"I don't even know who he is."

She put her hands on her head. "What are we doing here?" she whispered.

"Basra would have gone straight onto the no-fly list after we released him from Guantánamo. That's standard. He's a threat to the United States by definition. Even if he was a pacifist before we detained him, he has reason to harm us now. Maybe he wants revenge for the torture. Maybe some of the Saudis he met in the prison camp radicalized him. Point is, he's a suspect for life. We can't offer him money or an apology or anything like that. Can you imagine how that would go over in Congress? We've built a culture of loyalty in the intelligence community to our operatives on the ground. We can't let outsiders paint the soldiers and CIA officers and contractors who laid hands on these guys as sadists. They were following orders. You don't hang them out to dry."

"Have you forgotten they're hanging you out to dry? You're under investigation."

He sighed. "I told you I took steps to protect myself. The investigation will end."

Rebecca pulled her robe tighter around her chest. "It's after midnight. I drank because on our anniversary dinner I wanted to be where you were. Now I'm awake and I'm too tired and empty to think up a new story to tell myself. I'm seeing with clear eyes, Neel. There's no silver lining to your work, no higher purpose, no reform that matters. You're part of a machine that breaks bodies and souls."

Neel stood up. "I don't want to condescend to you, Rebecca, but you're being dramatic. We're both tired. Let's talk this through in the morning." He walked to the bathroom.

When he came back, Rebecca told him to leave the light on. "I'm not saying we had a perfect life before you joined the Freedom Center. But we had the girls, a beautiful house to raise them in, no real worries about money. I loved my work. Were you so unhappy?"

"Yes," he said.

She kept speaking through her tears. "Six months later a journalist is publishing a story about how you directed an attack that killed women and children in Pakistan. How did that happen? Don't you have cameras on your drones that show every detail on the ground? Did your people even look before they fired?" She wiped her eyes with her sleeve. "We're in a horror movie."

Neel sat on the edge of the mattress with his back to her. "We're all a part of this machine, as you call it." There was an edge in his voice. "I don't see you marching in the streets. Removing myself will do nothing. At least while I'm there I can do the job with honor."

"You've worked wonders so far."

He turned to her. "I feel terrible about every civilian death. But we've made the decision as a nation to send the soldiers and drop the bombs. We can't know everything before we pull the trigger."

"Listen to yourself, Neel. You're parroting an insane philosophy. It's all clichés and lies. Stop it. Save yourself. Leave the Freedom Center."

"I can't."

"Can't or won't?"

"I'm exposed. My options are limited."

She was silent for a minute. Then she asked a question in a softer voice: "Are mine?"

Neel looked at her from across the bed.

"It's not the Middle Ages. We're not living in the Punjabi villages you talk about. I can choose something different."

"We have time," said Neel. "We have years."

"I'm tired of being afraid. I'm tired of loneliness. I want friendship, laughter, passion. I want real life."

"Well," he said, after a pause. "I'm glad you told me."

He felt old as he drank his glass and stood and walked to the bathroom. He could think of nothing to say. When he came back Rebecca was lying down. The tension had disappeared from her face. She said good night to him. He switched off the lamp, put his head to the pillow, and waited for sleep.

THIRTY-NINE

THEY WOKE LATE in the aftermath, ordered coffee and croissants, spoke carefully to each other in bed. They put on their bathing suits after breakfast. Neel helped Rebecca with the sunscreen but used a light touch on her shoulders and back.

Rebecca called home. She switched on the phone's speaker. Maya said they'd been working in the garden with their grandmother. For Saturday's dinner they'd eaten butter chicken with chapatis. Their grandmother told them it had been Neel's favorite meal when he was a boy.

Neel stood at the window. He said little but before Rebecca ended the call he asked her to give the girls his love.

At noon, the traffic moved slowly on the Santa Monica Freeway. A breeze swayed the palms. Through the windshield, the sun pressed on Neel's eyelids like a drug. Rebecca slept.

South of Malibu, the air tasted of salt. They spread their towels on the sand. They undressed, lay on their backs. Neel covered his face with his baseball cap. When he sat up, half an hour later, Rebecca was gone. He stood, looked around. Eventually he saw her in the bay. She was treading water beyond the break, with her back to shore, while she looked out at the Pacific. There were cliffs to the east, ships on the horizon. She was safe, but the distance between them might as well have been miles.

By then the beach had grown more crowded. Children played at the water's edge. Shirtless men and women jogged down the sand. Families picnicked under tents and umbrellas. Everyone was talking and laughing, or dancing to music Neel could hardly hear over the waves and wind. He watched with his arms crossed. In his mind the holiday was over.

They drove back to the hotel late in the afternoon. Rebecca would fly to D.C. on the red-eye. Neel would spend a night alone in the hotel. Then, on Monday morning, he'd leave for Utah on official business.

He rested his right hand on Rebecca's leg. She didn't acknowledge him but neither did she push him away.

Rebecca wanted a light dinner in the room. She ordered salad. He asked for chicken soup and a bottle of beer. They showered separately. Her flight wouldn't leave until eleven but she was ready by eight.

The traffic had disappeared from the highways. At the airport, she held him tightly as she said goodbye. He watched her walk down the curb and through the sliding doors into the terminal. He realized, when she was gone, that they'd said almost nothing to each other that day.

Back in the hotel room, he watched baseball highlights in bed. His mind was elsewhere. He ranged from the BBC interview he'd watched with Rebecca to his own memories, his own dark places.

The Navy had sent him to SERE School before he ever flew a combat mission. The acronym stood for Survival, Evasion, Resistance, Escape. All airmen had to pass the course. They had to show that they wouldn't break down under interrogation—that they wouldn't disgrace the Navy if they fell into enemy hands.

One morning the trainers herded them into a van and drove out from their base near San Diego. They went deep into the Mojave. They stepped out of the van at a checkpoint on a dirt road. A man slapped Neel in the face.

"You're not in California now, comrade," he said, in a Russian accent.

Neel was so stunned that he laughed. The man punched him in the stomach. Neel fell to the ground.

The Russians, the pretend Russians, took the trainees to a bunker. They made them undress, squat, cough. Neel had to lift his testicles while one of his captors ran his gloved fingers beneath.

"Your asshole stinks, motherfucker," the man said.

A woman stood watching all this. The captors lined the prisoners up in front of her. She pointed at Neel.

"Are you cold, brown boy?" she asked. "Look at your little dick."

For ten days they told the candidates when to stand, squat, sit. They beat and choked them, tied them down, gagged them and poured water on their faces. They left them uncovered in the desert sun. By the second day the only things Neel cared about were shade, food, sleep, and the toilet. Though at some level he remembered he was in training, the experience had become real. His suffering was real. A week in, after one of the guards threatened to drown him, Neel revealed information he'd been instructed not to disclose. The trainers gave him a below-average score but not a disastrous one. He still received an officer's commission. All the same, he was a different man on the other side. From then on he understood that the opposite of power wasn't weakness but fear, that there was no more intimate relationship than that of interrogator and prisoner, and that in captivity one's own body became a wellspring of pain. He promised himself that he would never again submit to such a regime. He would not be a victim.

FORTY

ON MONDAY, NEEL weaved through the morning crowd at LAX. Business travelers moved with purpose. Others, young and old, ambled through the terminal in pajamas or sweatpants. Neel had a pass for the security checkpoint but there was no skipping the line at the coffee counter. Babies cried. The escalators hummed. The air smelled of disinfectant.

He sat in one of the last free chairs at his gate. He was sipping coffee when his phone rang. Vanderhoof's name appeared on the screen.

"Good morning," answered Neel. "How's the baby?"

"Where are you?" asked Vanderhoof. "Are you watching CNN?"

Neel glanced over his shoulder. A monitor mounted to the ceiling displayed a test pattern. There were no other screens in sight.

Vanderhoof didn't wait for Neel to respond. "An hour ago a domestic terrorist attacked a recruiting post in Little Rock. He shot two soldiers. One's dead, the other's wounded. The wounded man will survive. It could have been worse. Local police chased down the attacker's SUV a few miles from the post. He surrendered without a fight. I can't say too much on my cell but the guy had an arsenal in the car. Rifles, handguns, six hundred rounds. He was carrying a list of all the synagogues and military buildings in the region."

"Who is he?"

Vanderhoof said a name that Neel vaguely recognized. "An American kid, born black and Baptist in Memphis, converted to Islam as a teenager. Spent sixteen months teaching English in Yemen, radicalized, married a local girl. We let him fly back to the U.S. in January but had him watch-listed as a potential VERMIN. I mentioned him in a briefing at the Center. Remember?"

"Just about."

"Liar. You don't pay attention unless we're talking about the Pakistani tribal regions. The FBI interviewed the guy at Kennedy on his return from Yemen, sent the Joint Terrorism Task Force to visit him in Memphis, but in the end let him walk."

"So it's not on us."

"We could have done more. You have a watch-listed suspect buying arms, looking at all the wrong things on the web. Someone's going to ask why we didn't move him into a higher tier of the threat matrix. The silver lining is, having been out on paternity leave, I should escape the taint of your failure."

"Thanks, Jon."

"I'm driving to the Center now. Had another week booked for family time but fuck it, I'm done. The little guy doesn't care. He's a breast man."

"Should I come back to D.C.?"

"No. Cone said for you to stick to the program. But your afternoon itinerary is canceled. It's not a day to meet and greet. Monica's delaying her flight out. She'll meet you in Utah tomorrow. You're a free man. Have yourself a wild night in Salt Lake City. Let me know what happens in a Mormon strip club."

Neel returned his phone to his pocket. He felt disquiet more than guilt. The suspect had been under FBI surveillance. The Bureau bore the greater part of the blame. But if someone—the priest, a congressman, Cone himself—needed another scapegoat, Neel was vulnerable. His father had always urged him to stand strong before the world. He should never show weakness in front of whites, never wince, never falter. Everyone kicks at a broken branch, his father said.

A garbled announcement sounded over the public address system. Neel rubbed his palm on his forehead. He drank more coffee. Well, he reflected, a broken branch was also a club. There were limits to metaphor but he wasn't at the end. He knew things that made him dangerous. He would be ruthless and careful in the days to come.

The flight was delayed. The passengers boarded an hour late, then waited another hour on the runway. Finally they took off. It was ninety minutes to Salt Lake City. Brown hills and canyons gave way to desert, then steep, dark ranges.

They arrived at two P.M. Neel's first impression on getting off the plane was that he'd traveled to another country. Large, sandy-haired people spoke in quiet voices. There was space in the terminal. Every surface gleamed in the mountain light.

A man came running down the hall. He shouted Neel's name. He was black, older, heavyset. Neel recognized him, though he'd forgotten his name. They'd spoken on the street outside the priest's salon six months earlier.

"Sorry I'm late," the man said, when he reached Neel. Sweat glistened on his bald head. "I was tracking your flight. Knew you were delayed, thought I had time. Great to see you again."

"Great to see you too. What a surprise."

"Louie Horn, if you need a reminder. Special projects administrator at the Massive Data Repository. Remember to call me Horn. When I saw your name on the itinerary I volunteered to be your chaperone." He was panting. "I have a pass," he said, pointing at the lanyard around his neck, "but I had a hard time with airport security."

"Been there," said Neel, as they shook hands.

"All right," said Horn. "I bet you have."

They walked out together. The sky was a painted ceiling. Heat rose in waves from the blacktop.

Horn led Neel to a neon-orange Dodge Challenger. It had racing stripes and an oversized hood scoop.

"I like your style," said Neel.

They got in. Horn kept his seat reclined at a spectacular angle. He turned the ignition, put the air conditioner on at full blast, and switched off the radio. Soon they were past the toll gate and onto the highway, heading south through low-slung American sprawl: car dealerships, warehouses, chain restaurants. Mountains loomed on both horizons.

"Welcome to God's country. If you're a Mormon, which I'm not."

"I'm a heathen myself," said Neel.

"You're here for what, two, three days? That's enough time for the Mormons to work on you. They're still working on me. But I tell them I can't accept the tenets of their faith. It's not the ban on fornication. I'm a middle-aged black man in Utah, so celibacy is a given. I could consider giving up alcohol one day in the distant future. I can wear the funny underwear. Maybe I can even find it within myself to forgive the church for its history of racism. But Brigham Young doesn't want me to drink coffee? Man, forget it. Keep the keys to your celestial kingdom."

Neel was laughing. "No way I can work without coffee."

"Hell no."

The lanes were wide, the traffic light. Horn powered the Dodge over the flat, fast miles.

He began to talk about the NSA's new storage facility—the Massive Data Repository, or MADAR. ("Pronounced 'madder,'" said Horn, "not 'may-dar.'") The place was monstrous in scale. "You're talking two million square feet of floor space. A million gallons of water pumped in daily to cool the servers. On a plateau in the goddamn desert. And this is just phase one." Horn had retired from the NSA before MADAR opened. He'd planned to go to Silicon Valley, but the agency offered to hire him back as a private contractor at three times his former salary. He'd written the NSA's key protocols for managing big data back at Fort Meade. "If you want to get paid, you make yourself indispensable."

"My salary is dog shit," said Neel. "What does that tell you?"

"Come on, man. They're curious about you at MADAR. Mormons and non-Mormons both. More than one person has asked me what the Freedom Center wants from us. I know the official visit is canceled today because of that Little Rock nutcase but I can take you now. Answer your questions off the record. Otherwise we start up at eight thirty tomorrow morning."

"I'm good," said Neel. "I'll get something to eat, have an early night."

The city petered out. Eventually, Horn turned down an off-ramp. In the distance, a column of dust rose into the otherwise empty sky.

"What's that?" asked Neel.

"Couldn't tell you. Dust storm, sandstorm? I live indoors. I've been in Utah six months and I still don't understand the weather. I'm from L.A. originally."

"That's God's real country."

"Sometimes. When I was coming up we had the LAPD yelling at us to get the fuck off the street."

Horn pulled into the parking lot of a budget hotel. "This is your place. I don't think the Government Accountability Office is going to have a problem with your expense claim. We'll get a steak after you check in."

Neel asked him not to bother but Horn said he could bill a good meal now that he was a contractor. "Live a little, sir, forget that per diem. But no rush. It's early. Take a shower, change your shirt. I have the radio for company." He tapped the dashboard.

Neel got out. He lifted his bag from the trunk. A grittiness stung his eyes. He walked to the front desk through the strange, dry heat.

They put him in a room on the ground floor, facing the parking lot. He took a shower but didn't shave. He walked out of the bathroom with a towel wrapped around his waist. When he peered through the curtains, he could see the orange Dodge in the lot, though Horn disappeared behind the window tint. He dressed quickly. Before he went out, he sent Rebecca a text telling her he'd arrived safely in Utah. He hadn't heard from her since she'd left Los Angeles. Now, at five thirty in D.C., she would be busy with the girls. Still, her silence was not a good sign.

The pavement bristled with heat. Beyond the parking lot, power lines hummed over the sidewalk. Horn unlocked the doors. Neel got in.

"You smell good," said Horn. "I forgot to ask earlier. You're not a Hindu or some other type of vegetarian?"

Neel shook his head.

"Let's get that meat."

It was a short drive to the restaurant. It was too early for dinner, even by exurban standards, but pickup trucks and oversized SUVs filled the parking lot.

"Thirsty?" said Horn, holding Neel's gaze as they walked to the entrance.

"Hungry," said Neel. He hadn't eaten that day. "But I could have a drink too."

Inside was raw brightness: hanging lamps at each table, floor lights, ceiling lights. A hostess with white-blond hair and heavy makeup led them to their booth. A family of seven—grandparents, a mother and father who didn't look much older than their teenaged daughter, and a pair of bowl-haired toddlers—sat across the aisle. A waitress filled the family's glasses from a pitcher of fruit punch. The grandmother caught Neel's eye as he slid into his seat. She smiled at him.

"Good?" said Horn.

"Very wholesome."

Children's voices caromed off the tiles.

"Family hour," said Horn. "Don't worry. I've got something strong for later."

They ordered T-bones, medium rare, sides of creamed spinach and macaroni, and two pints of draft beer. The food came in a rush. It was all glazed, all sweet. The beer tasted like cold tea.

They talked about their families, the places they'd lived, and the lost days of their youth, or rather, Horn talked about those things while Neel ate. Horn had married in his twenties. It didn't last. All he had from that time was a shoebox filled with photos of his ex-wife. He looked at the pictures when he couldn't sleep. She had been pretty, Horn said, and a brilliant software engineer. "She wrote perfect, gleaming blocks of code—blocks that were like jewelry laid out in a glass case. Or poems from the Tang dynasty."

"Come again?"

"I'm talking about Li Po—also known as Li Bai—Du Fu, Wang Wei, all those Chinese cats." Horn wiped his lips with his napkin and straightened himself in his chair. "'We sit together, the mountain and me, until only the mountain remains.' That's for you, since you're the humanist type."

Neel peered at Horn.

"My ex-wife was always pushing me to work harder, to get deep into the algorithms. She told me to code from the inside, as if I was the machine. That's how the visionaries do it, she said. Think of Charlie Parker on the alto sax. He fused himself with the instrument, you see? Actually, I didn't understand what she meant. But she was one of the great talkers, she was an orator, so I never asked her to explain herself. The problem now is I can't remember what she sounded like. Her voice is gone. Smoke in the wind. It's driving me crazy. . . . I see everything, how she sat up in bed in her green pajamas, her brown eyes and little nose and black-framed glasses, the book on her lap. But when she speaks she sounds like someone else—like a TV actress. Then I think, Damn, dude, is any of the stuff in my head real? Did she have those eyes and that nose and that smile? Or did my subconscious just invent the details?" He rapped his knuckles on the side of his head. "I'm trippin'."

"Which actress?"

"Say what?"

"Which actress does she sound like?"

"Lisa Bonet, from the *Cosby Show* years."

Neel smiled.

"That girl was bad. Damn." Horn gave a little shake of his head. "But I only hear Lisa Bonet late at night. If I'm thinking about my ex in the afternoon, the voice that comes out is more like Mrs. Cosby. You know, Phylicia Rashad."

Neel laughed.

"She figured out pretty quickly I was a lost cause. Got sauced too often, couldn't code like she did. Lacked the ambition to be great. After the divorce she went to Palo Alto, wrote the bedrock software for a start-up that got bought by Oracle, made like ten million. That's middle-class out there but still. Shit."

"You could call her and hear her voice for real."

"It wouldn't do any good. No one sounds the same on a cellphone as in life. Anyway, she'd never pick up."

"I need another beer." Neel looked around for the waitress. The Mormon grandmother at the next table smiled at him again. It was as if she felt obliged to welcome him to Utah. "I'm not a refugee," said Neel, under his breath.

Horn shook his head. "Beer is water in Utah. Three, four percent alcohol. It has no effect except to make you piss. Don't get another. Like I said, I have a bottle for later." Somehow he'd finished his dinner despite having talked all the while. "Eat up, sir."

Neel worked on his pile of macaroni while Horn described his childhood. He'd been happy when he was a little boy, but in middle school the hard times came. His father died in an accident at the aeronautics plant where he worked on the line. Insurance and a pension paid the bills, but from then on there was no laughter in the house. His mother died of leukemia the year Horn started at Caltech. It was the same cancer that had killed her two older sisters. They'd all grown up in Port Arthur, Texas, a half mile from the largest refinery on the Gulf of Mexico. "Everyone gets cancer down there."

"I'm sorry," said Neel.

"Land of the free," said Horn. He rubbed his hand over his scalp. "You're looking at me funny."

"I'm not."

"Alopecia. All my hair fell out before I finished college."

That was it, Neel realized. Horn wasn't just bald. He had neither eyebrows nor eyelashes. There was no stubble on his chin.

"I look like a big baby, am I right?"

"I wouldn't have noticed."

Horn signaled the waitress for the check. "We'll have a real drink at your hotel. Me, I can't sleep until I've taken down a shot or two."

Horn parked the Dodge in front of Neel's room. The big engine ticked as it cooled beneath the hood scoop. Neel waited at the curb while Horn opened the trunk. Other guests walked from the parking lot to the reception desk or their rooms. None of them looked at Horn and Neel.

It was as if they were embarrassed to acknowledge the two men, or afraid of them.

"Should we call it?" asked Neel. He had to raise his voice against the rumble of trucks on the freeway.

"You serious?" Horn came around the car with a bottle wrapped in a towel. "I have a handle of white whiskey. Not easy to get in Salt Lake City. I keep it in the tire well for special occasions."

"We have that early start tomorrow."

"It's early now. You'll have plenty of time to sleep it off." Horn spoke in a plaintive tone. "At least have one for the road."

Neel unlocked the door. Inside, he gestured at the table and chairs by the window. He brought two clean glasses from the bathroom. His knees touched Horn's beneath the table when he sat. Each man had a leg wedged against the bed.

"They got you in a dollhouse," said Horn. He poured out two generous measures of whiskey. "No matter. See if this puts a shine in your eyes."

The liquor smelled as sharp and green as turpentine. Neel took a sip. It burned his tongue. He put down his glass. His ears were burning too. "Tastes like chili peppers," he said.

"This shit is deep. You drink too much, it'll make you crazy."

Neel took a second, smaller sip of whiskey. "The truth is, I don't have a reason to be here."

"There's always a reason. A higher-up wanted to check a box."

"It's not like I'm going to get in there and fix your code for you. I'm supposed to glad-hand, form relationships, give the tech guys the human touch. Not my strong suit."

Horn raised his glass. "Here's to forming relationships." He swallowed half the liquid in one gulp. He shook his head, wiping his eyes with the back of his hand. "When you see MADAR, you'll understand that America can still do whatever she wants. You talk about your foreign threats, the vanishing technology gap, China in the twenty-first century. Forget it. The future is open. Some sheikh builds an indoor ski resort in Dubai? High-speed trains in Japan, a tower in Kuala Lumpur, the biggest dam the world's ever seen up in the Himalayas? None of those things rate.

What we're doing in the high desert is at the same level as digging the Panama Canal." Horn swallowed the rest of his glass. "Woohoo," he said, smacking his lips. He poured himself another before he continued.

"Technology is not the problem. There may be an occasional blind spot, but for the most part the surveillance state has the access it needs. We have taps in the fiber-optic cable, geostationary satellites in high orbit. We can survey every square mile of inhabited Earth. We've got machines translating municipal reports out of Tehran. You guys asked for a world without secrets and here it is, boom, we delivered."

"But?" said Neel. He turned his glass on the table.

"But you can't engineer your way out of a machine. At some point an actual human has to look at what we've collected. The eternal bottleneck. You have to find the signal in the noise, as they say."

"You could argue there are too many signals. Signals everywhere. That's why we're letting the missiles fly. We need to stamp the signals out."

"Better you than me. I don't want to push that button." Horn finished his second drink and now poured a third. "I'm leaving you behind here," he said, as he added whiskey to Neel's half-filled glass. The neck of the big bottle slipped from his hand, splashing liquor on the table.

"Excuse me," Horn said. He raised himself to a standing crouch, bent his head over the table, and lapped up the spill. When he sat down again, his chin glistened.

Neel watched him without changing his expression. He was already starting to float. He hadn't yet crossed a line, but the critical moment wasn't so far away, either. "I have to slow down," he said.

Horn's nostrils flared. "We're just getting started. You said you have no real business at MADAR. You just need to smile and shake hands tomorrow. None of those NSA dorks have any social skills. They won't notice if you're hungover." He swallowed from his glass. "Do you mind if I change the lighting? Sun's in my eyes."

He stood up, drew the curtains, then walked to the corner to turn on the floor lamp. He returned to his chair. His face was now in shadow.

Neel took another sip. His thoughts drifted. D.C., work, family— they were all so far away.

Horn filled Neel's glass.

"How strong is this whiskey?" asked Neel.

"One hundred and twenty-five proof. Straight moonshine, baby."

"I should add water." Neel chewed his lower lip. He drew his glass close, drank a mouthful. The heat ran to his stomach. He asked Horn to excuse him.

When he stood up, his whole body was burning. The walls rippled as he walked to the bathroom. He closed the door, pissed, washed his hands, and splashed water on his face. A minute later he came back into the room. The scent of whiskey filled his nostrils. Also, the floor was moving. To keep his balance, he rolled his hips, as if he were walking on the carrier deck. Once again his glass was full. It might have been his last chance to avert disaster. His phone vibrated in his pocket. Silencing it, he took his seat.

"It got loud in here for a minute," said Horn. "I heard moaning, creaking. Whoever's next door is basically in the room with us. This is what bothers me. Look at MADAR, on the one hand, and then look at this hotel, ten miles up the road, on the other. The walls here are paper. I want to take the contractor by his ears. Slap him around, tell him, 'Take pride, boy, take pride in your work!'"

Neel cocked his head but heard nothing. "This room smells like an infirmary. This shit"—he picked up his glass—"is lethal."

"You still drinking it, though. Without risk, there's no reward. Pain for gain."

"Your voice is like a river," said Neel.

"What's that about?" said Horn. He smiled, but there was an edge in his voice. "The eternal wisdom of the Negro? *Show Boat*, 'He jes keeps rollin' along,' and all that?"

"No," said Neel, "That's not what I meant. I'm sorry." He closed his eyes. In his mind he saw the river he wanted, a river that had nothing to do with the Mississippi or the wounds of slavery. It ran deep in a desert valley, with sweet, clear water. Huge, hundred-year-old fish drifted beneath the current.

"Ah, you straight," said Horn. "Don't sweat it. You see how it is. I'm alone out here. A man gets his radar up." He poured another measure for himself. "I hope this is okay, but I need to move to the bed. My back is killing me. Old football injury."

He stood, glass in hand, without waiting for Neel to reply. He walked to the other side of the room. He put his drink down on the nightstand. He gathered two pillows, pressed them with one hand to his spine, and, holding his free hand out for balance, lowered himself carefully onto the covers. He kicked off his shoes, kept one foot on the floor, and swung the other onto the bed. He leaned his head against the wall.

"You wonder sometimes if you're a mascot. At Caltech, the NSA, out here in Utah. You think Obama hasn't felt that himself? But we don't have to talk about him. . . . The truth is—you know this, everyone knows this—whites need blacks like Puritans need sin. You can't have virtue without the fallen. Whiteness wouldn't exist without something called blackness. And without whiteness, what are these people?"

"You tell me," said Neel.

"Ordinary human beings facing the void. The same abyss you and me stare into every day. But the struggle to make meaning in a world that views us with contempt—that's a powerful thing. It can lead you to freedom."

"Hate takes a toll, though."

"You don't say. I saw the tension in your face, in your whole body, when I picked you up at the airport. Look how you're putting that whiskey away. You can drink, boy."

"I knew I was in trouble the first time I really got into a bottle," said Neel. "It was a fall night, sophomore year in college. On the fourth or fifth glass, the weight disappeared, poof, like that. I thought, Well, this is what I've been looking for my whole life. I actually wanted to talk to people at a party. I'd found a home."

"Home might kill you."

"You clean up after your family eats dinner on a weekend. You and your wife shared a bottle of wine; well, you drank most of the wine. You're tired, warm—you feel good. Your wife takes your daughters upstairs for their bath. Meanwhile you scrape out the plates, stretch plastic wrap on the leftovers. When you put the bowls in the refrigerator, you see there's a bottle of red vermouth that's been sitting three-quarters full for a month. Maybe you made Manhattans one Saturday night a while back. 'Ah,' you say, 'there you are, old friend.'"

"And you get an idea. I feel you, brother."

"It astonishes me that there are men in this world who've never had the urge to drink that bottle down, on their feet, while their girls are upstairs playing with rubber duckies in the suds."

"It's a rational response to the condition of our lives. Sometimes you want to annihilate yourself. Freud was on it a hundred years ago. *Beyond the Pleasure Principle*."

"I used to know things like that. But I've stopped reading books."

"Brother, that's a mistake," said Horn.

"I thought there was another path for me. I wanted to be part of something beautiful. I'm not talking about an imperial dream or anything like that. Just the idea that I belonged in the service next to all those fresh-faced white dudes. The guys in the squadron had the world at their feet. I wanted that feeling too. To live in *that* country. To be as goddamned American as they were. But putting on a uniform doesn't silence the whisper in your own head. *You're a fraud, a fool, everyone sees who you really are, dothead.*" Neel looked at his glass. "I'm drinking like a camel," he said. "Loose lips."

"You're a man in the wrong time. Like every thinking person in the history of humanity. Take Socrates. He asked the Athenians to consider the welfare of their own souls. How did the Athenians, his countrymen, thank him for that teaching? . . . They sentenced his ass to death."

"You lose me, Horn, when you get into the history of Western thought."

"I'm older than you. I'm trying to tell you what I've learned. Guys like you and me are not going to come out on top. Race is just the beginning. We don't have the arrogance, the entitlement. We think too much. People resent you for your solitude."

"I'm lonely, Horn, but I'm not Socrates."

"The one thing you cannot do is show weakness. Don't bleed in the water. Don't let the bosses play you. Smile, go along, do whatever, but don't forget that you've got hidden strength. I'm talking about *heft*. You have a big nose, thick eyebrows, big eyes. Heavy-lidded now with whiskey but that's all right. You've got a thick chest, big butt. I bet you put on color fast when they leave you in the sun. Some of you Indian cats are Third World as fuck. Let's see you open up your teeth."

Neel stuck his tongue out as far as it could go.

"Hoo boy," said Horn. "You're an animal. Must eat pussy like a motherfucker. Excuse me for saying that. Strictly off the record, sir."

"The thing is, I'm drunk." Neel stood and kicked off his own shoes.

"Bring the whiskey if you're coming my way."

They'd emptied a fair share of the big bottle. Neel passed it to Horn before he dropped onto the covers beside him.

Horn refilled his glass. "To friendship," he said.

He handed the bottle to Neel, who took a swig.

"Do you have them, though?" asked Horn. "Friends?"

"There's a Navy pilot I wouldn't mind seeing again. He lives in Houston. Otherwise, not really. What am I going to do, hit a Nationals game with some guy I know from law school? Leave work early, eat a hot dog, get heartburn? You spend a hundred bucks to check your watch for four hours. What's the point?"

"Friendship with Mormons is out of the question."

"I'm friends with my wife, though," said Neel. "I admire her."

"She doesn't know you."

"One night—this was years ago, when my eldest was a baby—I came home drunk and vomited on the floor. She cleaned that mess at two A.M. Scrubbed the bile and stomach juices and stinking chunks of food right out of the carpet. She's a rock."

"Truth is, I did a little confidential research before you came out."

"How so?"

"I'm not reckless. I wouldn't ask just anyone if he wanted a drink."

"What did you do?" Neel reached for the bottle on the side table and took another sip. "What are you talking about, Horn?"

"You know we collect everything. For my work, I need to audit the data. I have administrator permissions. I can't lie to you. I looked at what you've been up to. Damn, boy, you like 'em thick! Big blondes, Colombianas, sisters." Horn let out a burst of laughter. "Don't worry, I cover my tracks."

"You can't do that, Horn. You need a warrant. I have personal privacy. Apart from the fact that my work is classified. I'm a deputy director."

"I didn't read your emails. Just surveyed your internet search history, cellphone geolocations, that kind of thing. The metadata. Whatever else is happening, any deep state shit and so on, I'm the last person who wants to know." He looked across the bed at Neel. "Pass the bottle."

"Who are you, Horn?"

Horn took a swig. "I'm the keeper of secrets, my friend. Excuse me a minute."

Horn raised himself from the bed and walked into the bathroom.

He was gone for what seemed a long time. Neel caught himself drifting out of consciousness. He shook himself awake. The room rotated slowly around him. A beautiful light shone at the edges of the curtains. He should have been angry with Horn but somehow he couldn't bring himself to care.

When Horn came out of the bathroom, he was carrying his shirt in his hand. His head and chest were wet. He was heavy—his waist sagged—but Neel saw the strength in his arms too.

"I was on fire with that moonshine so I ran the tap to cool off," he said. "Excuse me for this. Excuse my whole performance. I need to lie down for ten minutes before I drive home."

He collapsed onto the bed beside Neel.

"You shook?" Horn said.

"No," said Neel. The whiskey had fixed him to the bed. "For as long as I can remember, I've expected the worst. You know I used to be a track star? My senior year in high school I only lost one time in the quarter mile. That time happened to be the state final. I busted it out of the blocks in lane four, made up the stagger by the end of turn one, flew down the back straight. People were screaming in the grandstand. My teammates were lined up on turn two, losing their shit. I had a nine-, ten-yard lead coming into the homestretch. But my legs turned to water in the final fifty. When that happens everything goes quiet—the crowd, the cheering—everything except the footsteps of the guy running you down. He caught me in the last few strides. I ended up losing by eight hundredths of a second. Afterward my father told me I had defeat written on my soul. I'm still hearing footsteps in my nightmares."

Horn was breathing heavily.

Neel was slipping under as well when an image flashed through his mind. He battled back sleep so the words could rise. "I have this wild idea," he said. "Maybe you can do something for me." Here it was: the moment of inspiration, a fleck of gold in the mire.

"I'm fading here, brother." Horn's eyes had closed.

"Hypothetically speaking. Say there was a guy in the threat matrix. Low level, didn't belong, so I took his name out. Say I did it because someone asked me to. Doesn't matter why. Say I don't want anyone to know what I did. Could you scrub the subject's data from the deep record? Erase him completely on the back end? And erase the fact that I ever looked at him? If you did that, maybe I could offer you something."

"Offer me what, exactly?" Horn opened one eye. It was red with drink. He rolled his head across the pillow to look at Neel.

"What do you need? Money?"

"Man, I have money. More than you got, anyways. What I need can't be bought."

"Tell me."

"Love, family, cardiac health." Horn laughed. "I'm messing with you. Neel, listen to me. There are lines you can't cross. Even if I wasn't worried about spending the rest of my life in federal prison, what you're asking for is impossible. Yes, I could delete the subject's data from the NSA's repository. But other agencies have their own records. I don't manage the FBI servers. Not CIA or the Defense Department either. I can't poke around at the Freedom Center."

"So it can't be done? You can't make that target a phantom, can't erase the connection between us?"

"Not across the whole government."

Neel had been sitting upright but now he leaned back against the headboard.

"Lucky for you," Horn said, "I'm drunk enough that I'll be able to forget our conversation took this particular turn."

"It's nothing. Whiskey talk. Ravings in the madhouse." Neel slid down the mattress. He curled an arm under his head. He resisted a minute longer, but the weight was too much and now the darkness closed.

When he woke, he sensed that many hours had passed. Horn had switched off the floor lamp at some point. He was snoring, though his eyes didn't seem to be entirely shut. Neel rolled onto his side. He looked at the clock and saw, with anguish, that it was three A.M. He turned on the bedside lamp. The bottle, on the opposite nightstand, was close to empty. Neel squeezed Horn's arm to wake him. Then he stood up. He wasn't sober but he was able to walk. He went to the bathroom to wash his face and drink from the tap while Horn stirred.

The room was empty when Neel returned. The front door was open. Horn stood on the narrow strip of grass that separated the parking lot from the walkway.

He turned as Neel came out. His shirt was half buttoned.

"Damn, dude, that was some gangster shit. Straight out of Faulkner. Or that other guy. *The Lost Weekend*."

"Are you okay to drive?"

The wind whipped against the building. Horn dropped to his knees.

"Are you sick?" asked Neel.

Horn had pressed his face to the ground. Now he looked up. "Utah dirt tastes like pussy. It's the salt."

Neel helped Horn to his feet.

"I felt the need," said Horn. "It's been a while since my last trip to Vegas."

"You might be the saddest man I've ever met."

"It's cold in this desert," Horn said.

Neel looked up. Looming on the horizon were the mountains he could sense but, in the darkness, not quite see.

Horn pulled Neel into a hug. "Thank you, brother," he said. "That was a great hang. I'll be back at eight."

"I'm going to need all the coffee in this place," Neel said.

"You're a killer. You'll be all right."

Neel watched Horn get into his orange car. It rumbled to life. Horn drove slowly out of the lot.

The room smelled of hot breath and whiskey. Neel took the bottle to the bathroom to pour what liquor remained down the sink. He brushed his teeth, drank more water, and undressed. He pulled the cover from the bed before climbing into the sheets. When he checked his phone, he saw that Rebecca had sent him a series of text messages earlier in the night:

> The children are asleep. Good luck with work!

> get home safe

> I know you're busy but I miss you

Then, at one in the morning in D.C., hours after she'd ordinarily have gone to bed, she sent a final message:

> I'm sorry. I can't go on. We'll talk when you get home.

He turned out the light, closed his eyes. The whiskey still burned in his throat. He'd met Rebecca when he was twenty-nine and she twenty-six. Now, at forty, he felt centuries older. He was wounded but not shocked by her message. Would their life together really end? He dreaded the tedium of separation: the negotiations, the untangling of their finances, the arrangements they'd have to make for the girls. No, he decided, if she wanted to leave, or wanted him to leave, she could have everything. He would not fight.

Despite the late, terrible hour, it was a long time before he fell asleep.

FORTY-ONE

HORN ARRIVED AT eight, as promised. Neel was waiting at the curb with coffee in a Styrofoam cup. He'd showered on waking but had been too tired to shave. Afterward he'd taken a Danish and an apple from the hotel's breakfast buffet, managing a single bite of each before he threw them out.

Horn lowered the windows. He wore a ballplayer's mirrored sunglasses. They covered half his face.

"I'm too old for this," he said, across the passenger seat. The engine rumbled.

Neel got in.

"I should have gone home after dinner to read Edward Gibbon," said Horn. "I'm on volume two, chapter twenty-four, Julian's expedition against the Persians. Eighteenth-century prose is where it's at, brother." He shrugged. "You all right? You don't look good."

"I was glad I could stand up this morning. A night like that can kill a man."

"I tell you what, I woke to the foulest smell. Couldn't place it. I lay in bed, letting my eyes go round the room. But there was nothing. No vomit, no misplaced shit dribbling out of the laundry basket. Then I realized the vapors were rising from my insides. With every breath I was polluting the atmosphere of my own bedroom. You can't shrug off a stench like that. It's six forty-five. I'm listening to the clock tick off the seconds. I know I'm not going to get anything done at work. I know I won't be able to read tonight. My energy is spent before the day even begins. I decide right there that I no longer want to be a human man. If Satan had appeared at the foot of the bed and offered to transform me into a sea urchin, I would have relinquished my immortal soul. Better to anchor myself to a rock for the rest of my days, waiting for the rising tide, than to live any longer as a Homo sapiens. I'm ninety percent there anyway. Writing code, auditing databases, reading long books, it's all about patience and stillness. You try to forget yourself so that your deeper mind, your reflexive mind as my ex-wife called it, gets to the truth. This is Zen shit. What I'm saying is that my core skills are perfectly suited to life as a spiny, poisonous, mostly stationary echinoderm."

"Horn, I'm not in a position to take this in right now." Neel wiped dried spittle from the corners of his mouth. "What I would appreciate is a few moments of silence."

"Let's go. We'll be as chill as a couple of Trappist monks."

Neel bumped his fist against the fist Horn offered. Then Horn put the car in gear and drove out of the lot. Neel sipped his coffee. He looked at the mountains and the sky.

They left the interstate after fifteen minutes. The exit dropped them onto a two-lane highway with a dirt shoulder. Horn drove another three miles before he turned onto a restricted road that was interrupted, a hundred yards on, by a military checkpoint. Horn and Neel handed their IDs to the young guardsman on duty. He walked into a booth where another guardsman waited. This second soldier made a phone call. Neel stared straight ahead. The horizon rippled. The first guardsman came back out, returned their IDs, and waved them on.

Next they reached a junction without signposts. The road on the right had broken asphalt; the road on the left was new. Horn turned onto the new road. It began to rise, gently at first, then steeply through a set of switchbacks. Neel lowered his window to feel the air on his face. Other cars and trucks climbed the switchbacks above. He closed his eyes.

"You okay, brother?" Horn looked across the seat. "Don't throw up in my car. We're not supposed to stop here but I will if we need to."

"I'm good," said Neel.

Horn was silent for a few seconds. "Meaning to ask. That stuff you mentioned last night. Scrubbing the databases, clearing the record? Do we need to get into it?"

Neel shivered. "That talk came straight out of the bottle."

"I'm here for you, is all I'm saying."

Neel kept his face to the window. "You haven't exactly colored within the lines either, my friend."

"Don't get upset now."

Neel opened his eyes when the road flattened out. It passed through an earthen berm before continuing, on the other side, into a valley of brown grass. Occasional white flowers swayed on tall stalks. Half a mile in the distance, a steel wall glinted. Behind it, on a plateau, stood a set of massive, tan-colored buildings. They looked like hangars or warehouses. Earthmovers and cranes were at work on a second, higher, plateau. Dry mountains loomed on three sides.

"There she is," said Horn. "MADAR, phase one."

Neel could hear the distant machines but also, closer, the wind in the brown grass. "Driving in this valley," he said, "looking at the grass, I feel like I'm on the sea again."

"The Utes never believed the white man would rule in the mountains. They knew about the slaughter of the tribes to the east and south but their situation was different, or so they thought, because in Utah the land doesn't end. The whites were looking for a route to the ocean. They preferred low places and didn't like the wind. The Utes thought that if the white man ever came, they could just wait him out in the next valley until he passed through."

"I guess that didn't work out," said Neel.

"Rivers of blood ran here."

The road led to an unmanned gate in the steel boundary wall. Horn lowered his window, reached out, and swiped his key card. The gate parted.

There were fewer cars than Neel had expected in the lot, given the size of the complex. Horn parked close to the entrance of a glass-fronted building that looked like the town hall of a small, newly prosperous city. The warehouses Neel had seen from a distance loomed on either side. Clusters of pylons and water towers stood in the lanes behind the warehouses. The pavement vibrated. There was no one in sight.

They walked to an array of lockboxes in front of the glass building. Horn swiped his key card again, opened a drawer, and deposited his phone inside. He asked Neel to put his phone in the drawer as well. Then he led Neel through the doors.

They walked past an empty reception desk and rows of empty cubicles to a briefing room.

Horn looked at his watch before he pushed open the door. "Eight thirty-one. All that moonshine and we're just a minute late. A couple of warriors here."

Monica stood inside, just by the door.

"I'm glad to see you," said Neel.

"I caught a charter from Andrews at four A.M. Eastern," she said. "It's been a day."

Neel turned to introduce Horn, but he was walking down the aisle.

"What's the mood at the Center?" Neel asked.

"It wasn't ideal to face a terrorist attack on a Monday morning. But it looks like the suspect was a lone wolf. It helps that the man he killed wasn't a civilian. I don't think Eliot will have to lop any heads."

"I suppose I should take comfort in that."

Monica handed Neel a sheet of paper. "Introductory remarks."

"You wrote them?"

"Eliot did."

The room fell silent as Neel walked to the podium. There were seats for a hundred but only twenty or so were taken. Monica was the sole woman present. Everyone, except Horn and Neel, was white. Two men in the audience wore desert fatigues. The rest were indoor types in chinos, short-sleeved polo shirts, and loafers. Many wore thick glasses.

Neel cleared his throat. He wished someone had thought to set a bottle of water beside the podium. He began by thanking Horn for his hospitality. He said that everyone at the Freedom Center hoped for a productive relationship with the NSA staff at MADAR. Then he said that Eliot Cone, the Freedom Center's director, wanted to share a few words. Neel put the paper on the podium, cleared his throat again, and began.

"No one in this room needs a pep talk from me, but I'm going to give one anyway. All you data scientists and engineers and administrators are soldiers in our long war—as crucial to our effort as any Air Force pilot or Navy SEAL. You are the invisible power beneath the visible power, the handle of the spear, the steel out of which we forge the blade." His voice cracked. "Excuse me," he said, as he looked up from the podium. His gaze fell on a man in the front row, a tall, sandy-haired Mormon—if you could tell a Mormon by sight—who was surprisingly broad-shouldered for a tech worker. The Mormon leaned forward in his chair.

"MADAR, the repository of secrets, is also a bulwark of our nation's security. Terrorists wounded our civilization on September 11, 2001, but make no mistake, our dominance and desire for vengeance are intact. The intelligence community relies on the information you collect and store. We need this data. Go forward in your great work with clear hearts and firm resolve."

Neel glanced up from the page. Monica, who sat to the side, looked at him with an ambiguous smile. The big Mormon was rapt. Horn, in a middle row, seemed to be asleep. Neel had gotten through less than a third of Cone's remarks but he was losing the will to continue. He'd felt uneasy since he landed in Utah. It was as if he carried a speck of gravel in his sock or suffered from an itch he couldn't reach between his shoulders. He was beginning to wonder if this trip—indeed, if his entire role as the Freedom Center's roving ambassador—was a smokescreen. Had he been exiled? Jones, who'd hounded Neel for months, had gone silent at the very moment that conspiracy turned to action. Cone seemed happy to keep Neel on the sidelines. The priest had vanished. No, thought Neel, not after the sacrifices I've made. I won't let them turn me into a ghost.

The audience stared. "Excuse me," said Neel, for the second time. "It's the altitude."

Horn, now awake, snorted from his seat.

Neel returned his eyes to the page. "The Freedom Center is a sister agency to the NSA, made up of brother and sister agents and officers. MADAR is crucial to our joint success. We aim to establish the closest ties, at the highest levels of agency leadership, to further our shared mission. . . ." Neel was hardly listening to the words he mouthed. He reached the end a few minutes later. "Thank you and God bless," he said, realizing only at that moment that the speech was over.

The audience clapped without enthusiasm.

Monica walked up to the podium. "Great effort," she whispered. "You're a born orator. Are you ready for the tour?"

A senior NSA manager, whose name Neel hadn't bothered to remember, drove them around the complex in a golf cart. First he showed them the data halls—those tan warehouse buildings. They contained tens of thousands of servers, he said. Collectively, the servers required more energy, and generated more heat, than the largest auto factories in the country. Without the cooling towers and chiller plants that pumped refrigerated water under their floors, the buildings would go up in flames.

"A million and a half gallons a day," said Neel.

"That's right," said the manager, a little sourly.

He stopped the cart thirty yards from one of the halls. Fans roared on the roof, sending heat waves into the air. Even at a distance, Neel felt the blast on his skin.

The manager pointed to the water tanks higher on the slope. Each had a footprint greater than a Manhattan city block. "We could flood the whole plateau. Turn it into rice paddy, if we wanted."

At that moment, two warplanes dropped into the valley. They roared over the grassland before climbing steeply at the range. They turned in a half circle over the mountains and soon disappeared in the white sky to the east.

"F-16s out of Hill AFB," said the manager. "A beautiful sight."

"Neel flew," said Monica, who was sitting in the front passenger seat.

"Right on," said the manager. He looked back at Neel with new interest.

"I was a naval flight officer, not a pilot. Electronics countermeasures in an EA-6B Prowler."

"That works. Welcome to Utah."

The manager started up the cart again. He drove to the power substation with its arrays of electrical towers, then circled the fuel tanks for the backup generators. Neel felt the thrum in his teeth. The noise reminded him of his time on the carrier. There were nights when he would have traded a week's pay for an hour of quiet.

When they had a little distance from the power plant, the manager resumed his narration. He gestured at the excavations underway in the distance.

"We'll double our capacity in five years, with phase two of MADAR. And we can double it again. Think of Los Angeles in 1900, Houston in 1950. You'd be a fool not to bet on growth. Take any angle: geography, labor, politics. Here you've got space. You've got a skilled U.S.-citizen workforce for construction. The people in the surrounding communities have the correct mindset. We won't face any environmental litigation. Every aspect is working for us. I don't think there's a location on the planet more suitable for this project."

Monica asked the manager questions as he drove. She was holding on to the frame with one hand, so that her silver charm bracelet slipped down her forearm. The manager answered her with grinning authority. Monica glanced over her shoulder to offer Neel a weary smile.

They returned to the glass-fronted building later in the morning. The NSA manager, Horn, and two young Mormon engineers joined Neel and Monica for meetings in a smaller conference room. Monica sat at the head of the table. She said that her director's dearest hope was to secure more intimate access for the Freedom Center's analysts to all of MADAR's resources.

"As I understand it, the NSA collects two billion communication events a day," Monica said. "We want to give our analysts the ability to look at that data without constraint, at the moment of collection and storage, even without a specific link to watch-listed individuals. Of course, we expect the analysts to exercise that power responsibly. But this is a question of agency freedom."

The NSA manager raised his index finger. "We actually store *twenty* billion daily communication events from across the globe. Emails, text messages, search engine queries, website visits, phone call metadata."

Neel sat across the conference table. He read the manager's name— "Scoot Baker"—off the pass he'd clipped to his breast pocket.

"That two-billion figure you cited only accounts for the domestic intake," the manager added. He stroked his mustache.

"Thank you for clarifying, Scoot," said Monica. "It's a magnificent achievement. Almost impossible to grasp. And presumably the scale of collections will increase going forward?"

"Sure," said Scoot. "Barring a civilizational setback like nuclear war or an asteroid impact, more and more human activity will move from the physical to the digital realm. So there will be exponentially more data to collect in the years to come. But with respect to global coverage, we're already comprehensive. As you know, industry, big tech, and the telecoms have all been patriotic actors. We haven't had a problem getting access to the choke points of digital traffic—the switches, routers, and so on. And for that fraction of global digital activity that doesn't pass through American-owned infrastructure, we have broad agreements with foreign allies."

"We've also engineered our way into unguarded segments of fiber-optic cable in the ocean to vacuum up any leftovers," added one of the younger Mormons. He blushed when Monica looked at him.

Now Horn raised his hand. "I've made this point in private." He nodded at Neel. "Yes, we collect it all. But the key is to find threads of relevant information. No agency, no matter how sophisticated its search and sorting algorithms, can effectively review billions of individual communications a day. I doubt that accessing a greater volume of raw data will help the Freedom Center in its mission." He turned to Monica. "Setting aside the legal issues, your analysts don't have the capacity to look much beyond the reports NSA already generates."

The smile Monica offered Horn was pure honey. Surround her with men and she was sovereign. Everyone was working together. All criticism was helpful.

"You understand the complexity of the mission," she said. "You're considering the practical side, the technical side, without which the enterprise doesn't function. But isn't there another, equally important, aspect?"

The younger Mormons stared.

"I'm speaking of a spiritual dimension. The question of empowerment. Even if our analysts spend most of their time looking at reports that come down through the agency pipeline, what harm can come from loosening the constraints? Why not leave room for intuition? The analysts toil through twelve-hour shifts, chipping away at a rock face. Shouldn't they have the chance, from time to time, to turn around and enjoy the view? We're building an index, and they have their magnifying glasses, but we want to give each of them a set of wings as well."

"Break their shackles," said Scoot. He was beaming.

"Speaking of intuition," said Neel. He felt the need to justify his presence. "Hunches and tips can save lives. If you sense that something bad is going to happen, give us a call. We want to open a less formal line of communication. It's not just CIA officers who should be allowed to trust their guts." His tongue was sticking to the roof of his mouth. The Mormons looked at him as if he was speaking with a foreign accent.

He pressed on. "Eliot Cone will pick up his phone. I'll pick up my phone. We came here to make friends." Suddenly, he felt ridiculous. His voice dropped. "We want to hear from you."

Silence fell. Someone's watch ticked off the seconds.

Scoot cleared his throat. "Well, I think we have made friends. I can see myself dialing up the Freedom Center in the near future." He smiled at Monica. "Let's break for lunch."

Caterers brought sandwiches and cans of iced tea to the meeting room. The talks resumed forty minutes later. Scoot and Monica discussed the legal clearances the NSA would require before it could open the data repository to a sister agency. The young Mormons spoke at length about the protocols the NSA employed to organize such a vast trove. Neel roused himself again to propose an analyst exchange between MADAR and the Freedom Center. Horn sat for most of the afternoon in a stupor. But when he did speak, correcting the Mormons on some technical point regarding, for example, the time lag between the collection of mobile phone metadata in Northern Europe and the logging of that data on MADAR's servers, or the NSA's capacity to monitor the internet activity of threat-listed targets in real time, everyone listened.

They ended at seven. Horn led them outside. They retrieved their phones from the lockbox. Monica's gray pants shimmered as she walked, or perhaps that was a trick of the evening light.

"Oh my," she said, on seeing Horn's orange coupe for the first time.

"Yes, ma'am," said Horn. He stowed her suitcase in the trunk. He turned to Neel. "Lady rides shotgun. Plus, she did all the work today."

Neel's legs were cramped on the rear bench, but he had headroom. He checked his phone: no message from Rebecca. He sent her a text saying he looked forward to seeing her and the girls the next day, in spite of everything. Up front, Horn and Monica were talking about D.C. and Los Angeles, the Atlantic and the Pacific, restaurants, wine. Horn said he'd offer to show her Salt Lake City's nightlife except that it all took place downtown, in neighborhoods that were hidden from him, living alone as he did, in a big house in the suburbs.

He asked if they wanted to listen to music. The first song he played was "When Doves Cry."

"You can't go wrong with Prince," said Neel, looking up from his phone.

"No, sir."

"My sister's only rule for my boyfriends was that they had to love *Sign o' the Times*," said Monica.

"The greatest album ever recorded," said Horn. "And have you followed your sister's commandment?" If he'd been shy with Monica earlier, at MADAR, he seemed at ease now.

"Not always. If you don't ask early, you lose your chance."

"Later on, you might be afraid to know the answer," said Horn.

"It would be like if my fiancé told me, 'Oh, by the way, I'm in Opus Dei and I've been wearing a hair shirt for the past decade. Don't let that get in the way of our wedding planning!'"

"Or if he told you he'd slept under a poster of Barry Goldwater in his childhood bedroom," said Neel.

"He probably did do that," said Monica. "But I'm sure he likes Prince."

Neel settled into his seat. With the engine noise, and the music, it was easy to drop out of the conversation. He looked at the dry plateaus in the distance. He thought about the desert, rock piles, salt, thirst. He thought about the people who lived deep in the empty land. He thought about the guns they owned and the hatreds they might nurture. An old fear passed through him. At that moment, he would have liked to be home. He wondered if he would ever again sit in the living room of his little house, listening to a classic—Miles Davis, Coltrane—while his daughters slept upstairs.

Horn left them at the reception desk. Monica had a dawn flight and would have to order a taxi. Neel wasn't leaving Salt Lake City until eleven thirty the next day. Horn said he'd return at ten to take him to the airport.

Neel carried Monica's bag. Her room faced his on the hotel's lower level, across a stretch of parking lot. At her door he asked if she wanted to go out to dinner, but she said she was tired. She would just eat an energy bar and some peanuts. She wanted to check her emails and talk to her fiancé.

"All right," he said.

He was outside. She stood in her room with the door partially closed.

"Call your wife," said Monica. "Talk to your daughters. You must miss them."

"It's late on the East Coast," he said. "The girls will be asleep."

She smiled, showing the gap between her front teeth.

He shifted his feet. The wind had picked up. It was blowing against the back of his neck.

"Bye, then," he said.

He looked over his shoulder when he was halfway across the asphalt. Monica was still at her door. She waved goodbye.

He showered, texted Rebecca again, and walked two blocks to a gas-
station convenience store. He bought a hot dog and a bag of chips. He
ate on the walk back to the hotel. The light was vanishing behind the
mountains. The wind made a lonely sound on the dirt.

Back in his room, his ears rang in the silence. Rebecca had not responded to his messages. No one had followed him, no one waited in the
parking lot, no one watched, but he was—he realized—afraid. He wished
he had a bottle of wine. My God, he wondered, is this all? This solitary
night, and a thousand or ten thousand more, until I reach the end?

He brushed his teeth, undressed to boxers and a T-shirt, pulled back
the covers on the bed. He couldn't face the empty sheets. He switched
off the lamp, went to the window, and pulled back the curtain. A seam
of yellow light glowed under Monica's door. Neel left the window. He
switched the lamp back on. He unzipped his suitcase, reached into the
slit he'd opened in the interior fabric, and pulled out the thumb drive
he'd carried from D.C. He took the drive and the key card for his room
and went barefoot into the night.

The asphalt was still warm under his soles. Dead leaves skittered
with the wind. The thirty yards seemed like three hundred. He knocked
twice at Monica's door. There was dust on his tongue. When he heard
no answer he tried the handle. It gave. He walked in.

The room was as small as his own. Monica stood in the bathroom on
the other side of the bed. The sliding door was open. She was brushing
her teeth at the sink. She wore the same white blouse she'd worn during the day, over a pair of white briefs. Their eyes met in the mirror. Her
face was calm, blank. She held her hair up with one hand while she
leaned down to rinse her mouth.

She walked out of the bathroom. "Why are you here?" she asked.
"Where are your clothes?"

"I want to give you something," he said. "I want to blow the whistle."

She shook her head.

It was the priest, he said. The priest and one of his CIA cronies.

Neel had manipulated the threat matrix so those two men could kill an innocent American without being discovered. If they hadn't killed the target yet, they would soon. Other killings would follow. There was no sense to it. His CIA contact had told Neel he was developing a program, honing a tool. But that part didn't matter. "They kill because they can. It's a reflex. A way to forget that they're old."

"That's absurd," she said. "I don't want to know this."

They were talking across the bed.

"I've done terrible things," said Neel. "But I can do one good thing now." He opened his left fist to show Monica the thumb drive. He put it down on her nightstand.

"If something happens to me. If they abandon the program and try to clean up the loose ends, try to silence me, it's all here. Proof, details."

Monica laughed. "They won't silence you. What does that even mean?"

"I'm in a dead zone. You feel it. The chill follows me into every room."

"Maybe they decided you're not the right man for this scheme, if it even exists. So what? You're better off. Do your work at the Center and forget about them. You have a family."

"Rebecca is going to leave me. I've ruined my life."

"You're being maudlin. You can rebuild your life."

"Rebuild my life." He looked down at his bare legs.

"Neel, you help the government kill people in Afghanistan, Pakistan, Yemen. Some of those people might be a threat to the United States but some aren't. We kill women and children. We don't mean to, but we do. You can live with that. Why are you so concerned about this other killing? The one you say you helped engineer, which might not even have occurred?"

"This one was murder."

"You're acting out of hurt feelings. That's not whistleblowing. That's not a moral decision." She walked around the bed to the nightstand. He gave way but there wasn't space. Her leg brushed his as she leaned to pick up the drive.

"I'm giving this back," she said.

"Please," he said. "Keep it until I decide what to do."

"It's dangerous for me."

He reached for her hand and squeezed it.

Sighing, she put the drive back on the nightstand.

He thanked her.

"I've been up forever," she said. "I'm on the first flight out tomorrow."

Neel didn't move.

"I feel sorry for you," she said.

"No, you don't." He lifted his fingers to her cheek. "I've been attracted to you from the beginning."

"And now your wife has given you up." She turned away. "This shirt is full of dust." She unbuttoned it and let it fall to the floor.

He looked at her naked shoulders.

"Switch off the light," she said.

Then they didn't speak for some time. Her skin was cool to his touch. She ran her nails down his back, put her lips to his neck.

He woke next to her. She lay on her side, facing him, with her eyes open in the dark. He asked how long he'd slept.

"Not long," she said.

"I always fall asleep after making love."

"'Making love.' That's what my mother would call it."

"What do you call it?"

She leaned over and bit his ear.

He pulled her close, kissed her mouth.

After a while she released him, sat up, pulled her knees to her chest. She reminded him that she had an early flight.

"I'm being selfish," he said.

He put on his underclothes, checked the window to make sure there was no one in the lot, and walked outside.

Satellites blinked in the sky. A crescent moon had risen over the mountains. For a night, or half a night, he'd been able to forget that he was alone.

FORTY-TWO

HORN LOOKED ACROSS at him from the driver's seat. Neel's suitcase was in the trunk, his seatbelt fastened, and the sun visor flipped down. They were five minutes ahead of schedule.

Horn moved his index finger to the ignition button but didn't press it. He turned to Neel again. "There's something different about you," he said.

"No hangover. Drank two cups of coffee, had a shave. Should we go?"

"If I didn't know better, I'd say you've been fucking."

"Come on, man."

Horn pushed his mirrored sunglasses up on his forehead. He leaned over the gear shift to sniff close to Neel's face.

"What are you doing?"

"You dirty dog. You can shower, brush your teeth, whatever, but you still smell of pussy. Pussy and perfume. I knew it."

Neel shook his head.

"Road warrior," said Horn. He straightened himself in his seat before he patted Neel on the shoulder. "Can I get the details?"

"No."

Horn laughed. "There aren't any secrets."

Neel shrugged. He'd had enough banter for one visit.

Horn started up the car. They drove the freeway in silence. But as they drew closer to the airport, Horn said he'd miss Neel. Though he was happy for the contract money at MADAR, life in Utah was lonely.

"You'll find your people," said Neel, without conviction.

"If you were here, we could get a drink once a week. See a movie. I could tell you about the books I'm reading."

"I'll be back. Or you'll fly to D.C. for work."

They entered the ring road to the terminal.

"Before you leave, tell me why they really sent you out here. Do you even know?"

"One of the big dogs wants me out of sight and out of mind. I'm not on solid ground at the Freedom Center."

"It went sour fast, huh?"

Neel didn't reply.

Horn pulled over in a loading zone near Neel's gate. He got out of the Dodge to wrap Neel in a hug.

"I'll remember our time together," said Neel. "My liver won't let me forget."

"Be careful, brother," said Horn. Now he held Neel at arm's length, with one hand on each shoulder. "We work with people we can't trust."

They shook hands.

Neel drank two more cups of coffee in the terminal, sent Rebecca a text, browsed unsuccessfully in the bookstore. The plane was only half full. He had a window seat near the back of the economy cabin, in an otherwise empty row. They left on time. Within minutes the city had vanished. From 36,000 feet, Neel looked out over the dry white land. When his eyes began to ache, he lowered the shade. He thought about his night with Monica. D.C. was three and a half hours away. For once, he wished it was a bigger country.

The taxi had him home by seven. At the curb he paused, suitcase in hand. Their beautiful row house looked as distant and self-contained as a small New England church. Would it also be as foreign to him, he wondered? Was he entering as a guest who should not outstay his welcome?

Rebecca came downstairs while he washed his hands in the kitchen. He said hello, switched off the tap, and dried his hands on a towel. She hugged him and asked him how his trip had gone. He couldn't meet her eyes. She said the girls were in their room. He could read them their stories and say good night.

They were lying on their stomachs on the floor. Maya was reading to Serena from a book of nursery rhymes, or reciting the verses from memory. They stood and ran to him when he appeared at the door.

"I missed you, Dada," Serena said.

"Me too," said Neel.

"Where were you?" asked Maya.

"Utah," he said, and both girls giggled.

The three of them lay down together on Maya's bed. Neel read the book of nursery rhymes from the beginning. It was still light behind the curtains. Serena soon fell asleep with her head on his shoulder. Her face was warm, her mouth open. There were blond streaks in her hair from playing under the sun.

"Keep going, Dada," whispered Maya.

He read the book to the end. Afterward he carried Serena to her bed. He left with tears in his eyes.

Downstairs he asked Rebecca if he couldn't just sleep on the couch. He'd leave for work before the girls woke up.

"I need space," she said.

"Is it over?"

"You chose this life. For months I've asked you to reconsider. But you had a plan."

"The plan isn't working out."

"You'll hang on to the bitter end." Rebecca shook her head. "I don't rely on you for money or companionship or to take care of our daughters. Where's our marriage?"

"I'm sorry."

Rebecca said she'd book him a hotel room while he packed his clothes.

He was folding his shirts in their bedroom when his phone chimed. Cone had sent him a text message.

Heads up. Wazir drone story drops tomorrow. Pics of crippled kids, pics of both of us. You're the star of the piece. Anyone calls, you have no comment. Ok?

He carried his suitcase, newly packed, to the front door. Rebecca walked him to the driveway. He told her about Cone's message. She patted him on the back and wished him the best of luck.

FORTY-THREE

CONE WALKED INTO Neel's office at nine on Thursday morning. The story was live, he said. An antiwar news site had published it. The site had a small readership, but this piece would find an audience. "Take ten minutes to review the story. Don't pick up the phone until we've had a chance to talk." He went out.

Neel typed the relevant terms into his computer's search engine. The headline, "SLAUGHTER IN PAKISTAN," appeared at the top of the news site's home page. Neel clicked on it and began to read.

The writer, Adam Buford, opened by evoking the desolate beauty of the village of Baz-Baral, high in a mountain valley in Pakistan's North Waziristan Agency. Few outsiders, wrote Buford, had ever visited Waziristan, an isolated tribal region on the southern fringe of the Hindu Kush. There were no cities and few roads in the Agency. The Pakistani government had no presence outside of a handful of military bases. Every householder, following Pashtun custom, owned a gun.

Fewer than two hundred people lived in Baz-Baral, wrote Buford, all of them members of the same extended family. The men routinely crossed the few miles of trails to the Afghan slope of the mountain. Shepherds grazed their goats where they pleased. To the villagers, the border did not exist.

The men of Baz-Baral earned hard currency through the opium trade. Some grew poppy. Others ran raw opium over the trails from Afghanistan. A few brave men smuggled truckloads of the drug, hidden under sacks of apples or boxes of scrap metal, to Pakistan proper. They drove north to Peshawar or south through the Gumal Pass and down to the great cities of Faisalabad, Multan, and Lahore. There, on the Punjabi plains, the opium was refined into heroin. Gangsters and industrialists—the distinction wasn't so clear in Pakistan—exported the heroin to India, or across the Arabian Sea and sub-Saharan Africa to Lagos, for eventual shipment to Rotterdam, Antwerp, Houston, and New York.

Opium made a few young men in Baz-Baral rich, by the standards of the place. They bought pickup trucks in Peshawar. One man owned a secondhand Mercedes that, according to his uncle, he never drove. Eventually, these vehicles brought the villagers to the attention of American intelligence.

Those villagers who didn't involve themselves in the opium trade remained subsistence farmers and herders. But every villager Buford interviewed, whether drug runner or orchard keeper, poppy farmer or shepherd, insisted that neither the Taliban nor Al Qaeda had ever established a presence in Baz-Baral. Of course, armed men crossed over the mountains from time to time. The villagers would always welcome and protect their guests. But guests, by definition, did not stay.

On the morning of February 4, 2009, an MQ-1 Predator drone, operated by a pilot who sat in a trailer on a Nevada Air Force base, launched two Hellfire missiles into the largest compound in the village. When the dust cleared, eleven villagers were dead and five horribly wounded. The list of casualties included six young children. Over the course of weeks, the villagers had gotten used to the buzzing of surveillance drones but they had never expected a missile attack.

Buford had taken photographs of an eight-year-old amputee who looked no older than four, as well as a young man, with only the beginnings of a beard, who had a mutilated ear and a face pocked by shrapnel scars. The village headman did not allow Buford to photograph the three surviving female victims: two women and a young girl. None of the wounded had received adequate medical care in the aftermath of the attack.

The incident might never have come to light, wrote Buford, were it not for the actions of a government whistleblower. The whistleblower had sent Buford a targeting memo that outlined the rationale for the strike: namely, suspiciously timed cross-border telephone calls, irregular patterns of human movement, and the incongruous presence of expensive vehicles. The memo was primarily the work of one man, Neel Chima, an obscure Freedom Center bureaucrat and Navy veteran. Buford noted that Chima had led an undistinguished seven-year career as a federal prosecutor before he joined the intelligence agency in 2008. A headshot of Neel, taken from the Center's press release announcing his hiring, appeared beside the text.

Eliot Cone, the Freedom Center's director, refused Buford's request for comment, other than to note that any intelligence product the agency provided to its sister agencies and the White House could not be attributed to one official but instead represented the joint efforts of a dedicated team of patriots. "We stand behind our work," he said. A small headshot of Cone illustrated his quote. A White House spokesperson refused to comment on the incident, stating only that the drone program was classified.

A high-ranking national security official, however, speaking on condition of anonymity, told Buford that such a poorly sourced document should never have survived interagency review. "We can't be killing on the basis of supposition and coincidence," said the official. "Incidents like this return us to the darkest days of the Bush era. You have inexperienced people acting out of ambition or ideology instead of the granular analysis of facts on the ground." According to the source, the White House had refined its targeting procedures in the aftermath of the Baz-Baral debacle. The CIA, with its greater resources and access to human intelligence, had since taken the lead in target selection in the tribal areas. "No more mavericks, no more getting out over our skis. We don't want to put the entire war effort into disrepute." The Freedom Center, the source said, had returned to its supporting role as a cross-checker and intelligence clearinghouse.

Buford concluded his article with the observation that no reform, real or imagined, could be of any help now to the traumatized villagers of Baz-Baral.

Neel turned away from the screen. The door was closed and he was alone in his office but the ambient noise—the hum of the servers on the floor below, the hiss of air through the air-conditioning vent, his own computer's whine—was suddenly intolerable. He put his hands over his ears until, feeling ridiculous, he lowered them to his lap. How should he feel now that he'd been outed as a war criminal—as well as a hothead and a fool? Rebecca would read the story. One day, Maya and Serena might read it too. The internet would preserve Buford's narrative forever. He didn't want to think about the victims. A man can descend to depths beneath remorse, beneath shame. There's a weight that flattens you and leaves you numb.

Cone walked in without knocking. He came over to Neel's side of the desk and patted him between the shoulders. Then he went back around to sit in one of the facing chairs. He looked delighted. After all, he had come through unscathed.

"Tough break, Neel. Keep a stiff upper lip, as our British friends would say. We've told the comms desk to route your outside calls to public affairs. If anyone reaches your direct line, just say, 'No comment,' and hang up."

"Okay."

"It'd be better for now to stay off the Operations floor. I don't want our people getting distracted."

The phone on Neel's desk rang. Cone leaned forward, picked up the receiver, and immediately put it down to end the call. "Or do it like that." He smiled. "You're on the road again next week."

"I leave Tuesday," said Neel.

"Wyoming, then Arizona the week after, and Nevada the week after that. That'll take us into July. Reporters at the big papers will start going on vacation. Readers will lose interest. Soon the big NatSec story will be the upcoming Afghan elections. By summer's end all this will be forgotten."

"But not forgiven."

"Neel." Cone stood. "The early part of this year was a whirlwind. I was new, I hadn't found my footing. Maybe I had some reservations about the strike that I didn't express forcefully enough. This mistake is on me as well. Look at the bright side. Our agency came out okay. Even Buford acknowledged that we've pulled back from targeting, made some reforms, returned to our core intelligence mission. You took one for the team but you'll survive."

"Sure," said Neel.

"Good talk," said Cone. He left.

Neel wanted to speak to Monica. She'd gone upstairs for another meeting after the early-morning conference that day. He hadn't seen her since. She was, at that moment, his only friend.

FORTY-FOUR

NEEL PUSHED OPEN the priest's door at three minutes to seven. A ripple passed through the guests—heads swiveled, silence fell. He stood alone for a moment at the entrance. Then the crowd parted. The priest walked to Neel with his arm extended.

"Well done," he said. "Brave of you to come. You're always welcome."

Neel shook hands without enthusiasm.

"Let's get you a drink."

"I'm fine," said Neel. He spoke in a quiet voice but his face was hot.

"Well then. Why don't we join our old friends?"

The priest led Neel to one side of the living room. There Tim Osborne and Peter Moore, the think-tanker and journalist Neel had met on his first visit, waited with eager expressions.

"What a pleasant surprise," said Osborne.

Moore, standing at Osborne's shoulder, licked his lips.

Flies to a carcass, thought Neel. Both the *Times* and *Post* had followed up Adam Buford's reporting on the botched Waziristan strike with articles of their own. In three days, Neel had achieved public infamy.

"The man of the hour," Moore said. He swirled the triple measure of liquor in his glass.

"One way to put it," said Neel.

"Now, now, old chum," said Moore. Four buttons were open on his shirt. "You're not the first man in this business whose trigger finger got a little itchy."

Osborne, who was sweating freely, grabbed Neel by the arm. "You have the full support of the American Institute for Global Democracy. Frankly, I wish you'd sent more missiles flying before the press sniffed you out." He raised his glass. "To Neel Chima. We have a twenty-five-year-old Laphroaig, if you're interested. It's a gift from our Emirati friends."

Moore looked fondly at his own glass. "Years of salt and wind in this one. Gulf Arabs always give a lovely bottle, despite the strictures of their faith. Tim's employers know their Scotch."

"Funders, not employers," said Osborne. "A fellow of the American Institute for Global Democracy is beholden only to his conscience."

The priest began to shift away from their circle. Neel pulled him back in. "I came to speak to you," he said. He held onto the priest's arm.

The other two men looked at Neel with astonishment. "You'll have your chance," Moore said, after a brief pause. "But before you arrived the three of us were discussing the situation in Afghanistan. Notwithstanding your efforts, it seems we're not at the happiest moment of the war. The countryside is in open revolt against Karzai."

Neel released his grip.

"Thank you," said the priest. He turned to Moore. "Give the surge time. We'll see an improvement this summer. Our soldiers will acclimatize. The officers will find their rhythm."

"Sounds wishful," said Osborne. He pushed his glasses up his oily nose. "There are those who say that Obama is questioning the mission. That he's lost his nerve."

"Tim, you know better," said the priest. "People like to gossip. But the president surrounded himself with the old hands for a reason. We've seen our share of ups and downs. We'll help him stay the course. I'm not breaching any confidence when I tell you that every American president has a necessary streak of machismo. Mr. Obama is no different. He doesn't want to look weak."

"I'm relieved," said Osborne.

The priest tilted his head. "Now if the president were to fire a general, perhaps even the top general in the theater, and if he were to replace that general with a real go-getter, I think the chatter will be very different. Everyone will see how bold Mr. Obama truly is. They'll understand that he's a man of action."

Moore's nostrils twitched. "Has the decision been made? Who's the replacement?"

The priest reminded Moore that they were off the record. There wasn't a story here for him.

"How about you, Neel?" said Moore. "What can you tell us? Are you upset that the CIA has elbowed the Freedom Center off the stage?"

Neel shook his head. He didn't want to talk to these men.

"The Company might have done you a favor. I don't think drones are the game changer we expected. We've been looking at this war through the wrong frame all along. Afghanistan isn't Vietnam or even Angola. This is another Colombia. Follow the money. We've opened the Central Asian front of the War on Drugs. I have a piece coming out that makes just this argument."

"You're wrong," said Osborne, raising his voice. "We're looking at a classic rebel insurgency. We must continue to use brute force against the brutes."

Neel had lost his patience. "Is your CIA friend here?" he asked, turning to the priest. "Because what I have to say concerns him as well."

"Let's go to the kitchen," the priest said.

They waited beside the bar cart until the room cleared. Neel stared at the priest all the while.

"There's no reason to be bitter," said the priest, when they were finally alone. "You stumbled into one of the hazards of our profession. But public opprobrium needn't be a career killer. Other men have suffered more."

"You pushed me into advocating for the strike in Waziristan. And then you pushed me into worse. It was all dirty work."

"I don't like your tone, Neel. I suggest you start to take responsibility for your actions. With the right mindset you can still rise from the ashes. But at present I'm not sure about your chances."

"What was the point?" Neel shook his head. "I don't want to hear from Jones ever again. I want written confirmation that the FBI will close its investigation into the missing documents. I'll finish out the year at the Center. Then I'll look for another job. You won't interfere."

The priest laughed. "Or what? You can't issue ultimatums to me."

"Or I might share what I know about your special projects. People will be interested. Federal prosecutors tend not to like interstate murder schemes. Congress, the public—there are many eyes and ears."

"Our work is secret. You will go to prison." The priest was clearly furious but he spoke now in a whisper.

Neel shrugged. "We'll see."

Moore appeared at the kitchen door, empty glass in hand. The priest waved him away before he turned again to Neel.

"I'm in the White House. I can't meddle with a federal investigation. I have to use a softer kind of persuasion. With the FBI it's a matter of give and take, courtesy, suggestion. You have to trust the process."

Neel moved closer to the priest. He took the priest by his suit jacket and lifted him to his toes. "That's not what you promised."

"Don't be an animal," said the priest.

Now Monica walked into the kitchen. She was all in white and carrying a bottle of wine.

"You have a week," Neel said, before he let the priest go.

The priest smoothed his jacket and shirt. He turned to Monica. "Welcome, my dear. Have a drink."

Monica put the bottle down on the counter. "Is everything all right?" she asked.

"Our friend has had a difficult few days."

"I've said my piece," said Neel. He looked at Monica. "Come with me." He reached for her hand.

"I just arrived," she said, brushing him away.

The priest leaned in to kiss her cheek. "Of course you'll stay," he said.

Neel looked at them. The priest had turned up his mouth into a sneer. Monica's expression was blank. He sensed that to leave the two of them alone would be disastrous for him. Though he'd put his faith in Monica he also understood that he knew nothing about her. He felt suddenly ill. In Neel's absence, the priest would draw Monica close, whisper in her ear, promise all he could promise. Neel wanted to drag Monica from the apartment. He'd seize her purse, check that she hadn't brought his thumb drive to the priest. Or perhaps she'd already betrayed him. He clenched his hand in his pocket.

"One week," he repeated, as he moved to the kitchen door. "Monica, we'll talk soon." He went out without another word.

FORTY-FIVE

NEEL COLLECTED HIS daughters in the morning. They were shy at first, but Serena took his hand on the walk to the playground. A few minutes later, both girls were laughing on the swings. They went from the slides to a seesaw to the climbing wall. Neel played tag with them until sweat soaked his shirt. Afterward they had grilled-cheese sandwiches and strawberry shakes at a diner. The girls told him about summer camp and their piano lessons. On the walk home Maya said she'd had fun that day. She missed her Dada but was happy that now, when he came to see them, he had to do whatever they wanted.

Kay had come over to help Rebecca make dinner. She asked to speak to Neel in private. He followed her to the garden.

"She'll have the best divorce lawyer in the District," Kay said, once they were outside. She wore pearls, a diamond tennis bracelet, and linen pants. "The others worth getting will turn you down, out of respect for George. This family is going to flatten you." She had a radiant expression.

"Rebecca doesn't need the best lawyer. I won't fight."

"'Stop the clocks,' I said, when Rebecca told me it was over. I've been in the most wonderful mood ever since. I'm so glad she didn't take your name. I knew you'd show your true colors in time."

"I prefer you, Kay, when you're drunk."

"George wanted to come with me today but I stopped him. He would have shot you with his Beretta."

"It's been a pleasure to know you both," said Neel.

He went back inside to kiss the girls and say goodbye to Rebecca.

His hotel wasn't far from the house. From his room that evening he called Lewis Maycock—Yoda—his old pilot. They hadn't talked in at least a year. But he wanted to hear a familiar voice, share a laugh, and, he hoped, clear the air.

"What's up, Tiger?" said Yoda. He spoke loudly, over shouts and laughter in the background.

"No one's called me that in a decade," said Neel.

Yoda apologized for the noise. He was watching his sons and their friends while they played in the pool. It was a hot weekend in Houston.

Neel asked about his work. Yoda had gone to business school after leaving the Navy. Now he was an energy trader in the deregulated Texas market. He'd come through the financial crisis with a six-bedroom house in Bunker Hill.

Everything was fine, said Yoda. Work, family, his health. "I'm just getting shorter and fatter and missing the Navy more every year. You?"

"Hit a rough patch."

"I read about the drone strike," Yoda said. "Makes me grateful we weren't in an attack plane. How're you holding up?"

"I'll live," said Neel. "The marriage won't." He was in bed, sipping from a bottle of beer. "Meaning to ask. Did you talk to a guy a while back? About the Navy? About me? Shore leave and all that."

Yoda was silent. Children continued to splash and shout.

Neel said he wasn't angry. He just needed to know. He was planning his next move.

"I haven't spoken to anyone." Yoda lowered his voice. "It's not the best time to talk. I'm here for you, Tiger, but I can't get dragged in." His wife was hollering at him to heat up the grill, he said. No doubt he'd be in D.C. in a couple of months for work. They'd go out for steaks, have a few drinks.

"I'll be on the road," said Neel.

"Another time, then," Yoda said. "Take care."

Neel walked to the window after Yoda hung up. He had a view of a rooftop parking deck, an alley, and the back wall of a conference center. There was nothing he wanted to read, no game to watch on television. He wasn't hungry and it was too early for bed. He rested his head on the glass.

FORTY-SIX

NEEL WENT INTO work on Monday morning as if nothing had changed. He read the daily intelligence briefs from the other agencies, edited the Center's own brief, and forwarded it to Cone with his comments. No one spoke to him on the Operations floor when he arrived. None of the analysts, it seemed, even looked his way.

He was a minute late for the 8:30 meeting. Vanderhoof had begun his presentation on the suspects he'd added to the threat matrix. He nodded at Neel but didn't pause. Cone looked momentarily startled by Neel's presence. Neel took his seat and listened quietly while Vanderhoof spoke. At the close, Vanderhoof listed the domestic VERMIN he'd promoted into a higher tier of the threat matrix in the wake of the Arkansas shooting.

"When in doubt, include and elevate," said Cone. "My predecessor was right to take an aggressive approach. I don't care if we have to triple the number of alerts we send out. No more slip-ups."

"Agreed," said Monica.

Neel had looked at her from time to time while Vanderhoof spoke, but she avoided his gaze.

"Anything else?" said Cone.

"What do you want me to achieve in Wyoming?" asked Neel. He was flying commercial to Denver that afternoon. He planned to stay in an airport hotel, then drive the hour and a half to Cheyenne early on Tuesday morning. There the Air Force had set up a squadron of drone pilots to fly Predators for the Afghan theater.

"Just don't get into trouble."

Neel laughed but Cone's expression didn't change.

"We've obviously taken a back seat on the drone campaign," Cone added. "But maybe you can make connections that will help us down the road. It won't hurt to see the war from a pilot's perspective. Study how the Air Force tries to minimize collateral damage. Lessons learned and so on."

Cone stood to signal the meeting's end. The others did too. Neel asked Monica for a word. She waited while Cone and Vanderhoof walked to the door. Cone, looking at her, tapped on his watch before he left.

Monica faced Neel across the table. It was the first time they'd been alone together since Utah.

"How are you?" he asked.

"Fine," she said. At last she looked him in the eyes. "Eliot and I have an appointment at Fort Meade."

"Then I'll call from the airport."

"It's a busy day. Let's talk when you get back from Wyoming."

He said he'd look forward to it.

"Safe travels," she said.

He hadn't wanted to leave a deeper trail through the electronic record or tie himself any more tightly to Ibn Muhammed's case. But now such wariness seemed naive. The internet had anointed him a war criminal. Rebecca had asked him to leave their house. He'd accosted the man who'd promised, not so many months before, to make his career. He had nothing left to lose.

At his desk, he once again typed Ibn Muhammed's name into the cross-agency search engine. The junior FBI analyst assigned to Ibn Muhammed's case had updated her summary report that very morning.

. . .

VIII. Conclusion

On June 2, 2009, a resident on the third floor of a
building at Rogers and St Marks called the
superintendent to complain of the smell of feces
emanating from a neighbor's apartment. When no one
responded to the superintendent's knocks, he entered
the apartment. There was a putrid stench in the
hallway. Flies swarmed at the half-open bathroom door.
The superintendent covered his face with his arm. In
the bathroom, he discovered a corpse. He ran out.

Two NYPD officers, responding to the superintendent's
call, found Ibn Muhammed slumped on the tiles between
the toilet and the sink. His hands and feet were bound
in cloth strips torn from a bed sheet. Another cloth
strip circled the lower third of his face. An electrical
cord ran from the doorknob over the top of the door and
around his neck.

Later that day a woman who lived on the same floor
told the investigating detective, in halting English,
that though her one-eyed neighbor never had visitors,
she'd seen "a big American" leave his apartment on
Sunday afternoon, May 31. She hadn't seen Ibn Muhammed
since. No other neighbor had witnessed anything unusual.
The detective noted that few of the building's residents
were at home for his follow-up visit on June 3 and none
responded to his invitation to call.

A Bureau examiner attended the city pathologist's
June 4 autopsy, since the deceased had been the subject
of a federal investigation. The pathologist discovered a
rag in Ibn Muhammed's throat, of the same material as
the cloth around his face, wrists, and ankles. In
addition to the abrasions caused by the bindings, deep
bruises marked Ibn Muhammed's chest and thighs. The
pathologist noted that, though it was theoretically
possible an intruder had beaten and tortured Ibn
Muhammed, his injuries were most likely self-inflicted,

perhaps during an autoerotic episode. The pathologist
surmised that Ibn Muhammed had tied himself up, placed a
gag in his own mouth, and then, panicking, had
accidentally swallowed the cloth. He may have sustained
the additional injuries when he fell. The Bureau
examiner concurred in the pathologist's determination of
the cause of death: traumatic asphyxiation by suicide or
accident. Ibn Muhammed was twenty-four.

The city released the body to Ibn Muhammed's only
living relative, his brother Faisal Jalaluddin, on
June 6. Faisal had Ibn Muhammed cremated at the Scolari
Funeral Home in Bensonhurst the following day, in a
private ceremony Faisal did not attend.

With the subject's death, the Bureau has closed this
investigation.

[Updated June 8, 2009, 07:13 ET]

. . .

So it had happened. Neel was an accessory to murder.

The air in his office had turned stale. He reached into his desk
drawer, where he'd put the bottle of bourbon the priest had given him
back in April. It still had a ribbon around its neck. Neel uncapped the
bottle, took a gulp, wiped his mouth, and drank again. Heat flooded his
chest. He put the bottle back in the drawer.

He covered his face with his hands. He wanted to tear off his clothes
or start a fight with someone who'd beat him bloody. But even at that
moment of dread, even while he ground his teeth, he saw through to
another truth. The FBI had closed its file. Ibn Muhammed was, in the
record, a suicide. Jones would not call Neel for help ever again. If the
FBI dropped its inquiry into the missing documents—if the priest made
good at long last—Neel would be a free man.

FORTY-SEVEN

NEEL DROVE NORTH from Denver at ninety miles an hour. The sky colored from pink to a wide, western blue. To his left, the Laramie Mountains rose over the high plains.

He reached the Air Force base, three miles from Cheyenne, at a quarter to eight. The two National Guardsmen in a booth outside the chain-link fence weren't expecting a special visitor. They were both teenagers. Neither had heard of the Freedom Center. Neel waited twenty minutes while one of them worked the phone. The second Guardsman stood beside the rental car with his hands in his pockets. Meanwhile traffic flowed through the gates: uniformed airmen and contract workers in their personal cars, cleaning crews, supply trucks.

"You know all these people?" asked Neel, through his open window.

"Sure," said the Guardsman. Braces covered his upper teeth. "I don't think we're supposed to talk."

Eventually a staff sergeant walked out from the base to the guard booth. He knocked on the passenger window, opened the door, and got in.

"I was finishing up my breakfast," he said. There were flecks of scrambled egg in his mustache.

Neel turned the ignition. The staff sergeant asked for Neel's phone. Then he guided Neel through the base. They drove at least a mile, past low corrugated-steel buildings, a control tower, and a pair of runways, to a second chain-link fence. A guard raised the striped barrier and waved them through. Beyond the fence, half a dozen trailers stood in a gravel lot. The staff sergeant told Neel to park. They got out.

"We have one bird in the air right now," said the staff sergeant, as he led Neel across the gravel. "It's an MQ-9 Reaper supporting a Special Ops customer in Logar Province. Night patrol, geared up for a raid on a Taliban-occupied village. There's a decent chance you'll see some action. Lotta gunplay out there. Logar Afghans like to shoot back. But there's nothing like dropping a laser-guided bomb to quiet the natives."

The staff sergeant knocked at the door of the first trailer. He waved Neel forward. "Go on. Captain Wade will come get you in an hour. You can talk to him about whatever you came to talk about."

The staff sergeant closed the door behind Neel. Inside, the lights were dim. Two Air Force officers sat in padded chairs facing the far wall, before a bank of screens. One of the officers looked over his shoulder. He had glazed eyes.

"Lieutenant Andy Connaughton. I'm piloting the ship. This is my S.O., Lieutenant Jasmine Day. We've been surveilling the target since 2200 hours Monday night. Militants in a fortified house. We're locked on the commander's cellphone. I've barely had time for a bathroom break."

"Don't mind me," Neel said. "I'm here to observe."

Lieutenant Day looked at Neel with a sullen expression. She offered the slightest of nods before she returned to her screens. Like Lieutenant Connaughton, she appeared to be in her late twenties.

Neel was relieved that the drone operators didn't know who he was. There were tens of millions of Americans, he remembered, who didn't read *The New York Times*. He moved closer to the far wall. He counted twelve screens. There were terrain and road maps. Two screens showed the landscape under a thermal imaging camera. Others displayed mission data and chat logs.

"We're talking to military intelligence in D.C. and Kabul," said Lieutenant Connaughton. "I have a chat going with one of the Rangers on the ground. We're flying at thirty thousand feet, but we'll drop down when the team engages. I'd say that happens within the next hour. They'll take out the two men on the wall, throw smoke into the courtyard, order the Talibs to come out with their hands up. Ever seen one of our birds in action?"

"I have," said Neel.

"It's satisfying as fuck. Any resistance comes from that compound, the Rangers will fall back and we'll drop a five-hundred-pound LGB on the main house. We'll clean up any leftover bad guys with the Hellfires."

"There's no civilian presence in the compound?"

Lieutenant Day laughed.

"It's all good, sir," said Lieutenant Connaughton. "Any noncoms in the place are keeping the wrong kind of company."

"If you're sure," said Neel.

The operators looked at each other. Lieutenant Day made a face.

"We need to lock in on the mission now," said Lieutenant Connaughton.

Lieutenant Day typed a message on her keyboard. Lieutenant Connaughton moved the drone and its cameras with his joysticks. Neel watched them work.

Ten minutes later, the door banged open. The staff sergeant stood at the entrance.

"You have to come with me right now, sir," he said.

"What's wrong?" asked Neel.

"Let's go."

Neel thanked the drone operators for letting him observe. He followed the staff sergeant outside. Two soldiers stood beside his car with rifles in their arms.

"These men are from base security," said the staff sergeant. "I'll ride with you to the entrance gate. Security will follow in the Humvee."

"I don't understand."

"As of now, you are not permitted to be in any secure facility operated by the government of the United States. That includes this AFB."

"I'm here on the government's business."

"Not now, sir. I strongly suggest you stop talking and follow my instructions. Unlock the car. The two of us will get in. You start driving."

Neel headed for the main gate. The Humvee followed a few feet behind his rear bumper. When they reached the perimeter fence the staff sergeant told Neel to keep going.

"All right. Stop here," he said, a hundred feet down the road. He gave Neel back his phone.

"Now can you tell me what this is about?"

"Just drive on."

The staff sergeant got out of the car. The two teenaged Guardsmen, standing outside the booth, stared at them with bewilderment.

Neel drove south toward Cheyenne. After a mile he pulled over on the shoulder. He checked his phone. He'd gotten a voicemail that morning.

> Neel, it's Eliot. The FBI has referred you to the U.S. Attorney
> for breach of the classification rules and violation of the
> Espionage Act. No charges yet but your security clearances are
> suspended until the matter is resolved. I'm disappointed for
> many reasons. Among other things, it's another black mark on
> our agency. I wish you good luck.

Neel slapped his hand against the dashboard. He looked at his watch. It wasn't yet nine. He had a flight out of Denver late the next morning. He could try to return to D.C. that night, but what he really wanted was a quiet room from which to make calls. He needed to retrieve the thumb drive from Monica. He needed a lawyer. He might need witness protection. He had forty thousand in the bank and more he could tap in his retirement fund. It was possible that Rebecca would still, after everything, offer to help.

He started driving again. There was no traffic, but within seconds a Ford pickup loomed in his rearview mirror. Neel glimpsed the driver's orange coat and sunglasses before the pickup swerved across the median to pass him. The truck accelerated, lurched back into his lane, and left him behind. Like Neel's car, the truck had Colorado plates with red letters—it was a fleet vehicle, a rental. It had only been a flicker, a moment, but Neel was left with the uncanny feeling that he'd seen the driver before.

Neel stopped two miles down the road at a motel by the interstate on-ramp. The desk clerk was surprised when he came in but she said they had clean rooms available. He parked right outside the room she gave him. He took out his travel bag from the trunk. Then he pulled back the mat to reveal the spare. He loosened the tire and lifted it to reach the jack and wrench below. He weighed the wrench in his hand. It was a foot and a half long, solid steel, with a satisfying heft. He carried it to the room.

Neel put his bag and the wrench on the bed. There were a table and two chairs by the window. He locked the door, then wedged a chair under the handle. He had to make lists, write notes, call Rebecca, find a lawyer. But he would take a minute before he got to work. He stood in the center of the room, drawing deep breaths into his belly. He swung his arms back and forth across his chest, touched his toes, and dropped to the floor for forty push-ups. When he stood up he was panting. The muscles of his arms and chest throbbed. Now that he'd reached the bottom, he felt a strange lightness inside. He picked up the wrench from the bed, walked to the window. For now his sedan was the only car in the lot. Still, he shifted the wrench from hand to hand, tightened and released his grip. He wasn't afraid. He was ready, at long last, for a fight.

ACKNOWLEDGMENTS

Thank you: Kathryn Davis, Aaron Coleman, Xuan Juliana Wang, Aja Gabel, Amad Jackson, James Bergin, Eyad Asad, Adam Poor, Kelly Marages, Trey Sager, Harris Lahti, Aaron Teel, Oliver Munday, Kristian Borg-Olivier, Joseph Raso, Sumir Sennik, Gabriel Louis, the National Endowment for the Arts, Dan Mandel, Caitlin McKenna, Naomi Goodheart; Harnam, Shiv, and Sim Grewal; Yasmin, A., and R. S. Grewal-Kök.

BIBLIOGRAPHY

Trevor Aaronson. "The 'Terrorist,' the Rapist, and Me: A Criminal Ratted Out His Friend to the FBI. Now He's Trying to Make Amends." *The Intercept,* November 26, 2022.

Spencer Ackerman. *Reign of Terror: How the 9/11 Era Destabilized America and Produced Trump.* Viking, 2021.

Lynsey Addario. *Of Love & War.* Penguin, 2018.

Henri Alleg. *The Question.* Translated from the French by John Calder. University of Nebraska Press, 2006.

Christopher Andrew. *The Secret World: A History of Intelligence.* Yale University Press, 2018.

Petra Bartosiewicz. "To Catch a Terrorist: The FBI Hunts for the Enemy Within." *Harper's,* August 2011.

Jo Becker and Scott Shane. "Secret 'Kill List' Proves a Test of Obama's Principles and Will." *The New York Times,* May 29, 2012.

Ben Brody. *300m.* Mass Books, 2022.

Jordan H. Carver. *Spaces of Disappearance: The Architecture of Extraordinary Rendition.* Terreform, 2018.

Rajiv Chandrasekaran. *Little America: The War within the War for Afghanistan.* Knopf, 2012.

Pratap Chatterjee and Khalil. *Verax: The True History of Whistleblowers, Drone Warfare, and Mass Surveillance.* Metropolitan Books, 2017.

Noam Chomsky. *9-11.* Seven Stories, 2001.

Andrew Cockburn. *Kill Chain: The Rise of the High-Tech Assassins.* Picador, 2015.

Steve Coll. *Directorate S: The CIA and America's Secret Wars in Afghanistan and Pakistan.* Penguin, 2018.

Luc Côté and Patricio Henriquez, directors. *You Don't Like the Truth: Four Days Inside Guantánamo* (film). 2010.

Crossing the Yellow River: Three Hundred Poems from the Chinese. Translated by Sam Hamill. BOA Editions, 2000.

Mark Denbeaux, Dr. Jess Ghannam, and Abu Zubaydah. *American Torturers: FBI and CIA Abuses at Dark Sites and Guantanamo.* Seton Hall University School of Law Center for Policy and Research, 2023.

Geoff Dyer. *Another Great Day at Sea: Life Aboard the USS George H.W. Bush.* Pantheon, 2014.

Charles Ferguson, director. *No End in Sight* (film). 2007.

Dexter Filkins. *The Forever War.* Knopf, 2008.

Peter Finn. "Documents Provide Rare Insight into FBI's Terrorism Stings." *Washington Post,* April 13, 2012.

Alex Gibney, director. *Taxi to the Dark Side* (film). 2007.

Ashley Gilbertson. *Whiskey Tango Foxtrot: A Photographer's Chronicle of the Iraq War.* University of Chicago Press, 2007.

Adam Goldman and Matt Apuzzo. "With Cameras, Informants, NYPD Eyed Mosques." Associated Press, February 23, 2012.

———. "Informant: NYPD Paid Me to 'Bait' Muslims." Associated Press, October 23, 2012.

Philip Gourevitch and Errol Morris. *Standard Operating Procedure.* Penguin, 2008.

Glenn Greenwald. *No Place to Hide: Edward Snowden, the NSA, and the U.S. Surveillance State.* Metropolitan Books, 2014.

Guantanamo Voices: True Accounts from the World's Most Infamous Prison. Edited by Sarah Mirk. Abrams ComicArts, 2020.

Janet Hamlin. *Sketching Guantanamo: Court Sketches of the Military Tribunals, 2006–2013.* Fantagraphics, 2013.

Michael Hastings. *The Operators: The Wild and Terrifying Inside Story of America's War in Afghanistan.* Blue Rider Press, 2012.

Michael Herr. *Dispatches.* Knopf, 1977.

Tim Hetherington and Sebastian Junger, directors. *Restrepo* (film). 2010.

Chris Hondros. *Testament.* powerHouse Books, 2014.

Alistair Horne. *A Savage War of Peace: Algeria 1954–1962.* NYRB Classics, 2006.

Scott Horton. "The Guantánamo 'Suicides': A Camp Delta Sergeant Blows the Whistle." *Harper's,* March 2010.

Kerry Howley. *Bottoms Up and the Devil Laughs: A Journey Through the Deep State.* Knopf, 2023.

Murtaza Hussain. "The Pariah: He Declined the FBI's Offer to Become an Informant. Then His Life Was Ruined." *The Intercept,* November 30, 2021.

International Human Rights and Conflict Resolution Clinic (Stanford Law School) and Global Justice Clinic (NYU School of Law). *Living Under Drones: Death, Injury and Trauma to Civilians from US Drone Practices in Pakistan.* 2012.

Sid Jacobson and Ernie Colón. *The 9/11 Report: A Graphic Adaptation.* Hill & Wang, 2006.

Kabir. *Songs of Kabir.* Translated from the Hindi by Arvind Krishna Mehrotra. NYRB Classics, 2011.

Michael Kamber. *Photojournalists on War: The Untold Stories from Iraq.* University of Texas Press, 2013.

Azmat Khan. "Hidden Pentagon Records Reveal Patterns of Failure in Deadly Airstrikes." *The New York Times,* December 18, 2021.

———. "The Human Toll of America's Air Wars." *The New York Times Sunday Magazine,* January 2, 2022.

Murat Kurnaz. *Five Years of My Life: An Innocent Man in Guantanamo.* Translated from the German by Jefferson Chase. Palgrave Macmillan, 2008.

Miles Lagoze, director. *Combat Obscura* (film). 2018.

James Longley, director. *Iraq in Fragments* (film). 2006.

Peter Maass. "Stanley McChrystal Accidentally Reveals the Dishonesty of U.S. Generals." *The Intercept,* December 4, 2021.

Chase Madar. *The Passion of Bradley Manning.* Verso, 2013.

Jane Mayer. *The Dark Side: The Inside Story of How the War on Terror Turned into a War on American Ideals.* Doubleday, 2008.

———. "The Unidentified Queen of Torture." *The New Yorker,* December 18, 2014.

Samuel Moyn. *Humane: How the United States Abandoned Peace and Reinvented War.* Farrar, Straus and Giroux, 2021.

Robert Nickelsberg. *Afghanistan: A Distant War.* Prestel, 2013.

Ian Olds and Garrett Scott, directors. *Occupation: Dreamland* (film). 2005.

Trevor Paglen. *From the Archives of Peter Merlin, Aviation Archaeologist.* Primary Information, 2019.

———. *Invisible: Covert Operations and Classified Landscapes.* Aperture, 2010.

Joshua E.S. Phillips. "Inside the Detainee Abuse Task Force." *The Nation,* May 13, 2011.

Laura Poitras, director. *Citizenfour* (film). 2014.

———. *My Country, My Country* (film). 2006.

———. *The Oath* (film). 2010.

Dana Priest and William Arkin. *Top Secret America: The Rise of the New American Security State.* Little, Brown, 2011.

Todd Purdum. "Guantánamo: An Oral History." *Vanity Fair,* January 11, 2012.

Daisy Rockwell. *The Little Book of Terror.* Foxhead Books, 2011.

Maxime Rodinson. *Muhammad.* Translated from the French by Anne Carter. NYRB Classics, 2021.

Jeremy Scahill. *Dirty Wars: The World Is a Battlefield.* Nation Books, 2013.

Jeremy Scahill and the staff of *The Intercept. The Assassination Complex: Inside the Government's Secret Drone Warfare Program.* Simon & Schuster, 2016.

The Senate Intelligence Committee Report on Torture: Committee Study of the Central Intelligence Agency's Detention and Interrogation Program. Melville House, 2014.

Bullhe Shah. *Sufi Lyrics.* Translated from the Punjabi by Christopher Shackle. Harvard University Press, 2015.

Hina Shamsi. *Command's Responsibility: Detainee Deaths in U.S. Custody in Iraq and Afghanistan.* Human Rights First, 2006.

Larry Siems. *The Torture Report: What the Documents Say about America's Post-9/11 Torture Program.* OR Books, 2011.

Jvala Singh. *54 Punjabi Proverbs.* Tattva, 2019.

Mohamedou Ould Slahi. *Guantánamo Diary.* Little, Brown, 2015.

Frank Smith. *Guantanamo.* Translated from the French by Vanessa Place. Les Figues Press, 2014.

Jean Edward Smith. *Bush.* Simon & Schuster, 2016.

Amy Davidson Sorkin. "Spooked: What's Wrong with the C.I.A.?" *The New Yorker,* October 10, 2022.

David Talbot. *The Devil's Chessboard: Allen Dulles, the CIA, and the Rise of America's Secret Government.* HarperCollins, 2015.

Larry Towell. *Afghanistan*. Aperture, 2014.

Declan Walsh. "Jihad Redux." *Granta* 116, 2011.

Eliot Weinberger. *Muhammad*. Verso, 2006.

Tim Weiner. *Enemies: A History of the FBI*. Random House, 2012.

———. *Legacy of Ashes: The History of the CIA*. Doubleday, 2007.

Craig Whitlock. *The Afghanistan Papers: A Secret History of the War*. Simon & Schuster, 2021.

Lawrence Wright. *The Looming Tower: Al-Qaeda and the Road to 9/11*. Knopf, 2006.

ABOUT THE AUTHOR

RAV GREWAL-KÖK's stories have appeared in *The Atlantic, Plough-shares, New England Review, Missouri Review, Gulf Coast, The White Review,* and elsewhere. He has won an NEA fellowship in prose and is a fiction editor at *Fence.* He grew up in Hong Kong and on Vancouver Island and now lives in Los Angeles. This is his first novel.

ABOUT THE TYPE

This book was set in Fairfield, the first typeface from the hand of the distinguished American artist and engraver Rudolph Ruzicka (1883–1978). Ruzicka was born in Bohemia (in the present-day Czech Republic) and came to America in 1894. He set up his own shop, devoted to wood engraving and printing, in New York in 1913 after a varied career working as a wood engraver, in photoengraving and banknote printing plants, and as an art director and freelance artist. He designed and illustrated many books, and was the creator of a considerable list of individual prints—wood engravings, line engravings on copper, and aquatints.